GUARDIAN OF THE VEIL

GREGORY SPENCER

AUTHOR OF THE WELKENING

A THREE-DIMENSIONAL TALE

GUARDIAN OF THE VEIL

A NOVEL

HOWARD BOOKS
A DIVISION OF SIMON & SCHUSTER
New York London Toronto Sydney

Howard Books
A Division of Simon & Schuster, Inc.
1230 Avenue of the Americas
New York, NY 10020

The Guardian of the Veil © 2007 by Gregory H. Spencer

First Howard trade paperback edition August 2007

HOWARD and colophon are registered trademarks of Simon & Schuster, Inc.

For information regarding special discount for bulk purchases, please contact Simon & Schuster Special Sales at 1-800-456-6798 or business@simonandschuster.com.

Edited by Ramona Cramer Tucker
Interior design by Jaime Putorti
Illustrations by Gregory H. Spencer
Cover design by UDG / Design Works

Manufactured in the United States of America

10 9 8 7 6 5 4 3 2 1

Library of Congress Cataloging-in-Publication Data
Spencer, Gregory H. (Gregory Horton), 1953–
Guardian of the veil / Gregory Spencer.
p. cm.
1. Friendship in adolescence—Fiction. 2. Marginality, Social—Fiction. I. Title.
PS3619.P4644G83 2007
813'.6—dc22   2007004428

ISBN-13: 978-1-4165-4341-1 (pbk.)
ISBN-10:   1-4165-4341-4 (pbk.)

For my mother-in-law,

Connie Siemens,

who was as much a mother to me

as any son could hope for.

Her later years are, in part, recorded here,

and all her life is honored.

THE CHOREOGRAPHY OF A COINCIDENCE . . .

—DAVID WILCOX, "BIG MISTAKE"
FROM THE ALBUM *BIG HORIZON*

CONTENTS

Contents

PART FIVE: AWAKENED, THE FAMILY

GRATITUDE

Six months after *The Welkening* was published, Denny Boultinghouse of Howard Books encouraged me to "set free" my desire to write a sequel. Thank you, Denny. I have indeed felt liberated. Two writer's settings deserve to be mentioned: Kirk and Bonnie Steele's Palm Desert house provided uninterrupted calm. Skipper John Coleman's competent sailing out to the Santa Cruz Islands allowed for the inspiration of many adventures on Justice Island. Thank you!

After I heard Bill Lindberg tell his story, I was so moved, I rushed home and wrote it down. He has generously let me retell it here—and (much more of a sacrifice) permitted me to refashion it for my own purposes. Thank you, Bill.

Two readers, Lauren Cano and Amber Ward, recent graduates of Westmont College, read the manuscript under significant time pressures. They supplied insightful observations and suggestions. Thank you, Lauren and Amber. With the ever-dependable Laura Wilson typing up my scribbles, I felt free to write the first draft in longhand. Ruby Jeanne Shelton closed out the typing duties with a smile. Thank you, Laura and Ruby Jeanne.

Westmont College provided assistance in the form of a Professional Development Grant during the summer of 2005. The myriad of pages produced therein have been thusly blessed. Thank you, Westmont.

Ramona Tucker, the most unwobblerated of editors, skillfully blended Bennu's sharp eyes with Angie's gentleness. *Guardian* is better for her efforts. Thank you, Ramona.

My daughters, Emily, Hannah, and Laura, are to be praised for their "is it done yet?" faithfulness. Laura was of tremendous help in costume design (someday, the runway?). Loves to you, daughters! My loyal companions, Mocha (curled up at my feet when not barking in fear) and Willie (at my side meowing constantly for more attention), deserve their due (an extra treat?).

GRATITUDE

Many friends inquired about my progress, encouraging me to keep at it. My closest and most loyal friend, the one who keeps me steady by pulling me back from frenetic overstatement and lifting me up from fits of melancholy, is my wife, Janet. You are a guardian of the veil. I love you.

PART ONE

TAKEN, THE FATHER

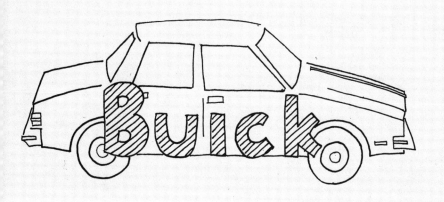

CHAPTER ONE
VEILS UNVEILED

I remain convinced that there are levels of worlds within worlds, seams and crosscurrents in which the old, worn rules shift slightly; that there are levels above us and below us, in which connections are made more easily, and that each of us occasionally passes through such seams.

—RICH BASS, "A WINTER'S TALE"

Only those whose hearts have been broken can remember anything before the age of four.

This is what he remembers.

From his bedroom, he awakened to a noise in the kitchen, a long, high-pitched screech with a barbed hook on the end. It snagged him and tore at him and reeled him in. Something was wrong, he realized. Something was wrong again.

He ran out of his room and down the dark hallway. The floor felt middle-of-the-night cold. He reached the end of the hall and looked to his left. The bare bulb in the kitchen hurt his eyes.

He felt something horrible was coming. He heard labored breathing, hard and trembling, so he started to cry. Then he turned to face the light and heard his father shouting at his mother. The words fell on him; they landed like flat stones pounding . . . pounding down upon his shoulders.

Under this weight, he staggered toward the kitchen but stopped. He did not enter it. An invisible boundary kept him out. A curtain that separated stage from audience, an impenetrable veil.

He does not remember his father's words. But he can still hear them. They

3

cracked open the sky of his mind. In the thunderous shouting, the boy fell to his knees. He reached out a hand to stop the storm. And when he did, he touched the veil; he felt its uncrossableness.

That's when it happened.

His hulking father stretched his broad hands around a stack of china plates on the table. He clasped the dishes and lifted them high above his head. The boy glanced at his mother. Her face screamed silently with the hard certainty of suffering. Her arms rose, hands up, fingers splayed out, trembling. Then his father heaved the plates down onto the floor, at the feet of his mother.

That crashing sound, that breaking and snapping, like a shattering of thin, brittle bones—this is how he remembers the sound.

Then the shards and chips flew everywhere, slicing, exploding into terrible shrapnel. One piece stuck into the wall beside his mother. One caught the frayed hem of her robe.

And one piece entered the boy's soul.

That's what he says now—that it sliced right in and cut him up. It left no mark on the outside.

But his father wasn't finished. He picked up the boy's mother like a sack and carried her to the front door. The boy reached out for her as she went by. His father opened the door, and the boy felt the freezing winter air rush over his hands and face. It held the coolness of death. His mother looked so helpless in his father's hands . . . as fragile as those china plates, beautifully breakable, her porcelain skin shining in the night.

His father paused for a second, as if he needed that moment to blow out the last flicker of conscience. Then he took two steps and threw the boy's mother into the snow on the front lawn. She screamed faintly. The father turned back into the house. He slammed the door and looked down at the boy as if the boy were the cause of his pain. As if he had broken the dishes. As if he were the reason that his mother lay bruised in the snow.

The father said nothing. His face raged with disdain, but his mouth did not form any words. He stomped with his boots down the bare-floored hall and slammed his bedroom door.

The boy dropped his head and cried. He cried on and on. He pounded his chest. And with each fist to his heart, he felt for the flying chip of glass that had entered him. He wanted to pull it out, but the shard cut deeper and deeper still. . . .

Lizbeth Neferti realized she was panting. She wiped the tears that came in the telling and ran her hand over the wrinkles on her flower-print bedspread. She did not turn toward her friend Angie Bartholomew, sitting next to her on the bed.

Lizbeth sighed. "So, that's it. That's the nightmare. I just had to tell you. It was like a horror movie that the boy told to me, whoever he is."

"I don't know what to say, Lizbeth. What an awful story. I feel like that broken piece cut into me too." She put an arm around Lizbeth.

"I know what you mean." Lizbeth glanced around the room. The softball trophies, the clutter on the floor, the stuffed-animal ox that Angie had added to her piled-high collection. These familiar things did not weaken her grief. They looked cheap and powerless. "It's not just this nightmare, Ang. It's everything."

"Yeah." Angie combed her fingers through Lizbeth's black hair. When she came to the end, she reached up and squeezed Lizbeth's neck gently. Then she let go and tugged on the cuffs of her own white shorts.

"After we came back from Welken . . ." Lizbeth paused, and her eyes brightened. "Can you even believe we were there—in that magical place, where we met Piers? The amazing Piers—with his golden skin and green-green eyes. Think of it, Angie! One month ago we helped defeat that awful, evil beast Morphane. He still makes me shudder. Here I was, in the summer before my senior year, and I felt so . . . I don't know, so sure, so confident. Piers told me I was wise. And all of us helped change everything with The Welkening. I made the land shake. I felt like I could do anything." She grabbed a softball with a torn hide and flicked at the stitching.

Angie pushed her hand under her own leg. "I felt like that too. I never felt more real than when I was invisible in Welken. I loved the mistiness of it, the silent, hovering lightness."

"You're weird, Angie."

"Yeah, I know."

Lizbeth tossed the ball into the air and caught it. "And I hate the McKenzie Butte Boys. They bug us. They bug everybody. Odin, Tommy, and Josh Mink, the McKenzie Boys. They're so demented.

Lizbeth slipped off the bed. She dug her fingers into the ball and pulled aimlessly on the torn leather. She flicked the ball back and forth in her grip—and on one hard flick, the ball flew across the room. *Bam!* Lizbeth's eyes grew big. She rushed to open the bedroom door. "It's okay, Dad! Don't worry, nothing broke!"

Shoulders drooping, Lizbeth picked up the softball again and sat dejectedly back on the bed. "Look, Angie, a month has gone by—and, and, and *nothing*. No message from Welken or Piers, no sense of what we should be doing. Then the worst of it, Percy runs away." She paused. "I'm so sad about it. He is a cat, you know, a cat that could get run over. I know he belongs to you and Len, but I'm scared for him. It's got to be something terrible. And I miss him. And now you and my brother together. C'mon, you're going to be a junior in high school and Bennu's going off to college this fall. It's so pointless."

"You're making me feel bad."

"I'm sorry, Angie. I just thought it would be different. I didn't think I'd crash back into my standard funk. It's a cliché, I know, but Welken feels like a dream to me now." Lizbeth tossed the ball in the air.

Angie caught it. She brushed her strawberry blonde hair out of the way, turned the softball over in her hand, and pulled back the torn section. "It's like this, Lizbeth. Here's the world. It's got a tear in it. And that's how we found Welken. Remember how I used to say that the fabric of the world is stretching? But maybe it's more like a tear. Maybe the rip's still going. And y'know, we're not supposed to make the rip bigger." She patted Lizbeth's knee. "Maybe we need to find the tear and sew it up. I don't know. Maybe Welken *is* a dream—but who says dreams aren't real?" She put the ball into a mitt so the tear wasn't showing.

Lizbeth grabbed the mitt and threw it into a plastic bin. "I want to know where Percy is. I don't want to dream about broken dishes, an abused woman, and a frightened little boy with a sharp chip of glass that cut into his soul. I don't want another month of bad news!" She jumped off the bed, rushed into the bathroom, and closed the door.

In the bathroom Lizbeth let down her guard even more. She knew that only a door separated her from Angie, but, to her in this moment, the door felt thick—a heavy, bank-vault barrier.

Lizbeth leaned over the sink and cried. When she peered into the mirror, she saw her anguished face and thought how ugly she looked when she cried, how ugly she was with her broad shoulders, thick thighs, and her dark Egyptian skin that reminded no one of Cleopatra. She put the top of the toilet seat down and sat on it, wondering if there could be a more humiliating position. It gave her one more reason to feel sorry for herself.

She thought about Welken. How she'd felt so full of strength and purpose when she had been transformed into a real ox. How she'd felt for once that she'd done something worth doing. She and her older brother, Bennu, and Angie and her older brother, Len—the self-proclaimed "Commiseration of Misfits," four inseparable friends—had made a difference in Welken. They had helped restore the tiles to the Tetragrammaton. They had joined forces with Piers and other Welkeners. Their bodies had changed into ox, falcon, angel, and lion, and together they had brought about The Welkening, that miraculous event that seemed to make everything right. That's where the meaning of life was—in Welken, with Soliton, that mysterious presence, the one who became "whatever love requires." Instead she was stuck in the economically depressed, rainy town of Skinner, Oregon.

Lizbeth stood up and walked toward the door. "Angie, I hate this place!"

"Lizbeth, c'mon, open the door."

"No!" She clenched her fists at her sides. "I don't want to be here!"

"Then come out."

"No, I mean I don't want to be in Skinner. I want to go back and see where Terz turned into stone. I want to see Mook and, most of all, I . . . I . . ." She leaned her head against the door.

"What, Lizbeth, what?" Angie's voice sounded like an open hand.

"I miss Piers."

"Me too. Lizbeth, please open up."

"No." Lizbeth turned back to walk to the toilet and *bonked* her knee on an open cabinet door. "Ahhh!"

Angie hit the door. "Are you okay?"

"I'm fine. But I'm so uncoordinated, it's like I'm drunk."

Lizbeth sat down again. She rubbed her knee and then her eyes as memories of Piers rushed by—his faithful leadership, his wisdom and eloquence, his way of calling the best out of each of the four friends, and how what made them misfits in Skinner had made them needed in Welken. Then, as she had for the last month, Lizbeth wondered about Bors, Piers's friend who was lost. She remembered that life-saving moment when she'd seen Bors inside the mind of Piers. And she worried about Bors . . . whether his soul had been reunited with his body.

Lizbeth had returned from Welken with hope that Percy, Len and Angie's house cat, would whisper Welken's secrets as he purred, and that Len's softened heart would grow more tender yet.

But her dreams hadn't come true. The worst of it was that the newness, the sense of being changed, had slipped away. She thought it was like trying to hold the good feeling of winning a softball trophy. The bronzed player kept shining on her bookshelf, but the glow from the high-fives faded like an echo, growing fainter with each retelling. Lizbeth's mother liked to say, "The Lord giveth and the Lord taketh away," but, Lizbeth thought, who wants a God who *takes*?

She didn't want to be at home, yet here she was with Angie, the one stable force in her life, her best friend. One year behind her in school, perfect Angie—the girl beautiful enough to have any guy for a boyfriend but who had, for the time being anyway, decided to make a go of it with Lizbeth's brother, Bennu. Now that Angie and Bennu were always together, Lizbeth felt that she'd lost both of them.

So Lizbeth felt alone, the thing she least wanted to feel. With all these familiarities gone, the weight of that absence fell on her oxen shoulders, like a yoke heavy and unyielding.

Then she felt a sharp pain in her stomach. She winced from it and stood up. She probed at the pain the way a doctor might, pressing here and there. She found it and winced again. She thought the pain had a shape, that its borders could be discerned with her finger. It felt solid, like a broken piece of glass or a shard chipped off a shattered china plate.

Just then a knock sounded on the door and startled her.

CHAPTER TWO
SAILING OVER MT. JACKSON

Remorse is a biting memory.
—HENRI NOUWEN, *THE LIVING REMINDER*

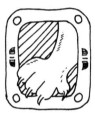 After returning from Welken, after being threatened by the McKenzie Boys, after waiting for some new Piers-inspired task, after listening to Lizbeth go on and on about everything going wrong, after applying for eleven summer jobs and getting turned down at all of them, after too many reruns and not enough river-rafting runs, Len thought he and Bennu needed to act like just-graduated high school seniors and do something irresponsible, like ignore the need to make money. So they headed up to hike in the Mt. Jackson wilderness, the home of the craggy peak Len called "the Prez."

Len liked the highway that followed the Lewis River up to the trail-head. The tight curves, the greenness everywhere, his favorite steelhead fishing spots. Then there were the logging trucks. He didn't like the logging trucks. He pictured each empty flatbed as a giant's jaw with its lower teeth sticking up. Once full of logs, the truck would roar back down the narrow road, a monster battering ram at breakneck speed.

Bennu stuck his elbow out the window. The wind played with both sleeves of his double-layered T-shirts. "OK, stupid question, but has this been a waste of a month for you or what?"

"You got it. No work, no money, no Welken. Pretty stupid and pretty boring."

"I know. Except for the fact that you thought Cindy Martinez actually looked at you, you have nothing to show for this whole month. Me, well, I finally hit it off with Angie, and I really enjoyed writing my college essays. Seriously. But I really miss the Welkeners . . . especially those gentle giants, Sutton and Zennor."

Len stuck out his tongue and blew. "*Pblibt!* What's with 'gentle giants'? Do you always have to sound like a stinkin' poet?"

After about an hour, Len turned his family's knock-kneed, powder blue Buick onto a dirt road, where he had to dodge potholes. He put on his infomercial voice: "Just imagine, Mr. Bennu Neferti, gliding over these ruts and holes in a brand-new Buick Skylark Sport Utility Vehicle. No other company can combine poor workmanship and ugly styling quite like Buick."

Bennu pushed up his glasses and pointed to a parking spot. Like a parrot, he said, "Park the Skylark. Park the Skylark."

"Bennu, you were a falcon in Welken, not a parrot. Act your species, will you?"

After Len pulled over, the two Misfits grabbed daypacks for the three-mile hike and started up the trail, cinching shoulder straps as they went.

Len loved being outdoors, especially on a trail. Hiking helped him forget his troubles and his limitations. So what that he was short and hot-headed? So what that Bennu was smarter and more exotic as an Egyptian? So what that his sister, Angie, was the most beautiful girl at Weyerhauser High? So what that he talked constantly . . . if not aloud, then relentlessly to himself?

The beauty of the place silenced them for fifteen minutes or so. Len picked at some leaves overhanging the path. He smelled the pine sap, listened to jays squawking, and squinted up at Jackson's flowing white mane of glacier and snow. Patting his shorts pockets to confirm that he'd brought a knife, he noted Bennu's eight pockets with envy. Between them, they'd packed enough water and food for two days, but Len worried they had not packed enough.

A few minutes later the silence became oppressive. Len knew he needed to have an important conversation with Bennu. This talk could change everything. He'd been thinking about it for quite some time. Although he didn't want to initiate this level of risk, this leaning over the precipice of friendship, he had to broach the topic. "So, Bennu," Len gulped and paused. "I guess you really like my sister."

"Look, I'm not getting ready to marry Angie, if that's what you're worried about. She's only sixteen."

Len felt his whole body relax. He kicked a pinecone down the path. He plucked a columbine flower and pulled at the tips of its starlike petals. "Yeah, Bennu, that's cool." Len smiled, picked up a rock, and chucked it at a tree, hitting it square in the center. Life would go on. He and Bennu could still be friends. *Guys*, he thought, *we know how to talk.*

Len yanked his water bottle out of its mesh sleeve in the daypack and squirted water into his mouth from as far away as he could hold his hand. Some dripped onto his shirt. Then he ate a protein bar in three bites, gobbled down four handfuls of trail mix, and sucked a day-old glazed donut out of a plastic bag.

Bennu pretended to throw up, then ate even more.

After another mile up the trail, Bennu pointed to a canopy of branches that lined the path just ahead of them. "Ah, Tolkien's Avenue, my favorite part of the hike. Just when you need some shade and a reminder of Hobbiton, here come the Arched Trees of Endolin."

"Yeah, just what I was going to say."

"When we get to the middle of it, I want to read you some lines from a new poem I'm working on."

"Bennu, maybe we're taking this friendship thing too far."

"Shut up." After reaching the densest section of branches, Bennu unzipped his pack and grabbed his journal. "OK, this is only a first draft, but here goes:

> *I know you won't believe*
> *me, that I've counted feathers on an*
> *angel's back and listened to a window*
> *sing in the starlight and watched a griffin graze.*
> *But I've left the simple addition*

of my life for the calculus
of visitation. And I'm quite sure that now
you know what I know, that
snow falls in August."

"That is so special, Bennu. Of the seven words I understood, I truly liked four of them."

Then without warning, it happened.

Len screamed first. At least his voice was audible. Bennu's mouth moved and his shaking hands dropped his journal and rose to his lips, but no sound came out. Len tried to shout again, but panic had swallowed his breath. His heart rammed his chest hard and fast, like it wanted to break open his rib cage. His breathing accelerated. His mouth dried up. He stood in the trail, motionless, eyes split open, staring at a tense, snarling cougar that had leaped from a branch overhead.

The cougar stood broadside to Len and Bennu, bent slightly in a taut crouch.

"What should we do?" whispered Bennu.

"I don't know." Len watched the cougar's claws extend slightly and retract, marking lines into the soil. The beast's face seemed utterly confident but brooding, like he was trying to remember when he'd last eaten. From the cave of its mouth came an awful moan, a call from the deep, guttural and ruthless.

"You growled down a cougar once before, Len. Do it again."

But as Len watched the cougar bare his teeth and poise his limbs for leaping, he could not find the strength to challenge him. The cougar circled back and started pacing.

Len swallowed hard. "Maybe this cougar is from Welken. Maybe we shouldn't try to make it go away."

"All I know is that I don't want to die."

The muscles of the cougar's hindquarters, then his shoulders, twitched.

"Len, c'mon, do what you're gonna do!"

"OK, fine." Len closed his eyes and imagined himself again a lion in Welken. Standing firmly, he roared so loudly that Bennu lurched away from him. Len thought he'd done well. If the cougar sensed that Len was also lion, he might slink away.

The cougar did become less threatening. He stopped pacing and sat. He licked the fur on his left leg.

Len took a step back. The cougar didn't seem to mind. Len slid another foot back, and Bennu did the same while bending over to pick up his journal. The cat lowered his head and growled like an idling dragster. The growl grew louder and louder. Then the cougar reared back and leaned into a roar that shredded the air and tore at them. Len felt sliced up, pierced to his center.

Yet the cat didn't pounce. Len and Bennu stood there, unscathed.

But the cougar inched closer. He took a few swipes at the shrinking space between them.

Len didn't know if he should roar again. He saw Bennu crouch down lower and lower. Len thought this was wrong, that they should try to appear bigger, but he followed suit anyway. He felt submissive. Yielding to the mountain lion's presence, they cowered down till their hands were on the ground.

The mountain lion stood defiantly before them, the picture of un-preyed-upon predator. He stared at them with power in his eyes. He furrowed his brow, coiled his body, and sprang. Reflexively, Len and Bennu ducked. As the shadow of the beast rose over them, Len braced for the first incision, then the tearing of flesh.

But the next thing he knew, the cougar's front paws flew above them. Then Len felt pressure and pain. The mountain lion grazed Len with his duller back claws, gouging deep enough to draw blood on Len's scalp before landing on the other side of the trail.

Bennu lifted his head. "You OK?"

"Yeah, but he nicked me in the head." Len felt the wound and showed Bennu the blood. "It's the same place I got nailed with the rock by the McKenzie Boys."

Len and Bennu stood facing the cougar, who was once again licking his paws.

"He's so calm," said Bennu, "as if he's waiting for us to figure this out."

Len looked at the cougar. "OK, big guy, we get it. You're from Welken, right? You want us to do something? Should we follow you somewhere?" He kneeled on one knee and reached out tentatively to pet the beast.

The cougar growled and snarled once more. He got up and, mouth open, charged at the Misfits. Now they knew what to do. They ran.

Lizbeth rapped on the toilet seat with her knuckles. "Angie, I'm sorry. I just want to be alone."

"I don't think you do."

Lizbeth glared at the bathroom door as if Angie could see her facial expression right through it. "So you know my feelings better than I do?"

"C'mon, Lizbeth, I *do* know you pretty well. And I *don't* think you really want to be alone. You want a friend to hold you. You don't want to sit on the toilet and feel sorry for yourself."

Lizbeth stood up and crossed her arms.

"You don't really want to cross your arms and look at yourself crying in the mirror."

Lizbeth dropped her arms to her sides. "Angie, how do you know exactly what I'm—"

Angie's cell phone rang. "Hi, Mom. Yeah, I'm at Lizbeth's. Really? You're kidding, how funny! OK. Can Lizbeth come too? OK. Fine. Bye."

Lizbeth unlocked the door. "What is it?"

"My mom just got back from the airport. She picked up my grandma. She says Grandma is worse than ever. Want to come over?"

"Sure! I love your grandma. She's so adorable. Do you really think she's getting worse?"

"It's that early Alzheimer's stuff. It's so sad to see her old self fade. Mom said that when she walked past security, Grandma held up her hands and said, 'No guns!'"

"Ha! What did security do?"

"They laughed. Grandma *is* eighty-two, y'know." Angie tugged on her pink bead necklace. "Still, she can say the nuttiest things."

"So can you."

Down the mountain, finishing the three-mile loop in record time, Len and Bennu scrambled as fast as they could. Whenever they slowed from a trot to a walk, the cougar closed ranks and snarled. The Misfits got the message. Panting heavily, they reached the Skylark and hopped in. The cougar sat about thirty yards away, acting uninterested and unwinded.

Len's chest heaved as he sat in the driver's seat. He fumbled for the keys then found them, but he couldn't get his hands to stop shaking enough so he could put the keys in the ignition. He put the keys on the seat and took a long draft of water. Then he saw the cougar charging toward the car.

"C'mon, Len, let's get out of here!" Bennu grabbed the key and stuck it into the ignition. "Move it!"

Len started the car and peeled out in a cloud of dust. He was quiet for a short while. After straightening his backward baseball cap, he said, "I don't know what to think. That cougar could have killed us at any time."

"I was so scared."

"Was? I still am."

"Me too."

"But the weird thing is that he didn't kill us. He just threatened us."

Bennu threw his pack in the backseat. "He did that really well."

"Yeah, maybe too well. I've got to stop shaking so I can drive."

In ten minutes, the Skylark pulled onto the two-lane highway and slowly reached the speed limit. Bennu leaned his head back and closed his eyes. "Wake me up if you need me to drive, OK? I'm exhausted."

"No worries. I *gain* energy from cougar attacks." Len sighed and mentally worked through what had happened—and why. The cougar had to be a message from Welken. Maybe this was Soliton himself, the orb of light that had visited them in Ganderst Hall, the one who seemed to watch over Welken, the one who had once appeared to them with the head of a cougar. But what did Soliton need them for? To turn the tide in a battle or to bring justice to some remote Welken village?

Len cruised down the highway, watching the cottonwood leaves flap light and dark in the breeze. Then he noticed the gas tank. "Shoot! Hey, Bennu, wake up. We need gas."

"What?"

"We're running out of gas."

"So? Why wake me up for that?"

"Well, *somebody's* got to do the windows while I fill the tank—with your money."

"*My* money?"

"Yeah, *I* drove."

"Your dad's car."

"Fine. I'll pay for a quarter of it." Len pulled into the one gas station in Old Blue, a river town with a population of eighty-seven. He hopped out, gave the guy at the pump Bennu's cash, and ran into the Food Mart. Grabbing the key attached to a rusty crescent wrench, he jogged out toward the bathroom.

Len unlocked the door and instantly gagged at the stench. He held his breath, took care of business, and depressed the push button on the faucet. A trickle of water came out, brightening the algae in the sink. A quick breath later, Len rolled his eyes and yanked hard on a paper towel. The whole dispenser came off the wall and crashed to the floor. "This bathroom stinks!" he yelled. "And nothing works!"

Then he heard a motor humming outside. It wasn't the Skylark, but he recognized it. He couldn't believe it. It sounded like the same guttural purr he and Bennu had left on the mountain twenty miles back.

That's ridiculous, he thought. *That cougar couldn't have followed us down. That's impossible. But now, how am I supposed to get out? Of all the stupid—*"Hey, Bennu! Bennu, get over here!" *Bennu can't hear me*, he realized. *What's the point?*

Len opened the door a crack. He saw a cougar snarling about ten feet from the door. Screaming, Len closed it fast, then heard a *whump* on the door. He jumped onto the toilet. One leg kept shaking.

When the growling subsided a bit, Len opened the door again. The cougar was still there, ten feet away. Trembling, Len opened the door a little wider. The cougar backed up. Len opened the door all the way, and the cougar retreated into some bushes.

That's weird, thought Len, *but maybe I can get out of here*.

Sprinting as fast as he could, he bolted for the car. He yelled, "Hey!" and tossed the crescent wrench key to the gas station guy with the nozzle in his hand. "That's enough. Keep the change!" To Bennu, he shouted, "Get in the car!"

"Keep the change? What's the rush?"

"Get in *now*."

The mountain lion leaped out of the bushes and ran at the car. Bennu threw the squeegee down, opened the door, and slipped in. Len started the car, watching the cougar all the while. He got the shifter in gear just as the cougar leaped over the hood of the car. They both screamed and pressed themselves back against the seat. Bug-eyed, Len held his chest. Then he jerked the Skylark back onto the highway.

Len turned the radio off. "I don't get it."

"Me neither." Bennu looked dazed. "Me neither."

When Lizbeth and Angie stepped into the Bartholomews' front room, Angie's mother, Charlotte, sat at the kitchen table while Grandma stood next to the coffeemaker looking impatient, her right hand on the handle of the carafe.

Angie held out her arms. "Hi, Grandma! I'm so glad you're here for a visit!"

"Oh, you dear-heart. It's good to see you." After a big smile and a hug, Grandma went back to the counter. "I'm going to have some coff' if this gadget would hurry up."

"'Coff'?" said Angie softly to her mom. "What's with that?"

"I don't know. All of a sudden, she's abbreviating everything." Charlotte smiled at Lizbeth, acknowledging her and winking in recognition of her mother's poor hearing. "Mom," she said louder as she gently touched her mother's arm, "you remember Lizbeth from next door?"

"Wha'd you say? Libby? Of course. Hi, Libby. I like that name 'cause it's like mine, Abby. I'm Abby, but you can call me Dear-Abby. I'm pretty good at advice. Now, Libby, get me some milk out of the reefer."

Lizbeth covered her mouth. "Is she serious? The 'reefer'?" She took the milk out of the refrigerator.

Charlotte threw up her hands. "I know. Everybody else says 'fridge,' but my mom has to say 'reefer.'"

Grandma grabbed the milk out of Lizbeth's hands. "You're kinda tender, getting the milk for me." She poured some into her cup and took a sip. "Now you girls come and sit with me for a spell. Dear-Abby's got to take a load off her feet. I'm not a saucy kitten anymore." She sat down ever so slowly and added sugar to her coffee. "I was just reading about Henry VIII, how he started the Church of England and knocked up all those Abbeys."

"Mother! He knocked *down* the abbeys. He ruined them so he could confiscate land owned by the Catholics."

Abby looked as if she hadn't heard a word. She fluffed up her over-sized sweater with a windmill on it. "Lilly, are you in junior high now? Oh, be a dear-heart and pass me one of those muffins. Char-Char, have you been writing any more of those darling Percy and Bones stories? I just love those two."

"I have, Mom, but I'm not ready to show anyone yet."

"Well, la-te-da-da. We're not good enough for you, Charlotte?"

Angie put a hand on Dear-Abby's knee. "Grandma, I think Mom just wants to keep it to herself till she's further along."

"What?"

"Till she's further along."

"Farmer John?"

"Mom's not done yet!"

"Well, she'd better hurry up. I could die at any moment."

The three younger women looked nervously at each other.

"Ha!" Abby shouted. "That's a good one! I could keel-keel before I finish this muffin-o."

"Oh well." Charlotte faced Lizbeth and wiped a tear. "The decline is so sad you might as well laugh at what you can."

Lizbeth let out a chuckle and sighed. She studied Dear-Abby's face, the layers of wrinkles, the wispy, gray hair, the deep-set, occasionally vacant eyes. Lizbeth was about to look away when Abby's eyes suddenly focused on hers. Lizbeth looked into those eyes that had seen so much. She knew that Abby hadn't had the easiest life. Then Lizbeth noticed something different about Abby's eyes. The shiny-wet gleam of her eye moved; it seemed to take shape. Lizbeth inched closer. The gleam became a sail, the sail a sailboat, and the sailboat bobbed in the turbulent sea of Abby's blue iris.

Angie stood up and took Lizbeth's arm. "Are you OK? What's going on?"

"I don't know. But I think we should get ready."

CHAPTER THREE
ONE CLAW AT A TIME

*For the rest of his life he would have to bear the burden of those looks
and judgment. From then on, he knew that . . . the poor,
the excluded, the bitter ones of the earth were watching him and
judging him.*

—PHILIP HALLIE, *LEST INNOCENT BLOOD BE SHED*

Len kept the Skylark floored till he rounded a bend and had to slow down for a bus. He hit the steering wheel in frustration. "OK, I'm officially spooked—and I'm dying from this exhaust. This mountain lion thing. It has to be Welken."

"Duh." Bennu fumbled through the CDs in his carrying case.

Len yanked the case out of his hand and threw it in the backseat. "Stop it! How are we going to figure this out with The Lemonheads blasting away?"

"You sound like my mom."

"That's a low blow."

"I guess I'm just trying to block everything out. I'm not a big fan of cougar attacks. And I'm not crazy about the timing of all this."

"What?"

"You know." Bennu took off his glasses and cleaned them. "Things have been going well—me and Angie."

Len added anger to his emotional melting pot. In the mixing, he felt himself wanting to erupt into his former volcanic fury. Since his last visit to Welken, he had been different. Everyone noticed. But now he felt the pressure rising and rising. He gripped the steering wheel till his knuckles hurt. He tried counting to ten but lost focus at four. He shook his left foot. Finally he rolled down the window, put his head out, and screamed as loud as he could.

Bennu grabbed the wheel as the car lurched a few feet into the other lane. "Are you trying to get us killed?"

Len looked back at Bennu, took his hands entirely off the wheel, and leaned farther out the window. He yelled again.

Bennu yelled back, "Stop it, you idiot! I can't keep steering forever!" Bennu slid across the bench seat toward Len.

Len plopped back into his seat. "Why, Bennu, I didn't know you cared."

As Bennu scooted back over, Len hit the brakes, hard. The car fish-tailed a little and came to rest on the gravel shoulder. Bennu flew forward but stopped himself with his hand before he crashed into the windshield.

"Hey!" said Bennu, "my seat belt was off. Now I *know* you want to get me killed." Len pointed to the cross street on the other side of the road. "Look. You're not going to believe it."

There was the cougar sitting at the corner . . . like he was being paid to advertise for a new zoo. He couldn't have appeared more natural or been more out of place.

"What do we do?" asked Bennu.

"I don't know." Len shifted his backward cap a quarter turn. "A few minutes ago he was chasing us, but now he's just sitting there. And how can he even be sitting there? I was going at least fifty."

"He's getting up. He's trotting away."

"A false alarm, I guess." Len cupped his hands around his mouth and shouted across the highway. "Hey, what's the message? What do you want from us?"

"Wait, he sees us. That's so bizarre. He's looking right at us."

"OK, here goes." Len jetted across the highway. "And another thing— where are the neighbors screaming about a mountain lion walking the streets? Doesn't anybody else see him? And why am I driving *toward* him?"

"And why is this cougar scaring us to death if he really is our friend . . . some messenger from Piers or Soliton?"

Len pulled up right next to the cougar. The cat seemed to be studying Len, sizing him up, assessing his character.

At the same time Len felt something come over him—a need to stretch, to curl up and sleep, to purr. He felt more feline than he had since The Welkening had taken place on Granite Flats. He squirmed in his seat because he wanted to switch his tail, the tail he didn't have. He took off his seat belt and pawed at the dashboard. Then the cougar bent his head slightly, and Len leaned half his body out through the open window.

"Len, what are you doing?" Bennu leaned over and grabbed Len by the belt loops.

Len arched his hand over the cat's head and scratched him behind one ear. As he touched the cougar's coarse fur, one of his own fingers became furry. A long claw came out to scratch the cougar. Len blinked in amazement. Nothing could have been more startling, yet reassuring. A deep chill ran from Len's leonine claw to his chest.

The cougar cocked his head, as if to acknowledge Len's friendly scratch. Then his whole body tensed as Len withdrew his hand. Len's claw again became a finger, and the cougar bared his teeth, growled, and took off into a dead run down the street.

Len flopped back into his seat and hit the gas.

"I saw that," said Bennu, his hands shaking with excitement. "I saw your claw. Wow, that's amazing! We're close. In some unthinkable way, we are *in* Welken but *not* in Welken. Maybe the cougar is a moving portal."

"He's a moving something, I'll tell you that."

"Nothing like this happened a month ago. We didn't have this much Welken in Skinner."

Up one hill and to the right, along a drainage ditch and over to the left, the cougar ran and the Skylark followed.

"Where are we?" asked Bennu.

"C'mon. You know this place, don't you? It's McKenzie Butte."

"I guess I don't usually come at it from this side." Bennu flicked his head, birdlike, from one window to another. "Hey, where'd he go? Oh, there, up that street. He's sprinting."

With graceful, athletic strides, the mountain lion turned onto a gravelly street. Behind homes on one side, engines and boxcars screeched on acres of train tracks. Mounds of moss clung steadfastly to most of the roofs. The cougar slowed to a loping trot before slinking into one of the yards.

Len had never been to this house, but he knew exactly where he was. It all fit. The faded, dark brown trim against the peeling white sides. The unmowed grass. The laurel hedge out of control. This was where the Mink family lived. Odin, Josh, and Tommy Mink, the disgusting McKenzie Butte Boys . . . the source of so much of the Misfits' pain and fear. And to prove it, parked in the gravel driveway was the rust-bucket, moldy green Ford LTD.

Len eased the Buick past the Minks' driveway so that the laurel hedge hid the car from the house. He took off his seat belt, but he was in no rush to hop out of the car. Staring out the windshield, he rubbed his head where the cougar had scratched him and felt again the horror of the afternoon a month ago, miles from here, at the Peterson homestead, when the McKenzie Boys had tied him up and knocked him out with a thrown rock. They'd said the Misfits had trespassed—but Len knew it had just been an excuse for cruelty. He flashed back to what had followed. The chaos, the peace. The sunlight, the rain. Their introduction to Piers in Welken.

"Hey, Len." Bennu shook Len's shoulder. "You OK?"

"Yeah, I guess. I'm not thrilled to be here."

"Me neither. Why would Piers want us to get beat up? I'm soooooo nervous."

Len opened the door and closed it quietly. He leaned against the car, not wanting to take one step closer to the McKenzie Boys. He could tell Bennu was less motivated than he was. He swallowed hard. "We've got to check it out. There's nothing else to do." He motioned to Bennu to follow him down the hedge that separated the Minks' house from their neighbors'. It meant being in the neighbors' yard, and he hoped that either no one was home, or that the neat rows of marigolds meant these folks were nice.

As they crept onto the grass, Len noticed rusted stuff at the base of the hedge—cans, gears, an ax head, even a license plate on the ground.

He brushed dirt off the metal. It was an Oregon plate from 1947: GFN 421.

Then they heard voices, familiar voices. Tough, yet whiny.

"C'mon, Odin, we need you."

"Yeah, it's not like we can pull this off by ourselves."

Since he was shorter and lighter, Len motioned for Bennu to give him a boost so he could peer over the hedge to see what was going on. After scrambling onto Bennu's shoulders, Len was grateful that the lazy Minks had not trimmed the hedge for years. It provided good cover.

Josh and Tommy, the two younger Mink brothers, had their backs to him. They were leaning over a makeshift table—a door and its frame supported by two sawhorses. Tommy turned and shoved his clenched fist toward Josh.

Len gasped quietly. He couldn't believe what he was seeing. Odin sat in a wheelchair, at the head of the table nearer to the back of the house. Odin, in a wheelchair! His huge head drooped forward, his slimy black hair shining in the sun. Josh faced Tommy. With his mouth slightly open as always, Josh slapped at Tommy's fist, reached for a Coke with a straw in it, and held the drink up to Odin's lips. Odin appeared pummeled, as if twenty bricks had fallen on him. But he didn't have a broken arm or bandages. He simply looked haggard, like he'd aged ten years in the last month since Len had seen him. Dark circles hung below Odin's eyes, and his lips were puffy.

Bennu wobbled under the weight of Len.

While Josh and Tommy gestured to various places on the table, Len tried to figure out what they were pointing to. Then he saw it—a crudely drawn map of downtown Skinner, one block in particular, between University and Eleventh, near the college.

Tommy moved one of the green army men standing on the map. "OK, I'm walkin' down the street, actin' normal, checkin' out babes. Then I take up my position here by that stupid coffee place, Java Jive. Hey, 'take up my position,' cool military talk, eh?"

Josh shook his head. "Shut up."

"You shut up!"

"Just stick with the plan," said Josh. "When you move in there, I'll drive by really fast about the same time *he* does. Then the accident happens."

Len's heart quickened its pace. *Are they planning to jump someone?*

"Yeah," said Tommy, "an 'accident.'" He said it slowly, sneering meanness into every syllable.

"No!" Odin pounded the makeshift table, and the army men fell over. The gesture seemed to take a lot out of him. He leaned forward, placed his hand on his chest, inhaled as if he were short of breath, and threw himself back. "I'm OK. Look, this is a stupid idea—and I don't think you idiots can pull it off anyway."

Odin, the hulking, muscular threat, shocked Len—not by his powerful presence but by his lack of it. Weakness was everywhere—in the wheelchair, in his mysterious wounds, and also in his tone and tormented expression. Len didn't know what to make of it. Odin clearly was in pain, but was it merely physical? He almost seemed oppressed, like he was acting on someone else's orders.

Len's racing heart made his knees wobbly and his hands shaky. When Bennu regripped Len's legs, Len squinted down at him. He saw the sweat on his friend's forehead from holding up his weight.

Len turned back toward the McKenzie Boys at the table. Josh and Tommy were chuckling. Josh leaned over and grabbed the doorknob. As Tommy snatched up the plastic soldiers, Josh yanked up on the door. They both laughed about their enemies falling down to hell as Tommy threw the army men into the opening.

Len expected to see grass. Instead, he saw a glimmer of light from the partly open door. Pressing his knees around Bennu's head, he prepared for Dracula to rise out of his crypt.

"Len," whispered Bennu. "I can't hold you much longer. My muscles are cramping up."

"Hang on. Just a second." Len leaned over as far as he dared. He saw something golden tan, something alive, something moving. As the bright light grew in intensity, Len struggled to discern the shape. Then a head appeared, a head he recognized—the square-jawed, menacing head of a cougar.

Once Josh lifted the door high enough, the cougar leaped out. The

McKenzie Boys seemed to take no notice, like they couldn't see that a cougar was now in their yard. But the cougar took notice of Len. He opened his mouth and showed his fangs. Frantic, Len slipped down, banging a knee into Bennu's shoulder.

"Ow!" Bennu yelled as he fell to the ground. He slapped a hand over his mouth and bugged out his eyes at Len.

Then the McKenzie Boys *did* notice. They turned toward the noise and ran up to the hedge, violently spreading branches to peer through. As Bennu labored to keep his breathing silent, Len grabbed a rusty gear on the ground and tossed it farther down the hedge in the neighbors' backyard. Tommy and Josh bolted toward the crash. After running a few steps, Len reached into the hedge, grabbed the license plate, and threw it like a Frisbee. It sailed over the hedge, circling into the Minks' backyard. Before Len and Bennu had scrambled back to the Buick, they heard "Yeow!" and guessed that Odin had a new bruise.

As Len started the Buick and lurched away, he looked in his rearview mirror. The cougar sat on the Minks' front lawn, licking himself.

"Now you listen to me, young lady." Dear-Abby wagged her finger in Lizbeth's face.

Lizbeth eyed Charlotte, who tossed her hands into the air.

"OK," said Lizbeth with uncertainty. "I'm listening."

"Will you look at that!" Abby leaned over and picked at the kitchen floor. "Cookie dough on the floor. I'll scrape it off with my finger-o. And crumbs and dust bunnies. I need to vac!"

Lizbeth's expression of fear relaxed. "Would you like me to get the vacuum for you, Dear-Abby?"

"Oh, you're kinda tender. That would be so nice. But first I gotta go pee. You know what I say, 'I drink, therefore.'"

As Abby walked out, Angie put her arm around Charlotte. "I'm sorry, Mom. It must be hard to see her like this."

"Angie, you're 'kinda tender,' as Grandma would say."

Lizbeth found the vacuum in the closet and set it in the center of the living room. She knew that one of Dear-Abby's many obsessions was vacuuming every square foot methodically four times. Then, stuffing both hands in the back pockets of her long brown shorts, Lizbeth motioned to Angie to follow her.

In the Bartholomews' backyard, the two walked among the intentionally casual plantings. Lizbeth plucked a cosmos flower that had come up in the peonies. She ducked under an arching 'Cecile Bruner' rose branch not tied to its trellis. Lizbeth snipped the unfragrant center of the cosmos and described to Angie her vision of the sail in Dear-Abby's eyes.

Angie pointed beyond the open gate, out into the Wilder, the Misfits' name for the land along the banks of the Lewis River. "And there's where it all got started."

"I'm not so sure. Sometimes I think Welken's been here all along, but we just didn't see it. Maybe we didn't want to. I know I usually miss the right thing." She plopped into Charlotte's Adirondack chair. Angie stood behind her, and they both stared into the Wilder.

"C'mon, Lizbeth, what happened to your oxen determination?" Angie pulled Lizbeth's scrunchie out and raked her fingers through Lizbeth's thick hair. "What happened to all that strength? Where's your Egyptian sense of authority? And what happened to . . . hey, it's Percy!" Angie sprinted around the chair toward the open gate. "Percy—oh, you kitten—you're back! Come to Angie. Oh, Percy, baby, don't go behind the fence."

Lizbeth picked up the scrunchie that Angie had dropped and ran expectantly. She charged through the gate and turned around. "Where is he?"

"I don't see him."

"Oh, c'mon, he was here a second ago."

With Len driving as quickly as the Skylark permitted, Bennu kept watching out the back. "No sign of them yet."

"Good." Len adjusted the rearview mirror. "If it's one thing we can't do, it's outrun the LTD in this hunk-a-junk."

"Well, the LTD's a hunk-a-junk too."

"Yeah, but it's a fast hunk-a-junk. The Boys may not have waxed the hood, but they've kept the engine pretty tight."

Bennu snickered. "As if you know anything about engines."

Len pulled onto the highway. "Bennu, they're planning something sick . . . a phony accident or something."

"Yeah, I heard."

"They drew a map of University and Eleventh."

"Huh. Well, let's remember that, I guess. I don't know what else to do right now."

After a few quiet minutes, they drove into Skinner. They were nearly home when, suddenly, in a panicked motion, Bennu slammed his hand against the dashboard. "Len! It's a red light!"

Len hit the brakes hard. The Buick screeched to a halt two feet into the crosswalk. "Sorry about that."

Before Len could back up, a homeless guy jumped off the curb and walked to Bennu's window. "It's the way of all flesh," he said, holding up a God Bless cardboard sign. "I know why you race here and there." He put one hand on the open window frame and leaned in.

"We don't have any money," said Bennu.

Len pushed Bennu back to the seat so he could lean over. He noticed the stark contrast of Bennu's dark skin with the homeless man's whiteness. "We have nothing to give you."

"And here is the first lie between us." The homeless man scratched his chin stubble. "You have more to give than you know."

Bennu jerked as if he'd been hit, and he scooted away from the window.

The homeless man poked his head inside. "You are rich, I tell you! You are chosen for this moment!"

Bennu pushed on the man's greasy head of hair. "Get out of here!"

The man bumped his head on the door frame and stumbled back. Then he grabbed his own shirt with both hands and lifted it up to his chin. His chest, as white as flesh could possibly be, almost blinded Len, who turned away and rubbed his eyes. When he opened them, the light had turned green. He floored it.

"Len, look out! You're going to hit him!" Bennu shouted and shielded his face from the impact. Then, from the other side of the intersection, he spun around to check out the damage. "Len, he's on the ground! You ran over him! He's reaching out a hand to us."

"What are you talking about?" Len hit the brakes. "I didn't hit him. I know I didn't." Flushed with both confidence and doubt, Len pulled over to the curb. "Look—there he is, picking up his cardboard! He's walking back to his chair. So there."

Len gripped the wheel and drove off. After the cougar and the McKenzie Boys, the homeless man had put his nerves over the top. His mind sped a thousand times faster than the Skylark. His shoulders tensed up. He couldn't relax. He thought about head wounds and wheelchairs, and about being chosen. He'd felt that way before, a month ago, when he'd endured the heat of the Wasan Sagad in Welken, and later when he'd turned into a lion and heard Piers talk about the meaning of all that had happened to him. Len had tried to hold on to everything he'd learned in Welken, to keep believing that even he could change, that somewhere in the universe was a place of magic and meaning—but he found it difficult. In Skinner, he just felt average . . . and boring. And, now, how was he to interpret what the homeless man had said? Chosen for what?

Traveling between dimensions, he thought, *makes a lot more sense in hindsight.*

Angie and Lizbeth searched in the Wilder, in the open spaces behind the Bartholomews' house that led to the Lewis River. They crouched down and peered under bushes.

"Here, Percy-Perce-Perce," Angie called. "Here, kitty-kitty. Oh, Lizbeth, I want him back."

Tired of calling Percy's name, Lizbeth scanned the flat spaces between the gate and the Bartholomews' dock on the Lewis River. "I don't think he's here, Ang. Maybe you were seeing things. Maybe it was Chester, the Garibaldis' cat."

"I know it was Percy. I know Percy. I saw him right here, walking past the gate. I saw his glowing fur and the wisdom in his eyes."

"Yeah, well, I saw his tail, the . . . um . . . curliness of his tail."

Angie looked back through the open gate to the house. "Hey, wait a minute. It's Bennu and Len. They're in the yard. Hi, Bennu!"

"You could say hi to Len too."

Angie waved but said nothing.

Lizbeth didn't like it. All of a sudden, Angie got all twirly. She smiled too big, and she ran her fingers through her hair. She was simply too beautiful.

When Len and Bennu approached the gate, when they were about the same distance from the opening as Lizbeth and Angie, they stopped. Lizbeth's focus shifted. She no longer looked past the opening at Len and Bennu. She saw something in the air between them. A thin veil appeared, a kind of membrane, a screen of images.

On it, Percy pranced by.

"There he is!" shouted Angie.

Lizbeth watched Bennu watching Angie.

Bennu scratched his chin. "Where'd he go?"

"Yeah," said Len, "to me it looked like he walked behind the fence, but he must not have—or you two would have said something."

"Wait!" Lizbeth pointed. "I see something else. It's my sailboat. It's floating down from your right. It's the boat I saw earlier, in Dear-Abby's eye."

"What?" said Bennu.

"Nothing. Just watch it."

The boat sailed across the veil. It tacked once, then appeared to bump into the fence post, as if the post had been a cliff on a shore blocking its way.

The scene changed. Images from Welken floated by. A goblet from Ganderst Hall. The tower of the Wasan Sagad. One of Vida's daggers. Before Lizbeth could get nostalgic, the body of a man drifted in, chest up with no shirt on. His sunken eyes frightened her. His skin, so pale yet dull, hung limply on his bones.

"There's the guy we saw!" shouted Bennu. "I thought Len had run him over."

"Guy?" Angie pointed at the vision. "You saw that guy?"

When Lizbeth said, "He looks homeless," the pale man's image grew larger on the surface. His face filled the screen invasively. His mouth grew until it overtook everything around it. When it opened, Lizbeth feared she would see a forked tongue or the hundred basilisks that had destroyed her Welken friend Alabaster. What if the mouth sucked them all in?

But the mouth pursed its lips to speak. "Spare change? A quarter? Just a quarter and you'll be whole." The mouth closed and faded from view.

Lizbeth reached toward the fading image and touched it. "Don't go. Don't go away."

Like polyester, the veil sprang back. The others came up and felt it as well.

"What's it mean?" asked Bennu. "It's like a silk shirt I have."

"Or nylons," said Lizbeth.

"See," said Angie, "the fabric of the world *is* stretching."

Len pressed on it slowly. "That's not funny."

But Angie wasn't laughing. She ran her hands over the screen dreamily, eyes closed, humming some tune Lizbeth didn't recognize. Placing both of her hands flat against the screen, Angie opened her eyes.

Bennu stared at Angie from the other side of the veil. He reached out his hands, and, before Lizbeth could say "Stop it, you're making me uncomfortable," he placed his hands on hers.

Now Lizbeth *was* uncomfortable. For a fraction of a second, they held the pose—then their hands appeared to clasp. But they hadn't. Lizbeth could see their hands somehow disappearing as they pushed in. Their hands just went through and vanished. Then their arms. Eyes locked, Angie and Bennu kept walking and, inch by inch, more of them disappeared. They stepped into each other . . . and were gone.

"Lizbeth!" said Len, snapping her out of her daze. "We have to act fast. Do the same."

Why? she thought. *Why should I do this? I don't want to merge into Len!*

But she ignored her thoughts. She put her hands on Len's and pushed through the veil. She looked at him and took a step.

"Don't get any ideas," he said. "This doesn't mean I like you."

Lizbeth sneered and pressed in. For a minute, she felt as if she were pushing her hands right into Len's arms. Things were dark and webby. She worried she'd get stuck inside Len, like when she'd seen Bors's soul from inside Piers's head. She forced herself to keep walking and sensed she was being pulled also. Then she felt the veil slip away from her, over her, like a sheath.

The next thing she knew she was in a forest. She looked around. There was Angie to her left, stroking her feathery blue angel wings. To her right a cougar paced and snarled.

PART TWO

BLESSED, THE BOY

CHAPTER FOUR
DON'T NEVER WELKEN'S ALWAYS

"Atmosphere in Deady still vilely polluted"
—HEADLINE IN *DAILY EMERALD,* UNIVERSITY OF OREGON NEWSPAPER
MARCH 15, 1911

 The next morning, when the boy awakened, his first thought was to open the front door. In his four-year-old mind, he thought his mother might still be there in the snow, wounded but waiting to be welcomed back in. He put on his slippers and ran down the hall to the living room. With both hands he turned the doorknob and pulled hard. When it gave way, he ran down the porch steps and into the snow. No one was there.

The morning sun had just reached the front yard, but it was still very cold. Cold enough that the light breeze felt like a blade scraping across his cheek. Too cold to be standing outside in pajamas and slippers. The boy gasped as the arctic air entered his lungs, but he crunched into the snow anyway. He knew where his mother had landed the night before. He knelt by the depression she had made in the snow and ran his hands over her contours. The stiff white powder glistened brilliantly in the sun. He felt where her legs had been and then her hips. He ran his hands up to her torso, then to her neck and head. When he kept his warm fingers on a spot, the snow melted just a little.

But the boy did not see it quite this way. As the tiny drops of water trickled down the sides of the impression in the snow, the boy cupped one hand against the side to catch the drips. He stood up and held the wetness to his face. He saw the drips as her tears. Then he bowed his head into his hands and felt his mother's tears against his own cheeks. He sensed her sorrow. He felt her rejection, her abandonment. Her tears seemed to multiply on his face—and then he knew he was adding his own tears to hers. He shook with great shoulder-lifting sobs.

Grabbing his stomach, he pushed on his skin till he felt it. The shard was still there. It hurt more now, but it was harder to find with his fingers. It had twisted in deeper. In his pain the boy fell to his knees and bent over the outline of his mother in the snow. He felt he had to do something. The pain was too great, so he pounded at the rim of her contour, breaking the edges into the center. He put both fists above his head and slammed them down on the rim. Over and over, he hammered the snow.

He felt better. It felt good striking blow after blow. Sometimes the hard snow hurt his fists, but he did not stop. The shard pricked at his insides, so he crushed the snow with greater strength, with power. The shard twitched again, as if it were growing sharper, more jagged. It gave him the energy to keep going. He was angry now, angry and resentful, resentful and bitter, bitter and tortured, tortured and cruel. He finished pounding at the entire rim before he sat back. Breathing heavily, he stared at the snow and the tiny red spots from his own bloody fists.

Then, suddenly, his body was lifted up. He turned to see that his father had grabbed him. The boy wrestled in the air to get away, kicking and twisting against the shackles of his father's hands. He felt helpless, but he flailed away anyway. As the father walked inside the house, he wrapped his arms around the boy's chest. Harder and harder, the father squeezed until the boy stopped resisting. The boy felt faint. He struggled to breathe. He thought he would die.

Then the father put his lips next to the boy's ear. In the father's deepest, sternest voice, he said, "Never tell anyone."

The boy started to black out. His head fell back on the father's shoulder. One more squeeze and he gasped out the last breath he'd saved in his lungs.

When he awoke, he found himself on the living-room sofa. The house was empty. The boy threw his face into the pillows and wept till he could weep no more.

"Wake up, Lizbeth. Wake up."

Lizbeth felt herself being shaken. She pushed herself up, a little too fast, and fell, light-headed, into Angie's arms. "I . . . I don't know what happened. One minute I saw you and the next minute I was back in the nightmare."

Angie patted Lizbeth's shoulders. "I guessed as much. You were moaning and shaking."

"It was about the boy again. The dream picked up right where the other one left off." Lizbeth rubbed her fingers across her brow. "I'll tell you about it."

"OK. But maybe we should get off this Welken trail. A cougar was here—or Welken's version of a cougar."

Lizbeth walked behind Angie toward some bushes. "Welken? Yeah, of course. We're here. Wow. It's amazing. The place where everything's the same but totally different."

"I know. Welken's like asking a coconut to drop from a palm tree and then the coconut plops into your hand."

"Angie, there are no palm trees here."

"I know. It's a feeling."

"The falling coconut feeling."

"Yes, it's Welken. It's the place where we feel whole and useful and where magical things happen."

"To me it's more like an extra inning softball game. Tense, exciting, a chance to hit the winning home run."

"OK, tell me about the dream."

Lizbeth sat and fluffed a fern back and forth while she told Angie about the boy. She stripped a frond clean. "So much all at once, Ang. This nightmare leaves me emotionally drained. And now we're back in Welken. It's weird. I thought you were the dreamer and I was the plodder—the one who can't escape from reality."

"I don't like labels. I'm the dreamer. You're the athlete. Bennu's the genius. Len's the leader. It's all too easy. Sometimes you're brilliant, and I'm the world-class sprinter. Remember, Lizbeth, we are all becoming *of* Welken. Maybe this is part of it. Maybe we will all dream dreams and fight dragons."

"Well, you can have the whole thing if I have to keep having these nightmares. They hurt too much, and I just don't get the point." Lizbeth rolled over and pushed herself up, feeling sharp pine needles digging into her hands. "Hey, where'd that cougar go?"

Angie helped brush her off. "As soon as you saw the cougar, you swooned, just like in an old movie. I caught you before you hit your head. Then I turned around and the cougar was gone." She grinned. "I guess you can stop complaining that nothing is happening."

"Let me lean against this tree a minute. Then we should probably head out. But which way? Where are we? Where are the guys? I thought Len and I would end up together—and you and Bennu. Oh, I still feel a little wobbly."

"You mean wobblerated?" The voice came from their right, up the path to the north. "I got so excited when I heard your voices. I untortoised my feet and rabbited right over."

"Vida!" said Lizbeth, "Vida Bering Well!"

Len felt himself falling. As he descended, he flapped his arms to slow himself down, and his arms met with considerable resistance. He wasn't falling through the air. He was in water. Accidentally he swallowed some. Then he switched his flapping into swim strokes to try to stop his descent. As the saltwater stung the scratch on his scalp, Len worried he wouldn't be able to hold his breath long enough. Gazing above him, he saw light and anxiously swam frogman-style upward. Gasping, he broke the surface and heaved.

Charming, he thought snidely. *This, Mr. Len Bartholomew, has got to be Welken—unless there's some other place to go when you slip through a membrane-portal stretched across your backyard. On the other hand, there are no identifying features yet. In fact, there's just an ocean. Here I am, the leader of the Lousy Swimmers Club, dog-paddling with no land in sight, not even a ladder out of the swimming pool.*

Len ran in place in the water. He saw nothing. No land, no boats. No Misfits. Only water and the bright fog to the west, and hot sun everywhere else. He tried not to panic as he swam over to his baseball cap floating nearby. He scanned for driftwood or low-lying land. Did Welken have sharks—or worse? Was he in some Soliton-forsaken ocean?

Then he heard a shout.

"Hey!"

It was Bennu. He was standing up about fifty yards away, in the direction of the blinding sun. Len smiled at the wonder of it and side-stroked over to him. Bennu appeared to be walking on the water.

Yeah, Len thought, *this is Welken all right. The land of miracles, and there's Bennu—walking on water just like the Messiah he thinks he is.* This thought made Len a bit peeved, a bit sorry for himself.

Wait a minute, he realized. *Of course Bennu's over the water. He can be a falcon in Welken. He can hover. But then, I don't think he's become a falcon yet. He's just dippy-looking Bennu. So what's up with that? How could he—*

Clunk.

"Ow! Why didn't you warn me there was a sandbar?"

Bennu held out a hand and pulled him up. "I tried to, but I guess you were absorbed in thought. It's just nice to know you have some."

"Very funny." Panting heavily, Len sat on the sand and put his head between his knees. "Oh, man . . . I'm such . . . a terrible swimmer. No wonder . . . Piers didn't make me a dolphin." Len looked with envy at Bennu's mostly dry clothes. "Where are we?"

"Welken, of course. After that, your guess is as good as mine. The water is so beautiful. If I were to write a poem about it, I think I'd call it Bahama-blue with a pinch of jasmine."

"*That* is the one-hundred-and-eighty-second dumbest thing you've ever said."

"Maybe, but I'm overcome with gratefulness for this loveable little sandbar."

Len took off his soggy socks and shoes. "So, why don't you fly up a-ways and see what a falcon can see?"

Bennu squatted down like he was sharing a secret. "That's the crazy thing. When I didn't see anyone else, I tried to switch into a falcon like before. I put all of my willpower in it, and all I got was this." In an instant Bennu's human head switched into a huge falcon head.

"Whoa. You are seriously spooky looking. No, I mean it . . . like an Egyptian god or a mummy case come to life."

"Crazier yet, I can talk aloud with this head, this beak. But who cares? I can't fly. At least I don't need my glasses. I put them in my pocket."

"I'm too tired to see about becoming a lion. But I'll tell you this: I'm as hungry as a lion."

As easily as all the Misfits had learned to do in Welken, Bennu switched back to human form. "I don't see a refrigerator here. My shoulders are still sore from the McKenzie Boys' place, but why don't you hop back up and see if you can see something?"

Len smiled. He took off his shirt and shorts, wrung them out, and put them in the sun to dry. Then he climbed up onto Bennu's shoulders and Bennu held his ankles as best he could. The first several attempts at stability resulted in flying tumbles and crumpled heaps on the ground. Among other things, Len still felt shaky, and neither of them had anything to hang onto for stability. Finally Bennu found his balance, and Len shielded his eyes for better vision.

"If your boxers stopped dripping on me," Bennu said, "that would be nice."

"You'd better hope it's just water." Len shook a little to make more drops fall.

"You are so funny."

Len straightened up with both hands held out like a tightrope walker. He sighed. "Nothing. I see water, water, and more water. Turn a little. Whoa, steady. Nothing there either. Turn. Don't buckle. Hold it! There. No. Nothing. Turn. Wait! I see . . . no, it's a wave or a fish jumping. Hand me those opera glasses you always take with you. Oh, you don't have them today? Rats. Turn. Hold it. I dunno, I see something way out there. It doesn't quite look like a wave. Hey, it's getting closer. It's . . . it's rectangular, I think. It's gotta be a sail. Yahoo! Let me down."

Bennu moaned as he bowed. Len flopped on his side onto the sand.

"Thanks for the smooth landing."

"No problem. OK, we need to get that boat's attention. Grab your shorts and wave them. I'll wave your shirt."

"Nice try. I'm not going to wave some boat over here while standing in my underwear. What if some cute Welken babe is on board?

You wave your shirt, and I'll wave mine." Len slipped back into his shorts.

While dark-skinned Bennu waved his black T-shirt and gold under-shirt and fair-skinned Len waved his blue-striped shirt, the boat kept a steady pace sailing right for them.

"Well," said Bennu, "we've got color going for us."

Len jumped up and down. "Saved! We're going to be saved!" He ran around the tiny island, throwing sand into the air. "Oh, dear God, thank you. I thought I'd never get off this prison. Me and Friday, we was about to go crazy!"

"Len?"

"Yes, dearest Bennu?"

"I think you might want to curb your enthusiasm a little."

"Why is that, may I ask?"

"Well, for one thing, your feet have claws and your tail is sticking out of your shorts."

Len looked down and spun around. He caught his tail like the Cow-ardly Lion in *The Wizard of Oz*. "What kind of a deal is this? Maybe you can't fly, but at least you get a falcon head. I get a lion rump. This stinks."

Bennu waved a finger in the air like a cheesy Boy Scout leader. "You never know when it'll come in handy."

"Yeah, like when I need to scare nearly blind rabbits." In a moment, by his will, Len made the tail vanish and his human legs reappear. As before, he was awestruck at the metamorphosis—but confused this time by the incomplete fulfillment of his leonine self.

The fat froggishness of Vida brought a smile to Lizbeth. All four feet of the Welkener from Deedy Swamp waddled over, her big-bellied body steadied by her large feet. She pressed against Lizbeth. Fat arms reached up around Lizbeth's waist. After shuffling over to Angie and hugging her, Vida rested her head briefly on Angie's stomach. Stepping back, Vida regarded the two of them like a proud mother would. She put her thumbs in her belt and wrapped the fingers of each hand around a dagger.

Then her face switched from a smile to a frown. "We'll have to get nostalgified as soon as we find some spare clockification. For now, all the gibbets are jangled and the whole chaos is catastrophizin'."

"That sounds bad," said Lizbeth, still holding Vida's hands. "I have no idea what you said, but it sounds bad."

"I'll speechify you this, you two misfitted fitters, Mook of the Nezzer Clan and I been wanderin' for the last calendarin', only to get off-roaded every time we seem to get within a blow-whistle of findin' Bors."

Angie's countenance fell. "You mean you haven't found Bors? How awful."

"We've smelled the roast cookin', but we can't seem to kitchen it. But like I was unveilin' but a freckle ago, we'd best be trekkifyin' back to Deedy Swamp. Mook's in a tidy mound of scaffoldin'." Vida slipped her wispy hair behind her tiny ears.

Lizbeth couldn't imagine why any urgency would be required if Mook were involved in some building renovation. So she stopped for a minute to brush herself off as Angie and Vida hustled down the path ahead of her.

"Angie, Angie, wait a minute, I get it!" As adrenaline surged through Lizbeth, she imagined Mook with a noose around his neck, his many ponytails hanging down his back. Lizbeth wanted to become as strong as she could to save Mook, as strong as an ox. Her biceps grew and her shoulders rose up on her bones. That beautiful oxen strength pushed against her stretchy top, and it changed into the short brown fur of oxen hide. Standing upright, Lizbeth's upper body swelled in size until her head seemed dwarfed by the powerful muscles around it. To her dismay, her still-human legs could barely support the weight. She stumbled a step, then fell forward. By the time she hit the ground, she had willed herself back into human form.

Lizbeth looked up and saw Angie and Vida rounding a bend ahead of her. No longer woozy from her dream, Lizbeth jogged to catch her friends.

Whoa, she thought. *So many questions at once. The dream, Vida, Bors, and now this weird half-oxen thing—or quarter-oxen thing. What's with that? And where are Len and Bennu? I hope they're OK. Heck, I hope we're OK. In*

Skinner, I couldn't wait to get back here. I thought everything would feel perfect. But I guess I don't get this whole Welken thing yet.

When Lizbeth veered left around a tree, she nearly knocked Vida over. "Oh, I'm sorry. I didn't see you."

Vida looked a little offended, hitched up her belt of daggers, and stood as tall as her shortness allowed. "Well, you'd best be gettin' better at binocularin', dearie. We've got to be trickery if we want to columbus Deedy Swamp without gettin' columbused ourselves. There's gotchas all along the way."

Laboriously, for the footing grew as slippery as Vida's words already were, the threesome hurried down into the lowlands. Along the way, Angie and Lizbeth learned that, after The Welkening, finding Bors had become more and more important. He had been spared the fate of being swallowed by Morphane, but now his soul was inside Piers and his body was missing. What The Welkening began could not be completed until Bors was whole again. He possessed some power or fulfilled some role that Angie and Lizbeth could not yet figure out.

Angie scratched her head. "Is Bors some kind of sorcerer or a prophet? Does he see the future or find out the truth of our hearts?"

"Oh, Angie." Vida reached up to touch the Misfit's shoulder. "You mark such a trail of verbifications. Bors is a watcher and a keeper. He's the whole caboodle of knowingness and gentle spirits. I rememberize one time, when he einsteined a lovely deed right before my visuals. I was trekkifyin' over to Welken's fairest city, Primus Hook, one day and was blatherin' all wide-eyed about some pilferizin' goin' on and on. The good man Bors snippified a rose, carried its scent like a bucket-o-sweetness, and handed me the redness of it all. He's got the knackification for good tidin's, he does."

"Vida Bering Well," said Lizbeth, "I'm so confusified by your speechification."

"I beg your christification." Vida pushed against a branch she'd turned into a walking stick. "I forget you aren't fully Deedy-ized—and I'm sick to my blood-pumper about Piers. He's not himself. He looks all gravel-and-rags. He's bent over, like a poet gone yonkers." Vida tapped a row of tree trunks with her stick. "He's been shaken and stirred up since you left, spit out for lost like so many amelia-earharts a-flyin' by."

"I'm so sorry." When Angie squatted, her blue wings pulsed in and out of sight.

Angie's powers seem more fully developed. Why? Jealousy stirred in Lizbeth.

"Hearing that about Piers makes me weak," Angie said. "I had no idea you wouldn't find Bors right away. That's so sad. In a whole month, you've not been close?"

Vida stopped and leaned on her stick. "In a whole month, missy? Just how have you been calendarin'? We've been binocularin' for Bors for a year now, almost to the very twinklin' you four twilighted out of Welken."

Lizbeth sat down. "We've been gone a year? That's not possible. To us, we've only been gone a month."

"Be careful about Welken's possibilities, young lady. All that is has been is-ing for as long as time needs be. Eternity's more a place for campfirin' a good story than it is just endless clockification."

"What's eternity got to do with it?" Lizbeth felt Vida had jumped on her for no good reason. "I was just telling you about time in Skinner. Is everything in Welken the way things are supposed to be? Is Skinner's clock wrong?"

Vida dropped the stick and put her hands on her daggers. "I only have one pointification. No, I'll show you four." She pulled four daggers out of her belt. In lightning succession she flung them at nearby trees. Two blades stuck into trees on the right and two into trees on the left. She pulled them out, each with one word. "Don't . . . never . . . Welken's . . . always."

"OK, Vida; I'll try. As soon as I figure out what it means." Lizbeth picked up a rock and threw it at one of Vida's dagger-struck trees. It hit. "All my friends back home are so cynical. I'm not used to accepting so much change so fast."

"It's like this," said Angie, grooming her feathers. "We just have a way of looking for the one faded flower in a field of blooms."

Lizbeth smirked. "Not exactly how I'd put it, but I guess you could say I'm not 'of Welken' yet."

Vida paused. She put each dagger back into its sheath and then looked down the trail. "Lizbeth, maybe oxen have a way of furrowin' their head too close to the dirt and such. But just as sure as we're trekkifyin' down this path, you are as much 'of Welken' as any of us inhabitants. Your heart is turned, Lizbeth, and that's just the best rotation anyone could edison. The rest of you will follow." Vida picked up her stick and pressed her thin hair flat against her round head. "Enough chatters-and-cookies. I've got a hunchination Mook needs us. In Welken!"

Lizbeth and Angie eyed each other. "*Of* Welken!"

CHAPTER FIVE
GARETH AND SLUGGY SLIDES

"Pass to, pass in," the angels say,
"In to the upper doors,
Nor count compartments of the floors
But mount to paradise
By the stairway of surprise."

—RALPH WALDO EMERSON, *POEMS, MERLIN I*

To Len and Bennu's delight, the ship kept coming closer. With sails full, the craft cut briskly through the water. Yellow and red flags fluttered from each mast, and the crow's nest bobbed to the rhythm of the swells.

By the time the sailors on the vessel could finally be seen, Len thought his arm would fall off from waving his T-shirt so much. He had switched hands several times and had even used his other hand to support the waving hand. "Do you have a flare gun on you, Bennu? That would be so much easier than waving and waving."

"'Fraid not. I do have an inflatable skywriting kit in my pocket—but I think I should save that for later. Man, I wish these guys would notice us. I keep picturing them scrutinizing us through a telescope and trying to decide if we are worth the stop. Len, maybe you should put your shirt back on. That skinny white chest could scare them off."

Len glowered. "No way. I know what these guys are thinking. They see the toughness and the heart inside this chest. They see my intelligence and wit."

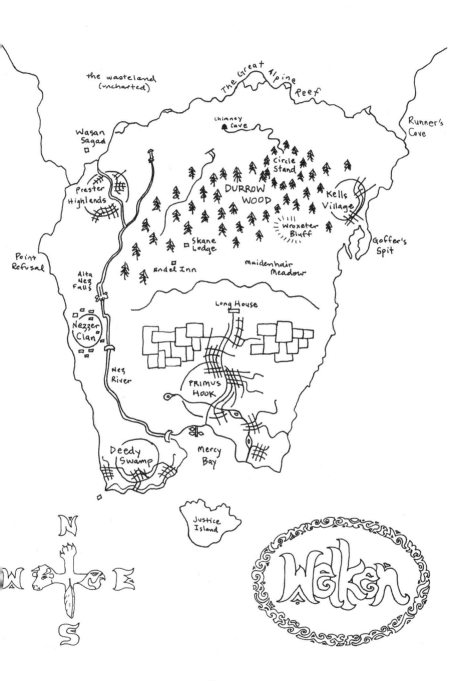

the wasteland
(uncharted)

The Great Alpine Reef

Runner's Cove

chimney Cave

Wasan Sagad

Circle Stand

DURROW WOOD

Kells Village

Prester Highlands

Wroxeter Bluff

Goffer's Spit

Point Refusal

Skane Lodge

Endel Inn

Maidenhair Meadow

Alta Nez Falls

Long House

Nezzer Clan

Nez River

PRIMUS HOOK

Deedy Swamp

Mercy Bay

Justice Island

Welken

N
W   E
S

"And that's why they're leaving."

"What? Oh, c'mon, they can't do that!"

Bennu angrily gripped a fistful of sand. "There they go! Sailing right by us, without a single compassionate impulse." He let the sand go.

Len threw his shirt on the sand. "Hey! You can't do this! You've got to rescue us! We'll starve out here! You idiots, come back!"

"I can't believe it." Bennu plopped onto the sand and rubbed his sore arm. "I just can't believe it. I wish Angie were here. Where are they, anyway?"

Len paced back and forth on the little strip of land. "This is just great. We get back to Welken, only to die in the middle of nowhere. I'm thirsty. Did you hear that, Piers? I'm thirsty!" He ran into the water and slapped his T-shirt on the surface. "Now what are we to do? I know what you'll do, Bennu. You'll write a stupid poem about it."

"Calm down, Len. Look what you did. Your clothes are all wet again."

Hanging his head, Len walked out of the water and plopped down on the sand. "Yeah, you're right. What good does it do to yell about it? I get mad, then I get mad at the fact that I just got mad. I don't know what else to do."

"I know what I could do. I could write a poem about it."

Len scooped up some sand and showered Bennu with it.

Bennu fluffed his hair to get the sand out. "You can't take anything, can you?"

After shaking his head, Len stretched out and made a sand angel by waving his arms and legs. Then a spray of sand hit him in the chest. "Hey!" Len sat up.

"Sorry." Bennu waded into the water. "I was aiming for your face." He dove in, turned around, and floated on his back.

Len dropped his head between his knees. He stopped to think how awful his situation was—and now he and Bennu were fighting. But he caught himself. Nothing truly terrible had happened yet. They weren't starving to death. Vicious beasts hadn't charged them. So he waded out to Bennu in the water, all the while watching his feet through the amazingly clear water.

Just then two dark rocks caught his eye. He stepped on them and stood a foot taller in the water. Before he could brag about his height to Bennu, the rocks moved and he splashed into the water. That's when he saw the beaks—turtle beaks—snapping at his feet.

"Bennu, get out of the water!" His heart racing, Len did his best to outswim the surprisingly fast turtles. Bennu reached the sand first and grabbed Len by the hand. The turtles kept coming. They crawled out of the water and, like herding dogs, backed Len and Bennu up into the center of the sandbar. Their flared shells had pointed rims, like a stegosaurus's, their long claws dug into the sand, and they were quick. They darted around, emitting a cackling *bark* . . . a cross between a crow's caw and a coyote's yip.

Len bent over and grabbed the two T-shirts next to him in the sand. If only he could throw the T-shirts over the turtles' heads. . . .

Bennu broke his concentration. "Another ship is coming! Look!"

"Yeah!" Len snapped his striped shirt at a turtle. "Now," *snap*, "we can," *snap*, "get out of here," *snap*, "maybe." Len glanced up and saw the ship coming toward them. "We must be near a good ocean current. Some shipping lane or something." When he looked back down to check the assault, he saw the turtles' backsides slipping into the water.

Bennu put on his shoes as Len waved his T-shirt. Then they reversed roles.

Len sighed. "I was really getting worried that our obituary would read 'Teenage Boys from Skinner Killed by Speedy Turtles.' Not a pretty thought."

"No, but that ship is a pretty sight. How can we get this one to stop?"

Not long after Len stood on Bennu's shoulders once more, the boys saw a flag wave back, the sails drop, and a rowboat make its way toward them.

"I hope it's somebody we know," said Len.

"Yeah, like maybe your dad or Cindy Martinez."

As the boat skimmed over the water, Len could make out three—he assumed—Welkeners, none of whom he recognized. In one sense, the scene reminded him of the famous painting of George Washington crossing the Delaware. One figure stood in the boat, one foot on the front seat.

It gave him the appearance of absolute confidence—and it also told Len that the Welkener must have absolute balance. In another sense, the scene would remind no one of George Washington. The standing Welkener wore a white sailor's cap with a slight peak in the center and a feather tilted backward, a bit of a cross between Robin Hood and Popeye. A navy blue vest came below his waist, and a blousy white shirt fluttered in the breeze.

With a final thrust, the oarsman powered the boat onto the sand. The one who appeared to be in charge stepped deftly off the bow and leaped past the water onto the sand. The oarsmen carried short swords, but the leader did not.

In addition to his dripping wetness, Len felt immediately under-dressed. The captain's vest looked regal, its deep blue offset with a gold border stripe. Ruby rings shone from each hand.

The leader dropped to one knee. "Len and Bennu, I greet you in Soliton's name, may his wisdom for Welken endure forever. I am Gareth, of Primus Hook. I was told of you by the Weary One, and I welcome you once again to Welken."

Len swallowed hard. "You know us? How did you know it was us? I mean, that we were Len and Bennu?" He squeezed the water out of the edges of his soggy T-shirt.

Bennu extended a hand and bowed his head. "Yes, I am Bennu, and this is Len."

Len shot him a don't-be-so-trusting look.

Gareth rose and pulled a folded paper from a pocket. "It is all here. Your story has been recorded and sent around the land. Some say it will be added to the Book of Quadrille. Your appearance is described in detail, as is your courage on behalf of Welken. But I did not need to read this document. I heard it all from the Weary One himself."

Len relaxed his stance. "The Weary One? Who is that?"

"Ah," said Gareth, "I forget that you don't know what has happened since you left. The Weary One is Piers, the Lord of Primus Hook, the High Ambassador of Welken. Come, get into the boat. I'll tell you all about it."

Bennu prodded Len by the elbow. "He's probably legit. Besides, what choice do we have?"

So Len and Bennu sat in the boat and learned that Welken had aged a year in the month they'd been gone, that Bors had not been found, and that Piers—the Weary One—had grown weaker under the weight of carrying Bors's soul within him. If this knowledge were not enough to make them squirm as the boat approached the ship, they also learned that Gareth was chasing the ship that had not stopped for them, a ship that had recently made enough passes through the channel to arouse Gareth's suspicion from Primus Hook.

As they traveled, the salty air smelled fresh and crisp, but bitter too. After a while, Len tested his sea legs and nearly fell over. He grabbed on to some rigging. With his elbow through a hole, Len realized he knew little about Welken's circumstances. But he knew this much: Welken was in trouble again.

At first the trail to Deedy Swamp felt appropriately swampy. More vines, more wetness, less sunshine. Vida led Angie and Lizbeth over the marshy path, sometimes hopping on rocks to avoid the mud, sometimes sloshing through the goo. Lizbeth was glad she had worn her tennis shoes. Here and there, short boardwalks provided relief from the "slickery" path and allowed for faster footwork. In the trees, exotic flowers bloomed, something like hibiscus or plumeria, only larger and each more fragrant than a gardenia. Some petals folded back when approached, as if aching to release their scent.

Lizbeth loved it. She skipped when she could. She drew in the aromas, holding a flower with both hands and burrowing her nose deep into the center, like a short-beaked hummingbird. She wanted to walk with her eyes closed and let her nose lead the way.

Vida sniffed repeatedly. "We've just outskirted the Swamp. Ah, the scentification, the delicious basement-and-dank coolnesses."

Angie stroked a hand-sized pink petal and put her hand to her nose. "It smells like watermelon, ripe and sweet. I want to eat it."

Vida wagged a stubby finger. "You're einsteinin' the swampification better than you know, but this one here is peaches-and-cream, not watermelon. Have a bite."

Angie plucked a petal and put it in her mouth. "It *is* like peaches, Lizbeth. Oh, I feel like a summer day."

Lizbeth tore off a petal and started to put it in her mouth.

Vida tugged on Lizbeth's belt loops. "Lizbeth, go ahead. But I'll paulrevere you this. The Meducer can look all taffy-and-toffee, but she's a right beaky snakification."

"The Meducer? A beaky snakification?"

Vida held out both hands and wiggled her fingers. "Starts off casanova-and-candles and then come out those ten tongues forkin' up the nectar."

"OK, Vida," said Lizbeth. "I'll try to be careful. I won't bite into any peachy petals that look like snakes with beaks . . . or . . . something." Lizbeth reached out toward another flower. "Vida, what about this one?" She spread her hands before a tall row of flowers. "And what about all these?" She ran ahead. "Angie, look at these flowers! Each a different flavor, probably. Vida, help me out here. Is the Meducer around? Can we eat?"

Lizbeth sidestepped joyfully, waiting for Vida's permission. She could barely contain herself. The thought of each delicious petal consumed her so thoroughly that she didn't notice the path shifting, slanting downhill. She reached back for a blossom and slipped. When she grabbed at the plant to stop her fall, it broke off. Lizbeth hit the ground and kept moving. Picking up speed, she slid down an inch of slime that covered the path. Faster and faster she fell.

Then she screamed.

She tried to dig her heels in to stop, but she flopped on her side, still sliding, still screaming. The yellow slime oozed up her socks and legs. As she searched furiously for something to grab, the slime gooped over her outstretched arms and splashed onto her face.

Then, *thwack*, she stopped feetfirst at a squishy, stinky, moving, living wall.

"Help!" Lizbeth pushed against the slimy skin of the thing. "Vida! Angie! It's sucking me in!"

"We're coming, Lizbeth!" Angie yelled.

"We're *not* coming, Lizbeth!" said Vida. "Freeze-tag it till we get set up."

"Freeze-tag it?" *What is that supposed to mean?* Lizbeth wondered. "This thing wants to eat me," she yelled back. "I need help now!"

Like a giant land anemone, the creature drew itself in. Lizbeth felt the suction, and she fought back. She pushed against the sluglike stuff that threatened to envelop her. Her hands kept slipping off. Lizbeth could no longer see her knees, and then her thighs. The walls sucked her down to her waist. She switched from pushing to grabbing, and that seemed to hold off the creeping yellow skin. But she couldn't keep a grip. The slippery body oozed between her fingers. It pressed against her. It sucked her in. Up past her stomach now in this living quicksand, Lizbeth struggled. She pounded at the thing. She screamed louder. "Angie! Vida! Where are you? Why aren't you doing anything?"

With all her oxen strength, she turned over onto her stomach. She grabbed on the ground for anything, a rock or a plant. She poked her finger through to a boardwalk plank and clung onto it with both hands. Looking up, she saw Vida's squatty self next to Angie. While Angie paced with pleading hands, her blue wings blazing, Vida stood poised with one dagger in each hand.

Lizbeth tugged on the plank. "Do something! Now!"

She thought she'd made some progress. She thought she'd pulled herself out an inch or so. An inch! An inch was good! Then the plank gave way, and Lizbeth slipped into the thing up to her armpits. She couldn't find breath enough to yell. With the broken plank in her hand, she pushed against the walls from the inside.

So tired. I'm so tired. C'mon, fight! She pressed the plank into the gooey wall.

Hold! she urged the plank. *Something's got to work.*

Lizbeth pushed against the plank and slowly edged her way up. She got her chest free. "Help! I'm losing it."

Then the plank gave way. The beast created another hole and sucked the board away from Lizbeth. The walls collapsed on her and drew her in. Her hope got sucked out too.

This is it. I'll die in this squeezing, sucking thing.

With her arms pinned to her side, all she could do was look out. She saw something curling toward her. It was a head, and it was opening its slimy mouth! Lizbeth saw teeth—dull, grimy, jaundiced teeth. She couldn't move out of the way. She couldn't cover her head. She couldn't bear the thought that this thing might come and chomp off her head. Why didn't Piers speak inside her and tell her what to do, like last time when Morphane had come to get her?

Lizbeth bowed her head. She didn't want to watch the head come any closer. Maybe the thing couldn't bite through her skull. . . .

Then Lizbeth heard a siren scream, a high-pitched, violent screech. It shook her so deeply that she glanced up. There, in the beast's mouth, was one of Vida's daggers. The head flailed back and forth. Lizbeth felt a sudden squeeze, then the sucking walls went limp. Gasping, she slimed her way out to her waist. She closed her eyes and tried to catch her breath. Her arms shook. Her legs felt numb.

When she opened her eyes again, a frantic Angie knelt at her side. "Lizbeth, are you OK? I'm so sorry we took so long. Oh, look at you. I started to run toward you, but Vida caught me." Angie wiped a tear. "She said I'd just get 'tar- babied' too if I tried to go get you. All we could do was wait till the head showed itself, till Vida had something to aim at." She yanked Lizbeth farther out, slipping in the slime as she did. "Lizbeth, I'm so glad you're OK. I felt helpless standing there. I wanted to fly over and drop rocks on the thing, but I couldn't. I have these wings, but I can't fly! I wanted you to become an ox and charge out of that stupid hole—but you couldn't. I saw your shoulders change, but that was all. Oh, Lizbeth, why aren't we whole this time? Have we done something wrong?" She scraped the slime off Lizbeth's legs. "And I just keep blabbing. Here—Vida gave me some water for you."

As Lizbeth bent forward to take a drink, she saw Vida pulling her dagger out of the monster. "Vida," said Lizbeth, still panting, "what is this thing? Why didn't you warn us?"

"I beg your christification, really I do." Vida wiped the dagger clean. "There's not enough clockification to do all the show-and-tell about what's happened since The Welkening. Some things got happily-ever-aftered, but other things got spookified." She and Angie pulled on Lizbeth, slipped, and pulled again. "Ever since you Misfits trekkified home, Welken's seen beasts of cruel teethification and wicked wanderin's. We've got more problems than we do solutions, if you drift me out."

Finally Lizbeth sat on the boardwalk. Breathing heavily, she scraped slime off her body.

Angie did the same. "I thought The Welkening was the end of Welken's troubles. And where's Bennu?"

"One chapter ends and the next one takes up the bookification. And, by Soliton's glow, Len and Bennu are page-flippin' in their own way. We've got to get to the end, y'see."

Angie and Vida supported Lizbeth as they shuffled cautiously down the trail to a pool deep enough for them to wash off in. Angie's expression troubled Lizbeth because it was so rare. Angie looked worried as she cleaned the gunk off her skin and Lizbeth's.

Though exhausted, Lizbeth did not linger in the pool. She kept imagining something from her last trip to Welken. Mook and Alabaster. Water. And basilisks.

CHAPTER SIX
TREMLINGS

In a desert land he found him, in a barren and howling waste.
—DEUTERONOMY 32:10a

 Away from the sandbar, the swells grew larger and occasionally slapped against the hull of the rowboat. Though experienced in a canoe, Len had never been in the open sea. Here his stomach followed the rising and falling of the waves. Bennu seemed to be fine. Len shot him a phony smile, then eyed Gareth with disdainful admiration. One foot on the front seat, he stood all the way, calmly explaining the past year's events to the Misfits. His balance as perfect as his clothes, Gareth did not vary his expression.

Len kept his eye on the teetering horizon. "Gareth, do you stand all the time?"

The boat rode high on a swell and hit the bottom of the next one with a splash, sending spray into everyone's face except Gareth's. "I've been sitting too much of my life, lad. I'm the Keeper of the Balance for Primus Hook. All my life, I've been adding and subtracting and balancing the books. Some say that's why I ride the waves so well."

Len studied the crow's-feet of Gareth's eyes and the creases of his mouth, but he did not detect the slightest sweet-wrinkling or smirk. "You got me beat, I'll give you that. I may be King of the Jungle when I'm at my best, but out here I'm Wuss of the Waves. What took you away from your desk job, Gareth?"

"After The Welkening, like all the villages in Welken, Primus Hook rejoiced for weeks, then went about the goodly tasks we'd been given to do in this life. Some cooked. Some told stories. Some made candles or threw pots or baked bread. All cared for the children and for each other. But something wasn't right—and the more time that went by, the more we knew the 'not right' was getting worse." Gareth picked at his fingernails with a knife. "Y'see, Piers never made it back to Primus Hook. Oh, we heard stories about him, brave adventures in search of Bors. But we heard other stories too, of Piers's halting speech, his hunched shoulders, his tired walk. We started calling him the Weary One."

Len turned his focus from the horizon to the ship up ahead. Though Columbus had fallen out of favor in high school history texts, here was a vessel to make the *Santa Maria* proud. The sails, the rigging, the crow's nest—everything inspired a sense of adventure. But Len mainly felt motion sickness.

Bennu tried to stand but quickly sat down. "So you decided you'd be more help as a sailor, as an adventurer of the High Seas?"

"We received news about terrible things happening in the Greater Wasteland, north of Kells Village. I'd always fancied the seagoing life," Gareth explained, "so I answered the call."

The oarsmen deftly pulled the small boat alongside the ship.

"Here we are, lads—our ship, the graceful, steady *Pelican*."

After a gentle *clunk*, the sailors grabbed the ropes that had been flung down from above. As the rowboat was tied on fore and aft, Len grabbed the rope ladder that swayed against the wooden hull. Climbing up proved more difficult than he imagined. Much of the way, the ladder pressed against the hull, making the rungs hard to grab and smashing his fingers once he did clasp them. When he reached the top and grabbed the hand of a waiting sailor, Len gratefully swung over the side and stumbled onto the deck. He turned back and looked down at the hesitant Bennu.

He might be able to soar the skies in Welken, but he's such a klutz everywhere else. I know how to speed him up. "Hey, Bennu, Angie's up here waiting for you!"

Bennu's head shot up toward Len. "Shut up!" He slipped in a foothold and hung by his arms. Frantically his feet searched for a rung until he found one. Pressing himself against the wobbly rope, Bennu climbed, rung by agonizing rung, until he reached the top. The others followed. Gareth came last, ascending the ladder with methodical athleticism.

Len leaned against some rigging and whispered to Bennu, "It's so small. I always pictured an explorer's ship much larger."

After Gareth gave orders to set sail, the deck erupted in busyness. Even Len and Bennu were asked to "hold this" rope or "pull this" line. Len felt so out of place he thought everyone was staring, that every glance in his direction meant, *You incompetent!*

Once they were underway, headed north by northeast, the fog lifted to the west. A coastline appeared.

"The eastern shore of Welken," said Gareth, pointing to his left. "We've passed Goffer's Spit. You can see the mountains of Alpine's Reef there."

"Where are we headed?" asked Len.

"To wild places farther up. It's all part of the Wasteland. But well past the desert are other villages. That ship sailing south—the one we're worried about? That was a merchant ship from Barmella, sailing to Mercy Bay. We're not always on friendly terms."

Bennu looked wistfully toward Kells Village. "Gareth, if The Welkening made things right, why are so many things now wrong?"

"Good question, lad. The Welkening turned the tide, but much more water needs to be pulled out to sea. The crimes of Terz and Morphane were not all that had been set loose, and they were not the first, either. Things will be made well, you can count on it—but folks like you and me still need to do the counting."

Bennu tapped Gareth lightly on the arm. "As Keeper of the Balance, you've got some good experience in the counting department."

Len rolled his eyes. He mouthed, "So cheesy."

Without a change in expression, Gareth grabbed a telescope from the bosun and surveyed the coast. "There's the destination, lads. Runner's Cove. So named, I believe, because visitors couldn't get out fast enough. We think there's been mischief here. Two villagers on a pilgrimage from Durrow Wood saw Barmella ships pull in and out of the cove. It's not a place to trade goods. There's no good reason to land there at all."

After a short time, the *Pelican* dropped anchor, and the rowboat skimmed over the water once more, Gareth standing tall. "We don't know much about this spot, lads. You can see the low-lying cliffs beyond the beach. We ought to get on top and have a look around. We're searching for evidence of Barmella's visits—could be a half-dead beast or a pile of bones. They don't call it the Wasteland for nothing."

Len thought of all the D-Day movies he'd seen, full of soldiers wading ashore on Omaha Beach getting cut down by Nazi machine-gun fire. Thankfully he could not see any bunkers or artillery. But he did see the beach, and it was not sparkling white sand.

When the rowboat *shushed* to a stop, Gareth hopped out and the others followed.

With his first step, Len slipped and fell directly onto the reason for his fall—smooth wet stones as gray as his mood was becoming. With some difficulty, Len stood and shuffled a few feet away from the boat. "Well," he said, "at least something is alive here. Algae." That's when he saw Gareth up ahead, walking as if on dry ground. He spoke just loud enough for Bennu to hear, "That guy is too perfect. He's starting to get on my nerves."

Then Bennu walked briskly away from him, and Len saw why. Ridges of dry, coral-like rock jutted out from the ground. As Len stepped onto the more secure footing, he realized the hazards of doing so. The rocks cut like coral, slicing off a piece of his tennis shoe. Len watched Bennu for a minute, then decided it was safe enough to step onto the firm rock and make his way toward Gareth. If he dodged the sharper parts, his soles would hold up.

Fifty feet from shore, Len discovered a gaping hole surrounded by coral. The opening was about two and a half feet round. He stopped to stare into it, then saw Gareth and Bennu doing the same thing up ahead. "What do you make of this?" he shouted to them.

"Well," Bennu called back, "they look like holes."

Len squatted for a closer look. "No wonder you win all those genius awards. Gareth?"

"I can't help but think they have something to do with this place being called Runner's Cove. Sorry, lads, I wish I knew more."

The closer the three of them got to the cliffs, the more holes they discovered. Between the slippery stones, the slicing coral, and the ominous pits, the rowboat started to look increasingly attractive. Len also saw an irony in the name Runner's Cove, since that was the one thing one could not do on this beach.

Len leaned over another hole. He picked up a slimy stone and tossed it down. He didn't hear it hit.

Then there was a *phissst!* A nearby hole blew like a whale exhaling, shooting spray fifteen feet into the air. Startled, Len fell down onto some slimy stones and slid backward into protruding coral.

"Ow!" he yelped. As he rubbed his hands, he watched the stuff that flew out of the hole. He couldn't tell if it was water, steam, or sand. At its zenith the substance formed into something recognizable, a humanlike shape, then broke apart as it fell back into the hole.

Another blast shot out. Then another. These elongated apparitions disturbed Len. Eerie, ghostlike, one sandy phantasm after another rose and fell, like imprisoned souls emerging for several seconds of daylight, then slipping back into their cells. But maybe they weren't ghosts. Maybe these beings were in their natural state, beach creatures that shot up like prairie dogs to see the world around them. No matter how he reasoned, his fear remained. The sand-ghosts terrified him.

Phissst! Another hole blew, this one right next to Gareth. He studied it, and then, stone-faced, glanced over at Len and Bennu.

Phissst! Phissst! Blowholes erupted all around them.

When I was in Skinner, I thought I might become a Wendy, a girl who wasn't allowed to return to Neverland. Yet here I am, back in Welken, walking in the swampy woods toward Vida's home. I should be happy, right? Lizbeth told herself. *But I'm exhausted from nearly getting eaten—and from cleaning the slime off, and I'm worried about the guys. What happened to them?*

"Vida," said Lizbeth, "I thought that after The Welkening, once Morphane and Terz were conquered, things would be peaceful here. Y'know . . . the lion would lie down with the lamb."

Vida pulled herself along the path with her pole, as if she'd been "punting" up an English stream. "Don't go all pearlygates on me, dearie. There *is* a golden threadification that's sewn into all things, but Welken's not tailor-made quite yet. And, besides, why would a finished Welken not have any lewisandclarkin' in it? If you think that everythin' in Welken should be all hammocks-and-tea, you've got more einsteinin' to do."

Lizbeth squeezed some water out of her ponytail. "I suppose I do."

Angie touched Lizbeth's arm. "Maybe it's just that one horizon gives way to another. We can't 'figure it all out.' That's not to say we shouldn't try."

Vida nodded. "I couldn't have saged it better myself. Now I beg your christification, but we really must get movin'. I've been questin' for Piers all snow-and-come-green things, but right now we got to get directly swampified. Word is that whilst I've been columbusin' for Piers, somebody's come and bejailed the goodness in Deedy, if you drift me out."

After walking swiftly for some time, Vida, Lizbeth, and Angie stopped at a curtain of hanging moss that hung over the path between trees. When they pushed the moss aside, the woods opened up onto a tropical marsh filled with blooming lotus flowers and water lilies. From high up on their trunks, mangrove trees sent their roots into the soil. When the path turned into a boardwalk rising above the water as a planked street, Lizbeth found herself smiling at everything. Roundish little boats floated here and there, some propelled with paddles, but most with poles for punting. Each gondola-styled bow resembled a giant hand leading the way. Colorful flags flapped out over the stern.

Lizbeth felt like all her strength had returned. "Oh, Vida, I love it! It's so, so . . . you!"

Angie ran up to the first building. "Lizbeth, come here quick! This is amazing!"

Lizbeth's smile grew larger and larger as she got closer. The structure, a general store of some sort, butted up against the boardwalk, but it clearly extended down into the marshy water also. The aboveground part looked like a giant teapot, with a suspension bridge coming out of the spout and leading to a building next door, a restaurant that reminded Lizbeth vaguely of a loaf of bread.

Deedy Swamp was Venice turned inside out. Venice's waterways were the boardwalks here. Everything else was in water, including the buildings. Vida pointed out that all the stores had a "ground-level" door that opened both to stairs that went up to a second-level "dry" floor and down into a "water-level" floor. Vida explained that Deediers lived just as well in the water as above it. They "amphibianized" their homes too, with at least two floors underwater for every one above it.

"So," said Angie, "that means you—all Deediers—can breathe underwater? I knew there was something fishy about you."

Vida smiled. "What do you Misfitters call that? Cheesification?"

To Lizbeth, the town grew curiouser and curiouser, wackier and wackier, evermore loraxed-and-green-egged. She came upon a basket-shaped flower shop and, while looking up, accidentally walked right into the water. Below the surface, she saw a store in "normal" business activity, with Deediers purchasing underwater bouquets.

Lizbeth came up to breathe, grabbed Angie's hand and the railing, and rolled over onto the boardwalk. She laughed. "The whole place is a crack-up."

Vida leaned over Lizbeth's wet body. "You might be jokified about ol' Deedy Swamp, but I'd advise you to show more respectification. Not every eye is what meets the eye. So, now, standify it." As Lizbeth suppressed her giggles and stood up, Vida greeted a few passersby. "Yes, yes, Miss Connie Sheekin Dream, butter-and-toast to you, my dear. Oh hello, Richard Terning Round, meet-greet and hand-shakerin's to you. By the way, Richard, have you columbused anythin' that truthifies all the gossipification?"

"Vida," said Richard as he waddled closer, "I can clandestine it no longer. The whisperin's tell the story. MaryMary Hardin Fast has as good as mussolinied her way to the very toppification. She's a ruthless oppressi-fier! One verbification can alcatraz you! She says we'd be better if we sounded all the same, speechifyin' like the lords and ladies of Primus Hook. And that's not the glass-half-empty-of-it, Vida. She's rallied a vi-cious forcification to her side, all handcuffs and spears, a whole host of outsiders from somewheres-no-one-knows-where. They want to cookiecut-ter every verbasaurus, but since they're so cruel, we just call 'em Cutters."

"I see what you're speechifyin', Richard." Vida put her hands on her ample hips. "The streets are scarce and shuttered-up. Must be these Cutters. And what about Mook of the Nezzer Clan? He trekkified here a fort-night yonder."

"Vida, there's no ollie-ollie-oxen-free anymore. Ears belabor every lily pad and barnacle. But I'll harken you this." Richard leaned in so Lizbeth could barely hear. "Mook's here. But the Cutters unquivered him. Mary-Mary Hardin Fast clinked him in the jailification. Scaffoldin' awaits, scaffoldin'!" With this, Richard opened the ground level door of a post office and dove into the water.

Lizbeth paced on the boardwalk, careful not to get too close to the edge. Nervously she stuffed her hands in her back pockets, then withdrew them to plead with Vida. "Mook's in some sort of prison, Vida. What are we waiting for? Why don't we stop standing around and go find him?"

"And microphone our allegiance to every Cutter a-squanderin' the air? We must be off and putterin', inspirin' no binoculatin'. Where'd Angie go?"

Lizbeth found Angie on her knees, studying the water as if it were a secret file. "Angie, we need to get moving. Didn't you hear about Mook? I want to see his brave face again."

"I know." She held one hand over the surface. "There are stories in these waters, Lizbeth, tales of struggle and loss. I feel the voices as they run between my fingers. I'm carrying their tears." Angie rushed to another place on the boardwalk. Lizbeth saw Angie's face reflected in the placid water over the side. Then Angie broke the surface with a finger. "The slightest touch will send a ripple, Lizbeth, the slightest touch." She stood, wiped her wet hand on her shorts, and gestured for Vida to lead the way.

Lizbeth started to ask Angie about what she'd seen, but Vida grabbed her hand and pulled her along.

Clunking down the boardwalk was not Lizbeth's idea of being inconspicuous. In fact, Deedy Swamp allowed for little privacy unless one entered a building or dove into the marsh itself. Occasionally a banyan tree stood tall enough to hide behind. Fortunately, the boardwalks teemed with Deediers, most of them squatty, sleek-skinned, more human than froglike but slightly green nonetheless. And chatty. Though conversation flowed, Vida told Lizbeth and Angie that these "greetifications" were subdued and well below the Deedy standard of friendliness. For the most part, no one looked them in the eye, and the Deedy faces looked "suspicionated."

At one point, when the threesome neared the Villard Jailhouse, Vida held Lizbeth and Angie back. She pointed to a Cutter stepping out from behind a stairwell. He grabbed the baker and handcuffed her, as well as the customer she'd been talking with. Lizbeth heard the soldier say, "You can't say 'hunchinateds' or 'pastrieds.' You know the law."

Lizbeth tried not to stare. She couldn't believe that someone would try to force Deedy Swamp to change its language—that anyone would care enough, or that they would use force. It seemed so out of proportion. What was the big deal anyway? If you wanted to take over, why not just get an army and do it? But then, she reasoned, maybe simple domination wasn't the only goal. Maybe MaryMary wanted to suppress a way of being. Deedy speech was such a part of Deedy life that robbing them of their language was like stealing their souls. It was a way to conquer their minds as well as their bodies.

They walked a ways farther, looking down side streets, before Vida told them to stop. "The Villard Jailhouse, an elder-building, a museum, a megaphone to a former lockification. Not used since Joseph Willy Ever kleptofied all the jewels kept in the vaultification of Deedy Bank. Epochs ago! Now the jailification's gone back to a regular hustle-bustle of shovings and gruntifications, all bricks and steely poles and such."

"Back off!"

The order came from a Cutter. His stiff green collar rose nearly to his ears, and medals of some sort hung from his wide belt. He carried a lance with an ax-head. "MaryMary Hardin Fast is holdin' court today."

Vida put up a hand. "No need to go germanshepard on us." She turned as if to walk away.

Before Vida could conk her forehead for being so careless right in front of the jail, three more guards charged out, handcuffed and disarmed her, and marched her into the jailhouse. Their knee-high boots slammed against the boardwalk.

CHAPTER SEVEN
GETTING IN, GETTING OUT

I think we are in rats' alley
where the dead men lost their bones.

—T. S. ELIOT, *THE WASTELAND*

 *Phissst!*

Another sand-ghost shot into the air right next to Len. The force nearly knocked him onto the coral ridge once more. As he caught his balance, one hand crossed into the path of the descending stuff. It felt like fine sand. And just as he stopped the progress of the shooting sand, he heard something, an anguished whisper, an *"Ahhh."*

"Hey!" shouted Bennu over the noise. "Listen carefully, when the blast is at its peak."

Phist! Phisst! Phissst! The explosions came again and again. And then Len heard it, in a gritty tone, something like a word. If he concentrated hard and tried to filter out the grit, he could make out words. "Must—*phissst*—help—*phissst*—fetters—shackles—chains—*phissst*—crying—trembling—death—*phissst*—Piers."

For a solid minute, the sand-ghosts stopped spouting. No one dared speak for fear of blocking out a crucial word. But the wait made Len go crazy. *Fetters, why? Death, how? Piers— When? Where?*

Phist-phisst-phissst! Three ghosts shot up at once. "Piers!" Then five. "Find!" Then ten. "Weary!" Then all of them. The explosions blasted Len's ears. The sand-ghosts turned their drawn, ghoulish faces to the three.

They shouted in unison. With the force of a hundred geysers, with grinding precision, they shouted, "Come!" Then they descended, every last grain, and not one reappeared.

Len listened down the hole but heard nothing. He stood and tried to intensify his hearing, but all he heard was the lapping of the waves. "Gareth, I don't like this. These blasts freak me out. What do they mean? What are we supposed to do?"

Bennu looked blankly down the hole next to him. "Okay, we already knew Piers was weary. What does this word, mean, Gareth? 'Come.' Come where? Where is he?"

"I'm only a bookkeeper, lads, not a sage. I'm adding up what I know, but it doesn't come to much."

Len kneeled next to a hole and listened, but he heard no new words. The closer he got to the hole, the louder the waves sounded, as if the hole were a giant seashell magnifying the sound. The rumbling grew louder. The crashing pummeled Len's ear, like a waterfall, then like a storm at sea, then like a blinding squall. He lifted his head away from the hole, but the sound still grew. He feared the whole beach would be flooded and they would all be swept away.

But the waves hadn't changed. Gareth pointed to the cliffs. "Lads, above us!" There, dust arose. The cloud grew taller and thicker as the din grew louder. Then Len saw "the squall," a line of big-headed, hairy desert beasts with long arms and pointed ears. They looked dull of mind. Some held clubs and some held rocks. They grunted out threats. The noise grew into a cacophony of pounding and shouting and dust.

One line on the cliff became two, and more came, and more, always yelling, always pushing. Some in the front line pushed back. They growled at each other as much as at the three on the beach.

Frightened, Len crouched down. He wanted to run, but Gareth just stood there, as if he were in the bow of a boat. The beasts' wide mouths opened to show spiky teeth.

"Gareth, what now?"

Gareth shouted over the din. "Don't move! They're called tremlings, I think. Fierce, stupid, half-blind. They make up for their poor eyesight by huddling together."

"OK," said Len, "they're tremlings. What about a plan?"

The tremlings at the front turned and raged at the ones behind. One clubbed another, then more shoving broke out. The front line edged forward, protesting wildly. Then one tremling jumped down the face of the cliff. Len thought for sure it would free-fall and get impaled on the sharp coral. But no. The tremling dug its big feet into the cliff. It used its club for balance as it half-skied, half-stumbled down. It dodged the coral daggers and came to a halt at the base of the cliff.

Then other tremlings followed, quickly, some tumbling down, others staying on their feet. A dozen slid down the cliff-face onto the loose dirt below. A guttural roar went up from the tremlings on the cliff. One flung his rock, and it zinged past Len. Then twenty or more followed the lead. Rocks came flying. The tremlings on the ground raised their clubs.

While watching the Cutters march away with Vida, Lizbeth tried not to act displeased. She didn't want to get arrested too, so she picked a lily growing through the boardwalk and played with the petals. Two more Cutters came toward them. They banged loudly on the wood with their boots. Lizbeth glanced up long enough to see their bowl-like helmets, the dull red ribbing at the shoulders of their uniforms, and the matching stripes on the pants stuffed into their boots. A shudder ran over her. The Cutters walked past them. Then she and Angie walked away.

"It's horrible," she whispered to Angie, "just horrible. I can't believe they took her. This whole thing is so stupid."

They climbed up to the dry floor of an inn and sat in a corner. The posted menu possessed not a word of Deedy speech.

Angie picked at a crack in the tabletop. "Now Vida *and* Mook are gone. We're two feet taller than Deediers, and we're obviously not Cutters. And all we're able to do is change into blue wings and wide shoulders. Not much help." She leaned back in her chair.

"I know. I feel helpless too." Lizbeth leaned forward in her chair. "On the other hand, if you think about it, Angie, we've always found enough of what we've needed."

"I feel so stuck right now. I want Piers."

"I know Piers isn't here to remind us—that's something else we have to face—but I don't think he would want us moping around like we can't do anything. We can *do* what we *can* do."

"You're right. I know you're right."

"Welken has taught us that if we get truly stuck, help will come." She stopped Angie's nervous picking with her own hand.

"I don't know why this one really gets me, Lizbeth. It all seems so pointless."

"Cruelty usually is."

"Thanks, Lizbeth. Thanks for the encouragement. OK, what's the plan?"

Lizbeth spied some food left at an empty table. "Let's get some leftovers and get out of here."

A few minutes later, they sat cross-legged, munching biscuits and cheese on a street just off the main boardwalk. They could see Villard Jail.

Angie finished a big bite. "We could charge through the front door."

"We could knock out the guards and grab the keys."

"We could get ourselves captured."

Lizbeth wiped the crumbs off her hands. "We could swim down and look for a way in. It's an old building."

"We could find some loose bricks."

"We could fall in and drown."

"*Aargh*, nothing seems like a good idea."

"If you're going to great-escape it," a voice came from the water, "you should be librarianatin' your voice."

Lizbeth recognized the man in the boat immediately. "Jacob! Oh, Jacob Canny Sea, we're so glad you're here!"

Jacob punted over in his roundish boat. Angie grabbed the wooden "hand" off the bow and swung the boat broadside to the boardwalk. Jacob said, "I heard it all, you Skinnerians. Now slip into my floatification before the day goes slanty and sick."

Although Angie's attempted hug of Jacob made the boat tipsy, Jacob kept it steady. Lizbeth hesitated. Worrying that her weight might be too much for the shallow-hulled vessel, she got in as carefully as she could and tried not to move.

"First off," Jacob said, "I've been un-Deedyin' my talk, so I'll be doin' my best to make it flat-and-sahara in case any Cutters are nearby." He maneuvered the boat over toward a bridge. "You two get under that blanket. We'll see if we can't houdini our way . . . oops, I mean, get out of the fix we're in. Quiet now. Angie, quick, slip one wing out from under the blanket if you can. That's it."

Lizbeth couldn't see, but she heard the boat brush against marsh plants. When nearby voices grew louder, she guessed they were near or under the bridge.

Then, "Stop right there! That's as close to the jail as you can go."

Jacob cleared his throat and spoke each word carefully. "I've caught an exotic bird for MaryMary Hardin Fast. I thought she'd like to binocul— I mean, to take a look at it."

Lizbeth felt Angie flap her wing.

"Looks like a beauty. MaryMary truly loves birds. I'll let you go if you tell her Karl Karlinski deserves part of the credit. Use the stairs in the back. And don't be too long."

"Thanks." Jacob pushed the boat near the side wall of the jail and turned to the right to punt along the back. "OK, ladies," he whispered, "this side has all kinds of alcoves and docks. The guards are going to be by the main stairs. They won't be einsteinin' anythin' else 'cause the windows are all too tall for us Deediers to look in or look out." The boat slowed down and gently hit something.

Jacob continued whispering, "Take your blankets off, Misfitters. Angie, you hold us steady by that ring on the wall. I'll snugify the boat on my end too. Lizbeth, gander up that window yonkers."

Grasping for any handhold the old building provided, Lizbeth slowly eased her way up from a crouch. The boat shook, and Lizbeth lurched toward the wall, finding a large nail to hold in the process.

Jacob grunted against the pole. "Don't be gettin' wobblerated, Lizbeth."

Lizbeth gripped the window ledge and pulled herself up. Then she grabbed the bars. The boat still felt unsteady beneath her, but she held most of her weight by pulling against the bars. She looked in. She couldn't see much because her eyes needed to adjust. Then she saw two prisoners pacing on the floor. They turned toward her. Their roly-poly figures told her Mook was not in the cell. Then she peered straight down. She could see the top of the head of someone chained to the wall. A centipede crawled over the dirty, bald scalp.

One of the other prisoners stepped into the light that came in from the window. He had a week-old beard, and his ear was red and swollen. When he made eye contact with Lizbeth, he came closer. He climbed up the body next to the wall. As the chained prisoner groaned, the other pulled his own plumpness up until he was face-to-face with Lizbeth. His shirt, torn at one shoulder, revealed a gash. Painfully he opened his bruised mouth. "Watch what you say, watch what you say." His chapped lips needed balm.

Lizbeth's own mouth went dry. "We're looking for Mook and Vida Bering Well."

More moans came from the chained prisoner. The other one opened his one good eye as big as it would go. "Watch what you say, watch what you say." He licked his lips. "We're all ingrates." He turned and showed Lizbeth an open wound on his neck.

Lizbeth saw a maggot in it, gasped, and lost her grip. She jerked her hands off the bars and turned her head as if the larvae might jump out of the wound and into her face. Wobbling mightily on the edge of the boat, she pushed it away from the wall with her feet and lost her balance. She fell to the left of the window, grabbed after anything she could on the way down, scraped her fingers on the bricks, the loose mortar, the moss, and plowed into Angie, knocking her from the boat. They both splashed into the water.

Lizbeth felt scared and stupid, because she had put everything at risk. She struggled to right herself. Then she saw Angie below her, sinking fast. She must have hit her head on something. After pressing her hand against the submerged brick wall, Lizbeth whirled around, pushed off the bricks with her feet, and shot toward Angie. Then she noticed that Angie wasn't sinking; she was swimming! Angie ducked her head through a break in the wall and swam through it. After watching Angie's feet disappear through the hole, Lizbeth followed.

As she grabbed both sides of the opening and pulled herself through,

Lizbeth felt a burning in her chest. She wasn't sure where Angie had gone, but she had to get air. She exhaled some bubbles. That made her feel worse—more empty. She kicked as hard as she could with her legs and pushed the water down with her arms. She needed air. She couldn't hold her breath any longer. Soon she would take a deep breath of water. She kept kicking. Then she saw the surface. One last push. Not enough. She wouldn't make it. Then she saw a hand—Angie's hand—reach into the water. She thrust her own hand into Angie's and gave one final kick.

Lizbeth blasted into the air and sucked up oxygen in one long draught. While coughing, she pulled herself entirely out of the water and onto the concrete steps where Angie sat. She put her head between her legs and breathed hard. Angie patted Lizbeth on the back. When Lizbeth lifted her head, Angie put her finger in the *Shhh!* position. Lizbeth nodded and, suppressing another cough, tugged her shirt away from her skin and wrung it out.

The ceiling above them, Lizbeth figured, must be the floor of the cell she had seen from the outside. The stairs led up in that direction, and brick walls greeted them everywhere else. Angie helped Lizbeth up. Then Lizbeth took the lead.

In dim light, the two Misfits dripped their way up about ten steps to a landing. The steps turned up to the left toward the dry floor. Before ascending the steps, Angie pointed to a tunnel at the landing that opened in the opposite direction. Lizbeth peered in. She could see light at the other end but couldn't tell how far it was or if the tunnel was truly passable. They nodded and mounted the stairs.

With each step, they heard more sounds. Groaning, the clanking of hard things against bars, occasional mutterings and outbursts. Soon they reached a doorless opening and cautiously poked their heads around the corner. The corridor was empty—except for rats, moldy straw, and an old tin cup. On either side of the hallway were five cells with bars . . . and prisoners.

Lizbeth gulped when she saw them, dirty and thin by Deedy standards. Most showed signs of a Cutter beating. Some of the prisoners rallied. They smiled and raised their hands joyously. Others seemed too hurt or numb to care. Lizbeth and Angie crept down the musty hallway, Lizbeth checking the cells on one side, Angie the other. Lizbeth saw a rat climb up the leg of a sad-eyed prisoner. She wanted to find Mook and Vida. She wanted them to be in cells near each other. She wanted the door at the end of the hall to stay shut.

At the last cell, Lizbeth looked frantically but still did not see her friends. She glanced back hopefully at Angie. She appeared crestfallen too.

Then Lizbeth saw them . . . keys, like in a pirate movie, hanging on a nail just inside the door. She couldn't believe her eyes.

"We've been lotterized, ha ha, sweepstaked," a prisoner said enthusiastically.

"Shush." Lizbeth drew a line across her neck.

The woman bit on her own finger and backed up into the shadows.

Lizbeth and Angie tiptoed up to the door. Lizbeth's hands shook. She backed against the door and squinted through the small window. She saw an elbow, its position indicating, perhaps, a guard in a chair, hands on belly, head down, eyes closed. But it was just a guess. Lizbeth nodded to Angie, and Angie lifted the key ring from the nail. She separated each key with a finger to keep them from clanging. Then they went to the locks.

As the prisoners waited to be released, Angie calmly explained that they should dive into the pool below, find the hole in the outside wall, and swim into the marsh. After that, they were on their own. When Lizbeth asked about Mook, one nervous Deedier said, "The Cutters roughhanded him from us yesterday. Made me feel all chills-and-fever."

Lizbeth grabbed the bars. "Where is he now?"

"Noosin' it, I'm afraid. If you're not flash-and-fury, he'll be planked and long-john-silvered, if you drift me out."

Just then the bolt of the prison door screeched and slid over. The door opened. As Angie herded the prisoners in the corridor down the stairs, Lizbeth tossed the keys through the bars of a still-locked cell. She saw the inmates' frightened eyes, their grasping hands. "Don't abandonate!" one cried as he fumbled with the key in the lock.

The guard yelled behind him for more guards, then charged, ax-staff in hand. As Lizbeth turned toward him, she heard Angie from the stairwell opening, shouting, "Lizbeth, no!"

By her will, Lizbeth's upper body became an oxen—her waist, shoulders, and arms, but not her head. She snorted, ran at the guard, dodged the ax-head, and swung at him awkwardly with her hoofs, banging the ax-staff out of his hands, then knocking him out with a blow to his head. She stood there panting, feeling proud she had knocked him out and feeling bad she had hurt him.

Since her oxen-self seemed no longer needed, Lizbeth switched back to human form and unlocked the remaining cells. She could see amazement in the eyes of the prisoners—amazement at her metamorphosis. She threw the keys to the prisoners to unlock those chained to walls, then darted out down the corridor. Angie wasn't there. Lizbeth tore down the steps, sending rats scurrying for holes. She hit the landing with a bound and turned to go down to the water.

"Lizbeth!"

It was Angie.

"Lizbeth, in here, in the tunnel."

Lizbeth got on her knees and poked her head in. "What?"

"We didn't find Mook or Vida. That's what we're here for. Let's see where this leads."

"Are you crazy? Into some rat-infested tunnel?"

"Look, it's our only option." Angie was insistent. "I just have a sense this is right."

"You and your senses. I have senses too—and my nose tells me this stinks."

"Then hold your nose and crawl in."

Lizbeth did . . . and the tunnel did not disappoint. Its moist walls stank of mildew. The floor was squishy and cold, a highway for creeping things, dirty things, nibbling and stinging things, an open sewer for vermin of all kinds. Lizbeth held her breath. The light at the far end stayed agonizingly distant.

I'm so tired of holding my breath. And I'm not very good at it. I hope this leads us to Mook. It could just as easily lead us to that MaryMary lady. Maybe I should keep some of this goo to chuck at her.

At the other side of the tunnel, Lizbeth groaned loudly at the stench. Angie held a finger to her lips. They stepped into a large musty room that smelled only slightly better than the tunnel. Though no Cutters greeted them, frightening bodies did. Old skeletons, some in piles, some in awkward positions, filled the room. Bones covered the floor. Leg bones, arm bones, ribs, bones! Bones upon bones!

Lizbeth felt faint. "This is worse than the tunnel. Let's get out."

"Shh." Angie put up a hand.

Above them, shuffling noises could be heard. Several sets of feet walked across the wood floor. Lizbeth could see light coming through spaces between floorboards. She heard voices too.

"MaryMary Hardin Fast, m'lady," said a man gruffly, "these here criminals are like the others. They won't obey the new laws. They keep talkin' in the old ways, Your Infinite Wisdom, and we can't get them to reform."

Another spoke with a whiny voice, like a drawer without grease. "And this one's not a Deedier at all. He comes to spy, and he won't tell us anythin' besides his name. He's Mook of the Nezzer Clan—and he brings a quiver of arrows and holds his head tall like he looks down on us."

In the silence that followed these accusations, Lizbeth imagined MaryMary's voice, a cold and barbed sound, echoing her name, Hardin Fast.

Then MaryMary spoke. "I appreciate you gentlemen doing your duty so nobly." Like a silk scarf slipping off a shoulder, MaryMary's words glided effortlessly into the air. They were soft yet strong, full of dignity and charm. "Because I am a merciful servant of all Deedy Swamp, I'm going to give these two a chance to clear their names, to establish their commitment to a sane and sensible future."

Lizbeth wondered what kind of face could go with such a beautiful voice. Surely not some sharp-toothed monster. Then Angie tapped her on the shoulder and motioned for her to follow. They had no choice but to step on the bones. Lizbeth searched for secure footing, quiet footing. She tried to place her feet perpendicular to the larger bones. She tried to tread lightly. One step, then another. She slipped once on a leg bone. It knocked another bone into the air. Lizbeth caught it.

When they were nearly underneath Mook, they passed an open pit. Skeletons circled around the hole, frozen in resistance, as if they had died in the act of getting pulled into a whirlpool. She couldn't tell for sure, but she thought she could see water in the center.

Lizbeth lost focus on her next step. She missed the dirt and crushed a bony hand, sending cracking and popping into the silence. Then Mook coughed. He coughed four times.

Does he know we're here? thought Lizbeth. *Could he? What would he have us do?*

From directly underneath the voices, she studied the floorboards. Light came through significant gaps. One floorboard sagged.

"I am Mook of the Nezzer Clan. I am a friend to Deedy Swamp."

The floorboard bowed under the weight. Looking quizzically at Angie, Lizbeth guessed Mook bounced on it.

MaryMary said, "I am glad to hear of your friendship. Here in Deedy Swamp, we have a way of declaring our loyalty. What do you think of our improvements?"

Each of these last syllables came punctuated by a grunt, a suppressed "ow." *Mook must be getting poked with something sharp.*

Lizbeth's eyes darted over the floor's underside. Then she saw what she hoped for—a cracked joist. The supporting beam looked full of dry rot. She pointed to it, and Angie nodded.

The floorboard sagged and leveled out as Mook spoke. "I am Mook of the Nezzer Clan. I am a friend to Deedy Swamp." He sounded tense, in pain, each word a struggle.

"I can see," said MaryMary, "that you would rather become a testimony to what a reformed Deedy Swamp is willing to do to become fresh and clean, to become one with the rest of the known world. I do hope you'll give me that lovely bracelet before you make your last walk."

Lizbeth grabbed a leg bone and turned her head as she twisted the bone off its pelvis. When she took a few practice throwing motions, Angie waved her off.

"And you," said MaryMary, with a hint of syrup, "Miss Vida Bering Well, what can you say about Deedy's reforms?"

Lizbeth wondered how it was that Mook and Vida were being interrogated together. Did MaryMary know they were friends? Was it a coincidence?

Angie moved over the bones till she stood on the highest point under the rotten beam. She got on all fours and materialized her blue wings, cupping them above her into two arches. Lizbeth climbed onto Angie's back. She hesitated. She did not see how these wings—or the more delicate Angie—could support her.

"MaryMary Hardin Fast," said Vida Bering Well, "so at last we meet. I'll tell you what I think of your reforms. You've judased Deedy. You've cracked a buggy whip on all the wrong horses and a dasdardization will follow!"

Lizbeth put one foot on the crown of a wing and did the same with her other foot. The wings held and, more than this, they pushed her up. With Angie breathing heavily below her, Lizbeth balanced as best she could and stood tall. If she leaped, she could hit the beam. But she was not close enough to smack it hard.

"Oh, Vida," said MaryMary, "how I long to have you as a lieutenant, as a leader of the good and useful changes to come. I have such plans for Deedy Swamp, and for all of Welken. Won't you make a pledge?"

Lizbeth nearly fell. She caught herself and realized Angie was moving the arches of her wings farther up. Lizbeth inched her way along the highest point of the moving curve.

"To the scaffold!" yelled MaryMary. "Have it your way!"

Then Lizbeth swung with all her might. The bone slashed all the way through the beam. Dry rot flew everywhere. In seconds the floor sagged, groaned loudly in all its still-attached joints, leaned down and down, and dropped six inches through the gap. Lizbeth saw scurrying feet and a body on the floor rolling toward her. She grabbed onto the sagging floor and pulled. Jumping off Angie's wings, she tugged as hard as she could. The floor gave way.

With a thunderous *crack,* the floor broke off another joist, tilted straight down, and jerked to a stop. Vida and Mook rolled into Lizbeth, breaking her handhold. She collapsed into Angie's wings and felt the feathers surround her as she thudded onto Angie's back. Then she and Angie both started moving. Sliding through the skeletons, they spun uncontrollably, twisting around and down, caught in a waterless whirlpool, careening, slipping, and circling down into the pit in the center of the room.

Lizbeth grabbed for a handhold. She found bones . . . and more bones.

She pushed them inside, kicked them out of her way. She could see Angie below her and dark water, dark enough to hide the demons no doubt swimming inside—sharp-teethed fish or shrieking eels. She glanced up and saw Mook and Vida at the edge, holding out their hands.

"Lizbeth!" Mook yelled, his ponytails dangling down.

Lizbeth heard a splash. "Ang!" she cried as she hit the water.

All went black.

CHAPTER EIGHT

BRICK BY BRICK

I've learned of life this bitter truth:
Hope not between the crumbling walls
of mankind's gratitude to find repose,
but rather, build within
thy own soul fortresses!

—GEORGIA DOUGLAS JOHNSON

 Len did not relish getting clubbed by charging trem-
lings. He ducked a flung rock, and then another. He
had no options, so he looked down, took a deep breath,
and jumped into the hole in front of him . . . a pit, an
abyss, a home of a sand-ghost geyser. Cold water, then
wet sand jolted him momentarily, slowing him down, but he kept going.
The sand retreated in grainy ripples. Was he falling into quicksand? he
wondered. No, the descent was too rapid.

Len shuffled his legs, hoping to find a floor with his feet. He reached
out to slow himself, but the few stray grains of sand he managed to grasp
moved away from him at his touch. Then he sensed sand underneath his
arms, sand that slowed him down. Was he falling *into* it—or being supported by it?

A gruesome thought struck him. Maybe he'd actually leaped into
the mouth of a sand-ghost. Maybe he was inside one, sliding down its
inner body. He imagined being inside a ghastly deep-sea fish, a translucent one with fierce bottom teeth, falling toward the stomach, to a

pool of acid, where he would float while he decomposed. Waiting to feel a decaying rib cage or a fish head, he wondered how slowly he would die.

Then, all at once, he stopped sinking. As he touched the bottom—of what he did not know—he looked up and saw a dim light, a light calling to him through the water. Yes, he was in water now. With newfound strength, he kicked his legs and swam for it. He hoped he would not become the next Jonah, or worse. The light grew brighter. Near the surface he felt something slimy with one hand and saw something dark, something rectangular, something wooden.

In a flash he realized where he was: at his own dock behind his own house on the Lewis River.

Len bobbed up and breathed in the lovely Oregon air. As the water chilled him, he grabbed for the dock and hung for a moment to gather strength. Then he pulled himself up and twisted in one fluid motion to land on his rear. He turned around to see Bennu, Lizbeth, and Angie, all soaking wet, all breathing hard, all smiling at his arrival.

Lizbeth took off her shoes and wrung out her socks. "Len, you're here! We're all here. We're back."

"Yeah." Len managed a two-second smile. "But I'm so exhausted."

"As am I," said Bennu.

"We fell into a whirlpool." Angie gestured excitedly. "We saw Vida and went to Deedy Swamp!"

"We saw sand-ghosts and tremlings," said Bennu, "and—"

"And," Len added, "we were rescued by this guy named Gareth." Without warning, tears welled up. Emotions rushed over him. "I don't know why I feel so overwhelmed. Everything came back so quickly—the comfort of being in Welken and doing amazing things. I didn't think, 'Am I dreaming?' Or, 'This can't be happening to me.' I just accepted it as real."

"Oh, Len." Angie lay down in the sun and closed her eyes. "If you weren't my brother, I'd hug you."

"Good thing, then." Len held his smile longer this time. He tried to warm himself by rubbing his arms. "Piers is in trouble, and there's lots more to talk about."

"Like ships on the move," said Bennu.

"And saving Mook," said Lizbeth, "we hope."

"And doing what we could against MaryMary." Angie shivered and brought her knees to her chest.

"I don't know about any of you," said Bennu, "but I'm cold. And, look, it's clouding over. Why don't we get into some dry clothes and meet later? We can compare notes without shaking."

"OK, fine." Len consulted his watch. "It's 3:05 now. Should we meet at our house in an hour?"

"Yeah." Lizbeth scrunched up her nose, as if remembering something unpleasant. "Our place is no good. You never know about Mom."

Bennu tapped the plastic cover on his watch. "Did we leave about 2:30? Seemed like we were about six hours in Welken, right? That's amazing. Gareth said we'd been gone for a year. We thought it had been a month, so the twelve-to-one ratio is still in effect."

"Thank you, Mr. Science," said Len.

Bennu stood up and brushed himself off. "The thing is, one hour here is twelve hours there, so we need to hurry. Who knows what trouble Piers is in! He's everything to Welken—their leader, their strength."

Len looked over at Angie, who was sitting up, leaning against Bennu's back. "And—it's starting to rain."

The Misfits walked briskly back to their respective back gates. For most of the way, Bennu and Angie walked behind, holding hands. This left Len paired up with Lizbeth, an increasingly common occurrence. He did not like the implication.

Lizbeth reached over the top of the fence and unlatched the gate on the other side. "We really ought to fix this, Bennu. I'm getting a callus on my forearm where the wood hits me."

Bennu didn't answer. Lizbeth looked back to see that he was still standing next to Angie, his eyes all ga-ga and weepy like she'd seen in a hundred romantic comedies.

Lizbeth slammed the gate so she didn't have to watch and so Bennu would have to reach over and maybe get a splinter. Alone in her backyard,

Lizbeth noticed the blooming dahlias. She also saw how many needed to be deadheaded and that the boxwood hedge should be trimmed. Her mother always obsessed about every detail in the yard—every fallen leaf, every drooping tendril. But Lizbeth knew why these tasks had not been completed, and the closer she got to the back door, the more dread she felt.

It's late enough in the day, she thought. *Mom could already be out of it. I don't know why she's doing this. I don't know why things have become so much worse this past month.*

She opened the sliding door quietly and swiveled back just in time to see Bennu kiss Angie by the gate. Disgusted, she ripped off her wet shoes and socks and tiptoed into the kitchen.

Maybe I can make it to the stairs. Maybe I won't have to explain myself. Maybe Mom won't see me.

The Nefertis' cockapoo, Sniffles, bounded in, barking and wagging her tail. She dribbled pee for the last three feet before reaching Lizbeth.

"Oh, you stupid animal!" Lizbeth grabbed some paper towels and wiped the mess with one hand while she petted Sniffles with the other. Sniffles put both front paws on Lizbeth's bent knee and licked her face.

"Sniffle-piffle wants to be your friend." Darlene leaned against the door frame leading into the kitchen from the dining room. "Don't yell at the poochie-woochie, Lizbeth-baby-dolls."

"Hi, Mom." Lizbeth glared at the drink in Darlene's hand, sighed loud enough to signal disapproval, and walked over to the wastebasket under the sink.

"Don't you want to give your dear mother a hug? I haven't seen you all day." Darlene took a wobbly step toward Lizbeth. She held out her arms, her gin and tonic spilling out a few drops.

"I just cleaned the floor, Mom!"

"Don't be so upset, Liz. Come here and give me a hug."

Lizbeth leaned over the sink with both hands against the countertop. She gritted her teeth, grabbed a wet rag, and turned toward her mother with her arms held stiffly to her sides.

Darlene threw herself around Lizbeth, slurred, "I love you, sweetie" with alcohol breath, and let her go. She took another sip of her drink. "You're all wet, honey. Don't you know enough to get out of the rain?"

Lizbeth wiped up the drips and went back to the sink.

In between swallows, Darlene said, "You can be so unfriendly. No wonder you don't have any boyfriends."

Should I gag her with this rag? Push her over? Or call AA? Aargh. And we all keep going to church, as if everything is just fine. Oh, how I hate this. I couldn't hate anything more.

Bennu walked in with a big grin on his face. It vanished immediately. *Your turn,* thought Lizbeth.

As she left the kitchen and rounded the corner toward the stairs, Bennu raised his voice. "What are you doing, Mom? Get your hands off me! I can't stand this. I can't stand you when you're like this. I mean it, Mom. Don't touch me. And don't give me that blubbering lower lip." Bennu continued as Lizbeth walked up the stairs. "Put the drink down. Get out of here! Get out of my life!"

With one foot on the top stair, Lizbeth looked down the hall. She saw her father, Martin, leaning out of his office. Clearly, he'd heard everything. He had an expression of resigned disappointment. And when his eyes met Lizbeth's, he turned away and stepped back out of sight.

Look what you've done, Mom. Look what we've become. Bennu—sensitive Bennu—is blasting you at the top of his lungs. He's so full of rage he's screaming at his own mother. And Dad. He sits in his office pretending that nothing is wrong. Is Dad's business not going well? Are you two fighting? And you? You've become a monster. . . . Wait a minute. What am I saying? What about me? What have I become?

Lizbeth walked into the bathroom. She'd like to talk to Bennu about it . . . get a hug from him. But since he'd been with Angie, they hadn't had the talks they used to have. Now he confided in Angie and, most of the time, Lizbeth confided in no one. She saw Bennu at the top of the stairs and started to close the door. His face was angry, his fists clenched. Their eyes met for a second, then Lizbeth pushed the door till it latched.

No, she realized, it wasn't Bennu's fault he liked Angie. She shouldn't punish him for it. But they should be able to commiserate about Mom. She missed their talks.

She put her hand on the doorknob to open it, to walk toward Bennu. But she did not turn it to open the door.

In that moment, Lizbeth felt that to survive in her aloneness, she would have to create a refuge for herself. She would have to become her own fortress. When she let the doorknob go, it was like placing a brick down, adding to a wall in that fortress. She pushed in the button lock and put down another brick. She turned away from the door and started the water in the shower. She got undressed. After stepping into the rising steam and putting her head under the hard spray, she let go and dove into her sorrow. She wept and wept, feeding the shower's stream with her own ample tears.

Len walked through the gate they'd left open when they'd crossed the veil into Welken. He looked through the misty rain to see if Percy might be curled up in a favorite spot under the protection of a rhododendron. He did not see a cat, but he heard snoring. Under a garden umbrella, Dear-Abby's head leaned against the back of the Adirondack chair, her mouth open, a magazine in her lap.

Len studied her and rubbed his chin.

Angie caught up to him. "Don't even think about it."

"Think about what?"

"I don't know. I just know you're plotting something."

"Oh, Angie, if you look for the worst in me, that's what you'll find."

"So what's your plan?"

"Look there. See the drool coming out of her mouth? It's swaying a bit in the wind. That's too funny."

"You shouldn't laugh at other people, Len."

"I'm thinking we should catch it in the rain gauge, run an experiment, maybe—see how much she drools at different times of the day."

"You're cruel. I'm going to wake her up and get her out of the rain." Angie gently shook Dear-Abby. "Grandma, Grandma, wake up. It's raining."

With a snort, Dear-Abby's head shot forward and her drool landed on her chin. She wiped her mouth. "What are you shaking me for, Angie?"

"You were sleeping, Grandma. I thought you would want to come out of the rain."

"I was not sleeping. I was dozing. But you are a dear-heart to want to get me out of the rain. But from the looks of you, you're not too good at it yourself. Now let's get back into the kitch-kitch." As she stood up, pages from Charlotte's latest Percy and Bones manuscript slid off her lap. Though Len caught them deftly, Dear-Abby did not seem to notice.

Len glanced at the pages. As he read about Percival P. Perkins, Detective Cat, he realized that although Percy the house cat was missing, Percival the book character wasn't. As they'd learned a month ago, in some bizarre way, these two and Piers were all the same person—though in Welken, Piers was not a cat. So, Len reasoned, the Misfits ought to find out about Piers wherever they could. And last time, the Percy and Bones stories had really helped.

Len went inside and read the message board that said his mom and dad were on an errand. He shivered in his soaked T-shirt and started to pull it over his head. But since it was wet, it got stuck on his back. He yanked on it and bumped into a wall.

"Len!" Grandma grabbed the T-shirt and pulled it a few more inches, incapacitating Len further. "For a grandson, you are simply too naked too much of the time. Go get some clothes on."

Len could hear Angie snickering. "Grandma," he said, "I'm not trying to be naked." He pulled one arm out and pushed the soaked shirt over his head. "And I have no idea what I just meant by that."

Dear-Abby opened the refrigerator door and turned back to Len. "It's just like the dumb ol' DMV."

Len and Angie exchanged "what?" glances.

"They took away my driver's license because I got one question wrong last time."

Angie whispered to Len, "She missed sixteen."

Dear-Abby leaned over and looked in the fridge. "The question was about being behind a truck in the middle lane on the freeway."

"OK," said Len.

"The question asked what lane I should use if I want to pass him."

"That's easy, Grandma," said Len. "You pass in the left lane."

Dear-Abby stood back up. "I know! But I didn't want to pass the truck!"

Len's eyes widened. "Can we go now, Grandma? I really need to take a shower."

"By all means, you dear-hearts. Now why did I open the reefer? Yep, good memory, just short!"

Well before the scheduled meeting time, Bennu and Lizbeth knocked on the front door, then opened it and walked in. "We're here!" shouted Lizbeth.

Dear-Abby grabbed Lizbeth with both hands. "Lettie, I didn't know you were a hoodlum, breaking into a house like that. Are you going to steal my truck?"

"I don't think so, Dear-Abby." Lizbeth wasn't sure what to say. "I didn't know you had a truck."

"Well, I do have to go to the bathroom. I drink, therefore." She went in but did not close the door.

Bennu ran to the stairs. "I'm outta here."

Lizbeth made sure she got to Angie's room first so that she and Angie could sit up on the bed. She did not want Bennu and Angie to sit on the bed together any more than she wanted to be there next to Len. Bennu and Angie seemed oblivious to the tension their relationship created.

Of course, obliviousness had always marked Angie, from her ethereal pronouncements to her dreamy inattentiveness. Her room made its own paradoxical statement. Next to her lacy, white canopy bed stood a bookshelf stocked with one row of fantasies and galactic thrillers, and the next row with biographies and histories. She read Harry Potter and Harry Truman, *Watership Down* and *Watergate*. It reminded Lizbeth of what her dad said—that she should read with the Bible in one hand and the newspaper in the other.

But the walls and ceiling grabbed most of the attention. In pinks, lavenders, and white, Angie had painted the room to look as if it were the inside of a feminine tornado. The colors swirled together, leading up to a still point in the center of the ceiling where the light was. She stuck labels here and there: Milky Way Galaxy, Betelgeuse, Eye of Horus, Mind of God, Window to Wonderland, Heart of Piers. The Heart of Piers nameplate made Lizbeth sigh. More than anyone in Welken, he had taught them who they really were. Her gratitude for him and Soliton wrapped around her like a blanket. She worried about Piers. She felt his loss deeply—most of the time.

Len twirled his pen repeatedly on the top of his hand. "I feel sorta stupid, like I'm calling to order the Misfit Club or something. On the other hand, we need to get going."

Lizbeth shrugged. "How do you do that?"

"Well, you hold the pen like this, spin it, and spend about a hundred lunch periods practicing."

"No, I mean, take charge like that."

Len raised an eyebrow. "Comes with being born King of the Forest, I guess. Speaking of, could you and Angie turn into ox and angel? All I could do was become a lion butt."

After Lizbeth and Angie reported about their own limitations, about Vida and the slimy blob and Deedy Swamp and the jail, Len and Bennu told of the sandbar and Gareth and the tremlings and sandghosts.

Len stopped twirling his pen and grabbed one of Angie's pink-flower notepads. "Let's write this down. What do we know? What do we need to know? Then we'll prioritize."

Bennu sat with his back against the cotton candy wall, with his knees up high. He picked at a scab on his hand. "The most important thing is about Piers. Gareth and Vida both talked about how tired he is, how nobody knows where he is, how the burden of bearing Bors inside him seems to take more out of him every day. We've got to find a way to help him. Gareth used the word *weary*, I don't like it. It feels like a pit in my stomach."

That made Lizbeth grab hers. At first she thought that maybe she was just hungry, as usual, but then she remembered the dream . . . how the boy felt the shard in him and Lizbeth had felt it too. Without any clear reason, she started to sweat. She didn't know why she hadn't told everyone about the way she seemed to be suffering along with the boy. Maybe it was happening again. She turned slightly on the bed and pushed on her stomach. She felt the shard.

Bennu got up on his knees. "Are you OK, Lizbeth?"

"I'm all right. I just suddenly have this pain."

Angie put both hands on Lizbeth's shoulders. "Try to relax, Lizbeth. Maybe if you stretched out instead of doubling over. I feel knots in your muscles. I'm going to push them out. Here's one knot. It feels to me like all the bad things done to you by the McKenzie Boys. Another knot, I feel it. It's the tension at home with your mom."

Why is she doing this? thought Lizbeth.

"—the father who'd rather play with words than with you—"

Stop it.

"—the mother who drowns her sorrows instead of talking about them with you—"

I can't believe you're doing this to me, Angie. Ow, my stomach, the shard.

"—and your own uncertainties. Let them go, Lizbeth. You are—"

"That's enough, Angie, that's enough. The pain is passing. I'm OK."

Angie ignored her. She closed her eyes. "You are the weariness of Piers, the lostness of Bors."

Lizbeth couldn't believe what was happening, what Angie was saying. Lizbeth had felt this idea already, and here Angie confirmed it. Then a rush of calm pulsed over her, down her shoulders, through her stomach, to her toes. She took Angie's hands. "I don't know what to say. Thanks, I guess. I don't know what it all means, but the pain stopped." She paused. "How can I be the weariness of Piers?"

Angie clasped Lizbeth's hands tightly before letting them go. "It's something to hang on to. Maybe he'll speak to you with his warm green eyes. I've been thinking we need to find out about Piers, but Percy is no-where to be found. The only thing we have right now is this." She held out Charlotte's manuscript. "I know Mom said she's not ready to go public with it, but it's all we've got. Since Piers *is* Percy, and Percy *is* Percival P. Perkins, I say we read it. We'll find clues. We always do."

"OK," said Lizbeth.

Len and Bennu nodded.

CHAPTER NINE

BONES ON BONES

Goodness is, so to speak, itself:
badness is only spoiled goodness.

—C. S. LEWIS, *MERE CHRISTIANITY*

Len scratched his back by squirming against a wall in Angie's room. "So who's going to read it?"

He tried to speak with a kind of self-centered openness, hoping it would communicate that *he* wanted to do what he offered to others. And he felt an urgency too. He wanted to resolve the tensions in Welken and in Skinner—and he couldn't wait to get out of his sister's weird pink room.

Angie flicked her hair behind her ears and straightened the manuscript pages against a notebook. "I will. I have it in my hands anyway."

"Fine," said Len, with enough force to say that he wasn't.

THE NEW AND IMPROVED ADVENTURES
OF PERCIVAL P. PERKINS III AND BONES MALONE
BOOK TWO: PERCY AND BONES GO TO HOLLYWOOD

CHAPTER ONE: Chugging Along Little Doggie

Bones Malone slammed the door behind him with his foot, then spread his stubby legs between the jostling cars of the speeding train. He put a basket and a sack and a box and a thermos into his left paw and said to himself, *Percy, you're gonna love all these goodies.*

Normally, bassett hounds from Virginia enjoy risks about as much as a grandmother in pajamas. This week, Bones was different. This week, Bones was brave. Hadn't he teamed up once again with the irrepressible Percival P. Perkins III, Detective Cat, the sort of orange-furred feline who had a knack for opening coach doors at the precise moment they are being pushed in?

"Yaaaa-eeeeee!" Bones fell nose-first onto the floor, his packages flying all over the room.

Percy snatched the thermos out of the air. "Bonesy, you are such a good chum." He opened the thermos lid. "You'll stop at nothing to help me feel better." He took a swig and placed the bottle on the coffee table. "Yuck and P-U! This stuff stinks like high heavens to Betsy!"

Bones rolled over and rubbed his sore knees. "It's called Malone Mash, a trusty brew of boiled spinach and crushed turnips. We Master Gardeners know these things."

"I appreciate the thought, Bonesy, really I do. My stomach hasn't felt right since we started west." Percy flopped onto the sofa. "Ah well, Ollie must be chased. Officer Hornbrook said Ollie told the prison guard he'd escaped from that he, Ollie that is, was on his way to Hollywood to become an actor. Something about 'talkies' and that if anyone could talk, he could. Indeed—like stealing candy from a china shop."

Bones put all the packages neatly on the dining table. The train lurched and the sack fell back onto the floor. Bones picked up a newspaper and scanned a few ads. "Lookit here, Perce. Here's a place we can stay."

"Be careful, Bones, you can't read everything you believe."

"But I can read *this.*" Bones showed Percy an advertisement:

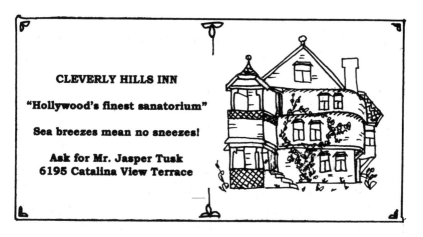

CLEVERLY HILLS INN

"Hollywood's finest sanatorium"

Sea breezes mean no sneezes!

Ask for Mr. Jasper Tusk
6195 Catalina View Terrace

"Good work, Mr. Malone. A right reputable place—and it's better to be safe than who's sorry now."

By the time the train jerked into the Hollywood station, Bones felt completely lost. He heard someone in a sandwich-board sign shouting about maps, so he asked the fellow if he knew the way to the Cleverly Hills Inn. The fellow said he should buy a map. Bones did, but it turned out to be a Map to the Stars' Homes. Bones still felt lost. And Percy felt sicker than ever. The usually effervescent cat seemed drained of all his typical bubbly fizz. All he could manage to say was, "Not a moment too good to be true, Bonesy."

After a short taxi ride to the Cleverly Hills Inn, Percy and Bones walked into the lobby and read the sign. "'Serving dogs, cats, and the occasional pig. No ferrets, please.'"

The desk manager, a slick-looking fellow with an enormous mustache, pulled a note from a cubbyhole. "Ah, Mr. Percy Perkins, sir, you have a message."

Percy and Bones exchanged uplifted eyebrows before Percy opened the letter.

PERCY,
I AM REFORMED
GIVE ME TIME.
OLLIE

"Funny," said Bones, "I thought you weren't supposed to put your name on an anonymous note. That varmint likes to be chased and caught more than a four-year-old in a tickle fight. Ah, he just wants to show off he can escape from prison."

Percy signed the register. "As I like to say, 'Don't bite the handwriting on the wall.' That note may contain a clue, Bonesy. But how do you figure he knew we were coming?"

"I'd give a bushel of pole beans to know that, Perce."

"Excuse me, Angie," said Len, "is this getting us anywhere? I mean, it's cute, but so what?"

"Well," said Bennu, "it obviously makes reference to Piers's suffering." Len did not like to be "obviouslied."

"And," Bennu continued, "I'm sure we all see that Ollie escaped." Len did not like to be "I'm sured."

"So," said Bennu, "any thinking person would ask whether or not the worlds of Welken and Percy and Bones are causally related."

After Len noticed that Angie looked proud of Bennu, he got up and started to walk out of the room. "*Obviously*, we're *sure* who the *thinking* person is. But what counts here is finding Piers."

Angie slapped the manuscript on her lap. "What's got into you, Len? It's a good question. You don't have to be mad just because you didn't think of it."

Len took two more steps toward the door and stopped. He put his hands in his back pockets. "Yeah, I suppose it is a good question." He relaxed his shoulders and turned around. Each step back to his spot felt momentous—reversing the tumbling gears of hurt pride and anger, a grinding away in Len, metal on metal. But he did it. He felt some shame at giving in, and then some shame at feeling shame.

A knock banged hard on the door. "I haven't seen those kids for a hundred years." It was Dear-Abby's voice, sounding anxious. Another knock—louder this time. "Are you in there, you dear-hearts? I want to show you some pictures."

Len pressed his finger to his lips, silently said *"Shhh,"* then gestured as if to say *"No way."* The others obeyed, and soon they heard Dear-Abby clump away, mumbling about teenagers these days.

"I feel terrible ignoring her like that," said Len, "but if Bennu's right, we should keep reading."

Angie found her place.

CHAPTER TWO: Venting One's Desires

Outside of the Cleverly Hills Inn, a slippery black otter paced back and forth. "Oh Mama, I do love being a giant Hollywood celebrity." Ollie admired a photograph of himself looking suave and adventurous. "They captured the masterful me in all my manly mystery. And I'll get big parts in movies, Mama. I'll be a productive member of society. I'll make mountains of money racing across phony sand dunes and smoking unfiltered cigarettes. I won't be called 'thief' ever again!"

Ollie stashed his Maps to the Stars' Homes sandwich-board sign in the bushes and dashed into the hotel. "You taught me well, Mama. 'It takes a first-class otter to be a first-class robber,' you used to say. Yes, indeedy, I've taken this to heart. Here I am right now, about ready to pay my respects to the ailing Percy Perkins. I already sent him a nice note, but I don't think that's quite enough, do you? But, dearie, dearie, doodles, Mama, what am I doing walking in the front door? I shouldn't-a otter do that, no sir."

Ollie found an open back door and strolled down a hallway. "Now, if I were a detective and sidekick, where would I be? Well, Mama, you are right. I would be so secret no one would find me. I would be as quiet as an empty vent. I would be . . . wait a tumbler-slipping minute. Here's a heating vent, and I can hear voices inside—the voices of Percy and Bones! Oh, no one's geniusier than your lil' ol' Ollie, Mama. I'll just cruise down this shaft."

With dogged persistence and catlike quickness, Ollie crept toward the end of the vent. "I'll have to whisper now, Mama. Bones is telling Percy forty-three ways to increase the yield of corn. I can see Bones but not Percy. I'm in a tunnel, a tunnel to Bones. Ha, ha!" He saw a steaming bathtub and scooted closer.

"I say, Perce," Bones shouted to the closed bathroom door, "a hot bath won't melt you. It'll do you a world of good."

"You can lead a horse to water, Bonesy, but you can't give an old dog new bricks."

"I reckon that's why you're a cat, Perce. This bath is Bassett's orders. Now, walk the plank or . . . or . . . or I don't know. I'm not very good with threats—except to cutworms, you know."

Percy pounded on the door. "Make no bones about it. You won't catch me with my pants down."

Ollie pressed his nose against the grate. "Maps to the stars. Maps to the stars' homes."

Bones looked around. "Did you say something Percy? I reckon you'll do anything to get out of a bath. Maps to the stars? Do you want to go visiting?"

Ollie did his best Perkins imitation. "Patty Pickford's house. A map in time saves nine. Yep, that's the one. Patty Pickford. Let's go before saved by the bell freezes over."

"All right, Percy, you win. I'll go get a taxi."

When Bones left, Percy unlocked the bathroom door and

looked around the room quizzically. Shaking his head, he shuddered at the sight of the tub, grabbed his derby, and walked out.

"All's well that the cooks don't spoil," said Ollie in his Perkins voice. He punched a fist in the air in triumph, hit the vent grate, knocked it out, couldn't find anything to grab, slipped down, saw the tub, flipped himself in midair, and dove with a smile on his face into the tub. When he surfaced, a great blob of soap sat on his head like a turban. "I will reform, Mama. It's all part of a twenty-two-point plan. As delicious as this water feels, I need to go pursue step number seventeen."

Lizbeth held out both hands. "Well, there's one clear link. Ollie said he was in a tunnel to Bones. That's exactly what Angie and I were in—that awful, rat-infested tunnel that ended up in a room full of bones."

"Then there's Ollie," said Bennu, "saying he will reform. Do you think there's anything to it? Do you think it means anything for us that Ollie might reform? Len, what do you think?"

Len jerked himself off the wall as if a spider had been crawling down his shirt. "The wall. Something's moving." He moved to the center of the room and watched Angie's painted walls swirl into motion. Slowly, then faster and faster, the pink twister gathered speed. It kept spinning until things blurred, until the dresser and bookcase couldn't be seen and Len felt dizzy. Would the tornado lift them all in its mighty force?

There was wonder on the faces of the other Misfits—the same wonder and awe Len felt, yet a belief that things would be OK. Here in Angie's room, the pink and lavender and white spun in cycloned frenzy. Though no one moved, the twister gave Len a sensation of being lifted up, caught up in the swirling glory.

He studied the ceiling. The magenta and soft pinks seemed to be traveling into a hole, as if they were being sucked into the light. Fuchsia sparkles shot out from the bottom of the twister. Then the spinning pinks rose. They swirled rapidly up to the center and vanished.

In one dramatic *poof*, everything went dark. And silent. The void lasted only a second, then crickets sounded and the night sky emerged, revealing ten thousand stars, all flickering vibrantly, as the moon rose on the horizon. It moved in time-elapsed speed, arcing up toward the center. But it did not enter the vortex; neither did the stars turn in their places and get drawn in. The pale moon dipped before it reached the center, dropped slightly, then slipped from the night sky altogether to hang in the room right next to the Misfits.

The man in the moon floated eye-to-eye with Len. The man's face took shape—not like the clichéd smiley face Len had seen in movies and commercials, but a face nonetheless. The craters refined themselves into cheekbones and a nose. Eyes appeared, and crow's-feet, and a wide mouth. Len knew the face, the furrowed brow, the serious expression. Here was the homeless man who'd stuck his head in his car. Here was the face Bennu thought Len had run over.

"I can't believe it's you," Len whispered to him. "I was worried about what happened."

The man's pale visage dropped its jaw like Jacob Marley in *A Christmas Carol*. "And this is the second lie between us. No caring marked your days or nights, no tears, no remembering your blessedness, not even gratefulness for your small world. There is pain beyond yours, ingrate, do not forget."

Then this gaunt man in the moon withdrew over the horizon. Dawn came, and with it the pink tones Angie had painted on her walls. The morning arrived, and the box of Angie's room reappeared out of the fading night sky.

CHAPTER TEN

A Surrounding Siren

Surely it was time someone invented a new plot,
or that the author came out from the bushes.
—VIRGINIA WOOLF, *BETWEEN THE ACTS*

 When Lizbeth realized the walls had stopped spinning, she closed her eyes and pictured the room swirling around her again. She preferred the beautiful pink cyclone to her darker reality. In the eye of her imaginary hurricane, she saw, as before, the unveiling of the night sky. In her mind, the moon stayed in its place. Then she heard something new—a lonely howl, like a hound dog, singing to the moon. It grew louder. The moon even seemed to retreat at the sound. The howling came closer, a more haunting moan, a challenge to the moon's brightness.

Lizbeth opened her eyes. The room sat motionless, its walls as pink as ever. Angie sat next to her on the bed, and the boys on the floor leaned forward.

Yet the howling remained.

Through the open bedroom door, Lizbeth gazed into the loft. It seemed darker than she remembered it. The howling came from there, so she got up from the bed and walked to the door frame. She saw not the couch or the desk but the same scene she had just held in her mind . . . of a night sky, trees dimly lit by lunar light. She smelled the night air, felt the cool breeze. She guessed the howling came from a place just out of sight, beyond the borders of the walls that had become screens projecting another place.

So she walked in. To her dismay, she was not in Welken but in the loft's open space between Angie's room and Len's. The other Misfits followed her.

Bennu pressed his hand into the scene. "It's weird. It doesn't resist like the screen we saw in your open gate."

"It's like the picture of Mercy Bay I saw in the tunnel in Ganderst Hall," said Angie, "but it feels more real, not like a movie."

Len pointed to the loft windows that faced north. "Look, more Welken." Through these windows, moonlight shone. A hillside could be made out. "Do you recognize it?"

Lizbeth walked up to the love seat below the window. "No, I can't tell where it is." She put both knees on a cushion and leaned toward the image. She wanted to stick her head in and turn it around, to see around the corner.

"Over here." Angie pointed to the door to Len's room. "A tree. A fir tree, I think. And at the landing to the stairs too. We're in this room, surrounded by Welken."

As Lizbeth glanced back to the stairs, the Misfits moved instinctively to the center of the loft. She heard footsteps. Someone walked in Welken. The steps came from Angie's door. They moved north to the loft window. Lizbeth's heart quickened. She tried to be perfectly still, totally silent.

The walking moved around them, over to the west, by Len's room. The steps sounded soft, a *crunch* cushioned by something . . . a carpet of old leaves or dry grass, perhaps? They got louder, like they weren't just circling around the Misfits but turning in on them, getting closer. The howling continued, competing with the steps for volume.

The soft *crunch* moved over to another tree, one with wide leaves, by the stairs. The walking and the howling came closer. Would this something or someone cross into their world? What would they do? The steps came on, to the very edge, to the skin of Welken stretched before them.

One step more and the walking stopped. A voice came out of the night sky. "It's not my fault, I tell you." A foot appeared through the veil and then another.

Lizbeth shrieked.

The voice came again, "Don't blame me."

Lizbeth grabbed Angie's arm.

"My word, Lizzie." Dear-Abby pulled herself up the last stairstep and into the loft. "You don't have to scream. I know I haven't fixed my wig right today."

The night sky vanished. Startled and embarrassed, Lizbeth released her grip on Angie and tried to look relaxed. "Oh, I'm sorry, Dear-Abby. You surprised me, that's all. I think your hair . . . um . . . looks great." Lizbeth felt her own hair standing on end.

Acting as if nothing had happened, Angie grabbed a comb off her dresser. "Would you like me to fluff out your hair in the back, Grandma?"

"So it looks pretty bad, eh? I can't do anything right anymore. I'm so stupid."

"Oh, Dear-Abby," said Lizbeth, gently squeezing the octogenarian's hand, "you look great. I need help on the back of my hair all the time."

Lizbeth saw Len's *we-don't-have-time-for-this* look.

"You dear-hearts." Dear-Abby patted the girls on the shoulders. "If these handsome men would just give me a pedicure, I would be in heaven-o."

Appearing panicked, Len and Bennu froze.

"Did I tell you the story about my wig?" Dear-Abby settled into the bold-striped chair in the loft. "I've probably told you a hundred times. Well, I took off my wig one night, as usual, and went to bed. About one o'clock, I started having terrible chest pains. I thought I might be keel-keel right there in my bed-o. Then I thought, *If I'm going to meet Jesus tonight, I can't be wearing this tattered old nighty.* So I got up and changed into that nice blue silky one. Remember, the one with the white collar? Well, of course you don't. So I fell back asleep . . . until my heart started flipping like pancakes again. And I couldn't breathe right. I knew I was going to meet Jesus that night. Then I thought, *Oh my stars, I'm not wearing my wig! I can't meet Jesus in my bald-bald with those ten strands of hair all matted down!* So I got up and put on my wig and makeup and went back to bed to meet Jesus."

"What happened?" asked Bennu.

"It's obvious, ain't it?" Dear-Abby put both hands on the chair arms and pushed herself up. "I died and went to heaven-o, and my flesh rotted till it became a heap of bones. Ha!"

Lizbeth rolled her eyes. "Dear-Abby, you can be so morbid."

"That's not the half of it, Lonnie, my bones were never found. Yep, the case has never been solved. Oh, they put a couple of detectives on it, but one thought my bones were hiding in an orange closet, and the other figured a nemesis had them under lock and key."

"You have a nemesis, Grandma?" asked Len.

"You're kinda tender for asking, dear-heart. But no, I don't have a nemesis. My bones do. That's why I walk all funny. OK, it's time for me to go to bed."

"But Grandma," said Angie, "it's not bedtime. It's still the middle of the afternoon."

"I guess it is still light outside. What's wrong with this head of mine? Sometimes I don't think I have every card-card in the deck-o."

On that note, Dear-Abby turned and walked down the stairs, muttering something about her teeth feeling like the Russian army had marched through them.

Len switched his hat around several times—it looked like a dog getting ready to lay down—and finally settled on the forward position. He fingered the curl of the brim. "Now that she's gone, we can go back to the howling in the night. Somebody's hurt, maybe Piers. We've got to get going, but we keep getting all these interruptions."

Angie sighed. "Are you calling our grandmother an interruption?"

"Well, I—"

"She's not. What other good thing could we be doing right now? Grandma is like a butterfly in the breeze, golden-winged but delicate, as fragile as the world. It's too bad we see the things we need to be doing as interruptions."

"Aw, Ang." Len tipped his head slowly from one shoulder to the other. "What can I say after you flowerize everything?"

"The thing is," said Bennu, "you're both on to something. What have we got so far? Ollie talked about a tunnel to Bones. Lizbeth and Angie crawled through a tunnel to a room of bones. Then Dear-Abby tells us this off-the-wall story about her own bones—and where they might be, in a closet or under lock and key. Bones Malone is Bors. And we've got to find him so Piers can get well."

"So, the howling," said Len. "Is that Bones too, a hound dog in the night? Is it Bors trying to give away his location? I don't know. We heard leaves crunching, or something—but that's not enough information. And who was walking around? And where? I think it's either the grassy mound, the entrance to the mine shaft in Welken, where I first became a lion—or it's someplace out behind the McKenzie Boys' house. I'd like to go out there. No, I *need* to go out there."

Bennu put his hands on his hips. "We don't have time for you to go out there. Every minute here is twelve in Welken. Every hour is half a day."

"I know, I know. But the image is too strong."

"Are you listening to me?" Bennu pushed his glasses up. "One minute you're telling us to hurry up. The next minute you're acting like we should stop everything because you have a hunch."

"This is so typical." Len gritted his teeth, then shifted his jaw forward and growled. "I get criticized for not caring about Welken. Now I get criticized for caring. I'm trying to control my temper, and you guys conspire to get me angry. I get no credit whatever I do."

Lizbeth saw the overstated truth in Len's reasoning. She knew what it was like to try your best and not get noticed. "OK, Len. You're right. You have been making progress. We're all feeling stressed, that's all. You go. Do what you need to do."

Len pressed his lips together like it was good to hear this from Lizbeth but somehow embarrassing at the same time. "Can you guys find something to do while I'm gone?"

"Are you sure you should go alone?" asked Angie.

"I'll be fine. I'll keep my distance. Lizbeth, why don't you read some more Percy and Bones? We didn't get very far before you interrupted . . . er . . . said what needed to be said. Angie, you could talk to Grandma. See if you can find out more about her bones—why she brought it up, what events she's really referring to. Bennu, you can . . . who cares? I don't know, take your pick, I guess. Help one of us."

Bennu took a step toward Angie. "I guess I'll help with the Dear-Abby interrogation. She can be tricky."

"What a shock." Len paused. "Sorry. I didn't need to say that. OK, meet in the backyard as soon as you can. You'll probably all be waiting for me."

In the Buick, Len changed radio stations four times, looked briefly at the CD case on the visor, then turned off the radio. He watched the smoke rise from the lumber mill at the edge of town.

Just like me, he thought. *I stink. I think I'm all "of Welken," then I yell at everyone to show that I'm not. Oops, don't miss the exit. Now here I am, headed to the McKenzie Boys' place by myself, like I'm some great spy or hero on a white horse. Who do I think I am? I'm going to get eaten alive. King of the Forest? What a joke.*

Len decided to park a block away. He thought it might be better to come at the house from the back, from the railroad tracks. Though homes on top of McKenzie Butte had nice views, the Minks lived at the bottom of it, with a view of idling engines and stockpiled railroad ties. Len walked toward the switching yard as fast as he thought he could without drawing attention to himself. Once he got to the tracks, he ran. Soon he knelt down behind the Minks' house and sized up the landscape. He could hide behind the hedge, like before, or he could sneak up directly behind a broken cedar fence, held up by wire and a few steel supports.

Len didn't like the idea of crouching in someone else's yard. He had gotten away with it once, but maybe this time he would be noticed. Maybe the McKenzie Boys' neighbors liked to take target practice on trespassers. What was he doing here anyway? Why was he searching for evidence to substantiate an image, a wispy, fading fairy-tale image?

Then he saw a mound in the Minks' backyard. With a sapling growing at its base, the tiny hill looked like a smaller version of the one in the vision in the loft.

So Len chose to come straight on, to hide behind the mound, then to get up as close as he could behind the torn couches, discarded plywood, and car parts littering the Boys' backyard. He looked around for a cougar but didn't see one.

Then he heard the Boys' mother shouting. Len crept up as close as he dared. He hid behind the hood of an old Chevy Monte Carlo. For once, it paid to be small.

"Josh, you are a pathetic excuse for a son. A family should stick together, but you want out. I won't have it! I won't have a boy of mine let down his brother. Oliver—oh, I know you call him 'Odin,' as if he's some stupid god—anyway, he needs you. Wouldn't you want him to help you if you were in trouble?"

What's Odin done now? Len wondered.

"Yeah, but this is different, Ma. What you're askin' for is big, real big. It's not like knockin' off a gas station. I got to think this through."

Tommy joined in. "You don't have to think about nothin'. You're a total idiot anyway, just like Ma says. Just do what I tell you."

"What if it doesn't work?"

"There you go thinkin' again," said Ma. "You didn't drop out of high school for nothin', Josh. Look, Tommy here is fine with it. Pa even got off his rear end and helped out."

"OK, Ma, fine. Stop yellin'. And you can put away the knife."

"Now get out of here. Take Oliver into the sun. It'll be good for him. Go over the details, son. Practice with Tommy."

Len looked around for another hiding place, a barrier he could escape from if need be. Wiggling out from under the hood, he banged his elbow on the metal. As he grabbed the hood to keep it from making noise, the back door opened. Len moved his hand off the hood. He tried to be "not there," to be absolutely silent.

Tommy led the way. "All right, ready, lift. I can't believe Pa hasn't made a ramp for Odin yet. He's such a lazy bum."

Josh grunted under the load. "Yeah . . . he . . . is. Uhhh . . . there. You OK, bro'? You look terrible."

Len could hear the wheels of the chair roll into the yard in front of him, by the door that sat on the sawhorses. He hoped for another cougar to come out of the door, one the Boys could see, one that would let him escape.

"Dude, you do look like crap." Tommy let out a big sigh. "Does the sun feel good?"

Odin worked hard to breathe and harder to speak. "I . . . guess."

"OK," said Tommy, "here's the plan. Ma says the key is to make it look like an accident. We go downtown and scope out a corner. We see who comes and goes and when. We find someone about the same size as Odin."

"Like all this is gonna be easy," said Josh.

Odin coughed.

"Then," said Tommy, "you get ready with the car—"

"And nobody's gonna notice," said Josh.

"Shut up. Yeah, nobody notices."

Odin coughed several times. The coughs sounded deep and weak. He continued to cough as Tommy talked.

"Then I push the guy—"

"Kill him."

"I make sure he gets hit."

Josh pointed at Tommy. "You kill him."

"*We* kill him. You hit him with the tricked-out Monte Carlo. I hop in the car and we get outta there. We call 9-1-1 on a stolen cell phone. We dump the car, toss the phone, get into the LTD, and come here. No one gets hurt."

Odin began wheezing.

"No one gets hurt? Tommy, you are so stupid. We're killin' a guy! We'll get caught and go to jail!"

Len swallowed hard. He had not pegged the McKenzie Boys as murderers, and he couldn't imagine how running someone over would help Odin.

"Where'd you get a conscience all of a sudden, Josh? And what choice do we have? You heard Ma, didn't you?" Len heard scuffling noises, pushing and shoving. He worried they would knock into the hood. "You think you're too good for this, Josh? You're nothin'! You're nothin' without Odin! And neither am I!"

"Shut up!"

"No!"

"No, I mean it. Shut up!"

"Ow!"

"I didn't hit you."

"I know. Odin did. He cut me with his knife. Man, that hurts."

"Look at him. He did it to get our attention. He's goin' down again. His lips are blue."

"Ma, Odin's in a bad way, really bad!"

"Call 9-1-1. Ma, call 9-1-1!"

Len heard the back door slam. Everyone was shouting in the house. Then he heard a train coming.

Josh yelled over the rumble, "C'mon, Odin, snap out of it. You're goin' to be OK. I'm sorry. I'll go through with it. You gotta get better."

The door opened and several bodies rushed by. The roar of the train came on. Ma said, "The ambulance will be here soon. Let's get him in front, in the driveway." The train whistle blew.

Then more shuffling feet and grunting and the squeak of the door. Len heard shouting and slamming. When the train reached the tracks in the back, the hood of the old Monte Carlo shook. Len slid out from behind the hood and ran out the back to the tracks. He ran as close as he could to the rushing train. His heart churned with the surging engine. He slipped on the gravel near the tracks and slid down the embankment. He kept running until he turned off to go to his car. As he started it up, he gripped the steering wheel and tried to catch his breath. That's when he heard the siren.

CHAPTER ELEVEN

THE EMERGENCY

*How many desolate creatures on the earth have learnt
the simple dues of fellowship and social comfort, in a hospital.*
—ELIZABETH BARRETT BROWNING, *AURORA LEIGH*

 Lizbeth walked into Angie's room to find Charlotte's manuscript, while Bennu and Angie went downstairs to find Dear-Abby. Right away Lizbeth saw the papers on the floor next to the bed. She picked them up. As she sat in Angie's desk chair, the "tunnel to Bones" line caught her eye again, and she remembered how she had used a bone to smash the rotten wood underneath Mook and Vida. She thought about MaryMary, about her silky words and barbed intentions. Then she felt the barb within her, the pain from the nightmare that wouldn't let her go.

She straightened the pages and started to read. She felt uneasy . . . distracted. As her mind wandered back to Welken, she forced her eyes back to the page. She reread the first sentence several times and thought how terrible she would feel telling Charlotte that the story did not keep her attention. She pushed herself closer to the desk till it bumped her stomach. She let out an "ow" from the impact against the shard in her side.

She tried to read again, but this time all she could think about was Bennu and Angie, together, holding hands—or more—and she couldn't concentrate. She thought about how they were changing the group, then she thought about how that wasn't the whole story. She knew she was jealous. One look at Angie's beauty had always sent her into a tailspin, and now having to observe Bennu's response led her to a full-on, all-alert nose-dive.

Mayday, Mayday, Mayday! I'm crashing! No matter how many things happen in Welken, I still come back here to me, to my ugliness, to my stupid thunder thighs. How can my blotchy, dark skin compare to Angie's creamy whiteness? Angie said I'm the lostness of Bors, the weariness of Piers. I don't know what that means—but I do feel lost and weary.

Lizbeth couldn't bear another minute alone in Angie's room. She grabbed the manuscript and headed quietly down the stairs. She walked a few steps down the hall before turning into the living room. She couldn't believe what she saw. She sure didn't want to see it. Bennu and Angie sat on the blue corduroy couch, kissing. Bennu held Angie's chin delicately in his hand. Angie gripped Bennu's elbow.

Lizbeth didn't know whether to cough and stamp her foot or say something that would end up sounding like somebody's mother. She stood there watching and not watching, feeling like an intruder, an angry one, a jealous one, wondering if anyone would ever stoop to kissing her. She opened her mouth, but no words came out. They didn't need to.

"I told you I'd be back," said Dear-Abby from behind Lizbeth in the hall, "me and MacArthur! I just needed to do a little flush-flush of the toilet-o. I drink, therefore! Oh, Lulu, it's good to see you, dear-heart. Bennu and Angie, I'll be with you as soon as I make myself another cup-o of tea."

Bennu dropped his hands like he'd just been caught touching some precious antiquity in a museum. Lizbeth thought it was a fake kind of shame, a modesty born out of being observed. But Angie didn't seem bothered. Lizbeth wondered if she'd ever seen her blush. Angie just never needed to.

"The water was still hot." Dear-Abby came in and sat in the maple rocker. "I just dip the tea bag in so it comes out like colored water. Now, what was it you wanted to know?"

"Well," said Angie, "you said something about your bones a little while ago." She flicked her hair back.

"I said something about my bones?"

"Yes, you did, Grandma."

"Good memory, just short. What did I say?"

Lizbeth drifted off. She looked out the window. She had this crazy physical feeling that she was about to get sucked into Welken. Closing her eyes, she saw Piers asleep, looking weak. Then she saw MaryMary marching through Deedy. She felt like she was in a cartoon, that boundaries and barriers were giving way. In that moment Lizbeth sensed that everything was malleable, that all the worlds—and all the world's stories—were as close as a door, as visible as any scene out a window. Veils were thin. Maybe they were stretching. Maybe they were contracting. She didn't know where to stay or where to go. She tried to slow her breathing.

"You're such dear-hearts."

Lizbeth snapped her head toward Dear-Abby's voice, her mind reeling, her body settling back into reality, this reality anyway, the Bartholomews' house in Skinner.

"It's so precious of you to ask me about the past." Dear-Abby leaned over and patted Bennu's and Angie's hands. "But don't think you'll get it!" Dear-Abby's voice thrust at them like a red-hot poker. "Some things best be left alone. You can't change the past—and I'm not about to tell you my secrets so you can go on a talk show and tell the world!" She took a sip of tea. "Now you 'dear-hearts and gentle people,' where were we? Good memory, just short."

Lizbeth wanted to know what Dear-Abby thought she should hide from them. Perhaps it was important. Then again, how could they trust Dear-Abby's memory? But all Lizbeth could think about was Piers, asleep, maybe dying.

She worried that if she read the manuscript, she'd miss clues from Dear-Abby. If she listened in on the conversation, something would happen so she couldn't finish the chapter. Messages seemed to be everywhere, speeding by so fast that no one could catch them all. And why? From where? Did all messages imply a sender? Did these clues flooding in mean that some cosmic dam had burst? Or did these multiplying wonders mean that worlds would collide?

Lizbeth slammed both hands on the manuscript. That got Bennu's and Angie's attention. "I'm fine," Lizbeth said in response to their worried glances, but she couldn't focus.

Len sat in the car and waited for the ambulance to leave with Odin. As he mulled over the McKenzie Boys' description of the "accident," he thought of Piers and his condition. Odin was weary. Piers was weary. For that matter, Len was weary of himself. Why all the weariness?

Then he got an idea. He started the car and headed toward the hospital. He would get there first, be waiting in the emergency room, find a good place for spying.

He parked the car and trotted into the ER, just in time to hold the door open for a man—had to be the father—carrying a screaming toddler. When the man said, "Thank you," Len caught his frantic, bulging eyes. No war, no famine, no crime could have made this father's eyes more terrified.

Len walked in and saw a world beyond his fears. Doctors pumped an old man's chest. A teenager with a head wound trembled in shock. Blood splattered the floor. The staff was clearly overwhelmed, a small-town hospital with big-city problems. Nurses ran with IVs on wheels.

Len shuffled in, afraid he would get in the way, afraid his queasy stomach would get the best of him and he would miss Odin. He found a wall to lean against next to a blue curtain hooked to the ceiling. Maybe he shouldn't be there, but the chaos kept anyone from noticing or caring. From there he could watch the door—and most everything else, including what he didn't want to see. He closed his eyes, but any new noise jolted them open. The loudspeaker, a moan, a crashing door.

Then he saw behind the blue curtain. He leaned his head against the wall and saw what the curtain didn't hide. A young boy, maybe ten, lay limply on the exam table. A doctor leaned over, and Len saw the boy's leg flat on the table. One of his forearms wasn't right. Len saw something sticking into it, something thin, like a blade. Maybe he had been stabbed. But the something wasn't metal, and it had no handle. Then Len made it out. It was the boy's bone. Len's knees weakened. He tried to draw a breath and nothing came. He started shaking. He knew he had to get his head between his legs before he fainted. He bent over. Along the way, he caught sight of the bone one more time.

The bone, that white bone, sent his mind spinning—to images of a sun-bleached bone in the desert sun, the skeletons of animals long dead. To the leg he broke when he was eight, that leg bone. Then to another leg bone sticking out, his own flesh recoiling from it and his hands tied and rats coming. No. No, that was a nightmare. Then he flashed on Gandric's bone, in Welken, white to the sky, a warning, an alabaster sentinel. Alabaster! He saw her shining, singing in Ganderst Hall . . . before she became dead, as silent as, as . . . this boy next to him, whose bone was right now being tucked back into its sleeve, his skin, the stuff that holds the planet together.

A great commotion startled Len out of his delirium. From his fetal position, back to the wall, Len saw the Minks come in, Tommy and Josh pushing the paramedics to hurry up, and Odin's father right behind.

Len wondered which poor patient would be ignored so a doctor could attend to Odin, or if Odin himself would not get treatment.

"Somebody see my boy now!" Odin's mother grabbed the arm of a nurse running by.

The nurse looked offended. "We will when we can." She tried to pull her arm away.

Tommy came up on her other side. "My brother's in a bad way. He may be dying. Get somebody here now."

"Let go of me. I'll see what we can do." The nurse went from station to station. When she came to the boy next to Len, the doctor said, "I'll come. Send this little guy up to surgery. They're ready for him."

As the medics moved Odin onto the table, the rest of the Minks came in. The physician turned to the father. "Has he been here before?"

"Yes," said Odin's mother. "Send some idiot to get his chart."

The nurse swept open the blue curtain as she left, exposing Len. The father noticed him first. Len looked at this man he'd never seen before. Strangely, the man did not look away. In his hardened eyes, Len saw a history of pain—and something else. Len couldn't put his finger on it, but Odin's father reminded him of someone or something. Maybe it was just the Boys, he didn't know.

When the father looked back to the table and watched the doctor work on Odin, Josh glanced in Len's direction.

"Hey, it's that runt, the Bartholomew punk. Get out of here. Get out of here now."

As the doctor said something about Odin's heart, Josh turned to Len. "Beat it!" He stepped out and shoved Len. "If I see you again, you're dead." Josh closed the blue curtain.

Len walked nervously toward the door. Peering back, he saw the curtain open.

Josh's eyes glared him out of the room.

Lizbeth realized that all she'd read was the title, "Chapter Three: Plucking Pearls at Patty Pickford's Place."

"Have I told you about the DMV test, you dear-hearts?"

"Yes, Grandma," said Angie, "you have."

"Of course, probably a million times. Have I told you about me going to meet Jesus in my best nighty-o?"

"Yes, Grandma, you told us that one just a few minutes ago."

"I did? I don't think so. You must be thinking about somebody else. Y'see, I was—"

Concentrate, thought Lizbeth, *Percy and Bones were at the Cleverly Hills Inn. They were met by Andrew McTrotter of Scotland.*

"Dear-Abby?" Bennu put both elbows on his thighs and leaned forward. "I study genealogies. I'd like to hear about your background, your ancestry. If Angie's all English, you must be too."

"You must be a detective, Bobby. Then again in England, we might have detective-bobbies. Oh, dear me, I made a joke-joke."

Tentatively Bennu pressed his case. "So, Dear-Abby, what was your maiden name? For that matter, what is your married name?"

"My married name?" Dear-Abby scowled back at Bennu. "The name that hung on me like chains? The name I got from that deadbeat? I won't say it aloud." Dear-Abby looked down, evidently saw that her own hands were in fists, and relaxed them. She placed them gently on her legs. She smiled like a grandma again. "No, my real name, the name I went back to, my true name-name, was Griffin. That's what I am, a Griffin. So Charlotte is half a Griff-Griff. And, Angie, you are a quarter Griffin-o. Makes me think of muffin-o. I'm hungry."

McTrotter? thought Lizbeth. *A horse? Are we going to learn something from a horse? Maybe the horse is like a griffin. Were there horse-gods in Egypt?*

As Dear-Abby passed Lizbeth sitting at the table, she dramatically snatched the manuscript out of Lizbeth's hands. "Oh look- look, it's one of Charlotte's Percy and Bones stories. I've never, ever, seen this one."

Lizbeth turned in her chair, suppressing her sense of being violated. "Actually, Dear-Abby, you were reading this story earlier today."

"I was? How do you know? Oh dear-dear-dear, sometimes I feel all funny in the head. I think I'm going crazy-o."

Lizbeth stood and put her arm around Dear-Abby. "Well, I think you're wonderful. I barely know my own grandparents. They're still in Egypt. I'm so glad I get to share you with Len and Angie."

"You dear-heart, you're kinda tender. Here, you can have Charlotte's story back. It's so, so . . . whatever! Now, let's see what's in the reefer."

Lizbeth took the manuscript and turned the page. She saw Bones's comment, "I'm lost, Perce. I couldn't find my way for a minute in these parts."

Hmm, she thought, *we already know this. Bors is lost. And I am so lost trying to get anything out of this. Clues! They're so, so . . . whatever!*

CHAPTER TWELVE

DRUNKEN VISIONS

Arise from my bones, avenger of these wrongs!

—VIRGIL, *AENEID*

 A knock on the door startled Lizbeth. She smiled and said, "I'm closest. I'll get it." When she opened the door and looked through the screen, her smile collapsed.

It was Darlene.

"Hi, Mom."

"Lizbeth, honey, sweetie-snoochums, I need you and Angie to come over and help me with something."

"Mom, you're swaying."

"I'm dancing in the wind, dearie-pie. Don't you want to join me?" She moved her hands in a pseudo-hula.

"Mom, stop it. You're embarrassing me."

"Kids, nowadays, you're just so worried about everything. You should get a little freedom." Darlene spun around on the porch, teetered, bumped into one of the posts that supported the overhang, and tripped down the steps.

"Mom! I can't believe you!" Lizbeth pushed open the screen door. "You come over here drunk and fall down!" Lizbeth's eyes welled up.

Angie came up from behind, brushed her hand across Lizbeth's shoulders, and gave her arm a squeeze. "Darlene, that step surprises so many people." She bent over Darlene and touched her hand. "Are you OK? Did you twist your ankle or anything? Let me help you up."

Lizbeth watched Angie get Darlene up to a sitting position. Angie brushed off her blouse, but Lizbeth couldn't find it in herself to offer a hand. She couldn't call to mind anything encouraging to say. What she wanted to do was slam the door and storm off, let her mom suffer the consequences of her own problems. Lizbeth bristled at Angie's assistance. Her mom did not deserve pleasantries. She deserved to be yelled at. It was a personal triumph for Lizbeth to keep her venom inside. Still, it excreted into her thoughts. The poison dripped from there into a small pool in her gut. She felt the shard of glass twitch in her.

Lizbeth looked back and saw Bennu behind the screen door, his arms folded tightly across his chest. His eyes caught Lizbeth's, and he shook his head in disgust.

Angie grabbed both of Darlene's hands and braced herself. "Up you go. There, steady, good. I think you're all right, Darlene. No broken bones."

Darlene closed her eyes and leaned on Angie. Her typical, exaggerated, happy face vanished for an instant. Lizbeth imagined her mother thinking to herself about how stupid and reckless she had been, how her life plunged faster every day into its free fall. Then Darlene smiled. "All I want is for Little Orphan Angie and you, my not-very-little Elizabeth, to come back to the house. I can't find the place mats I want."

The venom found the speech center in Lizbeth's brain. Several choice cursings sped to her lips.

But Angie ambushed her. "Sure, Darlene, we'll go. C'mon Lizbeth, this will only take a second. You can hold my hand, Darlene. Bennu, we'll be right back. Now, Darlene, which place mats were you looking for?" Angie glanced back at Lizbeth and nodded for her to follow.

Lizbeth took a long, deep breath. She shook her head no, but she walked down the step. She put one foot in front of the other. She walked and breathed and calmed herself. She felt the poison start to dissipate. She let it go, and as she did, the pain in her side subsided.

A phrase came to mind. She said the first half to herself on every step with her left foot, the second half with every right foot. "In Welken" with the left; "of Welken" with the right. She said it over and over.

While driving from the hospital to his home, Len's thoughts raced as fast as his heartbeats. He hated the McKenzie Boys, how they bullied their way through life, through the Misfits. He hated their scheming, their premeditated way of inflicting pain. He hated their perverted sense of superiority, how they called him "runt" and "Bartholomew-boy."

In that moment, as he turned onto Pershing Avenue and acknowledged a friend skateboarding past him, Len vowed to get back at the Minks, to get them first, to find a way to stop "the accident" before it occurred and to put an end to Odin's power over others. If he had ever sought help from some higher being, if Len had ever prayed, this was his prayer: *God, help me get them.* That was it, a simple, straightforward plea. Soon he would know if God existed.

Len saw his house up ahead on his left. The porch steps, painted red to match the trim, also matched his red-blooded anger. He felt fully alive, every sense searching for knowledge, hopeful that peripheral vision would yield an enemy to fight, that a sound would betray someone hiding, or a smell would reveal the rancid odor of evil. He wanted to become a lion, to roar and chase and pounce and shred.

Len gripped the steering wheel. As he released his hold, his hands stuck in the curved shape, his knuckles white with rage. When blood returned to them, Len pushed himself back against the seat. Wiping sweat off his forehead, he shivered with cold. He opened the door and got out.

Then he saw Percy on the blood-red porch. The cat paced like he was hungry. He opened his mouth to meow, but he didn't. He roared. He filled the air with a warning beyond Len's own lion-rage roar, beyond the cougar's feline fury, beyond the wild threat of Morphane's guttural explosions. Then Percy grew. He became as large as his voice, from bobcat to cheetah, from panther to lion—and he kept changing and growing. Len feared what beast would grow out of the lion, what Welkenian version of greatest cat, of King of King of the Jungle. The metamorphosis continued. When the top of the animal reached over six feet, Len thought wildly that Percy must be turning into another Morphane! This Percy was not their house cat but an apparition sent by an enemy, introducing a new Morphane into Skinner, a beast ready to devour.

Then the image slimmed down. The horizontal back became vertical.

The head refined itself on the top—and there, on Len's porch, stood Piers, his green tunic glorious in the Oregon summer sun, and his welcoming face smiling warmly at Len.

Piers said nothing. He gestured for Len to look around. It took everything for Len not to rush up to Piers and throw his arms around him. But the moment seemed to demand something else, a simple yielding to Piers. So Len looked, as Piers clearly wanted him to. And he saw Piers standing not on the Bartholomews' porch but on a grand entrance into a kind of palace. Piers pushed on the tall wooden doors decorated with carved vines. Len stepped humbly, tentatively, toward the doors. From the outside he could see many Welkeners seated at a table. Though he could only see part of the table, Len knew he saw the backs of Sutton Hoo and Zennor Pict, the gentle giants of Welken. They moved methodically, slowly. Beyond them, floor-to-ceiling stained-glass windows shone brightly.

Len wanted to speak. He wanted to run into the building. He couldn't bear waiting for Piers to give permission. Piers came to the edge of the entrance and motioned for Len to approach. He seemed to want Len to kneel. As Len came closer to the door, he saw Ellen Basala, Prester John's assistant from the Prester Highlands in Welken. She did not see him. Oh, how he wanted to call out to her. How he hoped he would soon be reunited with her and Prester John.

Piers took his satchel off his shoulder and gestured for Len to get on his knees. Piers pulled something out of the satchel and opened it up. Len bowed his head and felt Piers's warm hand fingering his scalp, searching until he found the scratch Len had received from the cougar. The wound seemed to stand up in a ridge, as if it were attracted to Piers's hand. Then Piers applied something to it—a bitter-smelling oil. The pungent scent shocked Len's nose. Its harshness burned so hot in his nostrils that his nose started to run. The burning increased. Len tried to wipe it away, to blow out the searing, invasive odor. He felt on fire, as if he'd eaten the hottest pepper or curry or mustard sauce. Then tears came. He couldn't stop the flow out of his nose and eyes. He wanted Piers to cork the bottle, to stop the penetrating smell.

The wound itself never hurt this much! It doesn't need to be healed. I'm fine. I don't want a cure that hurts worse than the wound.

Len couldn't take it much longer. He wanted to lift his head and tell Piers to stop, to tell him he was OK. He didn't mind the wound. He could live with it. The pain became so great that he had to risk disrespecting Piers. He didn't want his face to burst into flames. So he looked up.

Piers was gone. So was the Welken palace and the Welkeners. Len found himself kneeling on the front step of his own porch, his face hot with tears running down his cheeks.

Though the burning smell faded, Len's tears did not. Along with them, sorrow came. For what? Then an image accompanied the sorrow. It was Odin in pain. For the first time in his life, Len felt sorry for that monster, that thug, that sadistic predator. And Len didn't really like the sensation. It felt like he was betraying his friends and all Odin's victims. When he extended sympathy in Odin's direction, energy seemed to go out from him. He felt weak and vulnerable. He wanted to keep crying.

But he did not. He clenched his fists and slammed them against his thighs. Then he went back to the car, found one of his mother's ever-present boxes of Kleenex, and did his best to clean himself up.

Lizbeth leaned against a wall in the kitchen while Angie opened drawers looking for Darlene's requested orange-and-white-striped place mats. Lizbeth did not feel bad for not helping. It was all she could do to keep herself in the same room.

"Here they are!" Angie held one up to Darlene. "How many do you want?"

Darlene opened the freezer. "Five." She pulled out a bottle of vodka and set it on the counter. "Let's see, Martin, Angie, and Lizbeth, Sniffles, and . . . who am I missing?" She poured some vodka into a glass and added some juice that was already out. "Oh, yes, ha, ha, ha—me! I forgot me! Now, what would you kids like to drink?"

Lizbeth stormed out. She went out to the back deck and slammed the door behind her.

Drink? What do I want to drink?

She sat on the edge of a patio chair. She put her head in her hands and cried. From behind her, the door opened.

Angie came and knelt beside her. "I'm so sorry, Lizbeth." She tossed the place mats onto the glass table. "Should we just leave? I'm OK with that."

Lizbeth looked up, her bottom lip quivering. "I don't know what to do."

From inside, Darlene yelled, "Martin, I'm making some special lemonade!"

Lizbeth turned back and saw her father staring at her through the glass door. He looked helpless and afraid. That made her even angrier. Why couldn't he stand up to her, confront her? Darlene handed Martin a drink, then moved toward the handle of the sliding glass door.

"That's it," said Lizbeth. "I can't sit with her. Before she gets out here, let's go."

Lizbeth pushed off from the cushion and stood as tall as she could. In the middle of her huge sigh, Angie hugged her, then turned and grabbed her hand.

They faced the end of the deck and the backyard. As they walked on each plank of the deck, Lizbeth began to whisper.

"What are you saying?" asked Angie, imitating her steps.

"Oh, it's nothing. I'm just saying 'in Welken' with one step and 'of Welken' with the other."

Angie joined her in the repetition.

They reached the end of the deck and walked down the three wooden steps that led into the Nefertis' formerly manicured backyard. Lizbeth stopped on the second step and stared at the unkempt roses. Flowers had turned to rose hips and darkened. Dandelions had gone to seed. Darlene's good pruners stuck out of the ground.

"I can't believe she left her pruners out!" Lizbeth moved down to the last step. "They'll get all rusty!"

Lizbeth sprang to the pruners, as if pulling them out that instant would have saved them from destruction. She stepped off the last plank and onto . . . another plank. She expected to be walking on grass, so she looked down at her feet. She stepped out again and again, and with each step a plank appeared. She walked more quickly to see if she could outrun the advancing deck.

Plank, plank.

She jogged.

More planks.

Then she ran. Finally she looked up. She stood on the broadest boulevard of Deedy Swamp, on the sturdy planked boardwalk. Lilies bloomed on the water to her left and right.

"Hey!" Angie's voice came from several feet behind her. "Look over there! It's Mook!"

Lizbeth turned back toward Angie, and then, as she snapped forward to find Mook, she tripped. The front of her tennis shoe caught in a gap between planks and she landed hard, her head banging against the boardwalk.

Standing next to the Skylark, Len blew his nose and gently closed the driver's door. When it only latched partially, he gave it a push with his hip to finish the job. Filled with conflicting emotions, he kicked at an old wasp nest on the cement walkway. A dead wasp fell out. He'd never seen that happen, so he bent over to take a look. As he did, he heard a noise at the front door.

Bennu scratched on the screen. "Len, you gotta come in and help me out. I'm doing my best with your grandma, but I may go crazy in another couple minutes."

"Where are the girls?"

"Over at my house. Quite a scene with my mom. I'll tell you later. C'mon." Bennu held the screen door open for Len.

"Yeah, sure. Besides, I'm hungry."

When Len walked in, Dear-Abby was snoozing in the living room. He went into the kitchen. "What a wuss, Bennu. Look how harmless she is." He grabbed a bag of trail mix and broke the seal.

"Yeah, right. You try listening ten times to the same 'beautiful-amazing' story about the iris fields and then get blasted for asking about her childhood or how long she was going to stay at your house. Trail mix? Gimme some of that."

Len threw the bag at him. "No kidding. Welcome to my life."

"Oh boys! You dear-hearts!" Dear-Abby awoke and adjusted her bra in plain view. "I want to go on a walk-walk-walk. Want to come with?"

"Grandma, do you have to do that in public?"

"You mean I should go on a walk in private?"

"Oh, forget it."

"No time for the sad and decrepit elderly? Fine-fine-fine. Well, I'm compulsive, so I'll go by myself. Where'd I put my jacket? I'm so crazy."

Bennu elbowed Len. "Is she OK alone—with her Alzheimer's and all?"

"She knows her way around here. She walks the same route every time."

"I don't think you're going to be able to let her alone for very much longer. Why don't you get your mom?"

"Nah."

Dear-Abby pulled the hood of her windbreaker over her head and cinched it up tight. She resembled a blue astronaut. "Let us then be up and doing. I've got my jack-o, so I'm going to go-go." She pushed open the screen door. "Oh, by the way, Beppo, you'll find a book in the attic that tells all about the Griffin family, way back to old-old times. OK, I'm a-goin'. I shall return, me and MacArthur!"

The door slammed. Len and Bennu each downed a glass of milk, wiped their mouths with their hands, stuffed protein bars, red vine licorice, and string cheese into their pockets, and burped loudly.

Len said, "Wait here." In seconds he came back with a ladder and carried it up the stairs.

"I want to see the book," said Bennu.

"Yeah, but I should go first. It's my attic."

Len climbed the ladder and leaned his shins against the top rung. With both hands he pushed up on the attic's hinged door. It flopped back with a crash. "OK, what you have to do is balance on this top step, the one that says Do Not Use This as a Step, and then pull yourself up."

As Len straightened his arms and lifted his knee over the ledge, the light from the attic's dormer window blinded him. Shielding his eyes, he got out of the way so Bennu could get in. Then he stepped out of the direct sunlight.

But it seemed to follow him. The sun shone everywhere, on the wooden chest to his left and the mast to his right. The mast. The mast with the rigging. The mast that was broken in two, its upper half on the deck of the ship.

"Bennu," said Len with a smile, "we're not in Kansas anymore."

PART THREE

BROKEN, THE MOTHER

CHAPTER THIRTEEN

SPARKLINGS

"No, it was only a glimpse then," said the man;
"but you might have caught the glimpse,
if you had ever thought it worth while to try."

—J. R. R. TOLKIEN, "LEAF BY NIGGLE"

 *In the moon-filled night, the boy's mother felt the cold of the snow against her skin and through her thin robe. She hadn't shivered yet. Everything hurt too much. She lay frozen in the snow, not literally, but in fear. She kept still, as dead as she felt on the inside, until she heard the door slam. She waited longer in case he watched her from the window, gloating, hoping for another reason to show her his wrath.*

When she could bear the steely snow no longer, she hunched herself up, touched her bruises, took one look back, and shuffled off into the street. Gathering her robe around her, she started shivering, and then her teeth chattered. With each step, she hoped she would grow warmer. She shivered and chattered and walked on. Before dawn, she had made her way to a friend's house. The friend let her in and nursed her wounds.

Days came and went. Slowly, she got better. One morning the boy's mother looked in the mirror. She saw, as usual, the pain in her own eyes, the sadness she felt at not seeing her son. But she also saw that the dark circles under her eyes had faded some and her bruises had turned yellow. With makeup, she could cover the ones that showed. She could borrow a nice dress from her friend. She could go out into the white wind of this small town and do what she had to do. She could look for work.

She thought if she could find a job and live on her own, maybe she could bring her boy to live with her. Maybe then she could save him from the clenched fists of his father.

So she went out into the drifting snow, into the cutting wind, into the town where everyone knew everyone. She asked to be a waitress at the diner, but they didn't need anyone. She said she could be a secretary for the accountant, but he said no. She tried to get on at the mill, then at the beauty parlor. She saw a Help Wanted sign at the grocery store, and her heart fluttered in hope. But everywhere it was the same. The cold wind outside seemed to stay with her as she entered each place. The eyes she met were cold, the voices cold, the answers to her questions cold, cold, cold.

She learned why. In this small town, words were spoken, stories told. Someone had whispered here and there, someone not afraid of lying. He said she had been wicked. She had betrayed him. He said she had been with another man and then, when confronted, had run away. She had abandoned her family and her four-year-old son. That was the story her husband told.

So no one would hire her. After weeks of searching, after leaning as much as she dared on her friend, she had no money and no job. She did not know what to do. Then she got an idea, the saddest idea. It was the only option left to her, as impossible as it felt—like crossing a bridge made of air.

She went home. She walked the unshoveled frozen path to the front door. She forced her legs up the steps and did something she'd never done before. She knocked.

Her husband opened the door. She took a breath, as if it had been her last. It swirled swiftly into the depths of her lungs and curled up and tried to stay there. But the mother called it up. She brought it to her lips and used this breath to speak calmly to this man she no longer knew—if she had ever known him—this man who had thrown her out.

She asked him a question. Could she come to work for him? She had been turned down all over town. Could she come and be a maid in her own home? She would come in the morning to make breakfast. She would clean the house and care for the boy during the day. She would make dinner and then go home.

She waited at the door. The man looked at her with disgust and anger. No *pity filled his eyes, no compassion. He stared past her into the winter sky, into the gray street and the leafless trees. He said nothing.*

Then he opened the door wider and let her in.

And this is what the boy remembers.

For years, his mother came in the morning and left after dinner. He came to see this as his everyday existence. Other things happened over the years, terrible things, but he did not learn about all these events till later. For now, he felt the wound in his side grow larger. The shard twisted inside him. It cut deeper and, though he wanted to pull it out, he found that he had grown used to it. The shard carved him bit by bit, whittled at his insides.

In time, he feared nothing would be left if the shard were taken away. It had worked its way to the center of his being. So he looked after it. He cared for it and found that he could sharpen the edges. He protected it from its enemies. He learned it was his most loyal friend.

When Lizbeth opened her eyes, she wiped away her tears. Then she felt the bump on her head. She rested a few minutes in Angie's lap.

Mook knelt nearby, a worried expression furrowing his brow. "I can slay enemies. I can send many arrows to do what must be done." He adjusted his quiver. "But I do not know where to aim right now. I wish your tormentor would be brave enough to show his face."

Lizbeth strained to get off Angie's lap, and Angie helped her sit up. "Where'd you come from, Mook? I'm so glad you're OK."

"I have endured, thanks to you two. I'll tell you more later. What can you say about your dream?"

"The dream, the nightmare, is so sad. I know I need to pay attention to it." Then Lizbeth told them both the details of the story.

Angie pushed a leaf over the edge into the water. "Do you think it's real? I mean, of course it's real. You are feeling it and seeing it—but do you think it's a real family someplace or just a message?"

"I don't know. What makes me think it's not a real family is that no one has a name. But then—and I know you didn't mean this—it can't be 'just' a message. The story is too powerful. Even if it's not real, it has to be true."

Mook pulled his bow around his leather breastplate and smiled. "Now you are thinking like a Welkener . . . maybe even someone wise enough to be from the Nezzer Clan." Mook followed this comment with an unusual expression. He smiled.

Lizbeth knew that, for Mook, the reference to his home village was a daring joke.

Angie pointed down the boardwalk, toward a crowd or a parade coming toward them. "I don't think we'll have much more time here. Lizbeth, is there anything else you can tell us real fast?"

"Yes, I keep feeling the same pain in my gut, this boy's pain. I don't want to somehow get used to it or, worse, to need it. At the same time, it seems to follow a pattern. I mean, the more I think about Piers, the more the shard hurts me. And yet, that's when I see Piers best."

Angie helped Lizbeth stand. "You *see* Piers?"

"Well, yes."

"I know I shouldn't feel bad, but I wish I saw him. Last time, well, I saw things more clearly."

"I see him laying down, on a bed I think, his head in his hands. And I see warm colors—yellow and orange."

By the time Bennu climbed into the attic, Len's eyes had adjusted better to the bright sun. Even so, Len tugged his baseball hat around forward to shield his eyes. He walked over to the mainmast and ran his hand up the varnished wood. Above him, about fifteen feet up, the thick timber had snapped forward. It looked as if its fall had had something to do with the foremast's condition, broken higher up. Len found the torn mainsail draped over the starboard side, and part of it floating in the water.

Len's heart sank as he leaned over the side. "What do you think, Bennu? Do these look like the same markings as Gareth's ship?"

"I don't know. Could be. I was too worried about falling to pay attention to artwork."

"Must have been some storm, eh? We were gone about four hours. That's two full Welken days. Anything could have happened."

Tenderly Len drew two parts of the flapping mizzen sail together, as if by his holding the torn sections side by side, they might magically sew themselves up. Then he rushed back to the hatch where they'd climbed into the ship. He half-expected to see the top of the ladder and the carpet of his own house. When he didn't, when he saw more varnished wood and the ends of a few bunks, he feared he might find bodies below.

"What if," Len said as he slipped into the hold, "what if Gareth was ambushed? What if it wasn't a storm? What if he found Bors but had him taken from him? Dude, I wouldn't know Bors if I ran into him. I remember somebody once saying he was royalty."

Bennu followed him and held his nose. "You're right. Hey, is this what they call 'bilge'? Yuck! How could anyone sleep here? I don't see signs of fighting. Chairs and glasses are broken, but there's no blood and no bodies."

The ship swayed in the water, boards creaking and ropes stretching. Len felt claustrophobic down below. "Let's go back up. Maybe we'll find some poop on the poop deck."

Getting up proved more difficult this time. The ship groaned dramatically, tilting a few degrees toward the sea.

Len poked his head up. "Clouds are coming in. The water's getting rough." He steadied himself by grabbing a rope on the deck. "Look out there."

Bennu took his last step out of the hold just as the ship lurched. He tripped on the lip of the opening and fell, grabbing the end of the same rope Len held on to. Then he pointed out to sea. "Whitecaps. Maybe a storm is coming. It looks ominous. The dark sky out there, the sunshine here. But the swells are higher, that's for sure."

Len wondered what they should do. He'd seen old movies about sea squalls and how the captain would lash himself to a mast. It seemed a little over the top, but the ship shifted with each wave. The *eh-eh-eh* of the stretched ropes sounded like the slow firing of a machine gun. Increasingly Len felt that he and Bennu were the targets. Of course, the ship must be stuck on something. They weren't drifting. They could make a raft if they had time. They could swim to the island if there weren't any sharks—and if he were a better swimmer.

The island? Yes, he supposed that's what it was. He'd seen it right away but had been preoccupied with the ship. About a quarter mile away, imposing cliffs shot out of the sea. Len could not bring himself to say that the island welcomed them or looked like a refuge from a sinking ship-wreck. It didn't. From this vantage point, the island appeared unapproach-able. Sheer cliffs rose 250 feet. A jagged ridge marked the top. The island resembled a giant crown sitting on the water—or on the head of some un-derwater colossus, some aquatic king waiting to eat them.

OK, overactive imagination. Too many video games.

Then the ship jerked down on the port side, as if the underwater king had reached up and pushed the hull with a finger. But it wasn't a finger. It was a wave that smashed into the side, pushing the ship inch by inch over toward the island. Len tightened his grip on the rope. When the ship creaked like an old parrot and lurched again, Len's hands became paws and his own massive claws dug into the rope. His upper body had become leonine, but his head remained human. He couldn't figure out why he was only part lion again, and why it was a different part.

Bennu struggled to hold on to the rope. Len yelled at him to become a falcon, so he could at least clasp the rope with his beak. Then something snapped and the ship keeled over another few degrees. Len watched help-lessly as Bennu lost his grip. He slipped down toward the side railing, which had now become the only floor protecting them from falling into the sea. Len scrambled for a foothold. The rope hung flat against the verti-cal floor.

Bennu yelled, "Help!" and fell back. It wasn't that he slid down the rope; he appeared to lose his grip. Then Len saw Bennu's talons clasping the rope. Bennu swung like a bungee jumper.

The ship sounded a fierce *crack* and shifted more onto its side. As the sails tore loudly, Bennu's bungee fall stopped and he hung upside down by his talons, about twenty feet above the water.

"Bennu, are you OK?"

"Yeah, so far." Bennu grunted. "I can hold tight, but I don't know if I can pull myself up." He grunted again. "Falcons aren't gymnasts."

"I'll try to come down to help." Despite his good intentions, Len quickly learned why cats ascend so much more skillfully than they de-scend. When he retracted his claws in one paw, their curved shape made "grasping down" difficult, especially since he had to support all his weight with his one remaining grip.

The ship turned under more. Now Len worried it would capsize. "Hey, Bennu, what if the ship goes over? Should we let go now and take our chances in the water or try to go back up and get on top?"

"Oh man, the blood is rushing to my head. I think we should just drop into the water."

"But the ship might come over on us. I think we've got to go up."

The next wave twisted the ship side to side.

"Len, we should let go!"

"Why?"

"Because *they* will catch us."

"They? Who are you talking about? You're delirious."

"No, look on the surface of the water."

Hanging from the rope, his arms tiring, Len didn't see a rescuer. He saw the water moving, the backs of the waves heading toward shore. He saw the bright sun glistening off the water, dancing and sparkling in the blue-green sea. "Bennu, it's just salt water. I say we try to go up."

"No, Len, I'm not crazy. The sun on the water. It's alive. The sparkles are coming toward us. Look! Even in the shade of the ship right below, they're still here."

Len saw Bennu swing up and catch the rope above him. He held for a while, breathing heavily. Some of the sparkles seemed to fly off the water and hover near his face. He saw Bennu smile.

Bennu looked up. "Hey, Len, these are water glimpses. They're like the others we met last time—under the alders. They were land glimpses, I guess, and these live on the sea."

The ship groaned again, and the top of the broken masts above Len moved on the axis of the deck. Len guessed they'd break off or that their weight would tumble the ship all the way over.

"Jump!" Bennu yelled, and they both let go immediately. Falling with his back to the water, Len saw one mast high in the air, heading his way. He didn't know if he'd fall on Bennu or if the mast would crush them or if the ship would trap them underwater. He tried to turn over so he could dive into the water, but there wasn't time. He prepared for the splash, the pain against his back, the pressure on his lungs, the fear of not getting back to the surface.

But he barely got wet. He plunged into a sparkling net. The water glimpses, hundreds of them, thousands of them, caught him. They cushioned his fall, provided a barrier from the water as he sank below the surface, and then they swam him and Bennu to safety as the ship crashed down and broke apart.

Len tried to relax his stiff body. Surrounded by the buzzing, flapping water glimpses, he felt like he should trust them but couldn't suppress his fear. He wondered if they might open up a hole and drop them in. Finally he gave in and let these little creatures carry him merrily over the ocean.

The water glimpses shone so brightly that Len had trouble opening his eyes to see his rescuers. They were larger than the wasplike land glimpses. Tadpole in size, with shimmery fish tails and more humanlike upper bodies, these winged mermen and mermaids held Len and Bennu in their tiny hands. They flew and swam with equal ease.

One came up to Len's ear. "Mr. Len, I am Miss Noriadian. We know of your goodnesses to Welken. Water glimpses hear all that sparkles in the sea—and we get news from our forest cousins."

Len turned his head to see her, but she flew too close to his eyes. "Thanks for saving us. I mean, it sounds kinda cheesy to put it that way—but we are grateful."

"By Soliton's glow, grateful is a good thing to be."

Miss Noriadian flew back, and Len could see her shining teal tail. Its border of darker blue contrasted with the yellow dots on her teal-colored scales. Her upper body shone like a firefly. Every once in a while, Len caught a facial feature. Then Miss Noriadian bowed toward Len.

"OK." Len did not know what to say that would not sound trite. "What now?"

"What now, Mr. Len? Water."

"Water?"

"Yes."

Miss Noriadian turned her buzzing wings into a higher gear. At the sound, the other glimpses did the same, moved out from under the Misfits, and dropped Len and Bennu with a splash. Len surfaced first and rubbed water from his eyes. When Bennu popped up, the glimpses hovered up close to them. Their wings fell silent; their bodies held off the water by their sloshing tails.

Much less gracefully, Len and Bennu dog-paddled to keep their heads above water.

Len's tension returned. "Not to be disrespectful, Miss Noriadian— we're glad to be off the ship—but are you just going to leave us like this?"

Miss Noriadian fluttered her wings. Others flapped until the delicate hum wound up into a roaring buzz. Len thought he saw a smile on Miss Noriadian's sparkling face. Then the whole dazzling assembly sped across the open sea and vanished.

Len would have slammed his fist into the water if it hadn't been for the six-foot wave that crashed down upon him. He tumbled around in the water, not always knowing which way was up. He surfaced with a gasp, looked around for Bennu, then ducked under just as the next wave plunged him down. Len held his breath and did an underwater somersault. When he got a second to regain his bearings, he pushed off the sand and shot himself toward the surface.

He saw that the shore was close. Then another load of water hit. He rolled under and kicked hard but did not find anything to kick against. There was only water and foam and a long vine of slimy kelp that wrapped around his body.

Worried that the kelp was actually a sharp-toothed, eely basilisk, he yanked on it to get it off his body. He tugged and slipped, then hit the sand. With kelp still draped over his back, he got up on his hands and knees, crawled beyond the surf, and collapsed on the beach. Turning over on his back, he breathed deeper, coughed, and spit out some water. The sun above became shaded. Were clouds rolling in?

But it wasn't clouds. It was Bennu. "You OK?"

"I swallowed some water."

"Want me to push on your stomach?"

"No way."

"Sorry, but I'm not sure I've ever body-surfed so well in my life. What a ride! The next best thing to flying. I made it almost the entire way on that first wave. Cool, huh? How'd you do—besides swallowing water?"

Len coughed. "How'd I do? I may never walk again."

Bennu moved so the sun hit Len's face. "Why is it that you can skateboard and not surf? Both movements are 'swishy,' aren't they? But those water glimpses were the perfect rescuers. They caught us and carried us away. They were so beautiful. So many colors. And bright, like candles in the water."

Len held a hand up to the sun. "You are overwhelming me with your compassion. I'm speechless."

Bennu grabbed Len's hand. "Sorry." He lifted Len up. "I guess between the water glimpses and the ride, I'm just pumped. Sparkling mermaids. Their shimmering bodies, their flowing hair. Makes me think of Angie."

"Shut up."

CHAPTER FOURTEEN

WATER, WATER, EVERYWHERE
AND NO TIME TO THINK

Woe to him who seeks to pour oil upon the waters
when God has brewed them into a gale!

—HERMAN MELVILLE, *MOBY DICK*

 "Here she comes!" Mook's urgency sent Lizbeth's adrenaline rushing. As she watched the approaching crowd, Mook motioned for her and Angie to get out of view.

A parade of Deediers and Cutters tromped down the boardwalk. At the front, two musicians blew curlicued horns so plainly that Lizbeth thought the metal would straighten out.

Soon the throng occupied the open space. Marching Cutters followed the horns, some holding lances, others holding banners. The Cutters on the outside sometimes pushed against Deediers lined up to watch. To Lizbeth's surprise, instead of continuing on by, the parade broke up right in front of them, some marchers sitting on the boardwalk, some climbing to the balconies on the second floors of buildings. A few Cutters quickly assembled a portable platform right in front of Lizbeth, Angie, and Mook. The threesome drifted back and over to the side, trying to blend into the crowd.

Lizbeth watched flag-bearers mount the platform and stand at the corners, facing the street, away from her. Dignitaries stepped up and sat on chairs at the back of the platform. One chair, the largest one, with a high back and thronelike carvings, was empty.

Just as the crowd erupted with applause, Mook, Lizbeth, and Angie climbed up some unoccupied stairs on the side of a building. From there they could better see the honored one mount the platform, her long, dark hair covering the fur of a deep purple robe, its train flowing over the ground.

Many times in her life, Lizbeth had been stunned by beauty—on television, in movies, and in person, by Angie and others so geneti-cally blessed that Lizbeth wondered why the chromosomes couldn't have been a little more evenly distributed. But when Lizbeth saw this woman, this queen of some sort, she couldn't stop staring. The woman turned back to the dignitaries and smiled. It was a look to make Helen of Troy envious. She would have launched a thousand magazine covers back in America. Lizbeth had nothing to compare to this woman, whose shining, round eyes, soft caramel skin, glistening teeth, and silky, dark hair were perfection itself. Tall, thin, and shapely, the woman moved with a confidence Lizbeth knew would be hers if only she looked the same.

The crowd began to chant her name. It swelled in the air until it called even the lilies to tilt in her direction. Lizbeth couldn't believe what she heard—a name she'd reviled, a name she'd matched to a witch's face. The crowd roared, "MaryMary, MaryMary Hardin Fast." Lizbeth gulped at the contradiction, at the tragic paradox of outward beauty and inward ug-liness. She didn't want to believe it.

MaryMary stood behind a podium and hushed the crowd. "Good neighbors of Deedy Swamp. You know why we are here today." The crowd cheered. "You know of our promise to straighten out the crooked." More applause rang out. "We have taken the errors out of Deedy Speech and made them clear. We have remade boardwalks to be predictable and uni-form. And you know that we have much more to do—in music and archi-tecture, in business and in law. Deedy will no longer be a muddled old swamp but a shining city the equal of Primus Hook!"

Maybe she really does have a good long-range plan, thought Lizbeth. *Maybe she has rough methods but good motives. She doesn't look cold and harsh, just a little stern. Maybe she uses a "tough love" approach. Maybe she's warmer on the inside.*

Angie elbowed Lizbeth. "It's so sad. Can't they see how terrible she is? Can't they see her tiny heart and the hole in her soul?"

Lizbeth saw no such thing. She wondered how Angie could. Did Angie's own beauty give her insight into its limitations?

As MaryMary turned her profile from one side to the other, Lizbeth saw the awe in the Deediers' faces. They revered MaryMary's features. They saw in her a kind of holiness. All at once Lizbeth saw how she too accepted this face, this figure, this one feminine form to be true and sacred, an object worthy of worship and sacrifice. Hadn't Lizbeth herself been bowing to it for years? And if she could be taken in by MaryMary's beauty and presence, Len and Bennu would be reduced to star-struck admirers, weak-kneed and submissive.

MaryMary held up her hands to quiet the crowd. Then she bent down low behind the podium to whisper to an aide. When the aide whispered back, MaryMary slapped her. The crowd could not have seen it behind the Cutters standing guard, but Lizbeth had. MaryMary's fierce blow had knocked the aide to her knees. As she fell onto her side, MaryMary kicked her powerfully, then calmly turned back to her audience.

Lizbeth jolted out of her dream. She registered MaryMary's ruthlessness, her false claims, the fear in the eyes of the dignitaries as they watched the aide get punished. Lizbeth's pulse raced. She wanted to become an ox so she could gore this evil woman. She waited for her shoulder muscles to multiply and the brown fur to rise. But her upper body remained the same. A faint tingling moved in the middle of her shoulder blades, as if she had invisible oxen wings. Yet that was all.

Mook looked disgusted. "See, that is why they obey. No other reason."

"I have more to do!" MaryMary put her hands behind her back. "I have established a regime to make the province more productive, better able to compete. You must all lose your roundness and get more fit. We should all be perfect specimens of Deedy—sleek, toned, and beautiful. And I have decided to give you a picture of this transformation, an image of putting out the old and welcoming the new. I have exposed a Deedier guilty of treason, Vida Bering Well. We will dispense with her and her outdated views and usher in the new."

MaryMary gestured to some guards, who brought Vida onto the podium. Her hands were tied and her mouth was gagged, but she still looked defiant, standing as tall as she could next to MaryMary.

A hand gently pushed Lizbeth's right shoulder over to the left. She turned to see Mook pull out an arrow, strap the remaining ones tightly in the quiver, and draw the one arrow across his bow. It had a larger-than-normal arrowhead.

"Today," said MaryMary, "I will show you what happens to those who do not realize the goodness of our promises." Her cheerful tone seemed full of hope. "I give you a sight to remember, the hanging of Vida Bering Well."

The crowd cheered, some raucously, some halfheartedly. Guards wheeled a portable scaffold onto the stage and secured it to the edge of the boardwalk. The noose stuck out over the water. MaryMary asked those on the platform to stand to the side so the crowd could watch the "consequences" of holding on to the Deedy that "needed to change."

Cutter guards prodded Vida into position and made her face the crowd.

Lizbeth couldn't understand why Mook wasn't doing something. "Now!" she whispered. "What are you waiting for?"

"We have a plan," said Mook.

"We?" asked Lizbeth. "I don't know anything about it."

Angie's hands on Lizbeth's shoulders told her to stay still. "Lizbeth, shush. Mook needs a steady shoulder to lean against."

Vida got pushed back one more step onto the very edge.

"Behold the old!" shouted MaryMary.

Lizbeth thought, *Come on, come on.*

"Here is its destiny!"

When a Cutter kicked Vida with his shiny boots, she struggled mightily to maintain her balance. Angie grabbed Lizbeth. "Look, over there, in the cattails."

Scanning the reeds, Lizbeth saw the prow of a smallish, roundish boat and the crouched figure of Jacob Canny Sea.

Ah. That's the "we" in "we have a plan," Lizbeth thought.

MaryMary, with a flirtatious wink and a pucker of her full red lips, gestured to the rage in Vida's eyes. "That is last year's look, my friends. It is over. It will soon be just a part of our history. Executioner!"

As the hooded executioner grabbed the noose and walked toward Vida, Lizbeth saw Jacob slip his boat underneath the platform. He stood and raised a pole up to Vida's feet. Then he looked over to Mook.

"Very still," said Mook. "Become a rock."

Lizbeth hardened herself as best she could. Against her shoulder, Mook's muscular arm flexed into a tight, rocklike mass, as if to show Lizbeth what to do.

The order came. "Lower the noose!" shouted MaryMary.

In that split second, Jacob released a spring so that a rope attached to the pole wrapped around Vida's feet. As Jacob yanked Vida down into the water, Mook's arrow pierced the chest of the executioner. He let go of the noose and collapsed onto the platform. Chaos erupted.

As Cutters scurried about, Mook tapped Lizbeth and Angie. "Dive!"

They obeyed immediately. On the way down, Lizbeth looked out to Jacob's boat. He was not in it.

Panic. That's what Lizbeth felt once she was underwater. The swampy wetness chilled her as she watched Jacob cutting Vida's bindings. Lizbeth could not believe how well she could see. Next to her, Angie pointed to Cutters diving in behind them. Cutters! They had tossed off their helmets, but they had surely kept their knives. What would happen when they caught up? All Angie and Lizbeth had on their side were two roly-poly Deediers and an archer. Lizbeth turned ahead and saw that she swam not in a natural marsh but in a developed waterway. Trimmed plants created boundaries, boundaries of aquatic streets, streets that had intersections and rest stops and ladders leading up to shops. No matter! Cutters were coming!

Lizbeth swam with all her might. Then Jacob and Vida swam past her as if she and Angie were just paddling. Jacob let out a ribbon and indicated that they should follow it. Lizbeth looked back and saw Mook fending off two Cutters. One looked young and athletic, the other older with many medals on his belt. Then Lizbeth developed another problem. She needed to breathe.

Jacob and Vida's ribbon darted down a side street into the spreading roots of a tree. Lizbeth swam in total desperation. She needed air, and she needed it now. She even pushed Angie aside.

Jacob and Vida pointed to a leafy, flowering vine that hung from above. They grabbed its underwater blossoms and put them to their mouths, breathing out bubbles to show what was in the vine. Lizbeth took a draft and smiled at Angie. The air felt as solid and pure as water from a mountain stream. She wondered if Deediers needed to catch a breath as often as she and Angie did. She suspected not. When she looked around and saw these plants here and there, she felt better, but she didn't have a clue what to do next. Should they get back to a main underwater street? Go up to the surface? Get into a boat? Hide in the swamp's forests?

Mook swam in with no Cutters on his tail. He breathed through the vines and gestured that things were good but that they should hurry.

Angie pulled on Lizbeth's arm. Her face positively glowed, and her strawberry blonde hair flowed around her as if it were living. Lizbeth blew out a cascade of bubbles before taking another draft.

Swiftly they swam in a line: Jacob, Vida, Angie, Lizbeth, and Mook. They came out to the edge of a "street" and darted across it. Just like aboveground, the main streets were faster, but they could hide more easily "off-road" in the open fields of the swamp. They swam into an undeveloped area, finding another oxygen-supplying flowered vine. Lizbeth inhaled deeply, then turned away from the vine. After pushing her back, Mook swam in front of her. She could see why. Cutters.

"We don't have much time." Bennu sat on the sand, his back against a smooth rock at the base of the cliff.

Len walked on his hands and knees over to Bennu and sat next to him, his eyes closed to the sunlight. "You mean the clouds are coming in?"

"Well, that may be, but I meant the tide. It will wipe out the beach in a few hours. We should find a way up."

"I'm not going."

"What do you mean you're 'not going'?"

"I'm not going."

"Fine, I'll let down a hundred feet of rope when I get above you."

"I'm not going till I eat a protein bar."

"Me neither. Good idea."

The boys stood and watched the waves creep closer. Two bites into their bars, they walked to their left, toward the east. Bennu made a few observations comparing the ecology of Welken to the Oregon coast, and Len pretended to be snoring.

Len spotted a narrow trail that led up the rock face at a moderate angle. He walked on the dirt and loose gravel for about twenty yards. Scooping up a handful of pebbles, he tossed them one by one in a high arc toward Bennu, who sat down below on a driftwood log and picked at it as if he were collecting scientific samples of splinters for the crime lab back home.

Bennu jumped up. "Hey, cut it out!" He rubbed his shoulder where the pebble had hit. Throwing the driftwood slivers onto the ground, Bennu found the trail Len had walked up.

That moment was the end of their teasing for quite some time. After several switchbacks, the trail—or whatever it was—ended about two hundred feet up. They had at least another hundred to go. From the narrow ledge they were standing on, Len and Bennu peered down. The overturned ship rocked in the swells, and the tide had already conquered the beach.

"What do we do now?" asked Bennu.

"Focus on why we're here—to find Bors, to help Piers, to do what we can do for Welken."

"Wow, you're sounding patriotic. But I didn't mean that. I meant, what do we do from this ledge?" Bennu threw a few rocks and watched them fall and fall and *plunk* into the ocean.

"I knew what you meant. But I think we need to remind ourselves of why we want to get off this ledge. We're not just hiking. We have a mission, an important one."

"Len, sometimes you're downright impressive."

Len tilted his head. He wanted to make some wisecrack, some self-deflecting but nevertheless self-congratulatory remark, like, "Ah, shucks, Bennu, stop it with the praise, stop it some more."

At the same time, he felt an urge—heard a voice, sensed an inner presence, whatever you want to call it—that said, *"Don't."* That was it. A single "don't."

Len decided to obey the word, then didn't know what to say next. He put his hands in his pockets. "Look over there." Len pointed in the same direction they were hiking, but down a bit.

"I see it, a nice-sized overhang. Too bad the trail stops here."

Len leaned out toward it and lost his balance. He wobbled, reached toward the rock wall, slipped on the loose gravel, and fell. The path was wide enough to hold him, but he slipped back down off the end of the trail toward the overhang.

Before he could scream, Bennu grabbed his right leg and started to pull him up.

"Wait, Bennu."

"Wait? Don't you want to get back on this ledge?"

"Can you hold me tight?"

"Yeah, I've got a good handhold here. I can wrap my arm around your ankle and calf."

"I think I see something. Now, slowly, lower me down as far as you can." With his lower body somewhat level on the ledge and his upper body leaning over, Len inched his way down, searching for fissures to grab. He saw a good crevice and put as much weight as he could on his left hand. As he pressed deeply into the narrowing crack, his fingers felt crushed in the rock. His left arm started to shake, and he could feel Bennu trembling above him.

"That's it!" yelled Bennu. "No more."

Len saw another handhold. He crawled his right hand into it, twisting to partially face the cliff. He saw a solid place for his feet and stretched.

"I'm slipping! Len, I don't think I can hold you."

"I'm almost there. I see a clear way to the overhang. We just have to climb for a short while. Let me go."

"Are you crazy?"

"No, I see a great foothold, a ridge sticking out from the rock."

"You're gonna fall," Bennu warned.

"No, I'm not."

"Even if you don't, who's gonna hold *me* while I reach out?"

"Oh, yeah. Duh."

Len turned his head back toward the overhang. As he searched for another way down, he could not believe what he saw. Stairs. His own stairs. His own carpeted stairs in his own house in Skinner. The stairs that led down from his bedroom. The landing of the top stair was just below him. When he looked toward the base of the stairs, he saw his grandma, Dear-Abby, sitting in the living room, knitting. A cat brushed against her legs. It was Percy. Dear-Abby leaned over to pet him and looked right up at Len. She winked.

Bennu's grip slipped. "I've got to pull you up." His voice quivered. "I'm spent."

"Let me go."

"Len, I can't do that."

"Bennu, trust me. I see stairs and Grandma."

"You are *so* crazy." Bennu's arm shook. "I can't hold you any longer."

Len yanked his leg away. Bennu held on to Len's ankle but lost his grip on the rock. As Len fell off the rock, he reached out to grab a stair, snagging it with his lion's claw. He pulled hard. As he fell onto the stairs, Bennu followed, screaming.

Len tucked in his head and tumbled down. As Bennu rolled on top of him, Len sunk his claws into Bennu's arm, dragging him down until both of them rolled to the bottom.

As the dust settled, they moaned in pain. Len ran his hand over the ground. He did not feel carpet. He felt dirt and rock. He did not see Dear-Abby or Percy. He crawled over to the place they'd come from. He saw a four-inch shelf of rock that looked roughly like a series of steps.

Bennu grabbed his right forearm where Len had pierced it with his claws. "Ow. Those are sharp."

Len got up on all fours, flipped over, and surveyed his limbs. "You got me too." He rubbed his side. "Musta been a talon when you tumbled over me." Len tore off some of his T-shirt with a claw. He wrapped it around Bennu's wound. "Sorry about that."

Both of them sat against the wall near the end of the overhang. Len glanced out to sea, then toward the interior of the space that went farther in. They seemed to be in the mouth of a deep cave, a cave with a porch that dropped off two hundred feet above the ocean. They each took a swig of water from the plastic bottle in one of Bennu's pockets. Len leaned his head against the wall of the cave and sighed loudly. He did not want to say *What next?* He did not want to guess at what awaited them in the cave.

He did not need to. With an ugly growl, a tremling ran out from the dark. It stopped, raised its head, beat its chest, and roared.

CHAPTER FIFTEEN
CUTTING CUTTERS CUTTING

Rolling in the muck is not the best way to get clean.
—ALDOUS HUXLEY, *BRAVE NEW WORLD*

 When the Cutters attacked, Lizbeth was in the middle of taking a deep breath. She gasped and inhaled water. After coughing it out, she sealed her lips, but her lungs ached. She had no time to worry about having enough air.

Knife in hand, a Cutter slashed away. Lizbeth pushed back and dog-paddled so she could keep the Cutter in view. The strategy made her that much easier to catch. The Cutter swiped back and forth at Lizbeth, each swath in the water getting closer. All the while retreating, Lizbeth flailed with her arms. She dodged. She tried to find something to grab.

Then her feet found something solid—a tree trunk. Kicking against it, she thrust herself at the Cutter, surprising him. She snagged the wrist of his knife-wielding hand. As Lizbeth dug her nails into the Cutter's flesh, Angie grabbed his leg and twisted it back. Vida came in from above. She slammed the butt of her dagger onto the Cutter's head. He dropped his knife and pulled back, slipping out of Lizbeth's and Angie's clutches.

Lizbeth swam to get another breath. From that vine, she saw the other skirmish. Jacob tugged one of the Cutter's arms while Mook kicked him in the stomach. When Jacob flashed a dagger, the Cutter slashed with a short sword. He missed Jacob but caught Mook on his follow-through. Mook opened his mouth as if to scream. He grabbed the gash in his left shoulder with his right hand.

Then Vida surged forward and stabbed the Cutter in his sword-wielding hand. When the Cutter dropped the weapon, Mook hit him on the head. The Cutter swam away. It was over. The five triumphed over the two. Though Mook's wound bled, he shrugged it off, and they all congratulated themselves next to the breathing tubes.

But not for long. Vida led the way into a darker part of the swamp, farther away from the surface. When the fugitives stopped at flowered vines, sometimes Jacob and Vida didn't put the flower to their lips. Lizbeth got the impression that the Deediers could have gone a long time, maybe ten or twenty minutes, before needing to catch a breath. And they swam so effortlessly.

Lizbeth still worried about breathing. Though she had enough air to swim from plant to plant, she could not relax. The knowledge that the pressure in her lungs would be relieved before she reached a state of panic did not keep her from panicking. She wanted to breathe freely, to get off of these underwater roads and back to the dry ones an ox could sink her hooves into.

They crossed a narrow trench—Lizbeth could not see the bottom—then climbed back to street depth. Eventually they came to an intersection. Staying low in the grass, Jacob pointed to the wide street in front of them. Red-leafed plants swayed at the entrance.

With hand gestures, Jacob made it clear that they needed to cross the street and head toward a side road that appeared to go uphill. A few Deediers swam back and forth on the wide street, providing a degree of cover. One swimmer, a Deedy Swamp "trucker," towed three boxes behind him. Jacob gave the "come on" motion and led the way into the street. Vida gave Lizbeth a gentle push from behind and took up the rear. In the street, Lizbeth, Angie, and Mook looked like bicycles trying to keep up with Ferraris. Agile Deedy swimmers raced past them, some waving their hands angrily, an underwater version of road rage.

After reaching the center divider, a series of stout wooden poles about ten feet apart, all five took breaths from a vine and waited for a break in the traffic. As soon as they reached the other side, three Cutters swam down the boulevard toward them.

Vida yanked on Lizbeth's arm and pulled her into some flowing bushes; she saw Jacob tug on Angie and Mook in the same way. Lizbeth thought Vida would move her through the long leaves of the plant and into a freestyle sprint to outrace the Cutters. Instead, Vida pushed her head forcefully down into the center of the plant. Lizbeth did a full somersault, landing in a ball at the bottom. Vida plopped next to her and made herself as small as she could. Lizbeth followed suit.

Then the leaves of the plant moved. They flew up on all sides and curled around the two of them, not squeezing them down but creating a leafy room above them. Lizbeth's first thought was that this was step one in the plant's eating pattern. Soon the bottom would open up and a botanical throat would gobble them down.

Cautiously Vida pushed off the bottom and split open some leaves slightly. She pressed her face up to them, so Lizbeth did too. Her heart skipped as she saw Cutters swim up. An older one with raised gold bars on his shoulders pointed in two different directions, and the two younger Cutters swam off, their boots flashing like fins.

Then the Cutter who remained breast-stroked toward the plant. Quickly Vida and Lizbeth let go of the leaves and retreated into the center. As Lizbeth hugged her knees in the dark, she worried about when she would get another breath. Then she saw some light stream in through a hole, and a hand thrust in violently. Vida readied a dagger. Lizbeth felt like a magician's aide, waiting for swords to come slashing in from all sides. To her horror, the leaves of the plant moved on their own. Worse yet, they unfurled, opening the room to the marsh, exposing both of them to the Cutter.

Lizbeth just had time to think, *What are you doing, stupid plant? What are you doing?* before Vida grabbed Lizbeth's hand and swam out of the plant. Mook, Angie, and Jacob were already out of theirs, heading toward an oxygen vine.

Lizbeth glanced back to see how close the Cutter swam behind them. He wasn't there. Back at the plant, he struggled mightily in the leaves that had wrapped around him. The leaves were winning.

As the five of them refueled, Vida pointed back at one of the younger Cutters, who was returning to the trapped officer, then she nodded and gestured for the four to go on. Impulsively, Lizbeth pushed off to join Vida, but Jacob grabbed her. Vida swam swiftly back to the Cutter and sliced him with a dagger. Angrily, the Cutter bolted toward Vida, following her down into the boulevard, into the flow of traffic. The two of them disappeared as a thin red cloud of blood dissipated into the swamp.

Without hesitation, Jacob led the others "uphill." They swam as fast as they could, Mook's wound still bleeding. After two breathing stops, they broke the surface and, exhausted, dragged themselves onto the marshy ground.

Slowly, in deep measured breaths, Lizbeth felt her lungs return to normal. But her mind didn't. It raced at the thought of Angie lying motionless beside her and Vida being pursued underwater.

As Jacob attended to Angie, Lizbeth grabbed Mook's hand and watched while Angie's flattened wings slowly recovered their shining blueness. Jacob combed through them with his fingers, straightening them out. One large feather remained bent. Then Angie's wings faded from sight altogether. Jacob turned Angie on her back and pumped on her stomach till she spit up water and coughed and moaned and wiped her mouth.

Lizbeth smiled. She breathed in again and swore to herself that she would never again take air for granted.

And then, somehow, that ordinary promise took hold of her. Its halfheartedness became wholeheartedness, and gratitude rushed over her like a gust of wind. She felt weak before it, at its mercy. Vida might be captured or some calamity might any second put them at risk, but that did not matter. Lizbeth thanked God for Angie and her sweet mystery, for Mook's unswerving loyalty, for Jacob's roundedness. Then tears came. In this moment the tenderness felt like strength. Anyone could have said the harshest thing to her and she would not have minded. Gladness came next—a profound joy in life itself, in the sun, the pink lilies, the bees, the slosh of the water.

Mook pressed water off his pants, his oversized biceps mounding up and down. With a quizzical expression, Mook noticed Lizbeth. She wiped a tear and smiled at him, not knowing if his steadiness would ever give him permission for such emotional abandon. He nodded in sympathy with her. And his slight raising of an eyebrow spoke to Lizbeth all the richness of Welken's wisdom. He loosened the tie that had held his arrows together underwater.

Lizbeth examined Mook's wound. She daubed it with a cloth and pressed against it where it still bled. Watching Mook's gray ponytails drip on his shoulders, Lizbeth knew Mook would be fine. Welkeners seemed to heal so quickly.

Angie sat up. Jacob reached into a pouch tied around his waist. From its dry interior, he withdrew a tiny bottle and held Angie's head while she swallowed several drops.

Finally, they could rest and recover. They could minister to each other.

Into this quiet, an invasive splash broke the surface of the water. A head appeared. Then another. They were Cutters. Their heads bobbed in the water like buoys, then they took one more stroke and stepped out. From their gut they screamed a shrieking war cry.

Mook backpedaled. He snatched an arrow from his wet quiver and pulled it across his bow, but the bowstring's waterlogged state made the arrow wildly miss its mark. Jacob swiped at the first Cutter and kept him at bay. Lizbeth and Angie searched frantically for weapons, then each found a sizable stick. Lizbeth grabbed hers just in time to swing it at a charging Cutter. She dodged him, then skillfully flicked the stick twice and knocked him out with blows to the stomach and head.

Lizbeth turned to Jacob. She could see that his aboveground skills did not compare to his agility underwater. As the remaining Cutter closed in on him, Jacob shouted, "Go! Houdini it!" Just before he dove back into the water, he said, "In Welken!" The Cutter jumped in after him. In the silence that followed, Lizbeth, panting, dropped her stick to the ground. Mook released the tension on his bow.

Meekly Angie said, "Of Welken."

Lizbeth put her stick on her shoulder. "Mook, should we dive in and try to help Jacob and Vida—or do we 'houdini it,' like Jacob said?"

"They will do better in the water," said Mook, "without us to slow them down." He picked up his failed arrows and returned them to his quiver. "They can outswim the Cutters."

"I'm so overwhelmed by it all." Lizbeth tapped her stick on the ground. "The underwater city and the fighting. I need some time to process the whole thing."

"Think about it as we walk," said Mook. "Jacob jumped back in so we could escape. Let's go."

"But where?" Lizbeth backed up from the Cutter she had knocked unconscious. "We don't know anything new about Piers."

Angie rolled up the bottom of her top and wrung it out. "I still feel weak. Lizbeth, you seem to have made it through better than I did." Angie sighed. Her wings reappeared. They seemed to help her with her balance. "You said something earlier about the colors yellow and orange. Didn't Len say that the canyons around the Wasan Sagad were orangeish, like Bryce Canyon in Utah?"

"Yeah." Lizbeth emptied water from her shoes. "But the Wasteland is so far away."

Mook tied his gray hair back. "We should go see Prester John. He might know what to do. And if he doesn't, he will act like he does anyway."

Lizbeth and Angie laughed. It felt so good to Lizbeth. Weariness from the battle lingered, but she knew they had to keep pressing ahead. "OK, let's find the trail."

Lizbeth kept the stick and used it to part tall grass and push back bushes or low-slung tree limbs. She and Mook searched for a trail while Angie faced the sun, her hands outstretched, her wings hung out to dry. From the back, Angie looked as ethereal as ever, a blue embodiment of feathered purity. Like a Renaissance painting of a saint, her entire head emanated gold. She glowed like a sun, but Lizbeth did not worship Angie. She knew the glow was a gift, a radiance with a source beyond her winged friend. Angie bore the light, but she did not create it.

Then something else caught Lizbeth's eye. Beyond Angie, a low-hovering fog spread swiftly over the swamp. With a ceiling of ten feet, it split the sky into blue and gray and enveloped them in stillness.

As Angie retracted her wings, the silence became as tangible as the fog itself. It settled on them . . . *in* them.

That's when Lizbeth heard a voice. She had to strain to hear; it was as if someone were whispering in the far corner of a banquet hall. In the heavy fog, she listened with all her might—and heard Piers, so very faintly. She wanted to say *"Stand up! Shout!"* but she didn't dare miss what he was saying.

"Lizbeth."

Even softly, his naming her sounded like an evening by the fire, a balmy night under the stars, a day for opening presents.

"Lizbeth, you are indeed my weariness. Find me in you. Search for me."

With her concentration peaking, Lizbeth felt as if her hearing were enlarging, extending out in a larger circle.

"From the Book of Quadrille, one part is, 'The story's told by day and night.'"

Lizbeth leaned over toward the corner in her mind where Piers whispered. She nearly fell. She jolted forward, stuck out a foot to stop, and found her balance.

Piers's voice was gone.

CHAPTER SIXTEEN
DEATH AND THE ABYSS

Violence is not completely fatal until it ceases to disturb us.
—THOMAS MERTON, *THOUGHTS IN SOLITUDE*

 Len had felt vulnerable before. He'd been bullied by the "big kids" all his life, but this was different. This was a tremling. With his back to the wall of a cave two hundred feet up, Len stared at the tall, huge-headed beast, the dimwitted, strong-armed, long-eared hairy thing with a penchant for throwing rocks. Len didn't like the size of his mouth either, too large for his too-large head. His teeth were crooked, yellow, and dirty, his eyebrows long and pointed out toward the front. Len didn't like the tremling's fists, square, solid, three times the size of Len's. They hung on the tremling's arms like sledgehammers. Len didn't like his odds.

The tremling grunted. He seemed slightly uncertain of his next step.

Bennu whispered, "There's just one of them, looks like."

"Yeah, just one hideous monster with a huge mouth."

The tremling glanced around the cave and sniffed. He looked in Len and Bennu's direction but not exactly at them.

Len said, "Gareth said these guys don't see well."

"I have an idea." Bennu reached into his pocket. "Let's toss a chunk of protein bar in front of him."

Like a dog, the tremling got on all fours and sniffed again. He lapped up the piece. When he moaned his pleasure and picked at the chewy bits in his teeth, Len tossed another chunk to him.

As he gobbled it down, Len tore off another piece. "OK, he likes protein bars. How is this going to save our lives?"

"Lead him toward the opening."

"That's toward us, Bennu."

"I know. We'll make a break for it as he comes this way."

Len threw another piece at the tremling. It hit him in the foot. He looked up quizzically, stared at the motionless pair sitting in the cave, then sniffed and picked up the chunk on the cave floor. He bit into it and chewed noisily.

Len and Bennu scooted a few feet farther into the cave, but they couldn't go deeper or they wouldn't be able to throw the pieces in front of the tremling.

Len underhanded another piece of the bar. It landed in front of the tremling and skidded to about five feet behind the cave opening. The tremling sniffed and lunged for the piece. Then Len knew what to do. From his angle, with the tremling slightly ahead of him, he bowled a protein ball. It rolled toward the tremling. For a second Len thought it would hit the tremling's foot and stop. The tremling would turn and see them and come after them.

Then the bar hit a rock. It bounced to the left, missed the tremling's foot, and rolled in front of the beast. He turned his head toward it. The ball kept rolling. Just as the ball rolled over the edge of the opening, the tremling snatched it from the air.

And then he kept going. He screamed as he fell, an agonizing, deep-throated shout. Then a soft *thud* . . . and silence.

Len and Bennu rushed to the opening. They lay down and army-crawled to the edge, where they peered over. In the shallow water below, the tremling did not move. On his back, his mouth open, his arms wide to the heavens, the tremling held the ball in his fist. Then his hand loosened and the ball rolled out.

Len thought for a minute about the tremling, about his arched back and open mouth, about how cleverness had defeated animal strength. But the tremling was dead—and Len and Bennu had caused it. Len thought he should feel the glorious adrenaline of victory, like he did after blasting several hundred alien invaders in a video game. He thought he'd been toughened up by these tests of manhood.

Instead, he felt remorse. Why? Why should he feel sad to have saved his own life? Why should he regret seeing a monster expire? He didn't really know. The guilt twisted in his gut. He suspected that maybe even this clear choice was less than the best, that killing was not meant to lead to cheering, that death was somehow always tragic, a sign that something had gone amiss, that—as Angie would put it—the fabric of the world had received another thread-tearing pull. He thought that perhaps even this event was part of what was wrong in Welken that he was here to help get right.

Bennu leaned his head down, as if six inches closer would help his vision. "Death by snack food. Not exactly a manly way to go."

"Sounds like something I would say—but I'm not thinking like that right now. I'm thinking about the fact that he's dead."

"I guess I see him like an animal, like a bear that attacked us."

"Still, I feel weird."

Bennu elbowed Len's arm. "Look over there, under that arch."

Len looked below to his left. Because the cliffs rose almost perpendicular to the ocean, Len could see most of a tall arch that jutted out of the rock wall like a flying buttress. The turquoise water glistened brightly where the arch entered the water, and Len wondered if water glimpses scurried about right there on the surface. Then he saw what had caught Bennu's attention: the prow of a masted ship floating through the arch.

"Amazing," said Bennu. "Think how perfect the conditions must be down there: deep trench, calm water, skilled sailors. Wait. I see them, sailors with ropes, some on the beach and a couple where the arch goes into the sea. They're keeping the ship steady."

"They're also unloading cargo onto the beach. See it?"

"Tremlings. Dozens of 'em, in chains."

"Nasty. Sickening."

"Exactly. The ship Gareth was worried about is a slave ship."

Len pulled away from the opening and took a few swigs of water. "Wish I had a flashlight. Mom always said that between the two of us, we must carry just about everything in these pockets. But I don't have a flashlight."

"Me neither." Bennu got up and brushed himself off. "Well, there's only one way to go—into the cave. Ready?"

"Yeah, but if I wasn't already nervous, that ship put me over the edge."

Cautiously, Len and Bennu walked into the darkness. As their eyes adjusted, they saw a shaft of light coming from above, about sixty yards ahead of them. It came straight down. It illuminated something—they couldn't tell what—painted on the walls. Transfixed by the light, the two Misfits stepped methodically toward it, listening to the crunch of their feet on the cave floor and listening for any sound approaching them. They heard none.

Len walked close to Bennu, sometimes bumping him. In the dark, with the light up ahead, walking into the unknown, under threat of attack, wanting his feet to be quieter, Len almost wished he could hold Bennu's hand. Almost. Though every step in the dark brought them closer to the light, the light did not illuminate their steps. And every step sounded louder, more revealing of their presence.

Len squinted at the light. He could almost make out an image. He started to say *Look there* but it came out, "lookeyaaaaah!" because he slipped on gravel and fell, not onto the ground but down some hole, some crevasse. He grabbed after Bennu's arm. Bennu caught Len as one of his feet dangled over the chasm, a break in the cave floor.

Bennu grunted to hold on. "Is this going to be a habit with you?"

Len did not answer. He tugged on Bennu and scrambled back up, all the while listening to rocks fall down and down before hitting the bottom in the darkness.

Len patted Bennu's ankle. "Thanks."

"Yeah, no problem."

That's when Len saw that Bennu's feet had become talons and that they had cut into the floor in their attempt to grip. Len coughed. "We have to jump. I'm guessing it's about six feet."

"Yeah. I wish I had my wings."

They sat down to study the situation. Bennu pointed out how the low ceiling complicated matters.

Without any announcement, Len walked back a few yards. "We're wasting time. Let's do it." He skipped a step, then ran full steam, planted his foot, screamed, "Geronimo!" and sailed over the abyss.

Midflight he heard an echo—his words but, eerily, not his words. At least he thought he had. "Your turn, Bennu. Run as fast as you can and push off. You can't miss."

"You can't miss. You can't miss. Right." Bennu walked back, leaned forward like a sprinter in his blocks, ran hard, and leaped. Bennu pedaled one step in the air and landed with just his toes on the lip of the other side. He stumbled forward, turned his shoulder under like a judo fighter, and rolled on his back and up into a standing position.

Len mimed applause. "Good work, Mr. Neferti. But I was ready if you needed me." He showed Bennu his paw with outstretched claws.

Bennu felt his heel and ankle. "I heard something coming over. An echo . . . but not exactly."

"What did you hear?"

"Something like 'And you biss.'"

"Huh. I said, 'You can't miss.' Where's Angie the Interpreter when you need her?"

"You can say that again."

"Can't say that I will."

"Y'know, we need to be quiet."

Len took the hint, crouched down, and turned toward the light coming in up ahead. They walked quietly toward it until they came to a crossroads.

At right angles on both sides, paths emptied into darkness. Straight ahead, the light revealed a walkway that split on both sides of the wide shaft of light. They had to "cross the street," as it were, to get to the illuminated area.

Visions of tremlings waiting in the darkness took hold of Len's mind. He didn't know for certain that the light-brightened room was the right way to go, but they decided to start there. They walked to the edge of the intersection and listened. Len tensed up and said, "Ready?"

Bennu whispered, "No. Listen. Steps."

They backed up into deeper shadows.

The footsteps came on not quietly but confidently. The rock floor crunched. Sounds came from both sides, sounds too hard to be tremling feet. Boots, probably. One set of footsteps sounded larger, heavier. The noises came closer, almost in unison. *Crunch, crunch.*

Len saw a foot step out of the darkness to his right. Then a knee-high boot emerged. Len looked for a sword at the waist or a knife drawn or a club raised. A tall staff hit the ground, then the hand attached to it came into view. Finally Len saw the head . . . and the gentle, bearded face of Sutton Hoo.

Bennu bolted from the hiding place. "Sutton! Sutton Hoo! It's so great to see you!" He threw his arms around the massive Kells Villager. Sutton rested his chin on Bennu's head as they hugged, his beaded beard pushed back by Bennu.

Then Sutton held Bennu at arm's length, examining him. "Ah, Bennu. You look right handsome—and not a day older for the year that's gone by between us."

Bennu glanced back at Len, who raised his eyebrows knowingly. "Sutton, look, Len is here with me."

Sutton opened his hands toward Len. "The lion and the falcon together. You're good on the eyes, young friends. And I've heard you've met Welken's stalwart sailor, Gareth the Wave-Rider."

From the other side, Gareth emerged with as close to a smile as Len had yet seen. "Aye, Sutton, I'm glad to have Len and Bennu on our side. More tremlings have arrived. I'm afraid we don't have time for long conversations." Gareth held his stitched vest to his chest with both hands. "Sutton and I joined up on my way down from Runner's Cove. We followed a ship of Northerners and learned it was full of tremlings. They landed here, so we did too."

Len raised a finger to interrupt. "Then you know where we are?"

"Of course, Justice Island. We're in the crags that wrap around the place like a crown. You might say we're in the jewels of the crown, at the top." Gareth drew a map in the dirt by the light in front of him. "We are here, in the backside, by Smuggler's Arch. Sutton and I saw the tremlings march in toward the valley here. We were just now searching for a high place to look down on the valley, to see why the tremlings are being enslaved."

"Justice Island, eh?" Bennu rested his hands in his back pockets. "I guess you could say it's poetic justice that you found us."

Gareth's stern gaze grew sterner. "Perhaps. But the justice of Justice Island is more likely to be severe. It is a place without mercy. One wrong choice and you get justice all right—the justice of steep cliffs, little water, a labyrinth of confusing trails and tunnels. It is a towering, ruthless justice, so be careful what you ask for."

Len knew Bennu had not invited this admonishment, and he wanted to get going. "Gareth, Sutton, what do you say we find out what the light in this room's all about?"

Gareth bowed. "Well spoken, son. Into the light we shall go."

CHAPTER SEVENTEEN
COOLER HEADS PREVAIL

He who has been bitten by a snake fears a piece of string.
—PERSIAN PROVERB

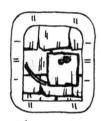 Lizbeth stood tall in the fog, like a Scotswoman poised on the moor, listening for the cry of a lost child. She strained so hard that she thought she could hear the flow of moisture through the air. She imagined tribal bands of Scots walking toward her, ready for battle, with war paint and tartan robes and blunt weapons.

But she heard no child crying; neither could she make out a trace of Piers's voice. No Scots came for battle—only Angie with her blue wings and plaid shorts, and Mook with his leather breastplate and his ever-ready bow.

"Lizbeth." Mook held his bow like a staff and tapped it on the ground for emphasis. "Lizbeth! Answer us. We have been calling your name."

Angie drew in her wings. She put her hand in the crook of Lizbeth's arm. "I know you are working on seeing, Lizbeth. Your eyes have a look—of recognizing what is not yet in focus, of being carried someplace without quite arriving."

"Yes." Lizbeth patted Angie's hand. "But it's not seeing so much as it is listening. I heard Piers. He said that I was his 'weariness.' That I should find him in myself." Lizbeth kept looking into the foggy swamp. "Then he quoted the Book of Quadrille, 'The story's told by day and night.' He said it like it was part of a riddle. What do you suppose it means?"

"I don't know." Mook strapped his bow over his shoulder. "But I don't like it here. Cutters will come. We should walk away from Deedy Swamp."

Lizbeth and Angie followed Mook. They stepped around bushes, searched for solid ground, and looked back to see if any Cutters were chasing after them. Lizbeth jogged and dodged. She powered through branches, knocking them back for Angie.

Then Mook stopped. Before him a curtain of hanging moss stretched as far as they could see. Lizbeth did not know why Deedy Swamp had this boundary. The moss seemed so useless as a barrier—just a slight, visual border one could easily brush aside. But then, maybe it was not meant as a defense. Maybe it was a veil that told travelers they were about to enter someplace new and different.

Yes, a veil, she thought. *We keep seeing veils. In my dream, the boy feels one. In the Bartholomews' backyard, a veil stretches out over the gate and we come back to Welken through it—and now there's this veil of moss around Deedy. Veils, veils, everywhere, and they're all thin, as easy to pass through as this moss.*

On the other side of the moss, Mook crouched down. He glanced up at the sun, which appeared white behind the fog. Then he motioned to the north, toward a well-worn path Lizbeth took to be the main route between Deedy Swamp and the Nezzer Clan.

"It feels good to be out of the water," said Angie. "I'm beginning to dry out."

Lizbeth nodded.

The threesome hiked along without incident for some time. The fog gave way to bright sunshine. Though worried about Vida and Jacob, and worried about Len and Bennu, and worried about her mom and long-lost Percy, Lizbeth tried not to worry. It was as futile as keeping ants out of one's house by putting up signs that said Go Away! So she and Angie talked about finding Piers and seeing Prester John again.

Mook took to survival education. "The root of the trundle plant can be pulled out from under the bush. You chop off what you need and slip it back in. Of course, there's also plenty of water here."

Lizbeth was not taking notes. "Mook, roots sound cool if you're about to die. But what about something tasty? Some nice fruit or something? I'm starving."

"Hmmm, tasty fruit." Mook jogged ahead. "I know just the thing." His jog became a run. "Stay on the trail. I'll meet you in a bit." He ran out of sight.

"He's a funny guy," said Lizbeth. "So serious—but you know he'd do anything for you."

"Yeah, I love the way his ponytails fly about his shoulders and that they look like they've been dipped in silver starlight."

"Right."

They walked past the place where Lizbeth had once been sucked into a land-roving anemone and past where they'd first met Vida. To botanists, the trail would have provided endless fascination. To Lizbeth and Angie, one stretch of flora and fauna began to look like the last one. They talked. They trudged. They trekked on.

Soon the scenery changed, becoming less marshy. Coastal redwoods stood tall and stately over the path, so rich with needles and decomposed bark that it felt to Angie and Lizbeth like a cushioned carpet. Bounding along, Lizbeth and Angie acted giddy. They skipped a few paces, then jumped as high as they could off the spongy floor.

Angie did a cartwheel. "I feel a little guilty."

"Yeah, I know. We should be focusing on finding Piers."

"We are, aren't we? Is it wrong to laugh if it doesn't slow us up?"

Lizbeth stopped. "Listen. Do you hear water? There must be a creek nearby." She rushed toward the sound, Angie at her heels.

In seconds, the source of the gurgling appeared just off the trail to their left—a gentle waterfall trickling down in a curve of green. The water emerged right out of the hillside and crept over the mossy bank in a wide sheet of drips, curling around large hibiscuslike flowers and flowing back underground in a pool surrounded by tufts of grass and white flowers that hung like streetlights for elves.

Angie and Lizbeth skittered off the path and walked up to the cascading wall. Lizbeth thought immediately of the old nursery rhyme "One misty, moisty morning." Though cloudy was *not* the weather, Lizbeth felt she had entered a mini–rain forest, an entire ecosystem ten by ten feet.

But biology was not on her mind. She ran her hand back and forth over the clover and baby's tears. Then she touched the base of an orange hibiscus flower and leaned over to smell it. The flower drooped. At first, guilt swept over her for having pinched this beautiful thing and killed it for no good reason. Then she saw it was still attached. The stem was like a hose that came out from the wall. When Lizbeth pushed it back in, the stem retracted.

She tapped Angie's elbow. "This is crazy, Ang. It's like these flowers want to be as accessible as possible, as nose-friendly as they can be."

"And the scent. It puts gardenias to shame. One good sniff is all I can take. The perfume's overwhelming, almost intoxicating." Angie held a flower to her nose, made a blissful face, and pulled the creamy petals away from her until the stem reached its limit. "Whoa. Lizbeth, look." Angie tipped the flower down and water came out.

Lizbeth started to put her mouth up to it. "Should we?" But she didn't wait for an answer. She pressed her lips up to the fluid and drew it in. It was more refreshing than anything she'd ever tasted. She felt its swirling path in her mouth. Every taste bud and tissue, every nerve in her gums came alive, as if they had endured seven years of drought and here came the living rain. Then she swallowed. She felt every inch of it going down. She wished she could slow the descent so she could relish the awakening. When the liquid splashed into her stomach, ripples seemed to wave out from there down to her legs and up to her arms. Even the tips of her fingers tingled. And she knew right then that she could not call the stream of life that had entered her mere "water." She thought of it as "the nectar of the gods," but that was cheesy, like an advertising slogan. Then her thoughts jumped to the bottling and marketing of the stuff—and how she'd make millions. She felt ashamed that her mind synapsed so quickly to this conclusion.

"Do you think," asked Angie, "that it would be wrong to do more than drink it? Should I let it flow through my hair? Could I shower in it? Should it be conserved, or is the supply endless?"

So Angie felt it, too. Angie's joy cleansed Lizbeth of any guilt she felt in enjoying the liquid. She did not know how to bring arguments to bear upon these questions. All she knew was that the water was good. So she answered by tipping her head under it. The water washed down her black ponytail and down her back. Angie did the same. They laughed and drank.

As she pulled her head out of the stream, Lizbeth enjoyed a contentment so full that she knew at once this sensation had only possessed her for brief moments her entire life. She let the flower retract. It seemed the right thing to do. Sitting in a shallow pool at the base of the waterfall, Lizbeth removed the rubber band from her hair and ran her fingers through the heavy locks. She licked her forefinger, then took it out of her mouth and pointed at Angie. "Your hair! Angie, it's moving. It's like fairies have the tips and are holding it up, or like it's totally electrified!" She covered her mouth and laughed, and Angie pointed back at her and laughed.

The strands moved as if controlled by an invisible hairdresser. They flew up and down. They weaved themselves in and out. In minutes both young women radiated with shining, vibrant hair assembled in a simple but elegant style. Lizbeth felt beautiful, inside and out. She was sure that she glowed.

Abruptly Angie sat straight up. "Oh, Lizbeth, we forgot. Mook might be looking for us. We should get back up on the path."

"Yeah, you're right. I hate to leave this place, but I feel ready for anything now: to march to the Prester Highlands, to rescue Piers, to fight off a hundred guards."

They found the path quickly and walked in silence. The dense trees gave way to more open spaces and more sunshine. Their clothes dried, and the lovely scent of the flowers rose in the steam.

"I hate to break this mood," said Lizbeth, "but I'm getting a little worried about Mook. He's been gone longer than I thought he'd be. And we're walking down this trail neither of us has been on."

Though Lizbeth and Angie did not know exactly where they were, they knew enough about Welken's map to guess that the Nez River should be nearby. If they could find it, they could follow it up to the Nezzer Clan. Maybe Mook was already there.

After walking a while longer, the two Misfits came upon a situation they'd feared—a fork in the trail. They talked about various reasons to go either way, then noticed a crude building up ahead, in a more forested area, right in the middle between the two paths.

It reminded Lizbeth of a prairie cabin. Hoping that the inhabitant could give them directions, they decided to knock on the door. The structure itself was square, with a fairly flat roof and shingles on the sides. The front faced the place where the paths diverged, and the back faded into the shadows of trees and bushes, which had been overtaken by a leafy vine that grew well onto the roof. It gave the appearance of a stage thrust in front of a theater's proscenium arch.

Lizbeth stepped off the intersection and onto the grass before the hut. "'You do not have because you do not ask,' right? 'Knock and the door shall be opened,' right?"

Angie joined her and put her hands on her hips. "Beware the stranger."

"Nothing ventured, nothing gained."

"Look before you leap."

In delicately bold steps, Lizbeth and Angie approached the door. Lizbeth's pulse increased as the shack loomed closer. She didn't like the overgrowth and the lack of windows. Then she noticed that shingles covered the door as well as the roof—and there was no doorknob.

As Lizbeth looked quizzically at Angie, one shingle, about peephole height, moved. It twisted up and revealed a dark opening. No voice came, no eye became visible.

Before her fear overcame her, Lizbeth said, "Hello. We are friends of Welken. We have come to these two paths, and we want to know which is the way to the Nez River."

Angie patted Lizbeth on the back.

The shingle closed. It swung on its single nail and scraped back and forth on the other shingles. Lizbeth noticed how the motion had left marks in the wood. Her shoulders fell. Angie shrugged as if to say, *"We tried our best."*

Then the shingle opened again and a hand came out. The arm seemed odd, like the forearm was too long for the hand. But the hand hung in the air, poised for a handshake. Lizbeth took it. She thought it was worth the risk. The inhabitant had made an overture, and she should accept it.

The handshake felt momentous—not a simple greeting but an investigation. She couldn't explain it exactly. The hand felt firm and fleshy, a good hand, one accustomed to greeting and welcoming strangers.

Then the hand let go. It pulled itself back in and the door opened. Standing just outside the entryway, Lizbeth and Angie peered in. Though no windows could be seen, the room reverberated with light. Like a smaller, dimmer version of the Window Under the Mountain—that space-condensed light show they'd used to escape from Morphane. Now, inside this cabin, glowing tubes pulsed with different colors. Most of these tubes shone from the top of the walls, like luminous crown molding. Other tubes glowed against the back wall, like a fireplace powered by a rainbow of electronic components.

Lizbeth stepped in. She just had to see the whole interior. The door nearly shut behind her, but Angie said, "Hey!" and stuck her foot in. Lizbeth let her in, and then the door shut tight.

"Lizbeth, remember, we're only looking for directions."

"I know, but why shouldn't we fill ourselves with more of Welken?"

"OK, but let's be careful."

"Aren't the lights wonderful? Aren't they glorious?"

Before Angie could answer, color dripped down from tubes where the walls met the ceiling. They blended and pooled together. Scenes emerged.

The wall to their left gradually came into focus, from the front to the back. Children played in fields of flowers, picked off petals, and skipped closer to the back of the scene. As they did, the whole wall seemed to move, the "film" moving from right to left, fading off the wall near the door.

Then the other side of the room sparked like fireworks. Its colors cascaded down the walls, creating images of Deediers swimming underwater toward the back. They stopped to breathe at a vine and swam gracefully out of sight.

"Lizbeth." Angie shook Lizbeth's arm. "Lizbeth, we came for directions."

"I know. We'll get them. What's wrong with watching this? Maybe it's a prophecy."

"OK, but I don't see anyone to talk to."

Lizbeth pointed to the glowing tubes in the center of the back wall. "Maybe the owner of the place is over there." As she approached the tubes, they grew like vines, straight up and then toward her. "Angie, it's like the flowers we just saw. Maybe these have nectar too."

Something pushed out from the center of the tubes. Lizbeth leaned in and saw leaves transforming the glowing cylinders into shimmering vines. The speed with which the vines grew amazed Lizbeth. Then, faintly, she heard something. She turned and saw Angie's face just as a vine wrapped around her mouth. One of the glowing vines curled around her like a boa constrictor. "Angie! No!"

Angie's eyes grew large with fear as the vine pinned her arms to her sides. Lizbeth tried to pull the vine off. She managed to pull it an inch away from Angie's body, but it slipped back and tightened its grip. Lizbeth pounded at the vine. She hit it again and again, and each time, Angie's head bounced around. Lizbeth didn't know what else to do.

Then Lizbeth felt a smooth, fleshy thing slide around her leg. A vine rose swiftly and pulled her to the ground.

More vines came and coiled around her. They squeezed in on her, but not hard enough to keep her from breathing. She found a crease and pushed her hand out through the gap. With her fingers she tried to pull off the vine. Then the very ends of three vines pulled away from Lizbeth's body; out of each came a small head with a small beak. They rose up and started pecking on her exposed parts. Lizbeth stung from the sharp pricks. The pecking hammered her in places and dug around in others. She rolled back and forth, but if one head became covered, a different one pecked away at another exposed part. Nothing worked, and she realized, to her horror, that these things would take a long time to kill her. She would stay bound in these coils, not squeezed to death, but waiting for these vines or snakes to peck away at her life. She wished she could at least talk to Angie.

Then a shout, a rumble and a great crash came from the front door. Light flooded in from the outside and the sound of several scurrying feet followed. Lizbeth saw blades above her and heard the *swish* of swords through the air, then squeals. And then her own heaving breaths.

Mook came to her and gently pulled the coiled thing off. "It's the Meducer—what Vida calls 'a beaky snakification.' Its mouth is weak, so it lures its prey in."

"It was awful." Angie rubbed her neck. "I didn't want to be nibbled to death."

Lizbeth breathed deeply. "It's so disgusting."

As Mook and a few other Nezzer folk carried Lizbeth and Angie out into the sun, the walls of the shingled room collapsed. They fell in on themselves and lay in colored puddles oozing from the severed heads.

Lizbeth wondered how many times she would almost get squeezed to death in Welken. Was twice a coincidence—or a message?

Mook held out fresh fruit, nuts, and dried meat. He didn't seem affected by arriving in the nick of time.

"We should have known," said Angie. "Vida warned us. We keep thinking that everything in Welken should be good. Maybe that's not a bad thought entirely, but Welken's got its own woes."

Lizbeth and Angie ate while the Nezzer folk tended to their beak-pecked wounds. Lizbeth's cuts hurt a little, and the salve felt good. But her pride kept hurting. She thought she should have recognized the temptations of the Meducer sooner. She thought she should have been more aware. "Angie, I don't know why, but all this reminds me of something."

"It reminds me too." Angie gingerly examined her arm where she'd been pecked. "It reminds me that we need to be more careful. We need to remember that some clouds are good for sunsets, but some clouds bring terrible storms."

"Yeah, and sometimes we're just plain idiots."

After eating and resting, Lizbeth, Angie, Mook, and the rest started down the trail to the right, the one that would lead to the Nez River. As they walked past the mysterious beast, the Meducer, Lizbeth counted ten heads. "Hey Mook, is it a beaky snakification or a snaky beakification?"

Mook simply shrugged.

CHAPTER EIGHTEEN

WHOSE HEART IS LIGHT AS A FEATHER?

In judgement be ye not too confident,
Even as a man who will appraise his corn
When standing in a field, ere it is ripe.

—DANTE, "PARADISO," *THE DIVINE COMEDY*

 When Gareth entered the light-filled room, Bennu followed, then Len and Sutton Hoo. The scene reminded Len of Ganderst Hall, the lavishly decorated underground room they'd found after fleeing out the back of Chimney Cave. He flashed on the murals in the room that housed the four tiles of the Tetragrammaton. The same artist seemed to have been at work. Before Len studied the story on the walls, he stared transfixed at the cylinder of light, rising like a chimney to the sky. Though glorious in many respects, the light also inspired fear, for the fireplace at the bottom of the chimney was twenty feet down, making their sojourn around the circle precarious at best. No guardrails had been supplied. There would be no stepping back to admire the art.

Bennu looked down the opening to the rocks below. "There's a design cut into the floor, don't you think?"

Len squatted and peered over. "Yeah, symmetrical curved lines coming out from the center."

Sutton leaned on his staff. "It reminds me of my fair Gildas's flowin' hair."

"No," said Bennu, "it's something else. I have this feeling I've seen the design before—but I can't place it."

Gareth tossed a pebble over the rim. "I would say it looks like a flower."

"I think you're right," said Bennu. "Now let's check out the mural."

Even though Len's first impulse was to give Bennu grief for once more posing as a scholar, this time he rather enjoyed seeing his friend step up as an expert. Bennu knew about ancient things, especially Egyptian, and how to study them.

Facing the fresco, Bennu paced on the ledge. "Let's keep the flower design in mind. If we know nothing else about Welken, it's that these kinds of things aren't accidental. *Coincidence* is not a popular word around here." A dragonfly hovered above Bennu's head and lighted on his shoulder. "These images look somewhat like hieroglyphics. There's a dog's head on a human body. I remember there was an Egyptian god like this, but it was a jackal."

Gareth ran his fingers over some lettering. "In the year you've been away, we've renewed our commitment to the Book of Quadrille, to the old texts and ancient languages. I have been studying—and I can try to interpret these lines."

Len brushed the dragonfly off Bennu's shoulder. "That leaves you and me, Sutton."

"I will protect us from fallin' into the pit," said Sutton.

"Good," said Len, "that means only one of us is useless."

Bennu took a few steps to his right. "It appears to be the life story of this doglike being. Here he is suckling his mother—hey, a bit like Romulus, right? You know, the mythical founder of Rome? . . . Oh, forget it. And here he battles his enemies, one against many." Bennu walked farther into the circle. "Look, a crown is put on his head. He's a canine king. Gareth, what's this say?"

"It looks like one of the king's titles. It says, 'He who is set upon the mountains.'"

"And here he is, standing on a mountain. His head is dark and strange—almost like a jackal's—and he is looking down on a bunch of people wearing hoods like monks."

Len got up close and squinched his eyes. "Who do you suppose they are? Just people in his kingdom?"

"More than that, I think," said Gareth. "This next title says, 'He who weighs the hearts.'"

"OK," said Len, "so he's some kind of judge."

Bennu grew noticeably excited as he pointed to the next painting, the one in the middle of the curved mural. "This explains it. He's a giant here and he holds a scale. On one side is a feather."

"But if he weighs the hearts," said Len, "whose heart is light as a feather?"

"Now I'm really freaking out." Bennu paced in an abbreviated way. As he approached the rim, Sutton held out a hand to keep him back. "OK. Wait. I see some bizarre parallels here to the Egyptian god Anubis, sometimes called Lord of the Dead. I wrote a paper on these gods this year for Mr. Kornelis's history class. He said it was 'interesting.' Anyway, Anubis guarded those waiting for the Judgment. If your heart was light as a feather—with goodness, I guess—you made it. If not, your soul went down to the Egyptian version of hell and got eaten up. Not pretty."

Absorbed in the painting, Len traced the scale with his finger, as if he could tip it with his touch. "So I was right. The question really is, Whose heart is light as a feather?"

Bennu crossed his arms. "Yeah, it is. You already asked it."

"I know. It's weird. I feel like I can't *not* ask the question. I mean, really, whose heart is light as a feather? Wouldn't everyone get sent packing?"

Len's eyes went from the scale to the dog-king. For some odd reason, the king, dressed in a long purple coat, was chained to the scale. Len thought it meant that he couldn't escape the scale, or that he couldn't leave until the Judgment was finished. Then something caught Len's eye to the right, from the crowd assembled below the scale.

Wait, he thought. *Did someone move?*

The person in the painting wore a hood over his head. And he *did* move. He stepped forward to the scale. As the dog-king bowed, the robed figure put his hand inside his robe and, in a matter-of-fact way, pulled out his heart. It wasn't gory, like a horror movie's bloody surgery, nor was it a

Valentine's heart. It was like a heart-shaped book, with tidy stitching pulsing a radiant blue. When the book hit the scales, it pushed the platform down dramatically. The scale jerked with the weight, and the feather on the other side nearly floated off. The platform holding the book reminded Len of another platform, the one he'd lain on underneath the tree house a month ago, the one on which he'd received a blow to the head from a rock thrown by a McKenzie Butte Boy.

Len stared at the platform. It spun just like the one he had suffered on. It swung back and forth and twisted around. He could almost hear Angie screaming in the background.

Then he did hear a scream. But it wasn't Angie. It was the judged one, the hooded one who had placed his heart on the scale. He reached up and removed his hood. As it slid down to his neck, Len gasped.

It was Odin. He grabbed the scales and jumped onto the platform. He climbed up to the center and leaped from there, throwing himself at the dog-king. Though he could not compete with the giant judge's size, he grabbed him by the throat. The giant dog-king staggered back but did not look surprised or threatened. He thrust a hand out to catch his balance. It fell on the feather's side of the scale, flinging the book-heart on the other side into the air. It flew open. As pages turned in slow motion, things dropped out—a blade, broken glass, a dead bird. Then words fell out. Len heard Odin curse his parents, his school, the Misfits, and, most of all, himself. The book landed on the platform once again.

Oh, how Len hated him. He burned with the memory of Odin hurting him, hurting his friends. He knew what he would have done if he'd been Anubis. He would have thrown Odin into the netherworld. He would have flung him into hungry jaws anxious to devour the condemned.

Odin looked at the book with disdain. He sank his hands deeper into the dog-king's throat. This time the giant canine reacted to the blow. He gasped for air. As Odin choked him, the king fell back flat against the mural's back wall. Though he should have been able to swat Odin away, the dog-king did not. His dark fur changed color as he lost breath. It faded as if it were skin, turning red, then an ashen gray, and, finally, a pale, clinging white.

Grimacing, the king held on to life. As Odin choked him, the king stretched his arm toward the scale. His finger found the feather-side and pushed it down. Odin's book rose slowly on the other side. Trembling, the king's finger kept the scales steady till they were perfectly balanced.

"Check this out!" Bennu's voice felt like a church bell gonging directly over Len's head.

Startled, Len looked at the mural. Nothing moved. The dog-king held the scales. The monks stood frozen in their places, none of them looking like Odin.

Bennu gestured to the king's finger pointing to the sky. "He's gesturing to a falcon. The king is sending the falcon to take his place on some kind of Olympus, some 'Company of the Gods.' I remember this from my report. In Egypt, Horus, the falcon-god, took Anubis's place."

Still disoriented, uncertain why no one seemed to be noticing things moving on the mural, Len wiped sweat from his brow. He didn't know what to do with this story about Odin. He wished he'd seen how the story had ended, what had happened next. He turned to Gareth. "Can you decipher this line, the one under the scale?"

Gareth bent over to study the writing. "I think so. Yes. It says, 'Guardian of the Veil.'"

"Really." Len sat down against the wall and put his head back. "I'm exhausted. And amazed. And confused. Guardian of the Veil? What veil?"

Bennu traced a line from Anubis to the assembled monks. "Well, first of all, he's Guardian over the veil between death and the afterlife. He protects those who are waiting to learn their fate. I guess you could say he's the Guardian of life and death."

"*Psssh.* I wouldn't want that job. What else?"

"There are other veils to think about too. Think of the veils we've been through. The veils between Welken and Skinner, between good and evil, faith and doubt."

Len stood up and put his arm around his friend. "Bennu, you're a genius. No, better than that. You are as light as a feather."

Bennu smiled and then, just as quickly, dropped the smile. "You know that's not true. I mean, thanks for saying it and all, but I'm carrying around way too much crud to ever pass the test. I'd need a lot of help to get past Anubis, that's for sure. Maybe Angie could dress like me and fool him. She'd be light enough, don't you think?"

"My sis is not—"

"Excuse me." Gareth stepped between the Misfits. "We don't have time for this argument. I know all about balancing the books. You can make it work for numbers, but for hearts that choose, well, that's another matter entirely. For now, let us say that Soliton—he who becomes what love requires—will care for the scales."

"True enough," said Sutton, "and wise enough for a simple man like me." He fiddled with a bead in his beard. "But I'd still like to know why this one you call a king is tied to the scales. Kings can do as they right please, can't they? What's a king if not a king?"

"It's strange," said Bennu. "On the other hand, he's also called *Guardian* of the Veil. Is he the original guardian of the Tetragrammaton, like those we found in Ganderst Hall?"

"And," said Len, "how does any of this help us find Piers or Bors? I mean, that's what we're here for, right? I don't see what we've learned from this." A wisp of shame came over Len as he said this. He knew he'd just learned something about Odin.

Bennu's face grew solemn. He appeared to be making calculations in his head. Finally he must have found the sum he was looking for. "OK, Gareth and Sutton, bear with me—with us. This won't make much sense to you. Len, we know that Piers is Percy. We learned that before. He's your house cat and the Detective Cat in your mom's stories. Wouldn't that mean that Bors is Bones Malone, the basset hound? And here—on this wall—we see a dog, or a caninelike person, even a dog-king. And if this is true, maybe we *have* learned something about Bors. Maybe he's chained up somewhere. On the other hand, if this mural tells us about him, it must mean that, well, he has a job to do. Maybe he is being held against his will. And maybe, at the same time, he can't get away until, I don't know, somehow certain scales are balanced, or until he finds someone light as a feather. If that's the case, he could be looking for a long time."

Gareth pulled on his bottom lip with two fingers. "My title of Keeper of the Balance seems important, but I don't know how. And, wait, here's another line, from the Book of Quadrille. It says, 'The sun is cold, the wind is white.'"

"So," said Bennu excitedly, "maybe Bors is chained up someplace in the mountains where it's cold."

Len shook his head. "No way. It's summer now, and hot." Shame touched him again. Why should he cast doubt on Bennu's hypothesis? More to the point, why should he not tell about his vision of Odin? But then, how could it possibly pertain to the question at hand?

In the instant of his decision to conceal, he felt loss, as if all his skin had faded to an ashen gray. When his right foot suddenly went to sleep, he wondered if his very life was leaving him. Was he, in that moment, leaning over some momentous precipice? The decision to speak seemed so small in the great scheme of things—yet it felt to him as if he was vacillating between life and death, between vibrancy and emptiness. He felt nervous, shaky, light-headed. No one else seemed different or seemed to notice. Sutton stood guard. He put his staff against the wall. Gareth and Bennu calmly discussed the mural.

Len clenched his fists. "I saw something!"

The others turned around and looked quizzically at him. Gareth seemed perturbed by the interruption.

"I saw something in the mural. It moved. I think I know why Anubis is chained to the scale." Len heard a faint pounding. He took it to be his own heart coming back alive. "I saw Anubis tip the scale."

"OK, Len," said Bennu. "Hurry up. Get to the point."

"He shouldn't have done it." Len felt that he was now present at the Judgment, that he was being weighed, that his telltale heart would reveal all. It drummed loudly in his chest. Len wanted to shut out the pounding, so he decided to tell the others about his vengeful thoughts.

But he could not. Another kind of pounding came, a rumbling that grew louder, moving in their direction. Then he saw why. Tremlings. A dozen of them were in the corridor outside the cave. They looked angry and confused. Then a whip snapped and the tremlings started down both sides of the circular mural. They growled and grunted their way around the ledge as Gareth stepped in front of Bennu on one side and Sutton slipped in front of Len on the other.

Gareth drew his blade, and Sutton grabbed his staff from off the wall. On the narrow path, Gareth swung his sword with fury and precision. He poked a tremling back until it crashed into one behind him. Then a tremling slipped off the edge, screaming as he fell. Sutton held his staff like a pugil-stick, smashing a tremling with one end and then the other. But as one tremling howled and collapsed, another stepped over him. Sutton hammered away. He knocked two into the hole, then pressed against the whole line, moving them a few feet back. He swatted a tremling in the chest. The beast staggered back but managed to drape his arm around the end of the staff. Then more tremlings threw their arms around the pole. With all his might, Sutton pushed against them.

From behind the tremlings, a soldier snapped a whip again and again. Len scrambled around for some way to be of help. He found a few rocks and threw them. Then he looked over at Gareth. While a tremling pierced by Gareth's sword staggered back, another grabbed up for the hilt and jerked the blade out of Gareth's hand. On the other side, the tremlings pressed in on Sutton. They grabbed him and forced him to the ground.

While the beasts tied up Gareth and Sutton, Len and Bennu frantically looked for some other way out. They ran to the center of the mural, as far from the approaching tremlings as they could get. Jumping twenty feet down looked awful. Desperately they searched the wall for handholds and footholds, scraping their fingers down the painted surface. They hammered the wall.

Len looked over his shoulder. Tremlings dragged Sutton and Gareth away. Others picked up the staff and the sword. They held the weapons over their heads and roared, their big feet pounding closer and closer to the Misfits.

Len and Bennu turned back to the wall. Len pushed on images in the painting, hoping for a secret panel or a key, a magic hole for his finger or a sliding shaft in the rock. All he saw was Anubis, the Lord of the Underworld, the dog-king holding the scales, the Guardian of the Veil protecting souls waiting for judgment. That's exactly how Len felt. Judgment approached. One tremling pulled Gareth's blade back and prepared to strike. A tremling on the other side held Sutton's staff like a battering ram and charged.

Len and Bennu slapped at the walls. They pounded with their fists. As the tremlings roared in triumph, the Misfits screamed.

CHAPTER NINETEEN

BACK DOORS AND RUMBLING FLOORS

Children should be led into the right paths,
not by severity, but by persuasion.

—TERENCE, *THE BROTHERS*

As Lizbeth and Angie walked away from the Meducer's trap, they kept about ten paces behind Mook. Lizbeth hung her head as if it were in a real yoke, then plodded more ploddingly than ever. She felt guilt, always guilt, an oppressive, smothering, suffocating guilt. "I'm such a loser, Ang."

"Stop it."

"No, really. It's an objective fact."

"Really. It's a fact, like gravity, or who won the last election?"

"Yeah. Why else would I fall for the Meducer's dreams? Why else would I be such a sucker?"

Angie put a hand on her friend's shoulder as they walked. "Do you ever get tired of listing all your faults?"

"Yeah. But it's just another one of my faults." She smiled weakly at her gallows humor. "I mean, why shouldn't I stab myself with each one? I'm good at it."

"You're funny."

"Yeah, hilarious. And I'm fat and stupid and unable to notice evil when it is dripping in my face."

"Lizbeth, stop it, really."

"Why should I? I'm a fool. I don't deserve to be considered a help to Welken. I don't measure up. I'm not perfect like you or insightful like Bennu or courageous like Len. I'm so stupid, I honestly believe that if I lost twenty pounds, people would like me. I really believe that if I hit ten more home runs next softball season, I'd be somebody. I actually think that if I had a handsome boyfriend, my life would radically change and all my problems would vanish. I am such an idiot. And don't tell me to stop. I'm just getting started."

"Lizbeth, you carry enough guilt for ten people."

"Hey, the ox is a beast of burden." Lizbeth kicked up some dust in the trail.

"You almost seem to enjoy it sometimes." Angie followed this comment with silence. Lizbeth felt awkward. Then Angie said, "Wouldn't you like to be free of it?"

Lizbeth's sense of awkwardness vanished. She pushed an angry breath through her flared nostrils. Then she bit her tongue. The blood tasted bitter, like a kind of venom that glided over her tongue. She wanted to hiss out the poison verbally, that Angie could not possibly know anything of what she had gone through, that Angie's question about freedom felt patronizing. Yet she didn't. She swallowed the poison. In the alchemy of her soul, the poison would gradually change into self-condemnation. Lizbeth knew how to mix this brew.

Angie moved her hand from Lizbeth's shoulder to her neck, where she worked on her stiff muscles. Angie's hand felt to Lizbeth like family, good family. It felt loving but protective and firm. "Lizbeth, I know I say a lot of goofy things sometimes—but hear me out. You are right. You don't deserve Welken's riches. None of us do. That's OK. Piers didn't ask for our résumés when we came, and Soliton didn't compare us to the worthiest Welkeners of the past."

"Angie, stop it."

"No, you need to hear all of it. You don't need to punish yourself for every little slipup. You feel guilty for everything. And you feel guilty for not feeling guilty. You probably feel guilty right now for feeling so guilty. But even if you felt the perfect amount of guilt, it wouldn't matter. I wouldn't love you any more or less—and neither would anyone else."

"Stop it, Angie. I get it. You can stop." Lizbeth's frustration grew. She didn't like just standing there and listening to this rebuke.

"I'm not done." Angie looked at Lizbeth with tender sternness. "I think there is one thing you do need to do."

Lizbeth tried not to blink. She tried to be brave and accept what Angie told her. She felt good that Angie said there was something to do. She'd known there would be. She wanted to start fixing the problem.

"There's someone you need to forgive."

"What?" Lizbeth was disappointed by this fix.

"You've got to forgive. I'm quite sure of it."

"Why? What difference would it make? How do you know?" Lizbeth paused. "And who?"

"I'm not sure. It's just this sense, I guess. No, that's not quite right. It's not *just* a sense. It's a good feeling and thinking. But I don't know who it is you need to forgive. Maybe you already know."

Then Lizbeth buckled over in pain. The shard inside her took this moment to leap into life. It felt stronger this time, more intense. Lizbeth thought she could discern the outline of the glass in her gut, the borders of this thing that entered from her nightmare.

The pain led her to think of Piers, the one she seemed to be suffering for. Did she need to forgive him? No. She could think of nothing he needed forgiveness for. She thought of the other Misfits, and the Welkeners, especially Jacob and Vida and Mook. And then she felt her body tingle. Of course. Alabaster Singing, her Welken friend, the silent one paired with Mook a month ago to help Lizbeth on her quest for the tile. Lizbeth realized she had not forgiven Alabaster. For what? For her beauty? Her steadfastness or her haunting song? No. Lizbeth knew the truth. She had not forgiven Alabaster Singing for dying—for swimming into the water and getting attacked by basilisks. She resented her absence. She resented the blame she felt for Alabaster's death.

The path took them into open meadows and over the Nez River. Mook, far ahead of them stopped and knelt down. By the time Angie and Lizbeth caught up to him, he was standing again, with a big smile on his face. "Here we are, at Nez Village." Mook's hand swept wide with grace and pride. "This is where my family lives."

Lizbeth didn't see much that resembled a town—only a rock path so precisely assembled it could justly be called a mosaic. Before the travelers had gone more than ten feet, Lizbeth remarked to herself how amazingly different Welken's communities were, and how fully they fit their inhabitants. At the same time, these towns were so close together that they had every reason to blend, to merge, to become a proverbial melting pot. But they did not—at least in her experience thus far. On the other hand, they were alike in many ways—in their commitments to count others' burdens as their own, to tell the truth with grace, and to heap gratitude upon all.

"Wait." Angie squatted down to examine the path. "Mook, this walkway tells a story, doesn't it? What's it about?" She ran her hand over the colored stones and put her finger on some turquoise eyes.

"It's a history of the Nezzer Clan." Mook offered a hand to Angie to pull her up. "We put the story under our feet where we can see it and be reminded of it every day. But I want you to look up. Friends are coming to meet you."

It seemed to Lizbeth like the whole village were descending upon them. Dozens of children ran to them with open arms bearing gifts—a bracelet, a slice of sweet bread, a shiny stone like those in the mosaic path, an arrow, a woven belt.

While overwhelmed by this generosity, Lizbeth wondered how they'd had time to prepare these gifts. Surely they did not greet every visitor this way. And surely the Nezzer adults did not always let the children run out to meet strangers to the village.

Then adults came. Two offered baskets to hold the gifts bestowed by the children. Others patted the Misfits on the back or asked questions or held out a hand to assist them in any way they could. And all of them kissed Lizbeth and Angie. And Mook too. Lizbeth felt awkward at first. They kissed her on the forehead and then seemed to wait to receive her kiss. She felt uncertain about so much affection. Then, despite her conversation with Angie, she felt guilty because she didn't deserve so much attention, so much love. Even so, she accepted the kisses and gave her own. Each one was easier to get and to give.

An elderly Nezzer man shuffled toward Lizbeth, with a thick blanket around his shoulders. It made his head look turtlelike, held aloft by his thin, weathered neck. The villagers parted as he approached, and the children quieted themselves and bowed their heads. Lizbeth shot a nervous look at Angie, but Angie did not see her. She held a child in each arm and whispered to them.

"In Welken." The old man spoke with youthful confidence. He waited, then said it again. "In Welken."

Lizbeth had not heard this as a greeting before, only as part of leave-taking. She looked over to Angie once again, and together they said, "Of Welken."

The man nodded in solemn acceptance of this reply, his crooked fingers tugging on the folds of his well-creased neck. His hands came down in an open gesture. "For Welken."

Lizbeth didn't know what to say. She'd never heard an answer to this phrase. Through Welken? Beyond Welken? No, these didn't work. The assembled Nezzer Clan seemed to be waiting eagerly. Under Welken? Over Welken? No, no.

"From Welken." Angie's voice pealed clear and bright. "Because of Welken."

Figures, thought Lizbeth. *I can't think of one and Angie thinks of two.*

But her envy faded quickly. She pondered the meanings in these phrases and processed them one after another. *In, of, for, from, because of.* There was a logic and a story in these terms.

The old man's head came farther out from his blanket-shell. As he strained his neck toward Lizbeth and Angie, his quiet, raspy voice sounded even older than he looked. "The Nezzer Clan welcomes you." He bowed his head, his hair falling forward. Like Mook's, it was a series of loose ponytails, only all gray, with a hint of black on the tips. "My name is Seff. I am Mook's great-uncle. We have been waiting for you for a long time. Come and see why." Seff gestured to the mosaic path. "Walk."

So they did.

At first, Lizbeth felt confused looking at these events and faces she could not decipher—and, at the same time, stepping on them. But some of the images made sense. She saw a hail of arrows rise and fall into some mammoth beast. A king or chief honored someone with a wreath. Then images of everyday life were recorded. A family eating a meal. Lovers embracing. Old men and women around a campfire. A child playing in the dirt. A dog howling at the moon.

When Lizbeth looked up, she noticed that they had walked into the village. Simple buildings dotted the landscape, with no apparent system of roads beyond the main mosaic thoroughfare. Lizbeth thought of the homes as a mix of English or Dutch cottages, African huts, and Native American tepees. A thatched roof curled as it ended, descending to the top line of the windows, about three feet above the ground. Some buildings had wooden walls. Others had no walls at all, just exposed poles in a foot of open space between the thatch and the ground. Some were cone-shaped and some were rectangular with crossed poles reaching high into the sky along a center beam.

Seff motioned toward the path. "Listen to the story. There will be time for meeting later."

Lizbeth looked quizzically at Angie. "I'm trying. I can pick out scenes and faces, but I'm not seeing a story yet."

"Me neither. Maybe Seff means for us to do more than look. He said, 'Listen.'"

Just like Angie, thought Lizbeth. *She gives advice no one in their right mind knows how to follow.*

Then two Nezzer women walked out of a house and came toward them. They played flutelike instruments.

Well, thought Lizbeth, *at least I can listen to this.*

The women acted like pied pipers, leading the Misfits down the path.

A Nezzer history of kings or queens or chiefs unfolded. As the line descended and the path led north through town, each ruler's contribution could be seen. Sometimes a new building or a better bow or arrow was pictured, but some of the time a quality of life seemed to be revealed. One family was known for peacemaking, another for bravery and courage. One queen led the clan in practicing forbearance.

Lizbeth felt a bit proud for figuring out the virtues. "I've never seen a history like this, Angie."

"I know. It feels so upside-down but so right-side-up at the same time. It's like saying that feathers will conquer the world or that we'll build our city out of stardust."

"Angie?"

"Yeah?"

"You're weird."

Then the players' tune turned doleful. The notes seemed to fall about their feet and pile up on each other, like burrs cast from a sack. They snagged Lizbeth and Angie in a kind of barbed melancholy.

Lizbeth decided she'd had enough Nezzer history. There was no Welken final exam to pass. She didn't need to know these facts. She grabbed Angie's hand and ran up the path. She wanted to put the mournful tune behind her. She looked to the right and saw trees along a thick line of green. She guessed it was the Nez River. "Let's go."

Before Angie could respond, before their feet had moved one step beyond the mosaic path, they heard dogs barking. From both sides of the path, snarling dogs stormed at them. Dust kicked up behind the dogs, and they closed the gap quickly, growling all the while.

Lizbeth and Angie turned to the center of the path and ran ahead to try to get away.

The dogs caught up to them in seconds. They charged to the edge of the path and skidded to a halt. No dog set a paw upon a stone. Lizbeth stared bug-eyed at their exposed teeth and snapping jaws. They snarled and growled. They paced and barked.

Lizbeth grabbed Angie's hand to walk back to Mook and the others who had greeted them so warmly. But when they turned to the south, the musicians stepped in and blocked their way. She could not see Mook or any of the others—and the dogs and musicians seemed to be teaming up to keep them going north. Lizbeth wanted to lower her shoulders and bowl them over. She wanted to become the ox she knew she could be.

But the music hurt too much. Curiously, the sad song weakened her. It nearly buckled her knees. And she saw that Angie felt wounded too. Already hunched over, Angie held a fist to her heart, as if to keep the music from penetrating too deeply.

When Lizbeth took one more step to the south, the shard in her soul cut into her, surprising her with the sharpness of the pain. Clutching her stomach, she fell back, stumbling two or three steps to the north. The pain went away.

Angie rushed to her side. "Lizbeth, what happened? Are you OK?"

"No, I don't think so. Help me up. We've got to keep walking north. I've got to get away from this music. It's cutting me up."

They rose slowly, careful to maintain their balance in the center of the path, as far as they could get from the yipping dogs. Arm in arm, they walked to the north. They saw some bungalows up ahead, their thatched roofs curling down over the eaves. Then Lizbeth picked up the path's mosaic story again. She followed the history for a few paces and saw a face that reminded her of Mook, complete with breastplate and foxtail hair. Then she saw something else, something that seemed to leap off the stones and grab Lizbeth by the throat. She felt she could not breathe. There, in the ongoing story of the Nezzer Clan, was Alabaster Singing, basilisks on her legs and back, set in tile, never to be pried off. And there was the land-bridge Lizbeth had created over the water.

Then Lizbeth held a hand to her mouth. She did not even hear the dogs barking. There *she* was in the mosaic. Lizbeth on the bridge. Lizbeth's hand reaching. Lizbeth too late.

She gasped. She looked at Angie in disbelief, tears wetting her cheeks. In the year that had passed in Welken, someone had made her a part of Nezzer history. And in that moment, Lizbeth knew that she had to do more than forgive Alabaster. She had to forgive herself.

The dogs snapped Lizbeth out of her reflections. They barked and barked. They leaned over the path and snapped at the Misfits. They growled low, in a grinding, steady threat. They seemed to be herding them forward, not wanting them to stand and wait.

Lizbeth glanced ahead at the huts. Angie pulled her up the path that wound around the closest two huts and led them to the door of the north-ernmost bungalow.

With the dogs hounding them on and the flute players marching mournfully toward them, Lizbeth noticed a familiar pattern. "Look, Angie, four huts, all facing the center, to the north and south, to the east and west. We've passed the south and west huts, and we are about to enter the one on the north."

"I wonder why. Why start here? Look at the way the path weaves around the backs of the huts and into the next one's front. It's like Ganderst Hall. No, it's more like the flower weave in the center of the golden scarab. Remember? It was carved into the amulet."

The oppressive barking became too great to bear. The girls approached the door, knocked, and went in.

A blast of cold air from inside the hut replaced Lizbeth's concern about the dogs with a simpler desire for warmth. She did not have to search for long. In the middle of the hut, smoke rose from an open fire and swirled up through a hole in the conical ceiling. Lizbeth and Angie ventured in, bracing themselves against the cold.

Lizbeth shut the door behind them. "It must be 50 or 60 degrees colder in here. I'm already shivering. I was shaking at the dogs and now I'm shaking at the cold. Isn't anything easy here?"

"So." A voice emerged from behind the smoke of the fire. "You want comfort and charm, do you?"

"Well," said Lizbeth, raising a *what gives?* gesture to Angie. "I don't know."

"No, you don't know. I'll tell you what. Bebba knows. Bebba's a-seein' eye in the darkness, she is. Bebba's the hard hand of truth in a world longin' for a soft embrace of its folly." The old woman from Kells Village stepped over from behind the smoke, her unkempt gray hair hanging in front of her blind eyes.

Angie ran toward the fire. "Oh, Bebba!"

"I may be blind, Angela, but I see you well enough. And Elizabeth too. Like loose shingles in a hurricane, you come a-flappin' to me. Well, let's have a look at you."

Lizbeth walked up behind Angie, then both approached the fire. Lizbeth could see Bebba's smoky silhouette on the other side, but the old woman was curiously unwelcoming. "I just want to warm myself by the fire, Bebba."

"Don't we all, lass, don't we all? Put your mitts right up to it, girl. Don't be shy. Bebba may bark, but she's got few teeth left for the bitin'."

Lizbeth crouched down and held her hands to the flame, but nothing happened. No matter how close her flesh got to the fire, she could feel no warmth. It looked warm enough, but it gave no heat.

"Bebba," said Angie, shivering, "the fire is cold."

"And that's where you're wrong, child. It's not the fire but the sun that's cold, and a hundred hearts besides. Come closer and see for yourself."

Lizbeth passed a hand through the flame and felt nothing. Then the cold grew colder. She never thought fire would make her shiver. Flickering up and down, these flames seemed to mock her desire for warmth.

A knock came from the back door. Lizbeth and Angie turned toward the knocking. When they turned back to the fire, Bebba was gone. The knocking grew louder. It pounded and pounded. Lizbeth and Angie didn't know what else to do, so they opened the door.

Brilliant sunlight greeted them. Without hesitating, they walked into it and held their faces to the sky. But no sooner had they stepped into the warmth than a familiar sound came at them. Barking louder and louder, the dogs rushed and herded them along the path, prodding them around the right side of the northern hut, into the middle of the four buildings, and facing them toward the door of the eastern hut. The dogs kept snapping.

Lizbeth and Angie knocked, opened the door, and shut it firmly against the annoying snarls behind them. In the middle of the furnished room stood Bebba—again—her white globes staring at them with unnerving emptiness. Along the sides, chairs faced into the center. A chandelier lit with dozens of candles hung above Bebba. The wax dripped around her but never on her.

Confused by Bebba's presence in this room as well as the other, Lizbeth waved, as if this gesture would tell her whether this Bebba was an apparition or not.

"I know you're here, child, you and the wispy one. It's as clear to me as a riddle unriddled, as a mind without straw, as the way the dawn cracks open the night."

"Yeah," said Lizbeth. "I see you too." She felt stupid, stupid for saying it, stupid for standing in another hut without having a clue why she was there or what she was to do.

"Lizbeth," said Angie, "do you feel it, underneath us?"

A mist came from the floor, not a swampy mist or a rising fog but a steadily thickening whiteness. A haze filled the room, then a fuzzier translucence. The air was disarmingly white, not white like a snowstorm, but thicker, like paint, almost solid, with a kind of porcelain opaqueness.

Angie grabbed Lizbeth's elbow as they walked forward. Lizbeth squinted to try to see Bebba. She tried to push away the whiteness with her hand. The knocking came again at the back, and they inched their way toward it. Lizbeth couldn't see her own hand. It was the darkest whiteness. As blind as Bebba, the Misfits felt for the back wall. When the knocking turned to pounding, they just knew someone was there to greet them. Lizbeth found the latch and pulled.

The day pealed into the whiteness as clear as any cathedral's bell. It cast away the white shroud, which fell to the ground like a robe before a shower.

Lizbeth sighed in relief, and Angie mirrored that sound with a smile—then the dogs started in again. Lizbeth and Angie knew the drill. They did not resist. They walked quickly on the colored stones, ignoring whatever Nezzer history lay at their feet. They stepped up to the third hut, the southern hut. Angie knocked once and Lizbeth opened the door.

They stepped in, shut the door, and immediately felt a strong, dry heat. Lizbeth thought how preferable this was to the cold of the northern room, then quickly changed her mind. *Preference* was a word she could not link to the oppressing, parched feeling that attacked every open pore. She thought she was evaporating. Angie seemed to be holding up a little better. Her shoulders were not as stooped, her eyelids not as heavy.

In the center of the room, as mysteriously as ever, stood Bebba, her head tilted up as if inviting more of the sun's scorching rays. But there was no sun . . . only heat. Heat that sucked them to powder. Bebba leaned over a copper cauldron. She dipped a ladle in and poured water into metal goblets. To Lizbeth, the fluid was surely more than water. It had to be life itself.

"Bebba knows, yes she does. She knows that you see what looks to be a crime, drops missin' the cup, water fallin' down, wastin' itself on the ground, dryin' up before your eyes. No meanness in that, really, 'cause the bowl is full, 'tis a spring as free-flowin' as an everlastin' waterfall. Come and taste."

With trepidation, Lizbeth approached. She put both hands on the tub. It felt redemptively cool. Angie clasped it too and leaned forward, as if Bebba would pour the water right into her mouth.

But Bebba didn't. She filled a goblet and placed it on a worn wooden table next to her. She filled a second goblet, put it down as well, then took a sip from the ladle. "Right handsome flavor," she said, brushing her stringy gray hair out of the way. "I think you'll find the water's worth the journey, my friends. It's not like anything you've ever had." She passed the goblets over the copper bowl to the thirsty Misfits.

Lizbeth glanced over to Angie as if to say "down the hatch" and drank as fast as she could. She gulped it down so hard she thought her loud swallowing would have awakened a sleeping baby. She held the empty cup out and smacked her lips. They smacked just as before. No, worse. Not only did the water not satisfy; it actually felt dry. It did not seem like hot air or grainy sand. The water felt thoroughly dry, like she had gulped down liquid parchedness. Like the water drew more water to itself, sucked her throat dry, and did the same all the way to her stomach.

She could not speak. She saw Angie holding her throat, about to dunk her head into the bowl. Lizbeth shouted, "No!" but nothing came out. She thought her throat would bleed at the attempt, but that would have required flowing blood. Lizbeth dove for Angie, tackled her around the waist, pushed her down, away from the water. Angie's grip on the pot pulled it down, and all the water spilled out. It vanished in seconds.

On hands and knees, Lizbeth looked for Bebba. She was gone.

Knocking came from the back. Knocking, knocking, more knocking.

Lizbeth and Angie crawled toward it. The knocking turned to pounding . . . desperate, frantic pounding. Lizbeth's body felt dismembered. She didn't sense any elasticity holding it together. She was certain the last drop of moisture in her would dry up and she would crumble into bits of rock and sand.

The pounding grew louder, but Lizbeth was too weak to get to the door. She reached back and pulled her legs up, then stretched out her hands toward the door. The pounding came harder and faster. She saw Angie on her side. It didn't matter. All that mattered was getting to the door. In one desperate heave, she threw herself at the latch and yanked on the door.

The sun shone in, and the outside air felt deliciously humid. As the moisture called Lizbeth and Angie back to life, they shielded their eyes from the brightness and crawled out of the hut. Then something came between them and the sun. Squinting, they saw the two musicians holding forth bowls of water. They drank greedily. It was not water. It was life, an elixir that animated every withered tissue.

They stood. The players withdrew and the dogs charged at them. Too tired to run, Lizbeth and Angie walked to the last hut, the one on the western side. The dogs settled down. As long as the Misfits walked steadily toward the hut, the dogs did not threaten them.

Angie put her hand on the latch. "This is the last one, Lizbeth."

"Yeah, whatever that means."

They walked in and closed the door. The room did not immediately impress them in any way. It was plain. Four walls, two windows, a dirt floor, and no assault on their senses. No pain, but no Bebba either.

"Bebba may be blind," came a voice from the center of the room, "but sometimes it's others who can't see her." Lizbeth and Angie looked around for her. Then Lizbeth heard a low rumbling under the ground. It started slowly and grew. As the floor trembled, Lizbeth spread her legs to keep her footing. Then the ground shook more and more violently. Lizbeth and Angie put their backs to a wall. The whole hut wobbled.

In the center, out of the dirt, a white spot bulged out of the floor, like a mushroom pushing up. In a furious burst, the white mound popped through the soil, and the white top revealed itself as Bebba's straggly hair, and Bebba's whole body followed until she stood before them, her vacant eyes laughing at the mysteries they held. "Bebba knows. She knows you ache to be sippin' tea and talkin' to Piers. She knows you want a way out—and here's the truth as wet as my own spittle. Bebba wants out too. We're on the move together, that's a solid thing. All you have to do is find a way in, and tell your story."

Then, like two Alices in a one-room Wonderland, Lizbeth and Angie became larger in the room. The ground shook, and Lizbeth could see that she wasn't growing. Instead, the room was sinking . . . getting swallowed up by the ground. Then a knock came from the back door. The door wasn't shrinking. The door stood there creaking against the collapsing walls.

The knocking turned to pounding and the pounding grew louder. As the dirt floor tumbled Lizbeth and Angie, they banged into each other and clawed toward the door as best they could. The pounding on the other side sounded furious, like a battle, like spears and clubs and a battering ram. It sounded like death on the march.

Dirt and splintered wood flew about the Misfits. Lizbeth pushed herself at the latch and stretched out toward it. Angie's hand was there too. Together they pulled, and the door gave way.

With a gasp and a scream, two bodies tumbled in, nearly flattening Lizbeth and Angie.

"Shut it!" yelled Len.

"Hurry!" shouted Bennu.

The four pushed at the hut's back door, pressed it hard, and latched it. Heaving for breath, the Misfits turned around almost simultaneously and leaned against the door they had just closed.

Lizbeth looked up to see Dear-Abby standing over them, hands on hips.

Dear-Abby wagged a finger. "I'll never understand teenagers. You can't get them to move an inch, then you find them by the backyard shed all out of breath and sweaty. Were you guys playing Frisbee-o? Oh, don't bother. I'll go get some lem-lem. Ya look thirsty. Even a crazy lady can figure that out!"

As if to jolt herself awake, Lizbeth shook her head. "Are you guys thinking what I'm thinking? No matter how many times we go back and forth, I'm always surprised, always amazed. I don't think I'll ever get used to it."

Dear-Abby took three steps toward the house, then turned back. "I shall return, me and MacArthur!"

CHAPTER TWENTY
RECOVERY TIME

Even sleepers are workers and collaborators
in what goes on in the universe.

—HERACLITUS, *FRAGMENTS*

 The Misfits sat in silence with their backs to the wall of the shed. Exhausted by her journey through the huts, Lizbeth leaned her head against the wood siding and sighed.

"You're always sighing," said Len.

Lizbeth sighed again.

"Every time you sigh I feel like something terrible is going to happen, or that you have some impossible burden that we should all try to fix."

"I'm sorry."

Len pulled himself off the shed wall. "No, really, that's it right there. You're always sorry." He paused. "Hey, you and Angie just saved our lives. You shouldn't be sorry for anything."

"Actually—"

"I mean it. No excuses. You should be feeling great about what you did."

"But—"

"No 'buts.' Bennu and I should start a parade in your honor."

"All I was going to say was that I was really tired."

"Me too," said Bennu. "I'm not sure I'm up for a parade."

Lizbeth propped her knees up to her chest. "I'm *so* tired. I know we have a lot to talk about, but I want to nap first."

Len turned to Bennu. "Who is MacArthur, anyway?"

"What?"

"Y'know, Grandma always says, 'I shall return, me and MacArthur.'"

Bennu rolled his eyes. "If you occasionally paid attention in class, you'd know that in World War II, General MacArthur was pushed out of the Philippines by the Japanese—but he vowed to return."

Lizbeth stood up to walk to the house. "You guys keep up the history lesson. I'm going to find a couch."

"General MacArthur was later fired by President Truman," said Bennu, "but that was in the Korean War. He—"

"Sorry I asked." Len stretched out on the grass. "Hey, Angie, how do you put up with this guy? Does he make you take notes? Does he give you quizzes?"

Lizbeth kept walking. She couldn't believe Len had the energy to debate. As she entered the Bartholomews' house, the corduroy couch looked more inviting than ever.

PART FOUR

GIVEN, THE DAUGHTER

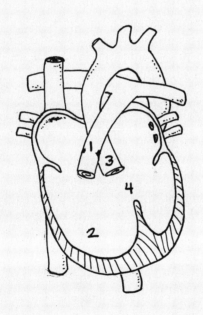

CHAPTER TWENTY-ONE

REPETITIOUS REDUNDANCIES

. . . not till the wound heals and the scar disappears,
do we begin to discover where we are . . .

—HENRY DAVID THOREAU, *CIVIL DISOBEDIENCE*

Sometimes the boy felt that nothing was really different. He saw his mother most days. When his father was at work, the boy's mother played with him and made him meals. By late afternoon things changed. Though only four, the boy could sense the way his mother's fear grew as the day went on. Soon the boy's father would come home. He always seemed to burst in, as if he hoped to catch someone in trouble. He often charged into the kitchen, pushed the boy's mother aside, opened the fridge, and got out a bottle.

Once, after a few months, he pushed her so hard she lost her balance and slammed with her back into the wall. She stayed there, her arms down, her hands pressed against the dull, worn paint. The boy wondered if his father would pick up some china plates and throw them again. It made the shard inside him twitch.

But the father did not reach for any plates. Instead he pointed and yelled at the boy's mother. He grabbed a frying pan and held it over his head, shouting, "Is it mine? Is it mine?" The boy did not understand. Why would his father be upset about a frying pan or ask about who owned it? Surely the father did. He possessed everything in the house. He possessed everyone.

Then the boy saw where his father pointed—at his mother's swollen tummy. With her back against the wall, her tummy's mound could easily be seen.

The boy does not remember what his mother said. He knows now that the baby had the same father he did, this raging man who stood in the kitchen that day and threw the frying pan onto the stove, knocking a pot of boiling potatoes onto the floor.

As the father stormed out, the boy backed up and bumped into the wall and caught himself against it with his hands. His posture became the same as his mother's. With his father gone, he rushed over to her. She cried and stroked his hair.

Then she took his hand and placed it on her tummy. He did not like it. The shard in his belly leaped, as if jealous. He withdrew his hand and ran from the room.

Months later, the boy's mother gave birth to a girl. At first, the boy did not mind. His mother brought the baby over when she came to work as a maid in her own home. The boy played with the child—and the mother did the most unusual thing. She laughed. The boy deeply enjoyed this.

Sometimes, after the mother of the baby had been in the house for a while, she walked up to the crib and smiled. She walked right by him without saying a word, and she picked up his sister. She held the baby close and kissed her. She brushed the baby's cheek with the backside of her fingers. And when the mother put her in her crib and winked at the boy and left the room to wash and cook, that's when the boy decided to go to his sister. He pushed on her stomach. He hit her on the head. He poked her in the eye. This, too, the boy enjoyed.

Years passed. The boy is not sure how many. He knows his sister could walk around and get into his things. He remembers that she cried louder when he hit her.

Then the day came when all of this would end. The boy had come home from school to find his sister playing with his trucks. She started screaming as soon as he opened the door. He remembers taking pleasure in her fear. He loved the wide eyes, the backing up, the arms raised for protection. But he hated the screaming. It was an alarm for his mother and, to his ears, like falcons descending from the sky. He threw a pillow at her to get her to stop, and then a doll. She cried louder, piercing the quiet, robbing him of his cruel secret. So he grabbed the toy truck and brought it down on her head. He heard footsteps and thought he should hit her as many times as he could before being discovered. He was good at lying to his mother. He would make something up.

But the footsteps did not belong to his mother. The door crashed open and his father had him in two strides. His father grabbed him by one arm and threw him on the bed. The boy fell on his side and rolled into the wall.

When he sat up to see what punishment would come next, he could not believe what he saw. His father held a pistol in his hand. He waved it over his head, shouting all the while. He asked the boy and his sister if they were ever once going to be good kids, if they could just for one day not be so stupid, so miserable, such hateful little brats.

The boy remembers these words. He tells them to himself every day and every night.

Then the father lowered the pistol. He seemed to relax, to smooth out the crazed winking in his eyes. He seemed to gather his wits, to focus—and he did, to take aim. He pointed the pistol at the boy and held it there, his hand steady. Then he switched to the girl and seemed confused. He went back and forth from the boy to the girl. He acted like the only thing stopping him was deciding which one he would shoot first. The boy's sister cried uncontrollably. The boy trembled and held the truck in front of him. He covered his face.

Another scream came from the door. The boy lowered the truck to see his father pointing the gun at his mother. His father looked panicked, as if he were surrounded by armed enemies, circling in for the kill. He moved the pistol from mother to boy to girl. He backed up until he was against the wall. The boy's mother stopped screaming, and in the boy's mind she did a very brave thing. She used softer words. She consoled the father, acting as if he were the victim. The father lowered the pistol, raised it up, then lowered it again.

That's when the mother motioned for the boy and his sister to leave the room. They slipped off the bed and walked like soldiers to the door.

The boy paused there and turned back. He saw his mother reaching out toward the gun. He remembers her saying something like, "It's OK. You are going to be fine. We all still love you."

The boy did not know why she would say such lies. His mother moved closer. She was but two feet from his father. He raised the gun again. The boy could not look, so he ran from the room. Before he made it to the living-room sofa, a single gunshot blasted out. It rang to him like a giant church bell, a death bell pealing loud and long, a bell that had been echoing for centuries.

A few days later, after his father's funeral, the boy had to gather his *things and move in with his uncle. His sister and mother packed up their things too and moved far away. He wondered if he would ever see them again.*

Lizbeth awoke but did not open her eyes. She lay on the sofa as if she were still sleeping. One part of her wanted to cry out the sorrow of the nightmare, to grieve for this family. Another part of her wanted to know what the dream was supposed to mean for her. Why did she keep dreaming this story? She thought about the mixed-up families she knew. None of them had suffered like this. The dream made her want to comfort the mother, to guide the boy, to protect the girl. But who were these people? Was she supposed to figure this out? She didn't have a clue.

Then she thought about these questions. What made her think that dreams had anything to do with reality? Was this nightmare another veil, a passage from sleeping to waking, a veil thinner than we typically suppose, a veil we should take more seriously? And why is it that we think these things ought to reveal some meaningful purpose? Whose purpose? Why? What good is a traumatic nightmare if you can't figure it out? Lizbeth settled on the idea that if there's a point, the Pointer could be a whole lot clearer.

An image came to her of the boy staring out his uncle's window, looking for the home life he'd never had. He grabbed his stomach, and his face took on a hardened expression. He ran his fingers tenderly over the deeply embedded shard.

Lizbeth opened her eyes. She saw Angie and Bennu on the adjacent love seat, his right arm around her shoulders. He leaned over to her, his left hand touching her chin. He held Angie, turned her toward him, fixed his eyes on hers, and maintained the gaze beyond Lizbeth's comfort. She was about to cough and sit up when Bennu pushed Angie's chin gently away from him. He moved in and whispered in Angie's ear.

Lizbeth had always heard that lovers were "radiant," but she wondered how that could be true for someone already as light-giving as Angie. She looked at Angie's eyes. There she was, smiling at Bennu's comments, giggling slightly, her whole being luminous.

"I can't take it!" Lizbeth sat up, rubbed her eyes, and held out her pleading hands.

"Sorry!" said Bennu. "We thought you were asleep."

"I had the nightmare again. I hate it. I'm starting to fear going to sleep. I didn't ask to know. I don't want to see these images in my head."

"Tell us."

So she did, sometimes racing through the story, other times pausing to gather herself for the next revelation.

Bennu put a finger to his lips. "Maybe the whole thing is symbolic. Maybe the dad stands for Morphane, that soul-sucking beast, and the mom is—I don't know—Bors's companion, Sarah Wace. Maybe the boy is Piers or Len or even you."

"Don't be ridiculous."

"Or maybe the boy represents America, raised on materialism and the media. Yeah, that's it."

Lizbeth rolled her eyes. "Bennu, sometimes you can be so academic, so abstract."

"Well, you never actually hear anyone's name, right?"

"So what? I hear almost no conversation at all. That doesn't mean each person represents a country. But wait a minute. Before we talk more about this, shouldn't we include Len? Shouldn't we spend some time all together going over everything we've been through?"

"Good idea." Angie scooted an inch away from Bennu. "The thing is, he took off."

"Yeah," said Bennu, "he can't sit still for a minute. He's compulsive. Maybe he needs medication."

Angie slapped his knee lightly. "Bennu, really."

"OK, he doesn't need meds, but he's not here. So, do we keep talking or wait? Since time is moving so much faster in Welken, we can't exactly sit around forever."

"So what you're saying," said Lizbeth, pulling her shirt down over some exposed tummy, "is that by leaving on some important errand, Len is wasting time while we are using it well, by napping or snuggling up?"

"Well, what I meant was—"

The phone rang. As Angie hopped up to get it, Lizbeth and Bennu stuck their tongues out at each other.

Lizbeth drew hers in first. "You are so immature."

"Am not."

"Are so."

"Nyaaa."

Angie held the phone in the air. "Lizbeth, it's for you. It's your mom."

Lizbeth sighed hard. She stood up, shook her head back and forth, and grabbed the phone. "Hi, Mom . . . You're what? . . . Why did you do that? . . . I suppose . . . OK, bye." Lizbeth turned to Angie and Bennu. "I don't know who is more needy—Dear-Abby or Mom. My mom is so clueless."

Bennu lowered his eyebrows. "Speaking of, where is Dear-Abby? She was here when we were out by the shed."

Angie frowned. "I think she's getting to the point where we can't leave her alone."

Lizbeth pushed open the screen door. "You two go look for her. I'll go help my mom. If I'm not back in ten minutes, someone come rescue me."

Len wondered what was worse, missing out on his friends' Welkenian tales or listening to his grandmother jabber on and on in the front seat.

"So, where are your mom and dad?"

"Grandma, they went out to a restaurant."

"How do you know?"

"There was a note on the refrigerator."

"On the reefer?"

"Yes, Grandma."

"Where is the restaurant?"

"Downtown, next to the performing arts center."

"Do they know how to get there?"

"Yes, Grandma. They've lived in this town for years."

Len tried to find something interesting about the intersection of Eleventh and University. He tried to take his mind off driving his grandmother to the pharmacy to pick up her prescription that was supposed to slow down her memory loss.

"Len?"

"Yes?"

"Where are your mom and dad?"

Len put his left palm on his forehead. "Grandma, they went out to a restaurant."

"How do you know?"

"There was a note on the refrigerator."

"On the reefer?"

"Yes, Grandma."

Len looked down Eleventh Avenue. He saw the pharmacy up ahead on his right. He wondered how many times he'd have this conversation before he got there.

"So, where are your mom and dad?"

"Grandma, they went out to a restaurant."

"How do you know?"

"There was a note on the refrigerator."

"On the reefer?"

"Yes, Grandma."

"Where is the restaurant?"

"Downtown, next to the performing arts center."

"Do they know how to get there?"

"Yes, Grandma." Len said it emphatically. "They've lived in this town for years."

Len pulled into the parking lot and put the Buick into park.

"Now what?" asked Dear-Abby, as if she had just come out of the Australian bush and had never been for a drive.

"Now we get out of the car."

"I will follow thee. Whither thou goest, I will go."

"OK, Grandma."

"Len?"

"Yes?"

"Where are your mom and dad?"

"Grandma!" Len could not hide his impatience. "They went to a restaurant."

Dear-Abby threw her arms into the air with exasperation. "Well, how should I know? You never told me!"

All Len could think was, *Never, never. May I never get Alzheimer's.*

It might have been his first genuine prayer.

Inside the pharmacy, Len and Dear-Abby discovered that they would have to wait a few more minutes. Not wanting to draw attention if Dear-Abby went into one of her crazy routines, Len sat in the corner chair.

Dear-Abby sat next to him. "So, Lenny-Benny, what do you think of your sister going out with that Bennu-Lennu?"

I don't get it, thought Len. *How can she be a lunatic one minute and more perceptive than Mom the next? Aw, so what? She's perceptive about something I don't want to talk about—not with her, not here.*

"What's the matter, Len-o? Why so glum-o?"

Len looked away in exasperation and embarrassment—and he saw, coming into the pharmacy, another reason to feel glum. Josh and Tommy Mink. Len sat back behind Dear-Abby, gripping the chair arms in preparation for the roller coaster.

Lizbeth clenched her jaw as she walked across the Bartholomews' front lawn and into her own front yard. Her tightened jaw hurt, so she opened it wide and rubbed the muscles at the hinge. With her jaw flapping repeatedly up and down, she had to resemble a laughing skeleton in a cartoon.

Yeah, a skeleton, she thought. *OK, Lizbeth, don't go there. Don't go thinking about how great it would be to waste away into nothingness. It's so ridiculous anyway, as if being a skeleton's a good thing. Hello! A skeleton is dead!*

She stared at the flower pots on the front porch. Real death was here. Lobelias fried in the summer heat, petunias keeled over from neglect.

That is so not like Mom, Lizbeth thought. *What's been happening to her this last month? She's always acted kinda looney—but why is she suddenly drinking so much? And Dad, he's gone from blurting out advertising copy every other minute to hiding in his office. He doesn't even yell at us anymore. I can't say I miss that, but it's got to be all about Mom.*

As she reflected on possible causes, Lizbeth was surprised to feel genuine compassion for her mom. She began to see her as a person—not just as a mom but also as a struggling, hurting woman. Someone who meant well and usually had her bearings but in the last month had slipped . . . a long ways.

Then Lizbeth stepped inside, and empathy vanished. Darlene sat on the kitchen island, her bare feet dangling over the side. Globs of mud dripped off her legs and formed chocolate kisses on the tile floor. Her blouse was open one button too low. Mud streaked her hair. While clinking ice cubes in her drink, Darlene put on a childish, pouty face. "Lizzie-poo, I made a mess. Will you help me clean up?"

Lizbeth hated being called Lizzie. She wanted to give her mother a time-out. She crossed her arms. "Mom, how could you? You've become a child—no, worse than a child."

"Oh, Lizzie, don't be mad. Sniffles isn't." Darlene pointed at the golden-haired cockapoo as the dog walked through the mud on the floor and tracked paw prints on the carpet.

"Dad's gonna kill you! Look at you!"

Darlene took another sip, put her glass on the counter, leaned back, and crossed her legs in a saucy way. "C'mon, Lizzie, he'll think I'm cute."

"Well, I don't. Get up, OK? Let's go outside and wash off."

Lizbeth grabbed her mom's hand, made her leave her drink in the kitchen, and led her onto the grass by the hose. Before she leaned over to turn on the water, she slumped her shoulders and took stock of her mother's muddy legs. She looked out to the garden, saw the drenched earth she must have slipped in, and then returned her focus to her mother's mess. Darlene stood there, wobbling, smiling as if she'd won a prize. Lizbeth knelt on one knee to reach in and turn on the water. She turned back. Eye-level with Darlene's legs, Lizbeth shook her head at the dark brown mud that covered Darlene's honey-brown calves and knees.

When she sprayed her mother's ankles, some of the mud wouldn't come off. She squatted closer and rubbed it. As water pooled at Darlene's feet, the drier mud softened and seemed to come alive. Lizbeth squeezed some between her fingers—and it lurched out of her hand and continued to move on its own. Startled, Lizbeth stepped back.

The mud kept moving. It wiggled around Darlene's feet, then slimed up her legs. It rolled itself into dozens of cylinders, and these cylinders changed from a fleshy brown to a shiny black. They slithered up and up. Lizbeth just stared at them. They wiggled and kept refining their shape. After a minute, the slimy, muddy cylinders began to look like eels.

Then Lizbeth saw them for what they were. Basilisks! Out of the water and the dirt, more basilisks came. They crawled up her mother's legs. Their teeth poked out their sides. Basilisks! Just like those that killed Alabaster!

Lizbeth glanced up at her mother. In her frozen posture, Darlene seemed not to notice, not to care that she was being smothered, being eaten alive. On and on the basilisks came. They crawled past Darlene's knees and reached her shorts.

Then Lizbeth snapped out of her stupor. She grabbed the hose and sprayed as hard as she could. She moved the water stream to the highest basilisk and blasted it. With the water shooting on them hard, the basilisks retreated down Darlene's legs. They left without biting. They were defeated easily, as easily as mud washes off one's body in a shower. As quickly as it began, it ended. Darlene was clean. The basilisks were gone.

Lizbeth threw down the hose. Her hands trembled. She knelt in the pool of water and pressed her hands against her thighs to stop the shaking. Everything swam together in her mind. Her guilt over Alabaster's death. Her anger at her mother. The sorrow she felt when she saw a drink in her mother's hand.

She cried a little, then tried to stop the flow of tears. Tired of crying and feeling helpless, Lizbeth hardened herself against this intrusion in her life. She decided to reinforce her defenses. She stuck a brick into the hole the enemy had made. She built up her fortress. Hitting her thighs with her fists, she pounded the tears away. She thought she had done it. She thought she had stopped the pain. She thought she had buried the last basilisk.

Then she felt the shard inside her twitch. It made her raise her head, and she noticed something touching her knees.

It was Darlene, kneeling beside her, her clean legs pressing against Lizbeth's own. "I'm sorry."

Lizbeth could not believe what she heard.

"I'm so sorry, honey. I've made a mess of things, I know." She patted Lizbeth's thigh. "Stay with me, OK?"

Lizbeth leaned her head into her mother's shoulder. Darlene put both arms around her and stroked her face. "Lizbeth, I can't help it right now. I don't know why. I'm more sorry than you know."

After a big sigh, Lizbeth pushed herself away from her mom's chest. She paused for a second before standing. She didn't know what to say—or she knew it but couldn't bring herself to pronounce the words. She shrugged. "I'm wet, Mom. I have to go change. And then I'm going next door."

In her wet pants, Lizbeth walked awkwardly back to the house. Just before she opened the door, she heard the squeak of the water being turned off. Then she heard her mother crying.

Lizbeth opened the door and let it slam shut.

CHAPTER TWENTY-TWO

HOLES

Pain wanders through my bones like a lost fire.
—THEODORE ROETHKE, *THE MARROW*

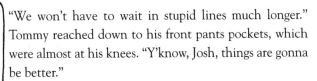 "We won't have to wait in stupid lines much longer." Tommy reached down to his front pants pockets, which were almost at his knees. "Y'know, Josh, things are gonna be better."

"Yeah." Josh turned around and glared at the middle-aged man behind him in line, a man with a pregnant-sized potbelly and a monkish bald spot. Josh stepped into him. "Don't crowd me, man."

Len slouched behind Dear-Abby, hoping not to be seen. As usual, things felt like slow motion when the McKenzie Boys were around.

Tommy snickered. "You are so tough, Joshua Mink. You can even push around an old man."

"Shut it."

"Yeah, yeah." Tommy clearly checked out the young woman in the white coat behind the counter. "Could we hurry it up here?"

The woman shot her head up toward Tommy. She had the look of a long day behind her, of strained patience, of dealing with ringing phones and the sad faces of the sick. Yet her expression was utterly composed, and her smile electrified her beauty. "Excuse me, Mr.? . . ."

"Mink. Mr. Mink." Tommy laughed. "But you, Gorgeous, you can call me Tommy."

After a pause, Len saw the woman do the most amazing thing. She leaned over the counter, almost eagerly. "Mr. Mink, I'm not sure what you don't understand about waiting your turn." She winked at the hunched-over, gray-haired, purse-clutching woman at the front of the line. "We'll just take all the time we need to do things right, won't we, Mrs. Dunn?"

Stunned by her composure, Len thought, *She's tough* and *beautiful. I want to marry this woman.*

Josh and Tommy both stuck their chests out. They folded their arms, pushing out their biceps with their hands. They widened their stances.

"I'm a compulsive walker," said Dear-Abby, "and when I walk, I swing my arms like this." Dear-Abby stood and made soldierly swings with her arms, with her fingers stretched wide and hard toward the ground.

"Not now, Grandma." Len squirmed in his seat. He pulled his hat around frontward so it covered his face.

"And I pray for everyone in the family as I swing my arms."

"Grandma, can we talk about this later?"

"Jim and Lisa." She swung her arms. "Tiffany, Kyle, Kirby."

Len tugged on her sleeve. He poked his head around to the left and saw the balding man staring. Len assumed everyone was.

"I'm not done. John and Joyce. Clare, Schuyler, Ethan, Janet."

"You don't need to do us, Grandma. I'm right here."

"But I pray for you every day when I swing my arms. Where was I? Jeff and Charlotte—"

"Grandma!"

"What?"

"What do you want for dinner?" It was a nothing question, but it was all Len could think of on the spot. He hoped to distract her, to change her focus. He peered around her and saw the elderly purse-hugging woman turn to leave.

Dear-Abby froze, like she was trying to remember someone else in the family.

"Next?" The unflappable clerk spoke as she would to any customer, though she addressed Tommy Mink. "Can I help you?"

"I think so. Josh, don't you think she could help me?"

Josh stepped forward. "We're here for a prescription for Oliver Mink."

Tommy hit him. "You're no fun."

"We need to get home. Odin's sick."

The woman turned to find the plastic bottle on the shelf behind her. Tommy and Josh whispered to each other as they watched her stretch to reach the drug. "Hmmm," she said, reading the label. "You need to talk to the pharmacist about this."

Tommy hit the counter. "C'mon! C'mon! It's just more waiting."

The pharmacist walked up. A fit-looking Asian man in his early thirties, with close-cropped hair, he slipped one hand into his white coat, his thumb sticking out.

Tommy's countenance changed as soon as the pharmacist approached. He lost his swagger. His shoulders drooped. He looked submissive and cowardly, as if he were the last one picked for an academic competition.

The pharmacist's serious expression grew even more serious. "I assume Oliver Mink is a relative of yours?"

"Yeah," said Josh, "our brother."

The pharmacist held up the orange bottle. "He needs to be very careful with this drug. The doctor faxed part of his file to me. He has an unusual condition, even more unusual for someone his age. Without surgery, few people survive past childhood with this problem."

Tommy wobbled his head. "I guess he wins the prize, Doc." It sounded falsely confident.

"This is no joking matter, young man. Your brother has a dangerous condition called tetralogy of Fallot. It's named after the person who learned how four problems in the heart come together. Oliver has a hole in his heart, which means his blood doesn't flow properly. This drug will help manage that flow. If your brother has any trouble with it, call immediately. I can't stress this enough, boys. At any moment, your brother could die."

Tommy threw down some money. "Like we don't know that, Doc." His hands shook as he waited for the change. "Like we're idiots, Doc. All you snobby jerks think that."

The clerk counted the change into Tommy's palm.

Tommy tried to grab her hand. "Thanks, Beautiful. And by the way, Doc, everybody dies."

The two McKenzie Boys strode toward the door.

Tommy turned back. "Even you, Doc. Don't forget it. Even you." The brothers pushed both doors too hard on their hinges. They creaked and banged, then swung back and shut.

"Oh my," said Dear-Abby, her fingers still stretched out wide. She swung her arms. "Oh my, oh my. I'm not done praying. Jeff and Charlotte. Lenny and Angie. There, that's what I do. And I thank God for you each time."

After Len drove Dear-Abby home and eased the Buick into the garage, he started his usual single fluid motion of put-it-in-park-unlock-the-seat-belt-open-the-door-and-roll-out. Then he glanced over at his grandmother.

She sat bolt upright in the seat, looking through the windshield as if at the open highway. "Oh dear, what do we do now?"

Len unfastened her seat belt. "We get out. We're at home, in our house."

"I know that. I'm not stupid."

Len withheld comment. He left the car and opened the door that led into the laundry room and then the kitchen.

Slowly, Dear-Abby got out of the car, came up, and poked him in the ribs. "I'll follow you."

Len took this exchange as confirmation that politeness was overrated. As he entered the kitchen, he heard the voices of the other Misfits from the living room. Walking toward them, he debated which story to begin with—the McKenzie Boys at the pharmacy, or the vision he'd had in the painted room.

In a second, he realized he would not be recounting either.

There, in the center of the living room, stood Lizbeth, pants wet, her arms held stiffly and unnaturally at her sides, her eyes unfocused, darting left and right. Bennu and Angie held her by her arms. "I saw them. Basilisks. I wanted to cram the hose down my mom's throat—that's how I felt—but *they* came. The basilisks came out of the mud, and I had to fight them again. But this time . . . this time they washed away. They melted or they drowned. I don't know. It was like I got a second chance to save Alabaster. I made the basilisks go away. I saved Mom. And then, and then . . . I hated her. I slammed the door and came back here."

As if these last words pulled the lid off her pot of simmering emotions, Lizbeth let the steam rise. She relaxed into Bennu's arms and buried her face on Angie's shoulder.

Lizbeth's heaving chest finally slowed down. She wiped her eyes and gathered herself. "I want to sit down. I think we need to talk about what's happened to each of us. I feel so much better for saying what I just did about my mom. So much has happened—and we need to see if we can make sense of it. No secrets."

Len sat down in the rocker. "What would be the point of keeping a secret?"

"I don't know," said Lizbeth. "I just know that I didn't want to tell you what happened with my mom—how I stormed off—but I think I needed to say it for my sake . . . and, who knows, maybe for ours too."

So Lizbeth told about hearing the voice of Piers, his odd words about finding himself in herself, and she told them more about the dream, and how she kept feeling the shard too. She ended with the line she'd heard, "A story's told by day and night."

"We heard something like that too." Bennu leaned in. He picked at a threadbare spot on his shorts. "'The sun is cold, the wind is white.' Maybe it goes with your line, like it's the second part of a prophecy or something. It's from the Book of Quadrille."

Then Bennu told the story of being on Gareth's ship, of the loveliness of the water glimpses, of the hike up the cliff, and how they'd tumbled down the stairs of the Bartholomews' house, right past Dear-Abby, and into a large open cave.

"That's so weird," said Angie. "I was standing in Deedy Swamp, and I had a vision of home too, only it was of Percy and Bones. Why is everything overlapping? Why is it so different this time, as if Welken and Bones Malone are just a squint of the eyes away from us? It's like the distance between these worlds is decreasing. We're getting closer. What we see here is the skin of Welken. And behind the skin is the flesh and bones of Mook and Gareth and, we hope, Piers."

"So," said Len cautiously, "do you think that's why our town's called Skinner?" It was the way his mind worked, seeing the potential ironies, the potential humor, in everything. But he didn't laugh. No one did. As Len pondered his own association, the possibilities overwhelmed him. He rubbed the dull ache that surfaced on his brow.

Angie kept going. She talked about MaryMary and the Cutters, how Mook had been injured and how Vida and Jacob had drawn the Cutters away so she and Lizbeth had been able to move up the trail. Then she told of the Meducer and the huts in Nez Village.

Bennu interrupted. "Bebba, huh? She keeps popping up. And you realize, of course, what happened in the huts—fire that wasn't hot, wind that didn't blow, water that didn't quench thirst, and earth that didn't bury you. It's our gifts at The Welkening, upside down."

"You're so smart," said Angie.

"Oh, stop it." Len shifted on the rocker. "The question is, what do we do now?"

"What about you, Len?" asked Lizbeth. "We haven't heard from you."

Len thought for a moment. He didn't exactly know why, but he didn't want to "reveal all." Maybe it was his natural rebellion. Maybe it was more. He thought about his conflicted feelings about Odin, about how he found himself sympathetic at times. He couldn't admit this even to himself, so he told about the McKenzie Boys picking up a prescription for Odin, who had tetralogy of Fallot, meaning a hole in his heart.

"No surprise there," said Bennu.

Then Len told about the painted room and the vision he'd had of Anubis, the Lord of the Dead, how he waited for the scales to be balanced by a heart as light as a feather.

"But whose heart is light as a feather?" Angie posed the question like a poet at a recital.

"Not mine." Len sat back in the rocker. "No surprise there."

Bennu smiled. "I know someone whose heart—"

"Look." Len rocked forward. "The point is that the question overtook me. It was like the answer to this question was all that mattered."

"Tea!" Dear-Abby stood at the opening to the kitchen, hands on hips as if she had been waiting for hours. "Which one of you dear-hearts is going to make me some tea?"

Angie shot up. "I will, Grandma."

"And I'll tell you another thing." Abby shook some rolled-up papers at the Misfits. "When I was a girl, a hundred years ago, we had to cut tea leaves with scissors. That's right. They came in a box, flat in a stack. We had to cut them up to make our tea."

Len looked suspiciously at Bennu. He opened his mouth to speak, but Dear-Abby bopped him on the head with the papers in her hand.

"Ha! I'm not crazy!" Dear-Abby's handful of papers flew all over the floor. "You kids believe anything."

Len rubbed his head, then noticed that the papers were pages of his mother's Percy and Bones story. "Since we're getting caught up with everything, maybe we should read the end of Mom's manuscript."

"Good idea," said Lizbeth. "I didn't get very far."

"OK," said Bennu. "I'll read it."

Len gathered up the pages and put them in order. The microwave beeped in the kitchen and, a minute later, Angie brought a tray into the living room. "Tea for you, Grandma."

"For me? Why, you dear-heart. And I didn't even ask! And a muffin-o too. You think of everything. You must be as smart as a whippersnapper."

Len wondered if things could get any loonier.

Bennu checked the order of the pages. "OK, remember that Percy is sick, Bones feels lost, Ollie wants to be an actor, and he has suckered Percy and Bones in to searching around for Patty Pickford's house."

CHAPTER THREE: Plucking Pearls at Patty Pickford's Place

A black Model T Ford pulled into the Cleverly Hills Inn circle driveway. The cabbie hopped out to open the door for Percy and Bones. "The name's Andrew McTrotter, lads. I'm not long from the Shetland regions of Scotland. Where are ye gallopin' to today?"

Bones gave him the map. "We want to see Patty Pickford's house."

"Saddled down with a Map to the Stars, eh? Weel, I can

get ye close, but ye won't be seein' her beauty up personal. Nay, she keeps a tight rein on that."

Andrew drove the Ford up the winding streets behind the inn. At first, Percy admired the mansions and gardens, then he felt sick to his stomach. "Too many turns spoils the soup, Bones. I just hope I can keep mine inside."

"And I'm so lost, Perce. I couldn't find my way for a minute in these parts."

Andrew looked back at them for what seemed to Bones like enough time to crash into two lampposts and three other cars. "Nay, you'd find your way in time. All it takes is a bit o' knowin' and a good guide. Whoa! Here we are."

Percy asked Andrew to wait as he and Bones walked up to the gate. Inside, a gardener trimmed roses. Percy winked at Bones, who winked back. Percy winked more obviously, then Bones took the hint. "Hello there, sir. Is that a 'Peace' rose you are trimming?"

A kangaroo gardener put some faded blooms into his pouch and looked around at Bones. "Indeed it is, mate."

Bones gestured with his paw between the bars of the gate. "I reckon that if you cut at a forty-three-degree angle, the new shoot creates a right fine bud."

"Is that so?" The gardener hopped over to the gate and unlocked it. "Mind showing me?"

In two whips of a whippoorwill, Percy and Bones were inside, strolling around the gardens, Bones giving horticultural advice, Percy peering around for a sneak peek at the famous and beautiful Patty Pickford.

As soon as they were a good distance closer to the house, a certain noisy burglar pushed open the unclasped gate. "Dearie, dearie, doodles, Mama. Here I am, right next to Hollywood royalty. When she meets me, I just know she'll want me to co-star with her in her next picture. But first, I'm going to please-and-pretty-please my way into Patty Pickford's parlor. I'll pounce on pearls and pilfer pendants. I'll pinch and plunder! I'll . . . oh dearie, dearie, doodles, I perceive a pressure to go potty!"

As Ollie searched a bit more frantically for a way in, Patty Pickford appeared on the front balcony, a parasol twirling in her left paw and a milk lollipop glistening in her right. She purred hello—and to Percy her voice flowed like an endless ball of yarn on a marble floor. "Oh, Joey, who are our guests?"

The gardener put his shears in a pocket and bowed toward the balcony. "Miss Pickford, I'd like to introduce a masterful horticulturist, Mr. Bones Malone, and his trusty sidekick, a certain Percival P. Perkins."

Percy raised a "dare he!" eyebrow at Bones, but before the ginger cat could assert his swaggering detectiveness, Patty turned back to the house with a scream. "Someone's in my house!"

Percy hung his head. "I should have known, Bones. I let my heart get ahead of my head."

Bennu put the pages down. "That's the end of chapter three."

Len sighed impatiently. "OK, so Percy has a crush on Patty. Big deal. While we are getting a cuteness fix, who knows what's happening to Sutton and Gareth and Mook."

"But don't you see," said Angie, "Percy, the one who always gets things right—just like Piers—has been fooled. If Percy is fool-able, then so are we. Maybe we've been going the wrong way or we've misinterpreted things. Maybe what we took for a silky coat is actually a weasel."

Len tried not to revert to his old self. He tried to keep from making a wisecrack about Angie's gibberish. He held the bridge of his nose and closed his eyes.

"You are so wise," said Bennu.

Len opened his eyes. "Wise? What's so wise about pseudo-psychology? Nobody has a silk coat! There aren't any weasels. There aren't even any minks!" He crossed his arms and pushed the rocker back. As he imagined

Sutton Hoo being tortured by tremlings, he knew all at once he was wrong. There *were* Minks—and he had not told the truth about them.

"Settle down, Len." Lizbeth looked angry. "Bennu, finish up. Go on to chapter four."

"OK, I think this is the last one."

CHAPTER FOUR: Oh, What a Tangled Mess We Weave

Percy and Bones ran into Patty Pickford's house and followed the screaming up the sweeping stairs and into the master bedroom, just in time to see Ollie climbing out the window, the stolen goods slung over his shoulder in a stolen sheet. "Forgive me, boys," Ollie said. "For your own good, forgive me." Then he vanished over the side.

Percy followed him out the window, down a trumpet-vine trellis, and onto the back patio. As Ollie hopped onto an available bicycle and sped away, Percy desperately opened storage doors until he found a fleet of bikes, grabbed one, and pedaled after him.

By then Bones and Patty had made their way out the back door. They also mounted the bicycles. Soon the bike caravan wobbled down a gravel path that cut between tall hedges on both sides. Ollie had enough of a lead that he quickly disappeared from view.

After about twenty yards, the narrow hall of hedges opened into a kind of courtyard with eight possible routes, all surrounded by hedges. Percy stopped, then Bones, then Patty.

His heart pounding from the bike ride and his proximity to Patty Pickford, Percy said, "Miss Pickford, I'm sure it's quite rude to skip-to-the-loo-my-darlin' and cut to the chase, but I'm afraid we know exactly just how slippery this robber is."

"I don't think he'll get far." Patty shielded her eyes from the sun. "You see, this hedge design is a cloverleaf maze. No matter which way you go in, you have to come out into the center."

"Ah, such foresight," said Percy. "Just the thing to catch a pedaling thief and put him in a lockup and save him for the Judgment Day."

Bones cleared his throat. "Perce, how about a plan of attack?"

"Oh, yes. Sorry. A little distracted. Sorry. A little flummoxed. We don't want Ollie to crawl out at the bottom of a hedge—so, Bones, you take the entrance to the immediate left. Miss Pickford, if you would, take the one to the immediate right. I'll take the one up ahead to the right. We have a seventy-five percent chance of flushing the rascal out."

The three of them raced down their respective hedge circles. Bones found that even with his short legs, he managed to pick up remarkable speed. Round and round his legs churned, and he cruised in the clover circle faster and faster. To his surprise, he suddenly pedaled recklessly into the center of the cloverleaf. He had come full circle—and had not seen Ollie anywhere!

At breakneck pace, into the center came Patty and Percy that very instant. And Ollie too! He had timed his escape from the hedges in the far left loop at precisely the wrong moment—and the four bikers crashed together in the middle, with screams and screeches and a billowing puff of dust.

Bones was the first to moan, a sick kind of hound-dog howl. The sheet Ollie had grabbed to hold the stolen treasures had come open and settled over the tangled riders. The sheet covered Bones so that only his feet stuck out. He lay on a bike and Percy had landed on top of him. From under the sheet, Bones could see that Patty had ended up sitting on the back of Ollie's head. The otter seemed to be knocked out cold.

Before anyone had the strength to move, Joey, the gardener, hopped into the scene. "What crazy thing's happened down under? Miss Patty, I see your head and the otter's paws. Then at the back I see Percy's tail and Bones Malone's feet. Quite a sight it is, like some sort of giant beast. But no worries, I'll have you out of this mess in no time."

Joey snatched off the sheet, untangled the riders from each other and the bikes, and he tied up Ollie with the sheet.

When Ollie woke up, he groaned in pain. "Oh Mama, this is just toodly too bad. But you wanted me to go to Hollywood, and I guess I am seeing stars . . ."

As Ollie Ollie Otterson conked out once again, Percy turned to Bones. "I don't know what it is, Mr. Malone, but I feel as fit as a fiddle while Rome burns. I do believe California is good for my health, Bonesy. I can't wait to read about this in the newspaper tomorrow."

Bones rubbed his head. "Don't forget, Perce. You can't read everything you believe."

With that, Percy laughed, put out the crook of his arm for Patty Pickford, and the two of them strolled as best they could toward the house.

Bones thought they made a rather dashing couple.

THE END

"Such a waste of time," said Len.

"Wait a minute." Bennu's eyes had that fuzzy look of interior concentration. "Two things stand out to me. The first is Ollie's odd comment, 'Forgive me, boys. For your own good, forgive me.' It just doesn't fit. It seems out of character for Ollie."

Len looked away. "Spare us the literary analysis, Professor."

"And then the last scene. I'm struck by Joey's comment that the bike accident ended up looking like a giant beast. Anyone else see something there?"

"Oh, this tea really hits the spot." Dear-Abby cleared her throat. "Your grandfather was a cad. I haven't told you much about him. He was a heel and a sneak and a no-good good-for-nothing. I know what I'm talking about. I was there."

Len put one hand alongside his face and pushed up so that his mouth and eyes appeared distorted. "Grandma, we're busy right now."

"Always busy. Oh, dear. No time for Abby stories. Oh, dear. The tea is so lovely. When I divorced my husband—the vileness of him—I took back my old name, my maiden-o. I left him all behind. I became a Griffin again. Abby Griffin, that name goes a-ways back. And I lived in a long, long house with three bedrooms and a septic tank."

Len ran his hand through his hair. "That's real nice, Grandma. We have work to do."

"Nice? The tea is nice. But not a-ways back. That's all darkness and blood, all sickness and the weeping of saints. I know you think I'm crazy. I know you do. Bebba knows. Bebba sees more than you think."

As the Misfits' mouths dropped open and they exchanged double takes, Dear-Abby put her tea on the coffee table, took one more bite of muffin, winked at the Misfits, and opened the front door. "Bebba knows. Abby knows. It's all the same. The truth loops on itself, and here we are to catch its tail. Grab on, children."

She opened the front door and walked outside. In disbelieving belief, Len jumped up and followed. He looked into the front yard and saw Bebba there, hunched over, her gray hair hanging limply to her shoulders, her dull eyes as blind as ever. Len couldn't exactly tell where she was. She walked with her stick along some cliffs. The sun shone brightly and he could smell the sea. Just as he put his left hand on the doorjamb to walk outside, Bennu pulled him back. "Ladies first."

Len didn't protest. He didn't have anything in him but wonder. No matter how many portals he saw, no matter how many entrances and exits he experienced, each time the glory showered over him. He wanted to bow and serve. As if from an everlasting spring, gratitude welled up in him.

With Bennu's hand still holding him back, Len watched Lizbeth and Angie walk into the front yard and onto Welken soil. Angie turned to beckon them in, then she and Lizbeth trotted to catch up to Bebba.

Len and Bennu looked at each other. Bennu motioned *"after you,"* so Len crossed the veil. When he did, he stepped down into someplace dark, lost his balance, and tumbled awkwardly onto a hard, gravelly floor. A rock poked his hips. As he shifted to move the rock, Bennu landed on top of him.

CHAPTER TWENTY-THREE

A SANCTUARY, STONE UPON STONE

Prosperity doth bewitch men, seeming clear;
But seas do laugh, show white, when rocks are near.

— JOHN WEBSTER, *THE WHITE DEVIL*

 "Bebba, wait up!" Together, Angie and Lizbeth ran toward the blind woman. Lizbeth glanced at Angie by her side and then down the way toward Bebba, this strange Welkener who was also, somehow, Angie's strange grandmother.

As usual, she had little time to try to fit this new piece into the puzzle of intersecting worlds. How could she? The puzzle kept moving and expanding. And she was clearly not the one putting the puzzle together. She was a piece in it. She couldn't get out of it, couldn't rise above it high enough to see the whole puzzle laid out on the table.

Hunched over on her cane, dirty hair hanging in her face, Bebba shuffled ahead with surprising swiftness. She seemed to know exactly where she was headed and she was in a hurry to get there.

Lizbeth looked around as she ran. "I don't know, Angie. I don't recognize this place. We're on some cliff. No trees, just rocks and dirt."

"And the ocean."

"Oh yeah, the ocean. I guess I missed that one small detail." Lizbeth gestured to her left, to the west, and nodded in acknowledgment of the great blue expanse and the unbroken horizon miles and miles away. "Well, we're not in Deedy Swamp."

"No." Angie sounded worried. "What's become of Jacob Canny Sea? I keep picturing the faces of the Cutters as they dove in after him. Faces full of fury and hatred, and mouths the shape of armies. I see troops of teeth biting and shredding, and tangled limbs and Cutters cutting."

"Angie—"

"Yeah, I know. I'm weird."

"No, I—"

Before Lizbeth could respond, Bebba pivoted abruptly and faced them just as they reached her. "One thing, children. Bebba wants you to remember one thing. The edge of the cliff is near. It comes toward us like a knife. Bebba knows how sharp it is, she knows it. She sees the slicin' truth of history, the stories of bangled death and heart-crushed fallin'. But this isn't what you need to know."

Bebba approached the edge with far less caution than Lizbeth thought safe. Would she walk straight off? Would she fulfill her own prophecy of bangled death? How would a blind woman know when to stop?

Lizbeth reached out to grab Bebba's left arm and saw that Angie lurched toward Bebba's right side. "Bebba?" Lizbeth spoke softly. "Was that really you in the hut? What did all of that mean—and why are we here?"

"Stand back!" Bebba threw up her arms, like a commander bringing her company to a halt. She walked right to the edge and stopped, Lizbeth and Angie a full step behind her. The ocean breeze caught Bebba's hair and held it aloft, then Bebba lowered her arms and ran her cane along the rim. She inched farther out until her toes hung over the edge. "Remember this, you chosen ones. Respect the silence." She paused long enough for Lizbeth to feel uncomfortable. "Yes, silence! The place below is hammered with glory. It is a churnin' holiness and a sacred tempest. Bebba says to hold it to the restless beast within. Listen for the crashin'—and be silent."

Lizbeth stared and did not think she needed the admonition. Trembling from the sheer drop-off, she saw the waves below and was speechless. In this noisy silence, her thoughts drifted from the hut to Piers. She felt weary as she held him in her mind, but she dwelt on him anyway. Then a wave crashed below. The water swept into a narrow cave and met the rocks and shore with violence, with white-foam force and swirling explosions. It seemed almost intentionally cruel. Chaotic and punishing, the waves gathered like reinforcements and dashed up the sides of the cliffs, an open and frightening assault.

"Point Refusal," said Bebba. "It's where we stand. I know what you are thinkin'. Bebba knows." She spit over the cliff and waited for the thick saliva to fall. "You wonder how a blind woman can lead you, how she can show the sighted where to go. I don't blame you. But we all look into the darkness, and some know the way out of it better than others."

Lizbeth could not bring herself to stand as close to the edge as Bebba. She felt foolish leaning back—and even cowardly as Angie stood at the edge too. In her ongoing quiet, she summoned her strength, her oxen strength. She wanted to become an ox, to gain the stability of standing on all fours. But this time all she could do was change her lower body into the animal. She teetered on her hoofs, inwardly cursed her inability to transform into her full Welken beastliness, and changed back into human form. She shuddered. From her place on the cliff, she dropped to her knees and shimmied closer. She lay down on her stomach and peered over the edge.

She saw the cove whole, the waves roiling in anarchy, the rocks that would be covered with water one second and drained of it the next.

Then she saw one distinctive part of it. Maybe this is what Bebba meant by leading them through the darkness. Maybe she wasn't referring to images of sailors tossed onto rocks. Maybe it was what stood on the largest rock in the cove—a stone structure, a kind of tiny outpost constructed on an island. Violent waves crashed through narrow openings on both sides. Lizbeth pointed to it, and Angie nodded.

How could it be there? thought Lizbeth. *Who could have made it? If one person could not survive for one minute in this water, how could this building, this miracle, rise stone upon stone?*

As Lizbeth pondered these mysteries, she held her silence tightly. She was overcome by the achievement of the sanctuary below.

Then her eyes widened. She kept thinking about Piers, about the line "find me in you." So Lizbeth entered her own soul. She kept looking at the sanctuary but didn't see it. She saw Chimney Cave, the first time she met Piers, and Ganderst Hall, the last time she'd seen him, when she'd had to say good-bye.

She saw herself petting Percy—and then, when no one could find him, going to the Bartholomews every morning to call his name. In her soul, she called Percy again, and this time he came. He looked tired and hungry. Lizbeth ran to him. She picked him up tenderly but struggled to lift him. Burdened by his weight, she took him upstairs. She pulled out an old doll's bed and laid him in it. He looked so human in the bed. She pulled the blanket up and put his paws on top.

Then, in her soul, she rose above him. She seemed to hover above the bed . . . and kept rising. She floated higher until she passed right through the roof. From above, she could see her house. But it wasn't her house. It was a building made of stone. It was the stone sanctuary below her.

A cold wind caught her and blew out her vision. She was no longer inside herself but standing on the barren cliff.

"Angie!" Lizbeth kept her eyes on the sanctuary. "Angie, Piers is in there! Look, the stone has copper and orange parts. I know he's there!"

Angie didn't respond, so Lizbeth turned toward her. Angie hadn't moved. She stood at the edge of the cliff, hands no longer outstretched but clasped to her chest. Her upper body—but not her head—was invisible. She did not appear to be held in place by wings, visible or not. She was weeping.

Then Lizbeth noticed. Bebba was gone.

Without speaking, without trying to convince Angie about the next step, without breaking the silence, Lizbeth scootched herself up to her knees and stood. She brushed off the rusty dust and walked along the rim toward the back of the cove, closer to the sanctuary. She heard Angie's soft footsteps behind her.

All the while she watched the pounding waves and inhospitable rocks. Sometimes the water shot fifty feet into the air and the mist rose higher.

"Angie, I found Piers inside me, just like you said."

"Really?"

"And I felt his weariness too."

"Good to be an ox sometimes, eh?"

"Yeah, but I can't make myself an ox. I thought I might be able to this time—but just my lower body changes."

"Sorry."

When Lizbeth pointed to a path, Angie began the trek down. In the open, on the narrow, rocky trail, Lizbeth felt exposed. She wished for a branch or two to grab along the way.

Thoughts of Piers kept her courage focused. Each step was one step closer to Piers. At least she hoped so.

About halfway down, with mist gathering on their faces, a large boulder on their left provided a screen between them and the cove. As they sat to rest for several minutes, Lizbeth rubbed her calves. The crashing of the waves was deafening at times, then it would retreat for a few seconds.

Lizbeth rose and took two steps into the open on the path, then hurriedly crouched back behind the rock. She motioned toward the ridge across the way. A line of soldiers marched over the crest and started down a path into the cove. "Angie, soldiers! What if they are coming to get Piers? Maybe this isn't a sanctuary. Maybe it's a prison."

"There's something familiar about the uniforms. I can't figure it out. Maybe it's just from pictures in our history books."

"But what are we going to do? We can't fight a whole army. You can't become totally invisible, and I just become part ox."

"Look, there's Prester John!"

"You're kidding. Wait. I see him too. Let's go!"

From the back of the line of about twenty soldiers, passing them deftly, came the prince of the Prester Highlands, the hero of most of his own stories, the irrepressible and lovable Prester John. He bounded down until he was at the front.

Lizbeth and Angie jumped out and scrambled down the path. More than once, Lizbeth skidded on the gravel, grabbed at the face of the cliff, and wished she'd worked harder at skateboarding. "This path is so frustrating." Lizbeth stumbled to one knee, then steadied herself. "We have to watch every step."

Once on the beach—a slim strip of pebbly sand, tide pools, and barnacled rocks—Lizbeth and Angie stopped to catch their breath.

Angie picked up a slimy rock. "I wish Prester John could hear us over the waves."

"Hey, wait a minute, Ang. Look, some soldiers are putting on chains."

"More than that. They're locking shackles around their waists. I don't like the look of it."

"Weird. It's got to be OK. It's Prester John, but let's hurry up and get over there."

They scrambled over rocks and dodged surging water for about twenty-five yards.

"Wait." Angie grabbed Lizbeth's sleeve.

"Whoa. You just about pulled me in."

"The waist shackles have rings on them—and they're sliding a heavy rope through the rings."

"Angie, I'm getting this terrible feeling, like these slaves are going to be forced into the water to drown."

"I know. But then I keep thinking, it's loyal, friendly Prester John who's in charge. He's the officer, right? He couldn't be involved in anything bad, could he?"

The two Misfits moved as quickly as they could over the slick rocks. As Lizbeth slipped on some algae, one foot fell into a tide pool just as she got hit by the last gasp of an incoming wave. She kept her balance, jumped onto a larger, taller boulder, and then over to another section of passable shore.

Angie, dry and stern-faced, awaited her. "Look, Prester John has the rope in his hands. He's going up the hill. What's he doing?"

Holding the end of the rope like a football, the lanky Prester John sprinted full speed toward the water. Just as the great force of a wave receded, he leaped into the water in full stride, bounding across it in four, long, even steps.

Wow, thought Lizbeth. *Prester John walked on water!*

But the soldiers did not celebrate. Looking worried, Prester John lugged the heavy rope across the water. He tugged with all his might, hoisted the rope over his shoulder, and pushed it into an iron ring secured to the stone sanctuary. Then a wave hit the rope in the water.

Prester John braced his boots against the stone wall and held the end of the rope. On the shore, a line of soldiers tugged on the other end. When the wave drew back, Prester John secured the rope on the ring and the soldiers tied the rope off on a boulder.

Lizbeth and Angie watched the most amazing thing. The four soldiers who were chained together with the rope threaded through the rings on their waist-shackles waited for one more wave to come and go. Then they shimmied into the water. Awkwardly they hopped in unison until each one stood on a flat rock just below the surface of the water, the same flat rocks that had given Prester John the appearance of walking on water.

The next wave crashed into the backs of the soldiers, swirling against and around them. As the water receded, the soldiers remained steadfast on the rocks, and the soldiers on land began lifting supplies across, hand to hand, until they reached Prester John.

After all the supplies had been passed, Prester John picked one up and carried it to the sanctuary. Before he got there, the door opened and out came Ellen Basala, his reliable aide. She seemed worried.

Lizbeth ran up to and through the soldiers on the shore. "Prester John! Ellen!"

Angie cupped her hands. "We're here!"

As soldiers grabbed them and pulled them back, Prester John looked over. He smiled, gestured for the soldiers to release them, and waved for them to come over. The next thing Lizbeth knew, she was the bucket in the bucket brigade, getting passed from one soldier to another over the water. Just as she was released from the last soldier, a wave hit. The water spun her like a wing nut, but she lurched through the water and up onto the rock island. She didn't see Prester John or Ellen. When that wave slipped back, the soldiers passed Angie over, and Lizbeth was there to grab her.

After pressing water off their clothes, Angie and Lizbeth walked up to the stone structure. Prester John stepped through the open door of the sanctuary. "By the Great Anuba of the Prester Highlands—may his name ever receive glory—what greets my eyes? Lizbeth and Angie!"

"Oh, Prester John!" Angie squeezed the tall, angular Highlander. Rather formally, he patted her back.

Then Lizbeth hugged him. "Prester John, we are so glad to see you. I mean, here we are in Welken, who knows where, and we bump into you." She fluffed out her shirt, which stuck to her skin. "Funny, you don't act surprised."

"Oh, dear one, in Welken what you call surprise is our daily fare." He motioned for them to walk in. "Why should one be surprised at goodness or shocked by the lovely guidance that fills our days? It reminds me of the many times I myself have been the brave rescuer who foiled the executioner in the rising of his ax. Why, not long ago, I—"

"Pardon me, your most eminent of princes." The voice came from deeper inside the sanctuary. Ellen Basala revealed herself, her face solemn and rock-solid, her white hair rolled up on each side like sheep's horns. "We must keep pace. The soldiers are being battered as you tell stories."

Prester John sighed. "Yes, I suppose you are right, but you do have such a knack for spoiling moments when hearts are open to learning."

Ellen bowed to Prester John and offered Lizbeth and Angie a firm handclasp each. The four of them walked down a short hall and into a room.

The interior of the sanctuary could not have been more different from the exterior. On the outside, all was threatening chaos and plain stone blocks. On the inside, peace and a kind of extravagant simplicity. Candles added to the dim light allowed in by the small windows. The painted walls shone in brilliant hues of yellow and gold, even orange. To Lizbeth, it resembled a sunrise. Then the colors shifted slightly, and she saw that it was indeed a sunrise—one that came over and over again. A gradually changing, softly illuminating light. A dawn that rose, receded, then rose again.

Angie put her ear to the wall. "Listen. The walls are singing."

Lizbeth heard a delicate tone, a humming like a sweet Gregorian chant.

Ellen grabbed Lizbeth's arm. "This is not a tour. Don't you know why you're here?"

Then Lizbeth remembered. Of course she knew. Where was he? How was he? Was he dying? Why didn't his weariness wash over her?

In the deepest room in the sanctuary, in the back, in a bed with its head against the wall that took the force of wave after wave, in a quiet so complete that not one crash or splash could be heard, in the colors of shifting dawn, flickering now and again in the shining of the candles, in this house of healing calm, lay Piers. His eyes closed, his hands folded on his chest, he looked dead, resting peacefully in this stone tomb.

Ellen left the room. As Prester John stood by the entrance, whispering about the Great Anuba's wisdom and the loving mind of Soliton, Lizbeth stepped forward, deeply feeling Piers's pain. Angie, tears flowing generously, took the other side of the bed. Both knelt.

Piers's ginger red hair had been combed out over the pillow. Though blankets covered his chest, his green tunic could be seen around his shoulders and the strap of his satchel was also exposed. His knee-high boots stood against the wall.

Lizbeth didn't know what to do. Calling his name seemed silly, shaking him even worse. Instinctively she slipped her hand under Piers's hand. Angie did the same, and they gently pulled his hands apart. Lizbeth felt warmth in Piers's hand. She squeezed tenderly. She prayed. She did not know whom to pray to—to Welken's God or her own, or if they were the same. Then her tears came too. They dripped on the bedspread, and she brushed them into the fabric with her other hand.

Lizbeth held on as long as she dared. At first she thought that maybe life would go out of her and Angie, and into Piers, but nothing seemed to happen. Her eyes met Angie's, and they exchanged glances. Moving Piers's hand back to his chest, Lizbeth and Angie started to pull their hands away.

Then Piers squeezed. He gently pressed his hands into theirs. Angie closed her eyes. Lizbeth leaned in.

Weakly, Piers pulled his hands across themselves, drawing Angie and Lizbeth onto the bed. He sat up. His eyes opened. They seemed fully alive. "The dawn," he said. "I want to see it." He paused and licked his lips. "Why are you holding me back?"

CHAPTER TWENTY-FOUR

FIGHTING FOR THE BATTLE

Be a good animal, true to your animal instincts.
—D. H. LAWRENCE, *THE WHITE PEACOCK*

"Hey, watch where you're going!" Len pushed Bennu off him.

Bennu coughed. "Kinda hard to do in the dark."

Len found the rock poking into his hip and moved it aside. "Yeah, and the dust. I'm getting tired of all this tumbling-into-Welken business. Why can't we step over a picture frame once in a while? I mean, it's not that I'm ungrateful. I—"

"Shush. We need to find Sutton and Gareth."

As Len's eyes adjusted to the darkness, he could see some light over to his left. He guessed by the rock floor that he and Bennu were back on Justice Island, back into the caves and corridors and prophetic frescoes, and back into the threat of wandering tremlings.

"I'd feel better about all this," Len whispered, "if I had some idea what we were supposed to be doing—besides presenting ourselves as fresh meat for the ugliest beasts ever."

Bennu approached a slender opening in the wall. "I feel the same way. All we know is, 'The story's told by day and night. The sun is cold, the wind is white.' Not sure how that helps us here. It's hot, and there's no wind."

"Lizbeth and Angie got to walk off with Bebba. I'll bet she— Grandma—is telling them all sorts of things. What gets told to us?"

"Well, we already know we need to find Sutton and Gareth." Bennu turned sideways and slipped through the opening.

"Yeah, I suppose. It's like all we're doing is trying to survive. I guess that's worth something."

Len followed Bennu through the hole in the wall and instantly forgot his complaints, because the place they'd entered needed his full attention. First, Len noticed light coming in from several windows on a wall a full story below them. The windows faced into the center of Justice Island, but Len couldn't see the view from his position. Then Len saw Bennu ahead of him, walking cautiously across a stone bridge. In fact, the only place to walk was on this bridge. It stretched the full length of the room and both sides fell off into an open area about ten feet below them. The only "railing" on the bridge was a three-inch lip that ran along both sides.

Bennu looked back at Len and put a finger to his lips. Len heard no strange sounds, but he tiptoed as quietly as possible. At the end of the bridge, a solid rock-face would have greeted the two Misfits, but a big hole appeared to have been punched out from the other side. Bennu crouched down to examine the broken rocks.

He picked one up, turned it over, and held one side up to the light. "Look at this. Paint. On this one, maybe somebody's arm. On this one something black."

"Here's a pretty big piece." Len brushed the dust off the painted side. "Looks like a bunch of people wearing hoods. Hey, I know—"

"Wait a minute." Bennu stuck his head and shoulders through the hole. His voice came back muffled. "Ust wad a thud."

"What?"

Bennu scooted back onto the bridge. "Just what I thought. This, my friend, is the back of the painted room we were in."

"Well, that's what I was going to say."

"Yeah, right. But go ahead, see for yourself."

Len tried to sneer and look hopeful at the same time. Then he sighed and pulled himself in. With the same fluid motion, he slipped back out. "Just as *I* thought. OK, what now? You and I both know we didn't break through a rock wall. We came through doors that Angie and Lizbeth opened. And if *we* didn't make this hole, then Sutton and Gareth did, or the tremlings did—or both. And where are they, anyway?"

Bennu started assembling the broken pieces of the wall, as if putting the fresco back together would yield some clue.

Len sat with his legs toward the bridge and his back resting against the wall. "You don't need to do that. I remember every detail, even the parts that moved."

Bennu shot a glance at him and worked faster. "Here's another mystery."

"Oh good, I was about to run out."

"Why would this bridge lead to the back of the painted room? Before the back was busted out, the bridge would have led straight into a dead end."

Len held up a finger to his mouth. He heard a scuffling from somewhere. It was getting closer.

As soon as Len could discern that the sound came from the floor below, and from the side opposite to where they now sat, he motioned for Bennu to follow him into the painted room. From there they could see part of what took place below.

From the other side, underneath the bridge, a soldier walked in. Len knew the uniform. It belonged to the guards at the Wasan Sagad, the tower in the Wasteland, where the heat had bored down and shown him who he was. Len wondered what the soldier could be doing here on Justice Island. Might he be a deserter? Then a large, broad-shouldered man lowered his head so as not to hit the top of the doorway. It was Sutton Hoo.

Bennu hit Len on the arm. "They got him," he whispered.

A shorter person, in a finely trimmed black vest and a torn shirt with blousy arms, followed. It was Gareth. A tremling followed. Sutton and Gareth had their hands tied behind their backs.

No one else came in.

Len had a sinking feeling that he and Bennu would need to fight. His stomach turned over.

The soldier unslung his water pouch. "We'll rest here for a minute. I'm thirsty." He took a long swallow, held it up to Sutton and Gareth, taunted them with it, then put it back over his shoulder. He walked over to the low windows that overlooked the middle of Justice Island. "Quite a sight, eh? Aw, why am I talking to you? I got two enemies and one idiot." He sat down with his back to the wall near the window. Every now and then he glanced out the window. "You won't try anything now, will you?" He laughed at his prisoners.

Nope, Len thought, *we won't try anything. We won't try standing here or breathing. We won't try a thing.*

Then he got an idea. He grabbed a rock from the pile and whispered instructions to Bennu. They waited.

The soldier grabbed his water and took another sip. He looked one more time out the window before closing his eyes.

Careful not to make a sound, Len and Bennu stepped out of the painted room and onto the bridge. Sutton tugged on a thin rope connecting his hands to Gareth's waist. The tremling stood just below the bridge, a club in his hand. He snorted.

Len and Bennu crouched low on the bridge, moving in slow motion. Len peeked up to see Sutton turn back toward Gareth, and that's when the Kells Villager noticed Len. Sutton began to hum softly.

Thanks, big guy. Smart of you to cover our movement with sound.

Len was right above the tremling, who was looking away toward Sutton. Len lay down on the edge of the bridge, and Bennu grabbed his ankles. Then Len thrust himself over the edge. As Bennu grabbed Len's ankles, Len nodded to Bennu and pulled himself up to the edge of the bridge at the same time Bennu thrust Len's legs over.

On his way down, his nervous stomach churning, Len smashed the rock on the tremling's head. The tremling yelled out and fell into Gareth, who yelled and fell into Sutton, who stumbled onto the soldier.

Bennu grunted out, "I can't hold on! What now?"

"Swing me over so I can fall on the tremling. Hurry!"

Groaning, the soldier pushed Sutton off and grabbed his spear. Then Len dropped hard onto the tremling, tucking his head in and rolling onto his right side. The soldier stepped aside and jabbed his spear repeatedly at Len.

Len dodged once and got up to his knees. He scrambled and dodged again and, panting, jumped into a crouch. The soldier poked the spear again and tore Len's shirt. When the soldier pulled the spear back, its edge sliced into Len's side.

Len screamed. The cut wasn't deep, but the pain shocked him. He reared back and roared, his head becoming a lion's head as he bared his fangs and growled.

Wide-eyed, the soldier took one step back. Len looked over and saw Bennu digging frantically through his pockets. Bennu's falcon wings flapped from his back, but the rest of him was unchanged. Bennu held up his knife.

With all the intensity he could muster, Len roared again. He tried to think what to do. He couldn't pounce or use his claws, because he had none. He had to get close, close enough to use his teeth.

The panicked soldier swung the spear recklessly left and right. It swooshed through the air as he backed up toward Sutton and Gareth. In between those two, Bennu sawed madly with his knife. He cut at the rope that bound Sutton to Gareth. It gave way.

Breathing hard, the soldier looked around. His head darted back and forth as if he were calculating the odds. Wildly he pushed his spear at Bennu, forcing him up against the open window. Sutton rolled over toward him, holding up his tied hands.

Then the tremling moved. Shaking off the blow, he staggered to his feet, rubbed his head, and pierced Len's heart with an angry roar. Len saw blood on the tremling's fingers and roared back. He felt exhilarated. He bared his fangs. Ferociously, Len charged toward him. The tremling reached for his club and Len leaped. He bit into the tremling's arm with the full strength of his lion's jaw. He set his teeth deep into the tremling's flesh. The beast screamed, but Len held on. He punched at the tremling's stomach. He shook the monster's arm and tried to sink his meat-shredding canines deeper. He dug in. He held on. He tasted blood. Screaming, the tremling slugged repeatedly at Len with his free hand. One roundhouse blow caught Len in his side, where the spear tip had snagged him.

Len let go. As he rolled over and winced in pain, the tremling fingered the gash in his own left arm. His oversized mouth grimaced and let out a deep moan. Then he faced Len with visible anger and resolve. Snarling, he took one giant step toward Len. Len backed up. Dust rose from his shuffling feet. Len put all his concentration and energy into his hands, hoping to will them into lion's paws and claws.

Nothing happened.

Bleeding from his head and arm, the tremling stepped again toward Len. He readied himself to charge. Saliva stretched across his gaping mouth. The tremling licked his teeth and gave a deep, gorillalike roar.

Len felt smaller and smaller. He roared back but knew he'd lost the advantage of surprise. The tremling slowly lifted his club. When it was waist high, Len saw something gleaming over the tremling's right shoulder. It was Bennu's pocketknife. Before Len could move, Bennu jumped up from behind the tremling and plunged the knife into the tremling's shoulder.

The tremling reacted by smashing back at Bennu with his fist. With the knife sticking out of his shoulder, the beast huffed out a growling heave with every breath. He tried to reach up for the knife with his left arm, but it was too damaged from Len's shredding bite.

All Len could think was, *Now. Now is the time. Go.*

He flew at the tremling, rammed him with his lion's head, and knocked him down. As the tremling fell over Bennu, Len completed the tackle with both hands around the tremling's chest. Sickened by the rank fur, Len raised himself off the tremling's body. He opened his mouth for the next attack. He could sense the size of his own lion's teeth and how they longed for something to tear into. He opened his mouth wider. Then he saw the knife in the tremling's shoulder. He reached for it and pulled it out. As he gripped it for a stabbing thrust, his eyes caught Bennu's for a split second.

A hundred thoughts debated in that one glance. Bennu looked worried and eager at the same time—worried at Len's savage fierceness, yet eager for Len to do the job. Len felt a flash of doubt and the weight of his whole history of unrestrained fury. He held the knife high. He knew he could stab the beast to death, but he hesitated. He wanted to thrust the knife downward and, at the same time, wanted to spare the tremling's life. For a second, he saw the tremling as a dumb animal just acting on instinct and fear, an animal not to be blamed. The next second, he saw the beast as a threatening predator. When he moved the knife up, he saw the tremling's stunned face and something else . . . the face of Odin. That sick grin, that contemptuous sneer, those eyes without a conscience.

Len gripped the knife tighter. He knew he could kill. And so he made his decision. He plunged the knife into the tremling's chest. Blood came out onto his hands. The tremling belched out one last gasp and crumpled onto the rock floor. Len stared at his bloody hands. He wanted to clean them. He wanted to wash his hands of everything. His lion's head became normal again.

For a little while, only panting, then hard, measured breathing could be heard. Bennu pulled his leg out from under the tremling's body. Len moved off the beast's chest. With a slow, deliberate lean of his head, Len stared glassy-eyed at the death he'd caused. He hadn't killed Odin. He hadn't killed his fears. He had merely killed one tremling. One bumbling, semi-innocent beast. He snapped his gaze away from the tremling and scanned the room. Gareth and the soldier were gone.

Sutton broke the silence. He asked Bennu to finish cutting his bindings. Len wiped the blade on his shirt—it was already bloody from his own wound—then handed the knife to Bennu. Soon Sutton's hands were free.

Len, Bennu, and Sutton sat on the floor and leaned against the wall.

Len started to shake. He pulled his knees to his chest. He tried to hold his struggle inside, to squeeze the shaking into calm. Once again, he doubted. "Did I do the right thing?" He lowered his head. "Suddenly I feel awful."

Sutton moved over next to Len and put his arm around him. "You did a right-needed thing, lad. Sometimes the good's not much better than the bad."

Len kept seeing Odin's face. He suppressed that image, and another took its place. "For some reason, all I can do is think about Grandpa Bartholomew." Len scrubbed at the bloodstains on his hands. "He told the story of being on a ship in World War II, in the Pacific. Grandpa was a navigator, and he'd never shot at anyone. Then a kamikaze dive-bombed them in one of those suicide missions. Grandpa was next to the artillery gun, so he grabbed it and fired away. The kamikaze kept coming and coming. Grandpa said that he finally downed the plane, but not before he saw the face of the pilot. That night he couldn't sleep, because he knew he had killed a man."

Len added the weight of his grandfather's actions to his own. "But here's the thing—I can't believe I'm going to say this—I . . . I wanted to do it. I tasted that tremling's flesh and . . . I wanted more." He paused and hung his head. "What's the matter with me?" Yet even as he held his face with his bloodstained hands, he knew he hadn't told the whole truth.

Sutton gripped him in his thick arms. "Nothin's the matter, good Len. The life I know back in Kells Village, and the life we all knew in Welken, before Morphane and Terz, well, that life—the freedom and beauty and neighborliness—it's all worth protectin', doon't you know?"

"I suppose," said Len. "But I thought I was getting better. I thought we would all just keep getting better and better. Now I've killed two tremlings. And the second was worse than the first. My conscience seems to be drifting away."

Bennu stood up. "If that were the case, then why are we talking like this?"

Len nodded and sighed. When he wiped his tears, some blood from his hands streaked his face.

Sutton patted Len's shoulder. "You're gettin' better, Len. I can see it all 'round the outside and inside of you. It's just that when you're climbin' uphill, it's not all one straight line up, doon't ya know. Sometimes the path takes us down as we're on our way up."

"And besides," continued Bennu. "You *are* a lion. That's got to affect you."

Len nodded. "I guess a lion has some beast in him."

Sutton helped Len up. "We all do, lad, we all do. And we must remember."

"Remember what?"

"We're in Welken. And everything that's got a sea-mist-bit-of-true-life is bein' remade. We're startin' to sing, and some day we'll lift our voices long and loud. We are gettin' to be of Welken. It takes time. That's why we say 'in Welken' and we answer—"

Len and Bennu hesitated.

"And we answer," repeated Sutton.

Together, with humble certainty, Len and Bennu said, "Of Welken."

When the echo of their voices faded, other sounds caught their attention. They heard shouts and the pounding of hard things on the ground. They heard growling and fighting and shuffling. The noise came from the windows.

Sutton, Len, and Bennu ran to look out. They saw the whole interior of Justice Island, like a giant ruined coliseum, with a valley floor and walls rising all around. The shouting echoed off the walls. It rose in intensity, louder and louder.

In the valley stood dozens, maybe hundreds, of tremlings, stamping their feet and pounding their staffs. Soldiers from the Wasan Sagad, Len guessed, surrounded the tremlings, threatening them and beating them. Most looked north, toward the one opening in the walls enclosing the valley. The opening led into the channel that flowed to Mercy Bay. The army raised their weapons toward Mercy Bay, toward Primus Hook. They demanded battle. They roared in readiness. They pounded their staffs, thrust them into the air, and yelled.

Over and over on the valley floor, the noise grew louder. It reverberated off the walls and into the hearts of the three at the window. Then the pounding changed. It became unified. As one, the tremlings and the soldiers pounded and yelled. They pounded again and yelled again and again. Each time they yelled the same word: "Fatagar!"

CHAPTER TWENTY-FIVE
FINDING THE WEARINESS

What language shall I borrow to thank thee, dearest friend . . . ?

— "O SACRED HEAD, NOW WOUNDED," LATIN, TWELFTH CENTURY

"Why are you holding me back?"

Lizbeth had longed for Piers's first words, for his tender wisdom and warm assurance. But what was this? How could she and Angie be holding Piers back? They hadn't even known where he was. Lizbeth worried she'd missed something important, some obvious request or clue.

Her brow fierce with doubt, Lizbeth kept her hand in Piers's hand. She wondered what Angie was thinking. Angie seemed troubled too, but in a different way. She looked "not there." She was drifting. Or she was already gone, transported.

"Angie," whispered Lizbeth strongly, "Angie, come back." She felt foolish saying it.

Piers released his grip slightly but held on.

Lizbeth felt something sharp in her hand. She looked from Angie back to Piers and saw something she had not seen for a month, something she had watched for every day, something she'd never expected to see here, now. She pulled back but dared not let go entirely. She was frightened, for here was Percy, the house cat. She couldn't believe it. There he was in the bed, the ginger cat with the warm green eyes, his paws in Lizbeth's and Angie's hands, his claws extended and scratching her skin. Lizbeth swallowed hard. She had prayed that Percy would come back. Was this the answer? She closed her eyes and rolled her eyeballs in the darkness. She wondered if she might faint. Then she forced her eyes open wide, bravely facing reality, ready to accept what she saw.

Percy was still there. Lizbeth grimaced. She wanted Percy, but she wanted Piers more. Then this Percy opened his mouth. He didn't meow. He said, "We are all here, in our own way, to make the Welken ring."

Lizbeth knew these words so well. She had said them to herself a hundred times since Piers had spoken them a month ago in Ganderst Hall. Then Lizbeth looked at Angie. She still seemed to be floating . . . to be "not there." Lizbeth wondered if maybe she was feeding Piers these lines. Maybe her life animated Piers or Percy. Lizbeth wanted to call out to her again, but she knew it was hopeless.

Piers, Percy, said, "Bones of my Bonesy."

Lizbeth flushed from head to toe. No, it couldn't be. It can *not* be. *He* can *not* BE.

Lizbeth turned again to the head of the bed. There he was, in the bed, Percival P. Perkins, the Detective Cat, his green vest, his pince-nez, his hat sitting like a hamburger on his head.

Lizbeth started to cry, partly out of fear, partly out of wonder. Awestruck, she froze. Too much strangeness. Too much goodness. Too much.

Then the cycle started over, back again to Skinner. The detective spoke, and in his speaking became Piers. "Sometimes I think Welken's been here all along, but we just didn't see it."

Wait, thought Lizbeth, *I said that. Piers didn't. And he wasn't there anyway and—*

Then she felt his claws again.

Percy the cat said, "It's a room full of bones."

Yes, me again, in Welken, in Deedy Swamp. I said that when trying to rescue Mook with Angie. How can he know this? Does he know everything?

Lizbeth stopped looking at the bed. The shifting bodies disturbed her even more than the shifting voice. She closed her eyes like Angie. Maybe concentrating on the words mattered more anyway.

Piers said, "I am reformed."

Who is reformed? Yes, Ollie said he was. So what? What's that to do with a room of bones? Yes, Bones Malone, a room of bones. Everything's spinning, colliding. I can't take it all in.

"You are the weariness of Piers, the lostness of Bors."

Yes, I know. Angie told me that. It made me depressed. Others get your joy, Piers. I get your weariness. I'm not sure I know what it means. I guess that's OK. I am here. I mean, here we are, Angie and me. The others don't get you at all. At least I see your weariness. I feel bad for you, but that can't be the point of all this. Wait. The shard. Is that your weariness? Is the lostness of the boy in my nightmare also the lostness of Bors?

"There's someone you need to forgive."

It's all coming too fast. Didn't Angie already cover this? Didn't I admit I hadn't forgiven Alabaster Singing? What more do you want from me?

Lizbeth heard the crunching of something, maybe leaves underfoot. She didn't know if she was dreaming or having a vision. The leaves crunched so loud! She opened her eyes and saw Angie, eyes open, noticing the crunching too, acting like she was trying to avoid stepping on the leaves, as if she wanted not to add to the noise. But they weren't in the bed next to Piers. They were in a place completely dark, yet Angie's body could be seen as if she were outside during the day. Lizbeth could see her own body too.

Another voice came out of the dark. "My flesh rotted till it became a heap of bones. Ha!"

Lizbeth shook with confusion and fear. "Angie, that's your grandma, Dear-Abby. Is she here? Bebba, where are you? How is your flesh rotting? What should we do?"

Angie motioned for Lizbeth to walk in deeper, to go toward the voice. Lizbeth followed. Where were they going? She couldn't tell. No entrance or exit could be seen.

Dear-Abby's voice could again be heard. "One thought my bones were hiding in an orange closet, and the other figured a nemesis had them under lock and key."

Lizbeth thought she must be dreaming. Things were just too weird. All these lines coming back to her. But she kept talking to Angie anyway. "Angie!"

Angie turned back toward her. "Shh." Then she shrugged. "Actually, wait a minute. I don't know why we need to be quiet. Do you know where we are?"

Lizbeth played along with her dream. "No, I was hoping you did."

"To me it's not a dark place like it looks. It feels warm and sunset-y. With some green too, and—"

Then another voice came. "No broken bones."

"Angie, you told my mom that when she was drunk and fell down the steps at your house. What are we to make of it? All these bones!"

"Lizbeth, come here."

Lizbeth looked ahead. Angie was motioning for her to catch up, as though she had reached a precipice with a grand view.

"Lizbeth, I am here."

This time, the voice wasn't Angie's. It was deep, a man's voice, a voice she thought she'd heard before but couldn't place.

Lizbeth stepped forward into the blackness, into this cave or hole or room where bodies could be seen without any source of light.

Angie held out her hand and pulled Lizbeth to her side. She pointed.

There, barely illuminated in the darkness, a ghostlike figure swirled into a smoky shape that seemed to be trying to form itself into a body but couldn't quite hold it. He had a long face and sad eyes.

"Remember me?" he said.

Lizbeth held on to Angie. "Yes. Yes, I do. I was at the Nez River. I'd seen Morphane. I remembered what Piers said, so I thought about him. I pictured him. I tried to enter into all I knew about him. Suddenly I was someplace else. Now I remember. I came here. I was here once before." Lizbeth swallowed. "Angie, we are inside Piers. We are walking in him, in his mind. And we are looking at the soul of Bors."

At this pronouncement, the wispy self of Bors seemed to bow. He turned his head as he did so, a respectful, elegant gesture, even in this moment, even in his lostness.

"That's it," said Lizbeth. "Angie, *now* I see how I am the lostness of Bors. I had to become a part of Piers to enter so deeply into Bors's lostness that I could sense more about him."

"Now you know what?"

"Now I know where Bors is, at least I think so."

Looking both serene and tired, Bors managed a translucent, wounded smile. He nodded in a smoky expression of gratitude. Then he added, "Respect the silence." After Bors repeated Bebba's phrase, he gestured to his right, near Lizbeth, then drifted away.

"Lizbeth, I think Bors wants you to find something."

"I think you're right, but it's so dark."

"Feel around for it. Let's get on our hands and knees where he pointed."

Lizbeth looked at Angie's bright, illuminated body. She noticed that part of Angie's upper torso was invisible. It flickered back and forth into view. And she saw that her own bottom half was oxen, her legs clumsily stretched out on the imperceptible floor.

Angie patted the blackness here and there. "Nothing. Nothing. Wait, I think I found something. Yes, this may be it."

"What's it like?"

"Here, feel it. I think it has straps."

"Really? Two or four?"

"Just two. I think they are for you."

"It seems too bizarre. I can't see it, but I guess I can put it on."

Lizbeth slipped her arms into the straps. She cinched them up and felt a weight on her shoulders, a difficult but bearable weight. "I know I need to carry this. I know what this is. It's the weariness of Piers."

As soon as she uttered this line, the darkness flashed into the sunrise hues of the room in the stone sanctuary. Piers sat up in the bed, looking relieved and grateful. When he opened his eyes, he seemed to study Angie, then Lizbeth. He seemed to be respecting the silence.

Finally, he spoke. "Oh, Lizbeth, you are a good friend. The longer I lived with Bors deep within me—since I couldn't find his body to reunite him with his soul—the heavier the task became. I grew too weak to move. And now you've spoken deep to deep and taken with you part of what only I have been carrying."

Lizbeth looked at Angie. She knew she bore no literal satchel or daypack or suitcase. But she carried a weight nonetheless. She had become Piers's weariness.

"Come, good friends. Now I can rise and walk. I can finish what I must do."

CHAPTER TWENTY-SIX
LOSING ONE'S BALANCE

But granted that we have all to keep a balance,
the real interest comes in with the question
of how that balance can be kept.

—G. K. CHESTERTON, *ORTHODOXY*

*Fatagar!* The name slimed into Len's psyche and gave it a squeeze. It slithered down into his stomach and made him sick. Fatagar—the toady despot of the Wasan Sagad, the failed soldier from the Prester Highlands who had taken Len's gift of fire and burned his way to Granite Flats. Len wanted to spit out the ugly fatness of him, his greasy skin, his knobby head, the rotten stink of his flesh.

Len shrank back from the window. He looked away from Fatagar's army of soldiers and enslaved tremlings and at the dead tremling over which he'd just agonized. In light of the army pounding their weapons, this one tremling's death seemed suddenly inconsequential. How could the Allies ever have won the war if they'd grieved over every dead Nazi? Yet something in Len told him that to dispense with remorse would be to throw off his humanity. How to fight for peace? How to fight for the peacemaker in himself as he fought to win, even to kill? The battle within mirrored the battle without. Good and evil. The virtuous and the beastly. The humane and the merely human.

Instead of inspiring courage, the whole scene saddened Len. He had not asked to be so close to death, to be standing over it in the form of a tremling or standing before it as it raged in the form of an army. His sadness turned to resolve as he saw a tear rise to the brim of Bennu's eyelid. It welled up higher and flowed over that cup. It edged down slowly to the cusp of his cheek, hesitated, then pushed over the rise. "Bennu, what's got into you?"

"I see these legs stamping for destruction, and these mouths shouting for death." Bennu wiped his face.

"Look, you don't have to turn everything into a poem." Len walked up to the doorway and cautiously turned into it. "We aren't in a dream. We're in a place where we can get hurt. Our friends can get hurt. The good thing is, we can try to do something about it."

Bennu sniffed and wiped his nose. "OK. I know we can't sit here—but I can't help how I feel."

"Gareth's down there somewhere. Feel that! 'I can't help how I feel.' How much garbage has been justified by that line?" Even as he said this, Len wasn't sure why he was so angry. He believed what he said: that they needed to act and not wallow in sorrow. But he also knew that his own tears were not far from the surface. He rubbed his sore side.

"Lads, lads." Sutton came between Len and Bennu. "The times are grave enough. Let's keep steadfast. We can't fight all these tremlings, to be sure, but a poem's not likely to rescue Gareth either. We're on the same side."

Len glanced up at Sutton, then over at Bennu. After a friendly slug to Bennu's shoulder, the argument vanished.

Soon the threesome left the room. They hid and skulked and walked their way through several empty passageways and other rooms. One minute, the whole place appeared to be a faded coliseum, much older than the Roman version, heaped over with mineral deposits and bird droppings, as if the giant building had been eaten away by natural forces. The next minute, the place seemed not constructed at all but more like "natural arches" run amuck, an impossible assemblage of wind-carved openings and hollowed-out rooms.

Len wasn't sure which explanation was less likely. "Have you been here before, Sutton? What do people say about this place?" He darted low, past an open window.

Sutton caught up to him, the beads in his beard clacking together. "I've heard stories since I was a wee lad. Goffer kept us awake many a night with tales that made our eyes open so wide, you'd think they'd roll right out. Legends about Justice Island could tame the wolf out of a boy and turn him into a lamb."

Bennu peered into a dark opening. "It leads down. Rough stairs, I think."

As Sutton checked out a different passageway, Len held the sides of Bennu's opening and leaned in. "The wind can't create stairs, that's for sure." He pulled back. "I'm hungry. Bennu, what have you got?"

"I restocked on our last trip home. We have boxes of cereal bars around the house. Dad wrote the slogan for the company. 'Desert Crunch: When water's dry and land be small.' How random is that? I can't believe my dad could say anything that's not corny."

Sutton joined them and eyed the food.

"You can have one too," said Bennu.

Sutton eyed the package. "Soliton's pleasures are indeed profound."

"Don't get your hopes up. The cereal bar isn't all that great."

"No, Bennu. I'm not speakin' about the food you've brought to share, though indeed I'm glad enough for it. Y'see, I was just fixin' to tell you how Goffer gathered us 'round and scared us with stories about Justice Island. With flames glowin' in his face, Goffer talked about the time Justice Island was a prison, a place to send the few too cruel to live gladly with their neighbors. Once a shipload got dropped off and were told to make their way on the island for a year. If they worked together, if they gathered to themselves Welken's ways, they could return. But 'twasn't to be.

"A pirate of the deepest meanness set foot on the island and meant to make it his own. The year passed, and when the sailors came to shore, they couldn't believe their eyes. They saw nothin'—no trees, no plants, no prisoners. Not a single livin' thing. Then one soul showed his face. As thin as a stick, he fell at the sailors' feet. They took him back to Primus Hook. In time, he told the tales of Karn the Slasher, how he loved death more than life, and how he'd made of Justice Island a bone with no marrow, a rock with no life in it."

Len swallowed a large bite of cereal bar. "Now I'm even more nervous. Shouldn't we be going? Who knows what Gareth's going through right now?"

"Soon enough, lad. What you need to be hearin' is how Goffer put it to us. As boys, we saw ourselves as conquerors. Justice Island was but one more mountain on which to take the flag of Kells Village. Then Goffer told us, 'All's bravery and battles won when you've got no enemies, lads. But when the water's dry and land be small, you won't be strong for long, not without the good hand of Soliton holdin' you up.' I never did forget how Goffer put it. And now—"

"And now," said Len, "Welken seems to have gotten inside your dad's thinking, Bennu. Wow. The connections get deeper and deeper. I've always wondered. Do you think Soliton orchestrates anything in Skinner? If he's like a god in Welken—or some super-being—maybe he can cross over easier than anyone. . . . Wait a minute." Len held up his hand. "I hear something."

The clumsy clunking could only mean tremlings. Silently, the threesome chose the only route available, down the stairs into the dark.

Hands against the cool walls, Len led the way, all the while trying to process the juxtaposition of food packaging and Welkenian prophecies. Martin's slogan had the rhythm of the other lines they'd heard about the cold sun and the white wind. As Len tensed his whole body with every step downward, the cut by his ribs ached.

The blackness grew blacker. Len wished they had a rope so they could be tied together. He worried about what creatures crawled across the walls, what shiny, spider-headed, scorpion-tailed millipede would snap at him, or if hundreds would drop from the ceiling, wherever the ceiling was. He knew he'd seen too many adventure movies.

Sutton grabbed Len's belt. "Don't move."

From above, the head of a tremling growled into the stairwell. He looked right at them but did not appear to see them.

Len figured they were deep enough into the shadows to be imperceptible to the poor-sighted tremling. The beast turned away, then came back to the entrance and kicked some rocks into the blackness.

Len ducked behind Sutton. There was almost nothing else he could do.

A rock hit Bennu with a thud. As a suppressed moan escaped Bennu's lips, the rock bounced off Bennu, missed Len, and banged down the stairs.

Len held his breath. He hoped the tremlings had not heard Bennu's moan, and he also wanted to listen to the rock's journey down. It bounced for a second or two, maybe spanning a dozen more stairs or so. Then *splash*.

Even though there was no question about it, Len felt around for another rock to throw to double-check. He found something to throw, then the "something" thrust out its legs in Len's hand. Len threw it so fast that his follow-through banged his hand into the wall.

But he heard a *plink*.

Len rubbed his fingers, then said, "*Ow*" with his lips but not his voice.

Sutton whispered, "Let's see where it leads, lad."

See where it leads? They were well past *seeing* anything. But they could hear the water.

Each step felt wasteful, one more step away from saving Gareth's life. But whenever Len slowed or stopped, Sutton nudged him gently from behind.

One hand overhead to keep from banging his head, one on the side to keep his balance, Len felt for one step and then another. He thought he had gone down enough to be at the water's edge, but nothing splashed. There seemed to be nothing overhead, then he felt rock. He leaned down to get under it and scooted along on his rear end. Then his upper hand gave way. Len pushed up and around and felt nothing.

But he saw some light. "There's something down here," he whispered behind him. "Maybe a way out. I don't know."

By the time Sutton and Bennu skidded on their bottoms onto the same step, Len's eyes had adjusted better to the dim light. They were in a large cave. Across the way, the light shone brighter, and illuminated what "the way" was. As the rock had revealed, the floor of this cave was water.

"I do *not* want to swim across this." Len watched the tiny reflections from the light on the other side. "I do *not* want to find out 'what evil lurks in the black lagoon.'" He felt a little sheepish using a funny voice to say this, especially when Gareth was probably suffering who-knows-what. He felt doubly worse sounding like a coward.

"I doon't mind a bit goin' first." Sutton put one foot in the water. "The water'll feel right refreshin'." As soon as Sutton put his weight on his foot, something moved around his boot. The water rippled out. In the blackness, something swarmed and attacked. Sutton pulled his boot out.

Basilisks!

Three deadly heads had sunk their teeth into Sutton's boot. He reached down and tore them off. One of them must have bitten into Sutton's hand, for he flinched. But he didn't yelp in pain. Instead, he simply threw each one back into the lagoon.

"What did you do that for?" Bennu showed his knife. "I could have killed them first."

"It's all right." Sutton fingered the marks in his boots. Blood dripped from his hand. "Basilisks have a way of carryin' on in the dozens. Three less won't get us across. Besides, they've got their life to lead."

Great, thought Len. *Sutton Hoo is the Albert Schweitzer of Welken.*

Len picked up a pebble, squinted to make sure it wasn't a bug, and tossed it into the water. *Take that you stupid basilisks!*

He also heard something besides a *plink* when the rock hit.

"Did you hear that?" Len reached for another pebble. "Shush. Listen." He tossed it into the light reflected in the water.

From the light where the rock hit came the faintest "Ouch."

"There. I wasn't imagining it. You heard it, right?"

"I did," said Bennu.

"Just so," said Sutton.

The glimmering light bounced and sparkled in the water. Then it moved. The swath of brightness came closer—and Len and Bennu exchanged smiles.

"Miss Noriadian, are you there?" Len covered his mouth, because he knew he'd been too loud. *Why is it,* he wondered, *that we shout at whatever is smaller than ourselves, as if their smaller ears make them half-deaf?*

A dozen water glimpses flew up next to Len, Sutton, and Bennu. Sutton pointed at one buzzing near his head.

The assembly flickered in a kind of V formation. "Miss Noriadian isn't here," one said, its golden bands shining in the dimness. "She sent us to be of use if we could. She is an open-sea glimpse. We stay closer to shore."

When Bennu held out his hand, three flew into it and rested on their floppy tails. "You're so amazing—and beautiful."

"Why, thank you, but we do wish you would tell us more. My name is Miss Maidinian."

Len put out both hands. The glimpses' tails tickled his palms. "Tell you more about what? About Gareth? Fatagar? The tremlings?"

Sutton put a hand on Len's shoulder. "No, lad. We see swarms of water glimpses—'sparklings' we call them—now and again off Goffer's Spit. They love to hear about themselves. They never tire of it. We should oblige them. It's the least we can do, doon't ya know."

Bennu wiggled a finger up and down at Miss Maidinian in his hand. "There's something about your size, little sparkling. You're the glimmer in someone's eye made large. You're like a moon shadow grown fairer yet and small enough to hold in my hand."

Miss Maidinian glowed brighter as she heard these compliments. She seemed to feed off them, to grow stronger, as did the entire swarm.

"The only thing more beautiful," said Sutton, "is my own sweet Gilda's tendin' to our own young babe."

As if a dimmer switch had been pushed up gradually, the water glimpses shone in greater gold-and-silver glimmeriness.

Len gulped. He knew he wasn't as poetic as Bennu or as tenderhearted as Sutton. "I can't make my words like flowers, but I know this. Water glimpses saved us once, when the ship we were on sank, and I'm so grateful my heart hurts. But more than that, my worry over Gareth makes me see that you are true glimpses, little windows into what we were all made to be, lovers of every good thing. And—I can't believe I said something so cheesy—and, well, we need you now to carry us across the water."

As an effervescence rose from the water, Len realized that he'd met the moment, that his praise, though not as fancy, had had an eloquence all its own. These sparklings seemed to need it, almost as payment for their assistance, just as the land glimpses needed a riddle.

Miss Maidinian bowed. "Of course. That's why we breathe and glow. Come, we can carry you now. You need not fear the basilisks."

251

First for Bennu, then Sutton, then Len, the water glimpses became a hovering hammock, a living ferry that traversed the treacherous water. More willingly than before, Len flopped onto the glimpses. They caught him and kept him aloft. He tried to feel each saving hand or wing or tail pressing against his back and legs. Of course, he couldn't. Instead, he felt illuminated, as if the light flowed into him. . . .

"Wake up, lad." Sutton shook Len's shoulders. "The ride is over." He and Bennu helped Len to the shore. " 'Twas like a bed of softest lamb's skin. I don't blame you at all for schemin' how to stay."

By the time Len got his footing and the three ferried friends stood on the bank together, the water glimpses had dashed over the water and out of the cave altogether.

Bennu waved. "I'm feeling it too."

Len put both hands in his pockets. "What?"

"Like it shouldn't end. The sense of being weightless, born aloft by light. It reminded me of flying. I miss it."

"Yeah, I felt good too. I imagined I was floating in a swimming pool. It's not as exciting as flying, I admit, but . . . hey!"

"What?"

"When water's dry and land be small."

"Wow. You're right. Amazing."

Sutton waved "C'mon," and they trekked up more stairs till they were level with Justice Island's valley floor. They got their bearings immediately, for there was Fatagar, clearly in charge on the dock. His back to the water, his voice bellowed out to his tremling troops.

"*Tck-tck.* This is the time. Our t-t-time." His many knobby horns glowed red. "We are the f-f-forgotten ones, the hated ones. *Tck-tck.* No longer! We will make them r-r-remember how they rejected us, r-r-rejected you for how you look, r-r-rejected me as general of Prester John's army." Sweating through his embellished Wasan Sagad uniform, Fatagar slammed his fist against the many medals on his chest. "We w-w-will show them I can rule. We w-w-will show them with clubs, with t-t-teeth. Come! We s-s-sail for Primus Hook."

Raucous cheering erupted. Tremlings, surrounded by Fatagar's guards, pounded staffs and growled into the air. The soldiers chanted his name.

Fatagar sat back on his blubber and smiled. He crunched on a stick for a second before throwing it aside. "The ships are n-n-nearly ready. We will go when G-G-Gareth says to go."

Len knew he must have misheard. He ran low from one rock wall to another, to get closer. Bennu and Sutton followed.

He saw Gareth step off a ship and walk toward Fatagar. Unchained, unguarded, his sword still at his side, Gareth strolled confidently till he stood next to Fatagar.

Len's jaw tightened and his fists clenched. He rolled out a steady, low growl. *Gareth? What is he doing here? Has he left us, betrayed us? Why? He's throwing everything out of whack, making everything more difficult.*

Bennu grabbed Len by the arm and motioned for him to cut the growling noise.

Len did. But he did not stop growling in his mind. He wondered how this Gareth—this steady seaman now whispering in Fatagar's filthy ear—could call himself "Keeper of the Balance."

CHAPTER TWENTY-SEVEN

PICKING UP THE WEARINESS

It is right that what is just should be obeyed;
it is necessary that what is strongest should be obeyed.

—BLAISE PASCAL, *PENSÉES*

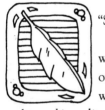 "So."

Lizbeth never thought one word would sound so wonderful, so full of hope, so . . . *so*. She sat on the edge of the bed, feeling tired. It made sense. She had just walked inside Piers's mind, seen Bors, and come back to reality—*this* reality, anyway, which was more than a Deedy's verbification away from Skinner. Then she thought about Vida and Jacob and Mook. She worried about MaryMary and the Cutters.

And there was the added weight she now carried.

"So. Lizbeth and Angie, my heart has ached for you." Piers leaned toward them. "I feel as if I have been walking in a hole for some time. With each step, a clump of dirt would fall on me from above. As I looked for Bors, all that happened was the hole got deeper. And the dirt kept falling on me, handful upon handful. I couldn't shrug it off. I kept walking in circles in the dark. That's what it felt like."

Angie hugged Piers. "And now you are better. The healing has begun."

Lizbeth thought about how Piers's strength had returned because she had taken on part of what had burdened him. Lizbeth, the beast of burden, measured the load on her back. Her oxen self didn't mind carrying the weariness of Piers.

After hugging Lizbeth and Angie, Piers motioned that he wished to throw off the covers. "It is fitting that I should regain life in this room, a place where the dawn is always coming on." He swung his legs over the edge of the bed. "But now that the sunrise has awakened me, I know we cannot stay here. What The Welkening set in motion must be finished."

"Piers?"

"Yes, Lizbeth."

"I know why you were walking in a hole."

"I suspect you do. Oxen get where they are going." Piers stood up and pointed to the door. "Let's talk about it after we get out on our own. I don't want all these soldiers to hear."

Just outside the doorway, Prester John sat on the floor, his head leaning sideways on his closed arms, his eyes shut. In jerky movements, he snapped his head up and stood, balancing himself with one hand on the wall. He hit his head on the arch of the doorway. "See, I have kept you safe!" He pushed his hair straight back. "A Highlander stands good guard. No marauding horde of stone-dwelling insects attacked. No flying armies found refuge here."

Piers bowed. "Thank you, Prester John. Your princeliness serves you well."

From another room came the voice of Ellen Basala, "And a nap feels pretty good too!"

Prester John stormed out past Ellen, and the others followed. Soon each one had left the sanctuary, been lifted over the raging water by the waiting soldiers, and set down on shore. Lizbeth noted how weak the soldiers looked, how they could barely keep their ground while passing her over the waves. Prester John untied the rope from the stone wall. Too weary to hold on, the soldiers-in-chains flopped into the surf and let the soldiers on the shore pull them onto land. Then Prester John took the excess rope, tied it around his waist, and waited for the soldiers to give the signal to leap.

But a monstrous wave struck first, yanking violently on the rope and pulling Prester John into the water. The soldiers hung on and reeled fiercely when they could. Prester John bobbed up and down in the tumbling water and foam. Each time he surfaced, he shouted something out.

"Don't worry." Then "I will serve." Then "Highlanders are strong." Then "A prince—" The last phrase got lost in a mouthful of water.

Hands on hips, Ellen shook the braided buns on her head. "Even the sea cannot silence the Royal Eminence."

After the soldiers tugged in Prester John, they removed the chains from the ones who had withstood the crashing waves. Prester John told of beastly fish he'd fought while under the water.

A few soldiers dug into packs and distributed food and water, handing Lizbeth a flat, stiff something-or-other. She wondered if this was what she'd read about in history books, what pioneering Americans had called hardtack.

One bite and she knew that no one in a wagon train had ever tasted anything so explosively good. With each bite, a new flavor burst forth, as if a seven-course meal had been compressed into a thick, chewy cracker. She tasted salad with raspberry dressing, green beans with almonds, and mashed potatoes. She looked over at Angie. Her friend was smiling widely. Lizbeth laughed with her mouth full of food, snorted, laughed again, then held up the Welkenian hardtack and pointed to its back edge. Angie took the hint, and they bit into it at the same time. Lizbeth laughed again. She had been right! Dessert!

Fully satisfied, Lizbeth took a long draught of water, which turned out to be a frosty lemon elixir. She saw Piers conferring with Prester John and Ellen and knew they'd soon all be on their way. After they climbed up the cliff, Ellen Basala started off with the troops, back toward the Prester Highlands. The Misfits, Piers, and Prester John trekked inland.

Angie picked up a stick and walked with it. "So, Lizbeth, you know where we should go?"

"Well, not exactly."

"Not exactly. Hmm. And you know why Piers was walking in a hole?"

"I think so," Lizbeth murmured.

"You think so."

Lizbeth bristled. "Are you interrogating me?"

"Not really. I was just trying to see if I could feel what it's like to be Len. I don't think I get it."

"It doesn't really fit you, Angie."

"I guess not. But it makes me wonder how they are. Is Bennu in trouble? Is he being brave?"

Prester John kicked at a rock on the path. "As I recall, Len admired the Highlander spirit. He regaled in my stories of valorous adventure. If he and Bennu are in a tight spot, no doubt they'll draw strength from these tales."

"Lizbeth?" Piers's voice sounded solid, as thick as Welken's hardtack, and just as rich. "It's time to talk about what you've learned."

Lizbeth moved her eyes from the path to the landscape before them. The treeless cliffs gave way to wind-sculpted bushes and then, ahead, a forest. "So many things came together for me in the darkness with Bors. I heard voices, some from our time in Welken a month ago, and some from this trip—and from home. From everywhere in fact, even my dreams.

"It starts with Bors being Bones Malone, in Charlotte's stories—oh, I don't expect you to be able to follow all of this, Prester John—then Angie and I were in a room full of bones, in Deedy Swamp. Then I started thinking about Gandric's bones on the hillside near the Window Under the Mountain. Oh, why did he have to get sucked into Morphane? Why did he have to travel so fast up the Window that he aged into a skeleton? . . . I'm sorry, where was I? Oh, yeah. Then Dear-Abby, well, Bebba, said her flesh rotted off her bones. Yuck. Why would she say that? When I saw Bors, I put all this together and realized his body must be in a cemetery. And, then, Piers, you explained your journey with Bors, like you were walking in a hole, and someone was throwing dirt in. Don't you see? You were being buried alive!"

Piers stopped.

Had her revelation brought him to a halt? Lizbeth wondered.

It might have, she figured, but he was also studying the trail in front of them. It split off into two paths—one going north around the forest, the other heading east straight into the woods. "Lizbeth, you have helped me more than you know. How should we decide which path to take? The only cemetery on Welken is behind Long House, above Primus Hook. It must seem odd to you from Skinner. We have only one cemetery because although there are many different villages in Welken, we leave this world together. The land has many faces, but we all see the same stars."

Lizbeth scratched her head. "Is that true for Alabaster Singing? A month ago, Mook said he was taking her back to the Nezzer Clan."

"The local clan makes preparation. They each have a ceremony to honor the living of their loved ones. Then they come to the cemetery. So. But we should keep going."

Prester John stepped to the front. "Allow me to risk the first step. Though I have never been lost myself, I have an imagination keen enough to serve those entrusted to me. Oh, how terrible it must feel to wander aimless and confused!"

Lizbeth whispered to Angie, "This could be a long trip."

"Thank you, Prester John," said Piers. "You do the Highlands proud."

Lizbeth followed Piers to the right as they stepped into the trees. "There's more. When Angie helped my mom get up when she fell, Angie said, 'No broken bones.' I want to believe that means Bors is OK."

"Well, why don't you believe it?" The answer came not from Piers but from Angie.

"What do you mean?"

"Lizbeth, you go to church. Of all people, I'd think you would understand faith."

"I think I do, Ang, at least parts of it. But is faith the same as wishful thinking? I mean, I want Bors, his body, to be fine. Can my wishing for it make it so?"

"There's that word we love to hear from Piers." Angie smiled at him. "So. I wonder if it has something to do with faith. In a way, aren't we believing things are 'so'? So beautiful—ultimately at least. So overseen by love. So kept alive by ginger fur and warm green eyes."

"You're losing me, Angie."

"Unfortunately, that's what I do best." Angie kicked the ground. "I don't mean to be confusing. Honestly, I wish I could be clearer. I wish people didn't always look at me like I'm crazy."

Snap.

It was an unmistakable noise. It wasn't a crow's caw or a squirrel's skittering. It wasn't a dead branch falling or thin limbs scraping in the breeze. It was a twig-snap, clear as anything.

In seconds, the foursome hid behind trees and brush, and they crouched low.

Footsteps came. A rush of feet, a pause, a rush of feet. They came from the direction Lizbeth and the others were heading, from the east, from the Nez River above the falls. More than two feet scurried around. Maybe six.

From around a bend in the path, the source of the footsteps came. They had a soldier's stride, a disciplined stretch of the legs. Lizbeth saw the uniforms and the cold, steely faces. Cutters. Four of them.

What were they doing up here? Why would they be so far from Deedy—and only four of them?

Prester John darted over, next to Lizbeth. "Who are they? In all my adventures, I have not seen these green uniforms. The one red stripe on the side of the pants could mean they are not from Welken at all."

"They're called Cutters," Lizbeth whispered as softly as she could. Her words were scarcely more than breaths. "They have taken over Deedy Swamp. They tried to kill Mook."

"My calling is to protect what's true and honorable." Prester John paused. "I'll face these intruders. You three go on ahead."

Lizbeth did not know if the Cutters had heard Prester John. She didn't know if she should listen to Prester John, or if each of the four should take on one Cutter. That seemed smarter, more likely to succeed. She longed for her horns and wished she didn't feel so weighed down.

The Cutters, in their shining helmets, strode boldly down the path. Two wore wide belts of daggers and short swords, Each of the other two had a quiver of arrows and a bow. They looked behind them and in front of them. They took a few steps into middle of the path, closer to the four in hiding. Lizbeth saw Prester John stretch his fingers, then clench and unclench his fist. He put his hand on the hilt of his sword.

Lizbeth glanced over to Piers and Angie. A few trees over, Piers sat with his back against the bark. He looked tired. Lizbeth thought about the weight she'd taken from Piers. She imagined herself carrying it—and tried to reach out to take more. Angie stood with her arms at her sides behind a wide fir tree. How Lizbeth wished Angie could become fully invisible.

Then Lizbeth heard Piers's voice, unmistakably, coming to her from inside her head. It made her gut feel a little weightier, the shard a little sharper.

Quiet your hands.

The Cutter scratched his neck where his collar touched it. He turned to walk up the path, away from them.

Quiet your hearts.

Then Prester John, without the slightest resistance, pushed his sword back into its sheath. He looked at Lizbeth and smiled.

Once the Cutters were out of earshot, the foursome regrouped behind Lizbeth's bush.

Piers spoke with some urgency. "Prester John, circle back through the woods. Get ahead of the Cutters to warn Ellen and the others. Go."

Prester John obeyed with the quickness of a private in boot camp. For all his bluster, Prester John had a singular sense of deference.

"Come, friends," said Piers. "We should not tarry. We must get to Bors. We need his judgment and his arms, his massive, swinging arms. I have seen him lift Vida Bering Well as if she were a flower. I have heard his wisdom silence an angry crowd. He is of judgment good and true. But enough for now. He is wasting away. If he becomes bones, he will never be reunited with his soul."

Lizbeth did not know what Piers meant, nor whether his "bones" had a capital B.

CHAPTER TWENTY-EIGHT
OF MICE AND MENTAL STRAIN

And little people know
When little people fight
We may look easy pickings
But we got some bite.

—HERBERT KRETZMER, "LITTLE PEOPLE," *LES MISÉRABLES* SOUNDTRACK

 Hidden behind the rock, Len took what chances he could, popping up to watch Gareth, then ducking down. He could not reconcile what he saw with his experience. Here was Gareth, the bookkeeper turned sailor who'd rescued them from the sandbar, who'd fought tremlings for the good of Welken, but who now looked to be Fatagar's lieutenant.

Whom could Len trust? Was Gareth's loyalty just a façade, a game he played to advance his ends? Or had he changed his mind? What persuasion could Fatagar have used to move Gareth's commitments? Bribery? Force? Or some darker appeal to power? Was integrity so easily compromised? Like a trapped fly searching for light, these thoughts banged around in Len's mind.

Fatagar stomped around the platform, his sagging underbelly bouncing almost to the ground. "*Tck-tck.* I need d-d-decisions, Gareth. We cannot take them all."

Bennu, looking stunned, sat with his back against the rock. "You know what this means? He's leaving some of the tremlings to die on the island."

261

Sutton softly beat his leather chest plate. "They are livin' things, doon't you know. He has no right to toss 'em aside as nothin'."

"Shh," said Len, "here he comes."

Gareth walked off the dock, his shoulders straight, his black vest at odds with the untailored Fatagar sitting in his own fat, ripping meat off a bone, then crunching the bone into splinters with his sharp teeth. He did not brush the droppings off his chest.

Looking officious, Gareth inspected a line of tremlings and culled out the lesser ones, pointing them toward the center. The others shuffled over to the opposite side of the island floor from Len, Bennu, and Sutton.

Gareth walked up the line, closer and closer to his hiding friends—at least Len hoped the friendship remained. Len did not see that they had any option. They would have to take a risk.

Gareth and several of Fatagar's guards broke through the ranks of nervous tremlings. Just twenty yards from Len and Sutton and Bennu, Gareth kicked at the dirt, and his chest heaved in a mighty sigh. While the guards turned back to enforce his orders, pushing some tremlings into the center, into the pit of this aging coliseum, Gareth put a hand to his forehead. He ran a finger back and forth as if massaging a tense mental anguish. It could have meant anything, but Len knew they had to act now.

"Bennu, give me some string cheese."

"This is hardly the time for lunch."

"Just do it. I have an idea." Len took the cheese and quickly rolled it into a ball. "It worked once. Maybe we will call this the Island of Rolled Food."

Len took a deep breath, slipped into the open, and bowled the cheese over the bumpy soil. He was accurate but much too fast. Len feared the ball would roll past Gareth and into the agitated tremlings. Peering around the rock, with his face almost on the ground, Len watched the ball roll. It hit a small rock, bounced up, and rolled straight for Gareth.

Too hard. Len thought, *too hard.*

Keeping his heel on the ground, Gareth lifted the front of one foot and caught the ball abruptly. He looked back and forth, then leaned over to pick it up.

Immediately Gareth turned toward the center and merged into the tremlings. Len thought all was lost. He couldn't imagine what Gareth was doing, or why he didn't come over. It made no sense, unless Gareth really had gone over to Fatagar's side.

Then Gareth emerged from the crowd. He said something to the soldiers before he walked deliberately toward the three in hiding. He came up to the rock they hid behind. He said nothing. Len did not know if he should peek over. Then he heard a trickle of liquid and smelled urine.

"I will create a diversion." Gareth sounded brave and frightened at the same time. "It's the best I can do. Then run to the ship. You do not want to get stuck on this island with angry tremlings."

Len crouched low and saw him walk away. Gareth straightened his shoulders as he walked and pointed at a tremling. The soldiers hit the tremling with a staff and prodded him toward the center. Other tremlings cowered in fear.

Sutton motioned for Len and Bennu to follow. Hunkering down, he ran from rock to rock till he was back in a passageway looking out on the valley floor.

Bennu pointed to a small hill of boulders fairly close to the dock. "We should run to those rocks. We can get pretty close if we follow this corridor to the end. Then we can make a break for it. We'll be in better position for Gareth's diversion."

Len and Sutton nodded in agreement.

The commotion on the valley floor kept them from worrying they would be noticed. From the end of the passageway, Fatagar and his guards could be plainly seen pacing around the dock. That meant Fatagar and the guards could plainly see them—at least once they left the shadows and darted into the open.

"I think you're right, Bennu." Len tried to sound resolute. "If we wait here for the diversion, we might not make it all the way to the ship. We have to get closer."

"Should we throw a rock to the other side?"

Sutton shook his head. "A good idea, Bennu, but I reckon Fatagar won't go fallin' for the same diversion twice. He's a shrewd one, he is."

Len watched Fatagar survey the valley. He scanned it like a searchlight, methodically, predictably. When Fatagar's gaze moved from the right toward the center, Len jumped into the open. "Run," he whispered.

Leaning over, trying to keep his upper body perfectly stationary and his lower body furiously active, Len ran toward the rocks. His heart pounded. His pulse raced. He thought that if he didn't soon stand up straight, his heart would come right up through his throat. He watched the path and dodged rocks. He looked up and ahead. He kept an eye on Fatagar.

He was nearly there. Ten more steps.

Five.

Then he heard a crash behind him and a muffled "*Uhn.*" Len looked back and saw Sutton several paces behind, carrying Bennu by the belt like a briefcase. In a few strides, all three reached the boulder. They slid down with their backs to it.

Len knew they weren't safe yet. Rising above them, a cloud of dust took flight, every floating particle a finger pointing down at them, exposing them. Len held his breath. He waited. He listened. Nothing.

He breathed out again, a long hard one. He tried to keep each breath quiet. Then he started shaking.

Bennu got to his feet but did not brush himself off. The threesome faced the rocks and crept over to their left. Len got down on his knees and looked at the dock. One guard turned on his heel and marched to the other side.

They did not need to wait long. An agonizing scream shot out from deep in the tremling ranks, followed by shouts and grunting.

It's a fight, thought Len. *This is it. This is Gareth's diversion.*

He leaned over to his left just in time to see Fatagar gesture toward the noise. The guards ran off the dock. Fatagar held his fat off the ground like a skirt and stepped off the platform.

OK, so far so good. We'll creep around these rocks. Stay low. Yes, Fatagar's going toward the fight. He's hitting tremlings. His head spikes are glowing hot. What an idiot. OK, on the dock. There's the ship. C'mon Bennu, don't trip again. Dock, don't make noise.

All around Len was the sound of feet pounding.

There's the ladder. C'mon, Len, up a step, two, over the side. OK, good, we're here. We made it. Now what? Is anyone on board?

"We know this ship," Bennu whispered to Sutton. "It's Gareth's. We've been on it."

Len scrambled along the deck, staying low. Beyond the mainmast, Len saw an opening to a storage hold. He stopped to listen for any footsteps, any evidence of the crew or guards. He heard nothing. With Bennu and Sutton crouched just behind him, he pointed to the hold. They nodded.

A seagull flew over them and landed on the deck in front of them. It walked around, keeping one eye on Len. Then another came, and another. The three gulls lifted their heads and squawked at each other. Three more came and squatted on the varnished wood.

Bennu tapped Len on the shoulder. He opened his clenched hand to reveal crumbs dug out of his pockets. He threw a few at the gulls, then tossed the rest behind him.

As the gulls flew to the food, Len ducked and moved out toward the hold. He stepped as softly as swift strides allowed and lifted the door. Pivoting, he backed down the ladder. Bennu came next, then Sutton. Then a gull.

Len swatted at it and tried to shoo it out. "Bennu, can you talk bird language? Get rid of this thing."

Bennu busily opened storage containers. "Too small," he said. Then the gull jumped in. "Get out of there." Bennu scooped the bird out. The gull squawked and snapped at him.

"Over here." Sutton held up the top of an empty rectangular crate. It had spaces between slats for breathing and for looking out. "It's big enough for the two of you lads. I'll find something else."

"Thanks, Sutton," said Len, "but hurry."

Before Len and Bennu pulled the lid over their heads, they saw Sutton step into a barrel. He smiled over at them as he squeezed himself in.

Then they waited.

And waited.

Len's knees hurt. He tried to shift positions silently. He could only imagine Sutton's suffering.

Bennu rubbed his feet. "I got a cramp."

More waiting.

Finally, clunking could be heard above. Soldiers shouted orders. Tremlings complained with grunts and groans.

Sitting on his legs folded to his right, Len felt something itchy on his calves. He scratched the spot and felt something scaly, something slick, with legs. He shuddered, grabbed the thing, and held it up to Bennu in the light between the slats. Some kind of cockroach. He stuck out his tongue and pushed the bug through an opening.

It fell to the ground at the same time Len heard louder noises, boot noises coming down the steps. And voices.

"Check the stores, soldier. Get ready for sailing."

"Aye, aye."

"And make it quick. Fatagar don't like waiting. Sticks—and other things—get snapped when he gets mad."

The soldier hopped down the last step with both feet. Then he was in the hold.

Len could see his knees and boots. He didn't know what he'd do if the soldier lifted the top.

But the soldier checked nothing. He sat down and pulled his flask out. After his loud gulps filled the room, the soldier burped and laughed a little.

Then the ship moved. It creaked and swayed in the water. As commands could be heard from above, Gareth's ship sailed away from Justice Island.

Len smelled tobacco smoke. The soldier must have lit a pipe. Then he heard the paddling of webbed feet. The gull was still there.

The soldier stood up. "Stupid bird. I'll get you."

The gull screeched and squawked as the soldier swiped at it. Then the bird landed on the wooden box. Len could see the soldier's waist coming closer.

Bam! Something hard came down on the lid. *Bam!* The soldier missed again.

Then Len felt something once more on his legs. As best he could in tight quarters, he turned his head to look. It was a mouse. It sniffed Len's legs repeatedly, its whiskers tickling him. It crawled onto his leg. Len held his breath. He tried to control his anxiety, his twitching leg, and his leonine instincts. His head started to change, his mane pushing almost willfully against the lid. He concentrated and made himself stay human. The mouse crawled higher up his leg. Nervously Len swatted at it, but the mouse kept coming. It sat on Len's leaning chest and gazed with black eyes into Len's face.

Squawk Bam. Crash. The soldier knocked over some dried corn, the seeds scattering.

The mouse skittered up Len's right shoulder and behind his neck. He tried to keep perfectly still. He imagined he was floating on his canoe, utterly content. Then the mouse climbed over to Len's left shoulder, which was leaning against the side of the crate. The mouse was so close to Len's face that his vision blurred. He could only see fuzzy gray fur.

"I'll kill you!" the soldier screamed.

Clunk. More squawking.

Then the mouse's tail flipped over into Len's face. He felt his canines grow. He wanted to bite and gulp.

But he resisted. He knew the mouse was looking out of a hole in the box. Carefully Len brought his right hand across his chest and up to his left shoulder. He pushed the mouse through the hole.

What happened afterward Len could only guess. Maybe the gull dove for the mouse. Maybe the mouse ran for the seed. Maybe the soldier saw the mouse and panicked and slipped on the seed. All Len knew for certain was that the commotion got louder and louder. The soldier yelled, there was a pounding and a skittering, a thud, and . . . silence. Len guessed—and hoped—the soldier had been knocked out cold.

Len shot a *what-now?* look to Bennu in the dim light of the crate and shrugged. Another mouse poked through a hole in the back. Then another. Bennu stretched his foot to cover the hole. Then another mouse came through a different hole and crawled onto Bennu. It sniffed Bennu's pockets. A mouse crawled up Len's leg again. He reached down awkwardly to hold his shorts tight against his leg. He was too late. The mouse was on Len's thigh, its tail on his knee. He tried to push it out. Then it bit him.

"Yuh," he grunted, trying to hold back. But he couldn't take it. His nerves on end, he pushed the lid off. He stood up, grabbed the mouse by the tail, pulled it out of his shorts, and flung it across the room. Then he saw the soldier, out cold, on the floor. A dozen mice foraged in the corn and carried kernels away. The gull sat on the top step of the ladder, its head snuggled into its feathers.

Len saw the sky through the opening to the hold. He wondered how close they were to Mercy Bay. He wondered how they could possibly get out of this mess. Then he saw a face fill the opening, a face grim and decisive, a face without a conscience, its greasy checks puffed up with blubber. *Fatagar.* His knobby head glowed with angry delight. "G-g-guards!"

The threesome gave up without resistance. The numbers were just too great.

On the deck, Len and Sutton and Bennu discovered how difficult it was to keep their balance with their hands tied behind their backs. Len saw Mercy Bay about a mile in the distance. Behind them, another ship sailed, no doubt filled with more tremlings ready to fight.

All were part of Fatagar's army. Fatagar's assault on Primus Hook. And Lizbeth and Angie had told them of MaryMary and the Cutters in Deedy Swamp. Welken was under attack.

Len did not have long to reflect on such things. With tremlings growling behind a row of soldiers, the prisoners were marched along the deck to the starboard side. Many of the soldiers poked them or spat on them. One soldier stepped up and pushed Bennu. He hit the railing and teetered toward the water. Sutton bumped him away from the edge—and into more soldiers. They spun him around until he stumbled and fell. In his helplessness, Len studied Sutton's face. The expression on the face of the normally softhearted man was stern, his eyes hardened.

They were brought to a stop in front of Fatagar and forced to kneel. Fatagar rubbed his bumpy head. "*Tck, tck.* You are still a t-t-troublemaker, Len. I tricked you in the tower of Wasan Sagad, in the W-W-Wasteland, but I-I-I won't need to trick you now." Fatagar squeezed a finger into a crease in his fat, looked at the slime he withdrew, and licked his finger clean. "You've met G-G-Gareth, I take it, when he p-p-pretended to be your friend."

Len looked up at Gareth. His eyes followed the lines in Gareth's coat up to his chin, his solemn mouth, and his unrevealing eyes. The point of a broadsword rested on the ground, with the handle firmly gripped by Gareth's right hand. As usual, he showed no emotion and no effect from the ship's movement.

"*Tck, tck.* T-t-trouble-makers, we know what to do with them."

Frantically running through every cubbyhole in his brain, Len searched for something to hold off Fatagar. He threw open drawers, flung everything out of his mental cupboards.

Bennu groaned from the pain of being pole-butted and mocked.

Len said the only thing he could think of. "Fatagar, you misunderstand. We are like Gareth here, loyal to you." He thought if double-spying was good enough for Gareth, then they should try it too. "We know many things about Piers and Primus Hook that might help you."

Fatagar dragged one finger across a line in his forehead. "I am not easily convinced." He grabbed Len's chin in his hand and yanked it upward, as if Len's neck would somehow yield the truth.

Len coughed. Fatagar's smell hit him a roundhouse blow. He felt faint.

"Y-y-you think you choose sides as you please, do you? *Tck, tck.* Gareth, what do you say?" Fatagar released Len and sat back in his fat.

Here comes the truth, thought Len. *Gareth will say he's with us.*

Gareth glanced at Fatagar, then out to sea. "I do not know these men, Fatagar. They are liars and not to be trusted. Dispose of them."

Fatagar's smell meant nothing to Len now. The stench of Gareth's words hit harder. He felt bruised and crushed. "Gareth," said Len, "what are you saying? Why?"

Gareth hit Len with the flat of his sword. "Fatagar, these men are enemies. You have my right hand on it." Gareth held out his hand toward the rancid beast. Fatagar smiled his crooked grin. He took Gareth's hand. As he squeezed it, Gareth's hand withdrew, pushed out, as it were, by Fatagar's sliminess.

Len's heart felt rammed, blindsided by an iron rod. He wanted to vomit.

Then Gareth looked at the gunk Fatagar had pressed onto his hand. And he put one finger in his mouth and sucked it off.

"*Tck, tck*. This ship d-d-does not have a plank, boys. And d-d-drowning is a death for s-s-sissies. G-G-Gareth will do the duties here." Fatagar snapped a stick with his teeth.

"I will go first!" Sutton scooted on his knees and pushed himself between Len and Bennu. "Welken is my home. If I must, I'll die for her."

"I do so love v-v-volunteers." Fatagar touched a knob on his head, and it glowed. "Gareth, d-d-do you swear to serve me?"

Gareth gazed out into the ocean. "I do."

"And do you, *tck-tck*, renounce the Welken of these three p-p-prisoners?" Fatagar raised his hand as his voice grew louder.

Len turned his head from the fetid odor excreting from Fatagar's mouth.

"I do, my lord."

Len couldn't believe what he was hearing. *Where is Gareth's great plan? Where are his own men? Where is his integrity, his loyalty, his conscience? Why would he stand with Fatagar rather than fall with us?*

"W-w-well put. Soon, we land in Mercy B-B-Bay. We take Primus Hook and L-L-Long House. *Tck-tck*. We join forces there. Then we r-r-reverse The Welkening. We give it b-b-back." He smiled falsely and bounced in his own blubber. "You'll see."

Join forces? Really? With Gareth's men?

"Sutton!" Gareth's voice clanged like the death bell it was. "Move forward." Sutton scooted up. "Put your head here." Gareth kicked forward a wooden block.

Sutton put his head on it. "Tell Gilda of my true and tender love."

"Who's he t-t-talkin' to?" Fatagar grabbed Gareth's elbow. "Lift the sword, *tck-tck*."

Sutton closed his eyes. "By Soliton's glow—"

"Sh-sh-shut him up!"

Gareth raised his blade. "I am the Keeper of the Balance!" He held the sword straight up to the sky.

Sutton opened his eyes. "In Welken!"

Len and Bennu shouted back, "Of Welken!"

Len could not bear to see Sutton's beheading or the fullness of Gareth's betrayal. As he turned his head, some movement on the deck caught his eye. Something scurrying around. His nostrils flared. He saw a carpet of gray, heard the flittering of tiny feet.

Then he saw them. Mice. And rats. Hundreds of them. All the bilge-feeders and grain-stealers on the run, rising to the surface and racing across the deck.

"N-n-now!" Fatagar's voice shot over the din.

Len turned back to Sutton. Gareth's sword began its descent. Len's head became a lion. Roaring into the sky, he saw flocks of seagulls swarming toward the ship. Then he looked back at the mice. The front-runners had reached his feet. They climbed onto his back. As they ran to the tremlings, the beasts growled and stomped. They hit at the mice crawling on each other. Yelling and fighting broke out.

All at once Len saw the gulls swoop down, the tremlings club each other, and the shining sword of Gareth slicing downward. Then, at the rear of the mice stampede, he saw another figure, a familiar one, pacing back and forth.

It was the ginger cat with the warm green eyes.

CHAPTER TWENTY-NINE
UNDER A VEIL OF DARKNESS

The evil that men do lives after them,
The good is oft interred with their bones.

—WILLIAM SHAKESPEARE, *JULIUS CAESAR*

With the fear of advancing Cutters pushing them ahead, Lizbeth, Angie, and Piers made good time. They arrived at the Nez River, well above the falls, without seeing any more soldiers.

While Piers filled his water flask, Lizbeth splashed her face and drank deeply. "Y'know, Ang, just once you could slurp or something—so we wouldn't feel like such slobs."

"Sorry." Angie quietly sipped water from her hands before daubing the back of her neck with the river's coolness.

Lizbeth stood up and walked down the bank for several yards. "Do we swim across? The river's pretty wide, and the current's not slow, either."

"You are right." Piers pointed to a spot. "The Nezzer Clan knows the path."

Lizbeth scanned up and down the river. "I don't see any Nezzer folk coming to help us."

"No, but we have Angie and the egrets."

Lizbeth watched Angie face the river. She appeared dazed, like she had in the museum and Ganderst Hall, like she always did when searching for an interpretation. Angie was a spiritual Geiger counter—not a tool

272

made to detect radio activity but an instrument designed to see the divine, even with her eyes closed, like now.

Angie walked into the river up to her waist. She floated her hands in the water and held them there. She seemed to be listening with them. An egret landed in the water upstream from her and floated down, stopping against her body. Angie stroked the bird's long white neck. She gently massaged the feathers between the egret's wings. The egret flapped farther into the river, and Angie followed.

Angie stuck her hands fully into the water, evidently feeling for something. Then her hands seemed to stop against something solid, and she climbed up what Lizbeth took to be underwater steps and stood knee-deep in the river about ten feet from the bank. She patted the egret on the head, left it standing there—on a rock, Lizbeth guessed—and descended into the river again. She seemed to be walking along a deeper ridge, holding her arms out for balance. Sometimes her chest became invisible and her head appeared to float a few feet above the water.

"Now that's bizarre," said Lizbeth.

"Ah, my friend. Purity is more practical than some would have us think."

As Angie rose in the water, another egret drifted into her. The long-legged bird stood on the rock, then Angie proceeded to the next. Soon a line of white elegance marked the way for Piers and Lizbeth.

From the other side, Angie waved them over. "It's not as cold as the Lewis River, Lizbeth. It's more delicious and it warms up as it soaks in."

Lizbeth waved back and thought that just once she'd like Angie to say something normal like, "Come on over! Just follow the egrets." *Yeah.* Lizbeth smiled to herself. *Like that's normal.*

Wading in toward the first birds, Lizbeth climbed the river reef. As she made her way past the first to the second rock, she looked back to see Piers on the first landing, stroking the egret waiting there. Then the bird flew away. Under the weariness she bore, Lizbeth labored through the river. Balance was difficult. After eight ascents and descents of the steps in the water, Lizbeth and Piers stood on the eastern bank of the Nez and faced the river. The walkway could not be seen—but a line of egrets circled in the sky.

Lizbeth sighed. "You're right, Angie, I feel warmer inside than I did at the beginning. It's almost like sunlight seeping in deeper and deeper." Lizbeth scratched her head. *There I go, talking weird again. I'm being Angified.* That thought made her miss Vida and Jacob. She felt renewed urgency. "C'mon, let's go."

Lizbeth headed toward the woods. Piers took long strides next to her. At the first tree, Lizbeth turned back. "Angie, we need to hurry. We need to get to Bors. Who knows what's going on in Deedy now."

Her back to them, Angie scanned the sky. She waved broadly with one hand as the egrets passed over.

Then an arrow whizzed by her. From the other side, a Cutter grabbed another arrow and pulled his bow. Angie ran. Her eyes bright with fear, she hustled up the bank toward Lizbeth's waiting hand.

Lizbeth took one step down and stretched as far as she could—and that's when the arrow struck, right between the two hands, clipping both and coming to rest about three inches from Lizbeth's left foot. Yelping in pain, they drew their hands in. Piers grabbed Angie's other hand and drew her into the woods.

They ran down the path, out of the Cutter's range, wary of more Cutters up ahead.

Piers adjusted his satchel to his front as he ran. "How are your wounds? Perhaps we should stop so I can look at them."

"It's OK." Lizbeth applied direct pressure to the cut. Some blood escaped, and she ran awkwardly. "I can keep going. Ang?"

Angie ran with her hand held up in front of her. Blood flowed down her fingers to her arm. "The blood is fine. All will be well."

"I guess that means you're OK too." Lizbeth's finger throbbed.

After several hundred yards, they slowed down, then stopped. Piers applied a salve to their wounds and tied torn cloth around each one. "The cemetery," he said. "It's not far."

They walked quietly for some time. When a twig snapped, Lizbeth feared Cutters would hear and attack them. When they were silent, Lizbeth worried they'd be seen. At last they stood on a slight rise and gazed down toward Primus Hook and over toward Long House.

Piers pointed to a copse of trees below them. "There's the cemetery."

"What cemetery?" Lizbeth threw up her hands, then winced from the jerk to her wound. "All I see is an orchard."

Piers smiled. "Yes, you see rightly." He began his descent.

Out in the open on the south side of the hill, Lizbeth felt vulnerable. Her eyes darted this way and that for Cutters. She took some solace in the fact that they wouldn't be able to hide very well either. She wished she could shrink into the tall grass. She wished she could slip down the hill in the stealthy steps of Piers and Angie.

Once under the canopy of the first tree, Lizbeth looked around for the cemetery. "Where are the graves, Piers? Where are the headstones?"

"Here, all around you."

Lizbeth studied the place more intently. She saw no crypts, no markers, no evidence of a cemetery. She did see trees, plenty of them, in rows. No two of them were exactly alike. An apple tree blossomed next to a ponderosa pine, and a tropical palm tree stood but fifteen feet from a leafy ash. "This is the oddest orchard I've ever seen, Piers. How can all these different trees grow side by side? What do you make of it, Angie?"

"I'm not sure." Angie touched the peeling bark of a birch. "It's not just the variety. Look around. The trees are in different seasons."

Lizbeth's heart beat faster. Here was an orange tree heavy with fruit, there a healthy, barren sycamore. She saw an elm with its first leaf unfolding and a maple aglow with the fullness of autumn color. "It doesn't make sense, Piers. And, anyway, where is the cemetery?"

"It's here, as I said. You are standing on the grave of Sally Tenders Till of Deedy Swamp."

"I am? Where's the marker?"

"The tree is."

"The tree is the headstone?"

"Yes, and if you look just right, you can see Sally in the leaves." Piers walked between two rows. "You see, my friends, we are all born with a seed. When we die, we discover what tree we've been growing into all our living days. So."

"It sounds so beautiful," said Angie. "I want to know what I'll be. Maybe a flowering plum or a lacy lilac."

"Piers, what about this?" Lizbeth pointed to a burned trunk with drooping limbs.

Piers grimaced. "The tree tells the story. You may not want to know more about this one."

"You mean," said Lizbeth, "that his shard grew into that?"

"You mean his seed?"

"What did I say?"

"His shard."

"Oh. I guess that's what it feels like."

"What do you mean?"

"I have this feeling that there's this shard of glass in my side. It's sharp and catches me sometimes. I must have thought of it when you said 'seed.'"

"Some are aware of their seed. Some are not. It does not matter, because the seed is preparing to grow. I think it is better to know. It is part of being in Welken."

"And so the tree belongs in Welken because it is of Welken."

"You are wise, dear one. But don't think that you are the only nurturer of the seed."

"What do you mean?"

"Oh, you already know. Did you come to Welken, or were you called? Did you face Morphane in your own strength only? Remember, there is a choosing and there is the chosen. So. It is as rich and full and mysterious as a dogwood in bloom."

"Piers?" Angie called for him from the end of the orchard, from the first empty space. "What is this?"

Piers walked over to a rectangle of barren ground. "This is what *you* would call a cemetery plot, an unfilled grave."

Unlike the surrounding orchard, this plot possessed neither tree nor wild grasses. The soil looked freshly turned and raked clean. Lizbeth noticed many such plots around them. "Piers, do no weeds grow, or is there a gardener?"

Piers knelt by a plot and fixed his eyes on the soil. "The place is tended to."

Lizbeth wondered if a new tree would bust through the surface. Angie reached out her hand toward the crumbly earth.

"Yes, Angie," said Piers, "brush the soil." Angie did so. "Now scratch the surface."

As Angie's fingers made rows in the dirt, Lizbeth knelt and picked up a small handful. The soil felt flaky, turning to powder when squished.

Angie closed her eyes. "It's like I'm pulling my fingers through hair, Piers. It's like I'm combing the hair of the earth."

"Keep combing, Angie. Dig with tenderness and love."

Lizbeth sat cross-legged and brushed the soil lightly back and forth, as if she were trying to get it out of the way of something deeper, as if she were an archaeologist expecting some treasure. She drifted off for a second. . . .

A rustling came from a short distance away. Flinging a glance back toward the orchard and beyond, over the grassy hillside, she saw Cutters! Maybe half a dozen of them, charging hard.

Grabbing a handful of soil and making a fist, Lizbeth pounded the grave-plot. "Piers, Angie. Look, Cutters!"

Piers ignored her. "You are almost finished, Angie."

"They're coming!" Lizbeth crouched low. "I think they see us."

"Don't pull your hand out, Angie." Piers held Angie's raking arm with both of his hands. "Do you feel a small hole there?"

"Yes," said Angie.

An arrow landed twenty feet in front of them and skidded along the ground.

"Hey," said Lizbeth, "we're in trouble."

"Pull the hole wider," Piers insisted.

Another arrow sailed over their heads. The Cutters dashed toward them, swords raised. They yelled, and a few stopped to shoot more arrows. Two landed on the other side of Piers. One whizzed past Lizbeth as she ducked. She banged on the ground with her fist. "Let's get out of here!"

As she hit the plot, her hand went through. The soil swirled over to Angie and ran quickly down a hole. Lizbeth held the edge to keep from falling in. An arrow hit a rock to her right and ricocheted near her feet. "Piers, what do we—"

"Jump!" Piers threw himself into the pit and disappeared. Angie followed. Then Lizbeth turned backward and slid down the side, grabbing with her hands to slow the descent. Her wounded finger ached.

Lizbeth hit the ground with a thud and rolled over. In the shadows, she saw Piers and Angie, their backs against the earthen wall. As arrows thunked into the ground where they were sitting, one flew into the pit and stuck in the ground. Lizbeth picked it up.

Piers stepped up to what appeared to be a thick rope hanging in the air near where he and Angie had knelt. He pulled on this "rope," and dirt shot out of it as from a hose. In seconds the soil returned to the plot above them, becoming a thin blanket that hid them from the Cutters.

Lizbeth's mouth dropped open in wonder. And her wondering continued. What else was down here? Why weren't they buried alive?

In the silence, in the dense, haunting quiet, Lizbeth's eyes adjusted to the blackness. It was not as dark as she thought. The blanket of soil let in a dim gray light. The blanket was more like a veil. Another veil.

Then Lizbeth saw movement at the grave's edge. Cutters.

"Where'd they go?"

"C'mon, they were just here!"

Lizbeth gasped as they walked right up to the grave.

"How could they disappear?"

"Maybe when they got hit with our arrows, they vanished."

"Don't be stupid."

One Cutter walked onto the plot, but it held, dropping only crumbs of soil onto Lizbeth, Angie, and Piers.

"OK, split up in twos. MaryMary said not to come back till we got 'em. Go."

As the Cutters ran away, Lizbeth realized she'd been holding her breath. "Now what, Piers? Do we just wait?"

"No, my friend, you are the one who said we should come here to look for Bors."

Piers took Lizbeth's hand. He walked toward the opposite end of the dug-out grave. He stepped into the darkness and drew Lizbeth through an opening and into another room, another empty tomb with faint light also coming down through the rectangle of soil above them.

The weight of Piers's weariness pressed down on her. She squatted briefly before pushing up. She could bear the load, but the yoke was not easy. Then Lizbeth saw something gray-white against a wall. She let go of Piers. As she bent down for a closer look, she let out a muffled scream. "Uhh! It's a bone. And another. Yuck."

Piers helped her up. "Bones. Good. We must be close." He walked on, stooped over, struggling with the remainder of his burden.

Lizbeth didn't know what to say. The whole thing was too ghoulish, especially for Welken. She didn't want to be creeping around in some underground graveyard, waiting to be scared out of her mind. She remembered Gandric's death, and his bones. She wondered what kind of tree he had become.

Piers took her hand again. "We are here to find Bors."

When he said this, Lizbeth's shard twitched. It added to the weight of Piers's pain. Even so, she clasped his hand and told herself that she could take on more of his burden, that she was willing to carry more on her broad shoulders. Given the sweat on Piers's brow, Lizbeth knew for certain that he could not have made this journey without sharing the burden with her. It was tough enough for the two of them.

Angie came up and squeezed her other hand, the one that held the arrow.

As Piers led them from grave to grave, bones became more numerous. Lizbeth didn't understand. Why would bones be in empty tombs? Where were the trees that came from the seeds that had been housed in the flesh that had once covered these bones?

But maybe these bones weren't from dead Welkeners. Maybe they were something else. Lizbeth couldn't tell.

Soon they came to a room filled with bones.

"Just like in Deedy," Angie whispered.

Then they heard something.

Piers stopped. Lizbeth strained her eyes and ears. Though bones covered the floor, she could not make out any skeletons. She didn't see any skulls.

Angie let go and walked toward the blackness on the other side. She did not look down at the bones below her, yet she did not stumble. "I see bones."

Duh, thought Lizbeth. *Wait a minute. What does she mean?*

Angie slipped into a dark passageway and disappeared. Top-heavy with her burden, Lizbeth managed awkwardly on the bones. Piers, groaning in duress, passed her and disappeared. Lizbeth started to panic. She imagined herself tripping, falling into the bones, and sliding between them. She saw herself grabbing onto a bone and holding on for dear life as she started to slide into a pit below her, a bottomless abyss.

"Lizbeth."

She shook off the daydream and saw Piers's hand reaching toward her from the darkness. She took it, stepped across more bones, and followed Piers into a much larger tomb.

Bones still carpeted the floor. A crack in the soil above them allowed a stream of light to shine into the far side of the room.

Something came between them and this light, something dark. They walked toward it. Sweat dripping down her forehead, Lizbeth held the shaft of the arrow above her, ready to stab.

Murmurings could be heard, dull groans and a melancholy hum. Then they saw the source. The darkness between them and the light was in fact a wall of bodies, the backs of dark robes with the hoods pulled over heads. They reminded Lizbeth of the cloaks Piers and the others had worn when the Misfits had first met them in the rain in Circle Stand.

Hunched over in pain, Piers pushed through the assembly. As he walked, the cloaks parted for him. Lizbeth struggled to keep her head up to see. At the same time, she was afraid to look ahead, afraid a cloak would touch her, afraid to see into the hood. Hanging onto the arrow, she followed Piers.

From up front, a howl startled her. It was an eerie midnight sound, like the moaning wind rustling through leaves. Lizbeth hated it. She turned her head away and stared right into the face of a hooded figure. She saw nothing, only darkness. She wanted to close her eyes, to stop stepping on bones, to get out of this mass grave, to make it, the howling, everything, go away.

Then Lizbeth heard a quiet clopping. It grew louder, clopping, clopping over the moaning.

At last she realized it came from below her—from her own oxen hooves, banging on the bones.

A hand on her back nearly pushed her over. She turned with the arrow poised to strike and shouted a guttural, bovine roar. She just knew she'd see a skeleton tugging at her.

But it was Angie, eyes closed, the light reflected off her face in blacks and grays.

When Lizbeth turned back, she couldn't see Piers.

As she yelled, "No!" a bone rolled under her, and she fell. Angie tripped over her, and they lay flat on the bones. Lizbeth didn't move. She felt better lying there, not having to carry Piers's burden as she walked. Then she remembered the vision outside Angie's room and the sight of Welken through the windows and the sound of the howling in the night. She pushed herself up.

Ahead, his body shining in the light from above, a stocky figure rested in a chair. He had a modest face, long with ample jowls, bags under his eyes, and brown hair that hung lifelessly to his shoulders. His rumpled, dirty coat, its insides tattered and smudged, hung over the arms of the chair. He did not look like royalty or like a person of greatness. In fact, he did not *look* at all, for his eyes had the dead gaze of someone who had seen Morphane, of someone whose soul had journeyed out of his body. Only one thing looked strong—his arms. With the coat hanging down to his biceps, Lizbeth saw his outsized muscles, the huge "swinging arms" that Piers had said he needed. Lizbeth knew this had to be Bors, but it was not how she pictured him.

Bones did not cover the ground near the chair. Piers knelt at his feet and put his head in Bors's lap.

More weight pushed down on Lizbeth until she groaned under the load. It was all she could do to turn her head toward Angie. As Lizbeth bore the burden on all fours, Angie knelt and watched. Lizbeth felt her own skin sink inward on itself.

She also felt no wind. In fact, it seemed like there was no air. A solid, deadening weight filled her lungs. She struggled to breathe.

Then Piers screamed. His hands on Bors's knees, his head thrown back in agony, Piers let out an otherworldly wail. His voice traveled deep to deep, and his face grew more and more contorted. In grisly imitation of Morphane's roiling muzzle, Piers did what he'd come to do. He called Bors's soul out. He pulled with his eyes and cheeks and lips. He brought Bors's soul—his very self—to the surface, to the edge of his own face.

Behind him, the hooded bodies moaned louder. Their voices grew in force like a choir, their dissonance echoing into the tomb.

Lizbeth buckled under the pressure and the awful sounds. She wanted all of it to stop—but she was willing to keep going, to endure anything to save Bors's life. And she worried about Piers. She tried to accept more weight. Her back bent under the pressure. She struggled to hold herself up, to carry the load, to not be crushed by it.

Then Piers's face changed. As if a thin, invisible sheet had drifted from him, his brow and nose returned to normal. He stopped screaming and bowed his head in exhaustion. The drifting thinness floated lightly in the air and molded onto Bors. He jerked at first, then stretched and groaned. Slowly he stood up and lifted his hands to the light. He shot his head up, as if surfacing from being underwater, and bolted open his eyes.

Bors's scream took over where Piers's had left off. Only this was a shout of triumph, of renewal, of resurrection. He clenched his fists in exultation.

As Lizbeth watched the color return to Bors's ashen skin, she felt instantly lighter. She got up off the ground, and so did Angie. Lizbeth thought she should feel completely free, so unburdened that she would be able to fly. She thought she would feel light as a feather. But she didn't. The burden eased, but the shard was still there, and some weight remained.

She expected Piers to be in a heap on the ground, panting over his ordeal. But he seemed full of energy—and, unlike her, utterly relieved of his weight, his weariness. He ran up to the rejuvenated Bors, hugged him, looked tenderly into his eyes, and led him off the chair. As Piers helped pull Bors's coat on, Lizbeth could see its magnificence—its deep purple richness, its square shoulders and golden buckle. It hung to his knees. As Bors tied the coat on, the hooded choir stopped chanting and bowed.

With Bors and his coat no longer covering the chair, Lizbeth saw its glistening precious stones. It was a throne.

Piers brought Bors over to Lizbeth and Angie. "Ah, good friends, here, at long last, is Bors, 'Aelred Broonsees, for the fullness of his name,' as Vida would say. Bors, this is Lizbeth and Angie, true travelers who have been helping us find our way home."

Bors pointed to Lizbeth. "I believe that, in a way, I have already met you." Bors bowed humbly. "Lizbeth, Angie, I reckon all of Welken praises your names."

Lizbeth felt utterly drawn to his side. Bors had no "airs," no sense of position. She knew at once she could be her whole self and Bors would accept her. "We are just glad we found you, Bors."

Bors smiled. The smile grew wider and wider until his mouth opened in laughter. He nudged the more serious Piers with his massive arm. Piers, caught off-guard, jolted over two steps. Bors laughed once more, then flung his head back and roared with laughter. He seemed at that moment to be the fount of all the joy in the universe.

Even the cloaked ones became animated. Their silence turned to light murmurings, and their moans sounded hopeful.

Lizbeth saw how much Angie was enjoying the moment. She twirled twice and stepped into the light. She seemed to soak it in, to swallow it up as nourishment.

Then Lizbeth looked back at the cloaked Welkeners. While Piers watched, Bors walked up to each hooded figure; each bowed when Bors approached and grasped the bottom of his purple coat, but Bors lifted up each seemingly vacant hood and looked warmly at each "face." He brushed dust off shoulders and hugged some hoods to his chest.

"Piers," said Lizbeth, "what is this place? What's he doing?"

"What you see, this room, is called 'The Between.' These hooded ones, they are waiting for their seeds to grow. They need care before they can shoot forth. That's what Bors does. He tends to these hopeful saplings. He's a gardener, you know." Piers sighed. "Ah, there he is, Bones of my Bonesy. And since he met Morphane, he hasn't been able to move them along, to provide good soil for growing."

Lizbeth stared dumbfounded at Piers, then made her way over to Angie. "I have as many questions as answers."

Angie kept her face in the light and her eyes closed. "It always seems that way. But it makes sense, don't you think? The bigger the truth, the less we know about it."

"And Piers. Look at him. Does he look bigger to you? His shoulders seem broader, and his hair is longer."

Before Angie could respond, Piers sat on the throne and held up his hands with his fingers curved, pointing out. He looked like he was getting ready to wave with both hands. Then his hands changed into cat's paws, his claws shooting out. Light emanated from him as his whole body shifted and reshaped itself. He became a cat, larger than Bors, larger than Morphane, powerfully muscular, and then, just as quickly, shrank down, smaller and smaller, until he was the size of a house cat, an orange house cat. He meowed. He jumped off the throne and paced back and forth on the ground. But the ground wasn't dirt or bones. It looked more like varnished wood. Lizbeth thought for a minute that it could have been the deck of a ship.

Then she glanced up from the wooden floor. She sat in her own backyard with the other three Misfits next to her. Percy paced back and forth on the deck. Then he curled up and purred.

PART FIVE

AWAKENED, THE FAMILY

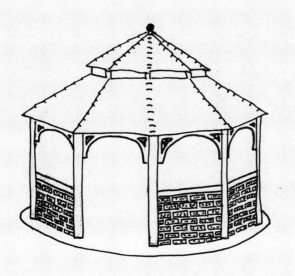

CHAPTER THIRTY

The Dream's the Thing

The net of the sleeper catches fish.

—GREEK PROVERB

 Somewhere far from her home, the mother wept. She looked at her daughter in the front seat. She rolled down the window and hoped the freeway wind would dry her tears. Draping her hand over the wheel, she felt tired as she crossed the border into her new state.

With miles to go, she worried she would fall asleep. She worried that the car would roll over and over and then all the pain would have been for nothing. But she also worried that she wouldn't fall asleep, and the car wouldn't roll over and over, and she would have to watch her daughter bear all the marks of sorrow. The bruises from a father who could not learn to love. The scars from leaving a brother behind.

The mother did not fall asleep. At long last, she pulled the car into a driveway. As the windshield wipers clunked and swished, clunked and swished, she stared at the garage door. Then she turned the car off, closed her eyes, and waited for the servants to come to open the door.

No one came. She laughed. She knew she would have to open this door—and all the doors to come. There were no servants. There was no jackpot.

Still, she had choices to make. She looked at her daughter asleep beside her, so peaceful, so free. But the mother knew better than this. The mother knew. And she knew that she could choose.

So she prayed. She did not know what this might mean. She did not have any clear idea of a God who listens or acts. She had seen gospel men in the street wave their hands. She had heard their pale shouting. They seemed crazy. And that's how she felt now, a little crazy, praying in the car at night, the rain gently falling, the water collecting and flowing down the same patterns on the windshield, as if tiny canals had been worn into the glass.

The glass. She would never forget that night. Her husband holding the plates. Her fear. Her terror. In the shattering of the china, she had seen her husband's madness, his anger, how it cut into grooves on his face. This time, when she remembered that night, she saw something else. She saw a wounded boy—not her own son, but her husband. She looked into her husband's eyes and saw a sad, frightened boy. For the first time, she pitied him. This did not excuse his violence or whitewash his bloody hands, but it did one thing. It helped her see her choice.

She could live the rest of her life with those plates above her, poised for harm. She could live looking into the cocked pistol and put up a shield. She could protect herself, build a wall, a fortress. She could tell the world that she had had enough, that she wouldn't take it anymore, that she would hide behind her past for the rest of her life. Or . . . or she could love. She could decide if her husband—her now deceased husband—would ruin her life or not. This was the gift his boyish sadness gave her. She could forgive him. She could yet love. This was her choice.

The mother picked up her daughter and went inside. The misty rain fell on her cheeks. It felt like answered prayer.

She closed the door and gazed into the entry mirror. She said to herself, I know what I will do for you, child. Momma knows. I will rock you, dear one. Momma knows what to do. Yes, she does. Bebba knows.

Lizbeth awoke to Angie, Len, and Bennu leaning over her. She lay flat on her back just below her backyard deck. Her friends shook her gently and said, "Wake up, Lizbeth," and "Are you OK?" She heard them, but she was too far inside herself to come out just yet. From that deep place she gazed out at them. She wondered how she had fallen asleep so quickly after arriving in her backyard. She wondered at the wonder of it all, passing through the veils, discovering revelations. She knew she could not stay inside herself much longer. She focused outward, seeing what she took to be the inside walls of her eyes framing her friends. Then she seemed to dive upward toward the opening, hitting reality with a belly flop, her eyes bulging, her body sore, and her breath short and desperate.

Angie put her hand under Lizbeth's back and helped her sit up. "How are you feeling? You had more of the nightmare, didn't you?"

"Yes." Lizbeth put her head between her knees. "Only this one was, well, more real."

"You started shaking," said Bennu, "and you said 'Charlotte' over and over."

"Yeah, wait till you hear about this."

Len crossed his legs and sat up. "Maybe you should catch your breath for a second. I just have one thing to say about being here. Arrooooooo! We were about to lose our heads when Percy saved us. I know, weird. Not Piers, but Percy. He came onto the deck of Gareth's ship."

"Was he pacing?" asked Angie.

"As a matter of fact," said Bennu, "he was."

"Just like he was in the cemetery when we found Bors."

Together, Len and Bennu said, "You what?"

"I know, I know, so many good things."

Len stood up. "I'm going to scream again." He put his head back. "Yaaaaaahooooo!"

Bennu picked up Percy. "OK, now that the whole neighborhood knows we're back, we've got to get going—y'know, share what we've learned—and somehow go back. Fatagar's army is going to attack Primus Hook."

Lizbeth snapped back to life. "Fatagar? That's terrible! Hey, let's pull some chairs together on the deck and sort things out."

Len leaped up and grabbed a chair on the deck. "We might not want to stay here."

"What's the problem?" asked Angie.

Len motioned with his head to the opposite side of the deck.

Darlene lay on her stomach in a flat chaise lounge, her bikini top unfastened, exposing her whole back and sides. A glass with ice and amber-colored fluid sat on the deck beside her right hand.

"I dunno," whispered Len, "I feel uncomfortable, kinda queasy."

Lizbeth grimaced. "She's probably passed out. She didn't say anything when Len yelled."

"I don't like it either." Bennu stared at his mother. "Let's go next door."

Lizbeth noted the disgust on Bennu's face, then her gaze lingered on her mother. "I don't want her to burn in the sun."

Bennu put a hand on the sliding glass door. "Let her. That's the price she pays."

Darlene lifted her head. "I won't burn."

Bennu hit the doorjamb with his fist. "Crap."

"You know I don't like that word, young man." Darlene brought her arms from her sides to the front and started to push herself up onto her elbows.

Len hit Bennu on the back. "Comin' through! Too much information!"

He and Bennu stumbled inside, and Angie quickly followed.

Lizbeth watched them go, then took one more look at her mother. Darlene was trying to sip from a straw in her drink while covering her front with one arm. Neither attempt was entirely successful. She sucked on the straw, pulling it out of the drink with a slurp. Then she smiled at Lizbeth with the straw in her mouth and shifted her arm so everything was covered.

Lizbeth was profoundly embarrassed. She couldn't understand how things had gotten to this point. They were churchgoers. They believed in family. It wasn't supposed to be like this. And she had enough stress— trying to understand the riddle of the nightmare and get back to Welken to help Piers.

When Lizbeth walked into the house, Martin was watching television in the living room. The others had gone out the front and left the door open. On one hand, Lizbeth wanted to shout at her father to straighten out her mom, to be a responsible husband. On the other, she remembered his sad, defeated look when her mother was drinking. She wanted to somehow broach the subject gently, to ask him what he thought. She wrung her hands.

And instead she said simply, "Hi, Dad."

"Hi."

"Whatcha watchin'?"

"It's a documentary about the Battle of the Bulge in World War II. It's strange. The Allies had really already won the war and the Nazis had to know they were finished. Yet here was this terrible, bloody battle. The narrator said that the situation is not uncommon. Sometimes the worst battles occur after the ultimate outcome of the war has become inevitable."

Lizbeth sighed. "It's summer, Dad. I'm not all that interested in a history lesson. I'm going next door. You might turn off the TV for a minute and go check in on Mom."

"She's fine."

"She might fall asleep while tanning."

"She's fine! I tell you she's fine!"

"Fine!" Lizbeth slammed the door on the way out.

Fine, she thought. *Watch some stupid war program while Mom slips into oblivion. There's the war you should be fighting, Dad. But if you won't, maybe I won't. I can make myself not care. I can prepare for a battle too. I can build a wall.*

As she approached the Bartholomews' front porch, Percy ran up, then stopped to lick his paws. He watched her with his beautiful green eyes and tilted his head. He seemed to be questioning her, expressing doubt.

Lizbeth picked him up and petted him. "How can I stay angry with you around, Percy? I know, I know. I shouldn't build a wall." She stroked his spine till his tail shot up. "I know. But I'm scared."

Percy meowed.

Len tapped his foot impatiently. He poured pita chips into a bowl and took a plastic container out of the refrigerator. "Anybody want some hummus?"

Angie snuggled closer to Bennu on the couch. "I can't believe my brother likes hummus. It's actually good for you."

"It's food, ain't it?" Len took a big bite as Lizbeth walked in the front door with Percy draped over her shoulder and facing behind her, his front paws kneading the air. "OK, we're all here." Len swallowed and stuck another pita chip in his mouth. "We need to review what we know. Lizbeth, you look a little frazzled. Maybe you should go first."

Lizbeth sat down and put Percy in her lap. He jumped off and lay on his side in the middle of the floor. "I guess I should begin with why I said 'Charlotte.' Well, we already know that Bebba and Dear-Abby are the same. That's weird enough. But in my dream, the mother and her little girl—remember, she left her son with an uncle—well, in the dream, the mother says she is Bebba, which makes her Dear-Abby, which makes Charlotte the little girl."

Len felt flushed. Adrenaline shot through him to his fingertips. "So, if we're to believe this nightmare, my grandmother had this disgusting husband, a jerk who beat her? No wonder she's crazy! No, I didn't mean that. Well, maybe I did. Maybe it's how she's coped with her past."

Angie leaned her head on Bennu's shoulder. "Poor Grandma. All those terrible things that happened to her. No wonder she doesn't want to talk about the past."

"But she found a way to survive," said Lizbeth excitedly. "That's the amazing part. She started over. She drove across the country to a new place. It was raining."

"Oregon," blurted Bennu.

"Yeah. I guess so. And she could only start over if she forgave her husband. My dream said she had a choice."

Angie lifted her head off Bennu's shoulder. "But what's this got to do with Welken? What good does it do us to know this story? Should we think of Bebba differently? Has Mom been traveling to Welken? And who are we needing to forgive?"

"Gareth, for one." Len stacked three cookies together and took a bite. "He told Fatagar to dispose of us, the jerk."

"There's more." Bennu leaned forward. "Fatagar's got soldiers, mainly tremlings—I know you haven't seen one yet—and he's sailing for Primus Hook."

"Where's Grandma?" Angie sounded startled. "She should be here, right?"

"I don't know," said Len. "Stay on task. She's probably out with Mom or Dad, or she's in the bathroom."

"I just don't like the way she left us." Angie looked out a window. "She just walked off without saying good-bye."

"Angie's talking about Dear-Abby as Bebba, how she left us at Point Refusal." Lizbeth sat on the floor and patted Percy. "We found Piers there. Then we hiked to Welken's cemetery and we found Bors. He's amazingly strong and gentle at the same time."

Before long, each had shared details from Welken, about the Cutters and the orchard of graves, about Justice Island and Sutton's sacrifice, about another line of mystery, "when water's dry and land be small," and more about Fatagar's intentions.

"And the way we got back," said Bennu, "wow. Piers and Percy were in two—no, three—places at almost the same time."

Len scratched his face. He thought maybe he had enough stubble to warrant a shave. He wanted to have some wise response to everything, to show his leadership. But all he could come up with was that things looked pretty ominous, that two armies were converging on Primus Hook, and that although Bors and Piers were well again, the bad guys outnumbered the good guys about fifty to one. Maybe the worst thought was that, unlike their first adventure in Welken, this time they didn't understand their mission. They had no tiles to search for. But maybe it didn't matter. They had helped restore the tiles, even though they hadn't found them.

"We need to focus on the positive," he said, as if this statement were insightful and resolved existing tensions.

Before anyone could follow up, the front door swung open and in walked a panting Charlotte. "Oh, I'm so glad you're here. We can't find Mom, I mean Grandma, Dear-Abby. She was telling us a story about her sister Louise, about her cemetery plot—and left the room. We waited a bit, then went looking for her. That was well over an hour ago. She's been wandering lately. It's a part of her dementia. I'm worried sick."

Angie brushed her forearm up and down. "What did she say about Louise?"

"Really, Angie, this is not the time. Grandma is missing."

"I know, Mom, but maybe there's a clue in the story."

"A clue in the story? This isn't a detective game. I'm getting upset."

"I'm sorry, Mom." Angie looked at Len. "We'll help you look, OK? But you know how Grandma talks. Sometimes she makes sense in spite of herself."

"Yeah," said Len, "she's got her own loony logic." When he saw his mother's look after this comment, he wished he hadn't said it.

"OK, real fast." Charlotte sat on the edge of the rocker. "Grandma's sister Louise never married. She lived with another sister, Betty. We always called these aunts the Twin Spinsters, but they were really sweet. They lived in a duplex next to an elderly couple. When the man's wife died, he stressed out because he hadn't purchased a burial plot. So Louise told him that she and Betty had two plots side by side. She said that she and Betty could be together in one plot and that the man and his wife could have the other. They'd be next-door neighbors, in a duplex, just like old times."

Len tried not to laugh—but he couldn't help smiling. "Sounds like a story Grandma would tell."

"OK, you geniuses," said Charlotte, "how does the story help us find Grandma?"

Bennu stood up. "This is maybe too obvious, but we could check out the cemetery."

"OK, fine." Charlotte ran her fingers through her hair. "Nothing else has worked. Why don't you split up? It's starting to get dark, so be careful. I'm going to grab a flashlight and look around in the Wilder. Maybe Grandma thought she'd take the canoe down the river. That's a horrible idea, isn't it?"

Len felt in his pocket for keys. "I'll take the car and go to the cemetery. It would be a long walk for Grandma, but she's got great legs. I mean, strong ones. Bennu, you coming?"

"I thought for once maybe I could go with—"

"Angie," said Charlotte, "I want you to stay here, in case Grandma shows up on her own. That way you can keep her here."

Bennu bit his upper lip. "OK then. I'll—"

"Go with me." Lizbeth turned him toward the door. "We'll go separate directions around the block and meet at the park to check it out. Where's Jeff?"

Charlotte opened the hall closet and took out the flashlight. "He's driving around. He'll probably drive by one of you."

Terrific, thought Len, *the Skylark once again*.

CHAPTER THIRTY-ONE

THE MAUSOLEUM

When we remember that we are all mad,
the mysteries disappear and life stands explained.

—MARK TWAIN, *NOTEBOOK*

 Lizbeth walked briskly down the street. She felt foolish calling out "Dear-Abby," as if Len and Angie's grandmother were a dog. So she didn't. Dear-Abby was hard of hearing anyway. Besides, Lizbeth knew that Bebba could take care of herself. Couldn't she?

Lizbeth saw an older woman coming toward her, silhouetted by the setting sun. "Dear-Abby, is that you?" Lizbeth ran up and saw that it wasn't.

The woman held her handbag to her chest as Lizbeth approached. "Oh, hello there. You scared me for a minute running up to me. I saw your broad shoulders and worried you were a mugger."

"Not to worry, ma'am. I just play softball." Lizbeth suppressed a sarcastic tone.

"Have you seen any muggers out tonight? I do hope to get home safely."

"Where are you going?"

"Just one more house. I'm visiting the Vaughans. I'm their old Aunt Vesta. I'm just an old biddy. Don't mind me. Walk me to the door, will you, sweetheart?"

Lizbeth started to tell her that she couldn't, that she didn't have time to help an old lady because she was busy looking for an old lady. Then she shrugged, took Vesta's arm, and said, "Sure."

They strolled slowly up to the door. Lizbeth saw the family crest on the door knocker, a shield held up by two griffins. She said good-bye and jogged away, remembering with every step wisecracks she'd heard about her potential as a running back.

Soon the park came into view. She saw Bennu twirling in a swing, the chains clacking as he spun.

"I thought you'd never get here." He pushed both feet into the bark dust to stop the swing. "Or that you had found Dear-Abby and taken her back."

"Neither."

"OK, slowpoke, let's look around."

In the Skylark, Len put his arm out the window and pushed his hand up and down in the airflow. He drove deliberately, glancing back and forth. As he turned off the radio, he chuckled at the possibility that the oldies station would play "He's a Wanderer" while he searched for his grandmother. Inspired, he tapped the side of the car and sang, "She wanders round and round and round and round."

Pulling into the cemetery parking lot, Len stopped singing. He was not a big fan of cemeteries. Something about death spooked him. Crazy that.

Well, no grandmothers so far. On the other hand, lots of grandmothers. Just none who are talking. I'll head up this hill, past the Skinner pioneers. OK, OK. Nothin' yet. The newer section's up ahead. Then I'll loop around back to the parking lot. I wish the sunset was brighter. I wish they had lights out here.

Len trudged up to the "view" lots. He wondered how much more they cost. He imagined himself six feet under, pacing underground and saying, "I can't believe they paid for the view lot and then didn't pay the extra for the periscopes. Cheapskates." He didn't know who he was talking to.

A sight a little ways off caught his eye. He walked over to where a backhoe sat next to a neat pile of earth. Plywood covered a hole.

This whole mortality thing. I don't like it. Cemeteries shouldn't include anyone from the last fifty years. *Hmm, I wonder who this is, was. I wonder who'll be buried here tomorrow.*

Then he heard voices, men talking from a gravesite nearby. Maybe they'd seen his grandmother. He walked past a couple of large monuments and a mausoleum in the shape of a small house. It had a sloping roof and a door that was open a crack.

How inviting. Too bad I don't have time to say hello.

The men argued loudly. Something about a gravesite. Len sat on a bench and pretended to be praying.

"In the morning, let's try this one."

"No."

"Look, Pa said we had to do it. Do you want to make him mad?"

"I don't care."

"Yeah, big bragger now."

"We don't need to buy a plot. He's not going to die."

"I know that. You know that. But Papa doesn't. Hey, this'll be like an alibi. We didn't know he'd get a new heart. We didn't kill the guy."

"Shut up."

"No one's here."

"Just shut it."

"OK, then, we're settled. We'll get this one in the morning. Pa says they're cheaper if you plan ahead."

"Look, the only name on a tombstone is going to be yours. I can see it now, Josh Mink, the Idiot Who Gave Up on His Brother."

"No, it'll say, Tommy Mink, the Brother So Stupid He Couldn't Stick with the Plan."

Len prayed for real now, to anyone or anything that would save him from being seen. He froze.

Become the bench. Become one with the bench.

"Let's go, dorkhead."

"Shut your face, Tommy. You are such a freakin' moron."

The McKenzie Boys slugged each other in the arm. They slapped at and blocked each other's punches. They walked straight toward Len.

LaRusso Park's several acres contained extensive play equipment, jogging paths, a Frisbee golf course, and rolling grassy hills. Although Lizbeth was fairly certain Dear-Abby was not playing Frisbee golf, she had no other intuitions. She and Bennu left the swings and headed into the fading light.

Bennu picked up a yogurt lid and spun it into the air. "This first hole's my best one. I always birdied it."

"Let's stay focused, Bennu. I don't think Charlotte cares about your scores."

"I know, but this feels like a waste. Abby is Bebba, and Bebba is as tough as they come. She'll be fine."

"OK, but if Piers needed help, then Bebba might need some too."

"Good point."

They crossed the fourth hole and walked down the jogging path.

"Someone's on the bench up there." Bennu quickened his step. "At least I think so."

"Yeah, you're right, lying down or something."

As they approached the bench, Lizbeth could see the person stretched out, a hat over his face. "Nope," she said, "not Dear-Abby."

Bennu picked up a piece of paper on the ground and ran to the Frisbee net for a dunk. He dropped the paper through, caught his hand on the rim, and brought Hole # 8 crashing to the ground. Then Bennu tripped. As he tried to right himself, he stumbled and landed in front of the bench.

"Graceful," said Lizbeth. "Too bad Angie wasn't here to see it all."

She went over to help him up, but the guy on the bench beat her to it. "Hey there, son, I'll give you a hand." The man held out his palm, his dirty fingers poking through a tattered glove.

"That's OK," said Bennu. "I don't need any help."

"And that's the third lie." The man's pale face could be clearly seen in the dim light, his bony cheeks pushing tightly against his bone-white skin. "We are all broken. All of us. We need help getting put back together. Someday you and your friend will see this for yourself."

Bennu got up on his knees. He gazed into the pale man's face and said nothing. Then he reached out and took the man's hand.

Lizbeth didn't like it. She didn't like the dark look in the man's eyes and his ghoulish skin. She didn't like the idea of Bennu holding that filthy hand. Yet she knew that Len and Bennu had talked about a strange man who spoke strangely.

The man lifted Bennu to his feet. "You have begun to tell the truth about yourself. Soon your friend will too."

Lizbeth stepped back, offended. *How have I been lying? What does he mean by that? He doesn't even know me.*

The man walked past Bennu, picked up the Frisbee net, and re-hung it on the tree. Then he walked away.

"He means Len." Bennu shook the dirt off his shorts and examined his knees. "It's not about you. He means Len."

Lizbeth and Bennu finished their tour of the park. On the way home, as darkness slowly prevailed, Lizbeth listened to every detail about the homeless man.

Len put his head in his hands. He hoped this way of covering his face looked like grief or fervent prayer. He hoped the McKenzie Boys would walk right by him.

Tommy and Josh stepped closer. Len heard every crushed blade of grass, every crunched pebble. He heard mosquitoes and crickets, and an owl somewhere in the distance. Then he heard a soft slap, like a hand on fabric.

Tommy said, "Y'know, a cemetery's a good place for a fight." A louder thud followed, and scuffing feet and grunts and "ows."

Aargh, he thought, *I wanted to be invisible—but not so invisible that they'd pick a fight right next to me. I am so stuck. And then these stupid mosquitoes. I'm really getting swarmed. I can't stand it.*

Len gently moved his hands over his forearms to sweep off the mosquitoes. Then he rubbed his legs. Mosquitoes buzzed in his ears and landed on his face. He swiped at them. He listened to the fight but dared not look. Some dust came his way. A mosquito bit his arm. Another bit him on his neck. He brushed himself all over now, his arms and face, his legs and neck. He felt like a mosquito magnet. He had to get away, had to move. Then he got bitten on both calves at once. He grabbed at them, rubbed the bites, and let out an involuntary "yeow."

He stood up. He did not turn around. Then he noticed that the scuffling had stopped. He must have missed something while he'd flailed at the mosquitoes. Maybe the McKenzie Boys had given up on their fight and walked away. Maybe they stood there staring at him in silence.

Len took one step away from the bench. Someone grabbed his left arm and pulled him around. He saw Tommy's scowl and felt Josh's punch in his gut. Len stumbled back. He grabbed his stomach and fell to the ground, his head landing between two headstones. His insides ached. He curled up into a semifetal position. Then Tommy yanked him up from behind by the T-shirt, lifting him off the ground. The collar choked him, so Len reached for his neck. He scraped his fingers into the shirt and pulled down.

Then Josh hit him in the kidneys. "You're right, Tommy. A cemetery *is* a good place for a fight." Len twisted and Josh hit him on the hip. "Not that this is much of a fight."

Holding the collar of his T-shirt with both hands, Len found the strength to kick wildly at Josh, landing a solid blow to his chin. Josh yelled and reeled back. Tommy dropped Len.

"Bro, you OK?" Tommy pushed his sleeves back.

"I bit my tongue. Blood's everywhere."

Crablike, Len scooted away on the ground. Tommy charged him, grabbed Len's foot, and spun him around on the ground. Then Tommy smiled. While Josh spit out blood and felt his tongue, Tommy gripped Len's foot again. He spun him on the path, stirring up dust. Len held out his hands on the bark-mulch and grass. He tried to find anything to slow him down. His finger clipped a memorial stone, and he yelled in pain. He brought the hand to his chest.

Suddenly, he was aloft. With a hand on each ankle, Tommy leaned back and twisted around and around. Len took in the swirling ground and screamed. Everywhere he saw bone-breaking, skull-crushing granite. The headstones spun by him like gear teeth sticking out of the earth—and with each revolution he saw the mausoleum.

Tommy said, "Uhh," and sent Len flying through the air. As the ground came quickly toward him, he tucked his head in and rolled over twice before stopping. Dizzy and aching, but with nothing broken, Len pushed himself into a crouch. He felt his aching side. He winced at the pain.

Tommy sat on the ground holding his head. Len thought he must have tripped and hit a marker. Josh brushed the blood on his hands onto his jeans. He skipped a step and ran at Len.

Len got up and looked behind him. The house-mausoleum stood about ten feet away. Remembering the open door, Len scrambled toward it, his head still spinning. He nearly fell once, pushed off the grass with his hand, and slammed into the stone wall next to the door. He looked back and saw Josh. Len searched frantically for the latch, for the doorknob, but he did not find one—he found only the crack in the opening. He yanked the heavy door back, slipped in, saw a handhold, and shut the door. He felt for an inside bolt or lock. In the dark, he found nothing. Facing the outside, Len slid toward the hinge and moved beyond the door. He put both hands against the wall and panted. He had no idea what he would do when Josh came in.

Listening with all his might, Len heard Josh cussing out the door for its lack of a handle. Then Josh called Tommy over, and Len heard both their voices.

They would find a way in, Len figured, and then he knew he was dead. *Well, good place for it.*

But they didn't come in. Len heard Tommy say, "Fine, we can wait. He's got to come out sometime."

OK, a breather.

Len turned around and sat with his back against the wall. He felt his sore neck, bruised kidneys, and mosquito bites. Then he saw light coming in through the angled roof of the room. Soon Len saw things in the darkness, strange things—and strangely familiar things.

The inside of the mausoleum reminded him a little of Ganderst Hall, with skylights above and a door in the center of each wall. But instead of ornate tables and chairs in the center, the mausoleum housed four crypts, two side-by-side lengthwise, their "feet" facing the "feet" of the other two crypts about a yard away, also side-by-side. The dusty light from above illumined the tops of the crypts.

Len pushed himself up off the wall. Not eager to look at the crypts, he wondered if there was any way to know if the dead people were already in there, inside their caskets, inside the crypts.

Did the workers leave the lids off until the caskets were placed inside? he asked himself. *I doubt it. Would the tops move and reveal murderous mummies? Nah. Why did people want to get buried above ground? Did they think they'd rot slower? That's a nice thought, rotten flesh falling off bones. OK, another connection to bones, to Bors. And here I am in a tomb like the one Lizbeth and Angie talked about. Maybe. So, is there a Guardian of the Veil around here?*

Len whispered, "Bors, are you here?"

Nothing.

Len forgot his pain when he saw two of the crypts, stone images of sarcophagi raised up in relief on their tops. The sculpted Egyptian eyes were closed, and their hands were clasped at the center. He thought about his great-uncle Kieran Bartholomew's attic and the museum display where they'd found the golden scarab.

Len looked closer. Each pair of hands held something. The female Egyptian held a miniature yoke. It wasn't carved out of stone. It was made out of metal and leather.

Yes, yes, thought Len, his heart racing. *Lizbeth. But how could she be here? She's not dead. Duh.*

Then he leaned over the male Egyptian. The sarcophagus clutched something in his hands, too, something small, bonelike, and curved. It was a talon. Len felt its sharp point. *It's Bennu.*

His eyes wide, Len turned to the other two crypts. These, as he expected, bore images of a medieval man and woman. Len stood above the woman's body. Her head framed by a hood, the woman looked blissful, at peace. In her hands, she held . . . nothing. Her hands were simply clasped.

Of course, thought Len. *Angie's invisible. She has nothing to "show" for her angel's body.*

His heart pounding harder, Len lurched over to the last crypt, to "himself." The jerk in his leap stretched his wounds and shot a stabbing pain through him. He put both arms around his sides as if he could keep the pain locked inside. Grimacing, he shuffled over to the middle of the knight's crypt. He wondered what symbol of a lion the knight would be clasping. The armored gloves held something, but it wasn't a claw or a bit of mane as Len expected. Instead of something leonine, the knight held a feather.

"Curious, ain't it, lad?" Blind Bebba emerged from the shadows in a corner.

Len gasped.

"No need to be scared of old Bebba. I won't spit on ya—and my eyes don't bore through stone. They just feel like they do. Ha!"

Len grabbed his sides again. "Have you been here all along?"

"Weel, lad, it's where I live."

"In a tomb? C'mon, I know that's not true."

"We're in Welken, child—or somewhere's in between. The veils are thin, the passageways like silk. I can't see 'em, but even I can feel the smooth sides. We go slidin' back and forth."

"But where are we in Welken? Is this the future? Am I dead?"

"Oh, son, there's much more dyin' y'll need to do before y'll find your last death. And that of your own choosin'."

"What?"

"Look down."

Bebba pointed to the center of the room, to a flower-weave mosaic set into the floor between the four crypts. It was the same flower design as in the amulet, and the same as on the floor below the painted room on Justice Island. The weave turned slowly and changed shape. The petals became two ovals, two disks held together by a frame. The ovals shifted too. They teetered up and down on the frame. Len could see that the flower weave had become a scale. It was the scale he'd seen on the painted wall, the scale of Anubis, the dog-king, the guardian of the dead. Then an image appeared in one of the ovals. Fatagar and his army stormed through the streets of Primus Hook. Gareth, sword raised, commanded the tremlings. The other disk also revealed an image. Another army marched, led by a stern but beautiful woman. Len guessed this had to be MaryMary and the Cutters.

MaryMary's army moved toward the center, marching in silent fury. The Cutters traveled out of one oval and toward the other, joining Fatagar. When she appeared on Fatagar's side, the oval dropped down, like more weight had been added to the scale.

Len looked back to the disk the Cutters had come from. It was empty. Then he saw something, a speck on the surface. He could not tell what it was, but he could hear something, a cry gaining volume. Like nothing he had heard before, the thing screeched louder and louder. Whatever it was, somehow it counterbalanced the weight of MaryMary and Fatagar. Its haunting voice pierced right through him.

Len looked up. The light in the tomb seemed dimmer. He couldn't see Bebba. He couldn't see much of anything.

"Bebba?"

Nothing.

"Bebba? Grandma? Are you there?"

Len strained his eyes into the dark. The crypts were gone. He put his hands in front of him and walked back to the wall he'd entered from. His hands found it, the hinges, and the handhold in the door.

He paused before he opened it. Tommy and Josh might be there, but that didn't matter to him right now. He'd seen something so much bigger. They were nothing compared to advancing armies and the mysteries of Bebba the Blind. How could he fear them?

Len put his shoulder on the door and pushed. It yielded. He took a deep breath and stepped out of the mausoleum. Tommy and Josh weren't there.

Len found his way down to the car and drove home, the glow from the headlights feeling to him like the light of Soliton himself.

CHAPTER THIRTY-TWO
I'VE BEEN SO MANY PLACES

Every good and perfect gift is from above.

—JAMES 1:17a

 As she stepped onto the Bartholomews' front lawn, Lizbeth rubbed her chilled upper arms. She tried to generate enough heat to push the goose bumps back in. "So what you're saying is that this homeless guy has been in your face three times now—and you still don't have a clue what he's talking about, or even if you should be paying attention."

Bennu stepped onto the porch and wiped his feet on the mat. "Oh, Len and I have been paying attention. How could we not? The guy is too weird *not* to get our attention. Each time he sounds so, so, eloquent, yet harsh. His words are beautiful in their own way. To me, he talks like a prophet."

Lizbeth held the screen door open. "Then what's the prophecy about? Who is lying about not being broken, and what difference does it make?"

"All the way home I've been thinking that it must be related to me. I'm the only one who's heard all three corrections of the lies. I've been tormented by it, really."

"What did Len say about the first two?"

With his head Bennu gestured to the car entering the driveway. "Ask him yourself."

Lizbeth raised her eyebrows and followed Bennu inside. There, knee to knee on the corduroy couch, sat Angie and Dear-Abby, laughing.

306

Bennu rushed to sit next to Angie on the sofa. He put his arm above her shoulders on the back of the couch. "What's so funny?"

Angie put her right hand on Bennu's knee. "Grandma was telling me about her encounter with a cell phone. Go ahead, Grandma."

The front door slammed, and Len banged kitchen cupboards open and shut.

Dear-Abby got up and walked to the kitchen table. "I was right here having a cup-o of tea, when I realized no one else was home, not Clark Gable or Robert Redford or even sweet Lenny Bartholomew." She hugged Len, who was now busy dipping an apple slice into thick caramel sauce at the table. He gave her an obligatory pat. "So I decided to call Char-Char. I dialed her number and just then a cell phone on the table rang. I thought, how inconvenient. Someone is calling the phone at the same time I'm making a call. So I hung up this phone and picked up the cell phone. It said, 'Home.' I answered it but no one was there. How rude! Then I picked up the cordless phone again and called Char-Char's cell phone. The phone on the counter rang again! It said 'Home' again! Now I was getting suspicious!" Dear-Abby raised a finger to the sky. She laughed, and everyone joined in.

"When did you figure it out?" asked Len.

"Figure what out?" Dear-Abby paused and walked out of the kitchen.

Lizbeth collected herself. She rubbed her eyes and let out a deep post-laughter sigh. She was struck by the absurdities of life—how we can receive a prophetic threat one minute and be laughing at silliness the next. The veil between seriousness and levity appeared to be thin as well.

Len wiped his mouth with his sleeve and launched into a description of the cemetery, the McKenzie Boys, and Bebba the Blind. He showed his welts as evidence. Then Bennu and Lizbeth told of the homeless man and his rebuke about brokenness.

"I learned a few things too." Angie flicked her hair back. "Not long after you left, Grandma came in from the back."

Just then, the door to the bathroom opened and the toilet's flushing could be heard. "I returned, just like MacArthur." Dear-Abby grinned as she walked into the kitchen, zipping up her pants in full view of everyone.

Lizbeth struggled to hold Dear-Abby the Fool and Bebba the Wise as the same person in her mind. She tried to imagine Bebba inside Dear-Abby's body moving her arms and legs. But the more she did this, the more she realized it couldn't work that way. Dear-Abby wasn't a puppet. She couldn't be. She'd led a whole life here. Was Dear-Abby the truer self, or Bebba? Or—was it possible—neither?

Percy strolled in and rubbed against Angie's leg. She picked him up. "When Grandma came in from the back, she petted Percy just like I'm doing right now. And then she looked at me with such piercing eyes."

Dear-Abby laughed. "Pierce-o, pierce-o."

"The same eyes that can't see in Welken, and she said she had just seen a griffin."

"I can tell my own story, dear-heart. I'm not speechless, you know. Ha! That's a good one, me mute! I was walking in the wild, up the Lewis. I'm a compulsive walker. Sometimes my feet hurt so bad, I just *have* to walk. So I walked and walked. And then I saw a griffin-o. I says, 'Feasle, fisle, fuzzle, fome; time for this one to come home.' Oh dear, I need to go to bed." Dear-Abby walked away. "See you all in the morn-morn."

Angie gave her grandmother a good-night hug and turned back to the Misfits. "It made me remember our time with Soliton in Ganderst Hall, and how I had a vision of a griffin speaking to me." Angie closed her eyes as if trying to picture the scene.

Len shook his head. "She's just mixed up. Her last name is Griffin."

Bam! The noise of the back door hitting the doorstop startled everyone. Lizbeth jerked up to a ramrod-straight position. Angie dropped Percy.

Big steps banged down the hall, and Charlotte burst into the room. "I— I—I have to tell you." She held herself up in the arched opening to the hall. Panting, she raked her hair back with her fingers and placed the still-beaming flashlight on the floor. "In the Wilder, I walked down the Lewis looking for Grandma. I got all the way to the back of the Ruths' house. It's that four-acre place that's stupidly still zoned for cattle. I heard some rustling noises, so I shined the flashlight up ahead. I couldn't believe what I saw. Through the barbed-wire fence, a mountain lion was attacking a cow. I'm not making this up! I wanted to run and hide, but I had to keep

308

watching. The cow bellowed in pain as the mountain lion tried to pull her through the fence. Then a woman came out of the house and starting yelling. It was Janet, Janet Ruth, and she screamed at the mountain lion and threw rocks at it. Then she ran back to the house.

"After that—you're not going to believe it—an owl flew down. So amazing! I was shaking now! The owl dive-bombed the lion with his big talons. He swooped again and again, but the lion hung on. Then Janet Ruth came running out with a gun. She got close, and fired a shot into the air. That did it. The owl flew off, and the mountain lion let go of the cow. I thought, *Oh. good.* But he turned and came running right at me!"

"Oh, Charlotte!" said Lizbeth.

Charlotte threw her hands up. "I ran! I could hear the cougar behind me. Then I thought how stupid this was. Two leaping bounds and he'd have me for dinner! So I turned back and waved the light at him. I shook the flashlight violently, trying to make myself big, y'know, like they tell you to. And it worked! The mountain lion turned real quick and ran back the other way. Then I came back. I'm still shaking."

Angie grabbed Charlotte's hands. "Mom, whew! Are you OK? Do you want to sit down?"

Len handed Charlotte a glass of water. "That's so awful, Mom. Right here—in the Wilder."

Bennu helped Charlotte to the wingback chair. "Len and I saw a mountain lion up on Mt. Jackson. They're everywhere! Is there somebody we should call? A wildlife authority or something?"

"It's too late right now." Charlotte rubbed her eyes. "I'm OK. I'm starting to settle down. Where's Dad?"

Len made awkward work of consoling his mother, patting her on the back as if she were a child. "He's still out looking for Grandma. We called to tell him that she's back, but his cell phone must be on silent."

"I'm OK. I'm OK." Charlotte went to the sink, splashed water on her face, then lifted her head at the sound of her husband's car. "I'm going outside to talk to Dad."

Bennu waited a minute for her to leave, then looked sternly at the others. "Something about griffins. I don't know what, but we can't ignore it." He yawned.

Lizbeth yawned back. "Maybe we should go to bed. We have to sleep sometime. I know I'm wiped out. If you want to research griffins on the Internet, Bennu, go ahead. I think we should all get some rest. We'll work better in the morning."

"Maybe you're right." Bennu stood to go. "I *am* exhausted. But I think we're real close."

"Before you go." Angie grabbed Bennu by the elbow. When Lizbeth took this as a cue for her to leave and Bennu to stay, Angie reached out for her elbow too. "I mean all of you. I have something else to tell you." Len stepped up so that the four Misfits were almost in a huddle. "When Grandma came in, I said, 'Oh, Grandma, where have you been? Mom and Dad have been worried about you.' Grandma closed her eyes and raised her chin, like Bebba does sometimes, and she said, 'Child, I have been so many places. And I want you to know that my heart has been looking for you all day.' Isn't that just the sweetest thing! I think she meant all of us."

Percy walked into the middle of the huddle.

Lizbeth and Bennu said good night and opened the door into the balmy air. Though it was after ten o'clock, the western horizon still resisted the fullness of an indigo sky. As she looked over to her porch light, Lizbeth remembered her dad's comments about the Battle of the Bulge.

That's how I feel right now, that things are going to be OK, that the victory in the war is, in some sense, already certain—The Welkening made sure of that—but that here we are, preparing for a big battle. We still have to fight it. Some will get hurt, some will die. In fact, maybe the battle's going on right now.

"Lizbeth!"

"What?!"

Bennu put his hands on his hips. "I've been talking to you, and you haven't said a word. You haven't been listening to me, have you?"

"There's a first time for everything."

"*So* funny." Bennu showed her a flip-pad. "Look, I've been cataloging questions. Here's my list."

1. What will happen now that Bors and Piers are better?
2. How can we stop Fatagar and MaryMary?
3. Why is the pale homeless guy haunting us?

4. What do those poetic lines from Welken mean?

5. What are we supposed to learn from your experience in the huts?

6. What are the McKenzie Boys up to?

7. What do we do about your dream?

8. Why all these references to griffins?

"OK, now let's explore possible answers for each question."

"Bennu?"

"What?"

Lizbeth put her hand on the doorknob. "You missed a question."

"Really?"

Lizbeth opened the door. "Yeah. Why has Mom been drinking so much?"

In the living room, the TV blared. Its flashing lights softened Darlene's features as she lay on the couch, asleep. Her head bent forward awkwardly, and her bathing suit cover-up left her legs exposed.

Bennu grimaced. "Maybe knowing why doesn't matter so much. Maybe we just need to know what to do from here."

"I know the thing to do right now is to get a blanket and cover her up." Lizbeth pulled one out of the hall closet and draped it over Darlene's oily, bronze skin. Lizbeth gently lifted her mom's head, pushing a throw pillow more securely underneath at the same time.

Bennu shrugged and left.

Lizbeth stood back and looked at her mom. Then she knelt and stroked her hair. She thought about what Bennu had said, but she couldn't shake her need to know why. She wondered about her parents' marriage, if one of them had had an affair. Or maybe her dad's business was falling apart. She didn't know. Maybe her mother had discovered a dark family secret. Maybe it wasn't anything big. Maybe the little struggles and irritations of life had become too much to bear. Maybe she was disappointed in Lizbeth and Bennu.

In those quiet minutes, Lizbeth saw her mother as a wayward child, an insecure adolescent looking for stability. For all the sympathy this inspired, at bottom, she wanted her old mom back. She missed her mom.

Lizbeth dropped her head and cried. She cried for her mom and for Bennu and her dad and herself. She cried for Mook and Vida, for Piers and Bors. She cried about Bennu and Angie, about her own awful fatness. Then she wiped her eyes and whispered, "Mom, my heart has been looking for you all day."

The little girl grew up in her new rainy town. She didn't remember the old life, the life of broken glass and beatings, of anger and guns. And her mother decided not to tell her. She would make for her daughter the home she did not have for herself. The mother did what she could to bring this about, even though she had little money. She invited neighborhood children to the home for treats. The mother made of her home a refuge, a place for all to be loved, but most of all her daughter. And the girl loved her home.

In time, the girl grew older. She learned to drive. Her mother worked long hours, yet she still invited the neighborhood children for cookies. As much as the mother tried to forget her past, the scars would not go away. Sometimes she dreamed bad dreams and woke up with the terrors. Sometimes she heard voices. At times the mother spoke oddly. She said things that led her coworkers to tell stories about her, to laugh at her behind her back.

The daughter did not know what was happening to her mother. She called it a disease. But it didn't matter. She loved her mother deeply, though she guessed that secret wounds that had been pressed down were beginning to rise.

One day, when the daughter was not at home, a young man came to the door. He had small black eyes and a thin mouth. His look said, I am weary of my pain, but it also said, I can make you join my pain. He acted as if he knew the mother, and he said that the mother owed him something, that she had been cheating him for years.

"Why did my sister get this life and I didn't?" he said. "Why was I left behind and then sent to this home and that school? Why would no one keep me?"

The mother knew why her son had been moved here and there. She'd heard stories of the fighting, of how he'd kicked at his uncle and hit his aunt with books and bricks and pans. She knew of attempts to reform him, and of the arrests and probation and jail time. She'd sent along letters and all the money she'd been able to spare.

The son pushed his mother aside. He wanted to know where the money was and anything that he might be able to sell. He knocked over a lamp in the living room and then stormed into the kitchen.

"I'll tell you what I hate," he said.

He opened drawers and dumped the contents on the floor.

"I hate this silverware," he said.

The mother shook her head and called out for him to stop. She had not cried in this way for so many years.

The son pushed his way into her bedroom.

"I hate how neat you keep this room," he said.

So he ripped the bedspread off and threw his mother's special things—little plates and dolls—against the wall.

The mother fell to her knees. She said, "Don't, Jesus, please. Please don't break my things."

"I hate how you talk," he said.

He took her small jewelry box and emptied it on the bed. Only a few trinkets fell out.

"I hate that you have nothing to give me," he said.

She reached out to him from the floor. "I gave you everything," she said.

"Name one. Name one thing you gave me," he said.

"I gave you all I had," she said. "I gave you myself. I gave you my love. It was not enough for you. I know that I left and I don't blame you for thinking I abandoned you, but I didn't. Your uncle gave me no choice. I called you. I sent money. I sent for you. Did you never get my letters?"

"I hate you," he said.

Then a pin caught his eye. He picked it up and turned it over. It was a golden bug of some kind—a little beetle. He put it in his pocket and walked back to the front door. His mother followed him. Then he turned back and slapped her.

"And I hate one more thing," he said. "I hate that you changed your name. You wanted to shake him off, and you wanted to shake me off. You wanted to leave me behind, but you won't. I won't let you. Your last name is Mink. You will always be a Mink."

The son slammed the door on the way out. The mother sat on the couch and rubbed her chin and wept. After she had cried herself out, she stood and straightened up the house. It was still there. It was still a refuge.

313

Lizbeth rubbed her eyes. She realized she must have been crying in her sleep. She'd never done that before, but the revelation in her nightmare led to real tears. She had trouble focusing. As she wiped away the wetness, Angie's face came clearly into view. Lizbeth said, "What are you doing here?"

"When I woke up, I was here next to you."

"Oh, I see. I'm not in my bed. Where are we this time?"

"I don't know yet. Not in Welken's cemetery, and I don't see Piers or Bors. Why were you crying?"

"You're not going to believe it."

Angie helped Lizbeth to her knees. "Maybe. Maybe not. I'm trying to keep my hands open."

"Well, catch this. Your mom has a brother. He's in town. His last name is Mink. So Odin is your cousin."

Angie put her open hand over her mouth. "What?"

"That's what the dream says. The little boy who watches his mother get beat up, the little boy who enjoys poking his sister, who likes to see others in pain, it's Odin's dad. What do we do with that?"

"Oh my."

"Yeah, oh my." Lizbeth picked up some leaves on the ground. "I guess this isn't my bedroom."

"No. We've awakened into Welken." Angie stroked a blue flower. "I guess that's true in a number of ways. And now I've awakened into a mystery—and I don't really like it. I don't like knowing this."

"I could be wrong. It's just a dream."

"Just a dream? I don't think so."

CHAPTER THIRTY-THREE
AWAKENING INTO THE ACCEPTANCE

Facts are stubborn things.
—JOHN ADAMS, QUOTED IN *JOHN ADAMS* BY DAVID McCULLOUGH

When Len awoke the next morning, he did not want to open his eyes. He did not want to know what time it was or whether Angie was already up, waiting for him to join the other Misfits. He wanted to sleep ten more minutes. He wanted . . . breakfast. Maybe his dad was up making his traditional Saturday morning pancakes. Len breathed deeply, hoping to smell the banana-and-walnuts buckwheat variety or the blueberries with whipped cream.

What he smelled was seaweed. Its pungency jerked his eyes open. Then he heard something. As the sound roared up to him, he thought he should move, but he didn't, and a wave swept over him from behind. The wet and cold doused any lingering desire to remain prostrate. With a shout, he jumped up and ran for dry ground.

Stumbling in the deep sand, Len saw a log up ahead—and Bennu sitting on it, not nearly as wet as he. Len slowed down to a walk and brushed sand off his legs. "Why didn't you wake me?"

"I thought it would be nicer to let you sleep."

"No, you didn't. You thought it would be wetter."

Bennu looked away. He pointed out to sea. "Justice Island. It's like we washed up on shore, like we were shipwrecked."

"Weird. I haven't read *Robinson Crusoe* or even seen a movie

315

about him, but I have this image of him on the sand with waves coming up."

"Yeah. But our ships weren't wrecked. There they are in the harbor."

Len turned his head to look at them. "Gareth's probably sitting in the captain's quarters, getting fat off Fatagar. I don't get that guy."

"Me neither. Keeper of the Balance? More like Stealer of the Balance."

"Man, I'm cold."

"Well, there's no point in staying here. Let's go. Moving around will warm us up."

"Good idea." Len brushed more sand off and trudged up the rise toward town. He held his T-shirt off his stomach and flapped it to dry it out. "Do you have any blueberry pancakes in your pockets?"

Bennu unsnapped the side pockets on his shorts. "Fresh out. But I do have a good supply of cereal bars. Can't get enough of those. Here."

Len gulped one down. "Not enough syrup."

"Sorry."

A hundred yards up, Len turned back to the ships. "Maybe we should set some traps for Fatagar. We can't fight them all, but we could slow them down."

"Too late." Bennu's voice crashed down like a stone wall crumbling. "Quick. Look here." Bennu pointed at a body on its stomach.

Len looked at the awkward angle of the legs. "Oh man." He could not bring himself to look at the head. Then he saw a second body. He felt colder, a chill rippling over his skin and pushing inside. It landed with an icy thud in his stomach. "I can't believe it. Look at this. It's terrible."

Bennu knelt near one body.

"How can you do that?" Len turned away. "I think I'm gonna lose it."

"The fight's not more than a few hours old. The blood's still fresh."

Len wretched into the blackberry bramble. He felt woozy, so he plopped onto the ground and put his head between his knees.

Bennu came up behind him. "You OK?"

"No. How can I be OK? I am not OK seeing the dead of Primus Hook. Are you? You're like some TV detective: 'The blood's fresh.'" He wretched again. "We're too late. Too late."

316

"Let's get out of here." Bennu helped Len up.

Weak-kneed, Len walked a few steps before grabbing Bennu's arm. "So much for the cereal bar."

By the time they reached the first building in town, screams and scuffling could be heard from a good distance away down the street. Len held his stomach and kept pace with Bennu. With every swift change of direction, Len felt the blows he'd taken from Tommy. He winced but went on.

At first they saw no signs of life, only evidence of assault. The metalworker's shop door hung on one hinge, and flower baskets in front of the meat market lay smashed on the ground.

Len didn't know how he would handle another body. For the most part, he didn't need to. He figured that residents must have run or made their attack from a distance. This surprised him. He'd expected Primus Hook to fight hard and long, to marshal a brave army, at least set up some snipers. Then he realized that though he'd seen weapons in Welken, he hadn't seen an organized force. Prester John talked about soldiers—and he was one, presumably—but Prester John always talked big.

Len and Bennu gained on the rear of Fatagar's force. They saw a tremling at the back leap up and hang from the baker's sign until the sign came off in his hands. The tremling fell to the ground. Then, holding the captured sign high over his head, he brought it down on the shop's shutters, breaking slats and knocking the shutters down. He looked up the street to the rest of the army and seemed to be struggling with a decision. He waved the sign over his head and growled at the pack ahead of him. Then he entered the bakery.

Len stretched his neck. "Let's see what we can do. We have to do something." Len looked over at Bennu. His upper body had become a falcon, except without the wings.

Bennu looked disappointed. "This won't help much, will it?"

Len responded by flexing his triceps, then his biceps and forearms. He'd hoped for leonine power, but all he got was his mane shooting out over his shoulders. "This lion gig ain't so dependable either."

They both returned to human form, ran up to the shop, and ducked down below the opening by the broken shutters. Peering in, they saw the tremling with bread in his hands. He ripped loaf after loaf in half and bit into the centers. Sometimes he buried his face in the bread. Sometimes he tossed it on the ground. Then he broke shelves down with his fist. If all of this didn't make him repulsive enough, his hairy skin looked abused or diseased. His "fur" had holes here and there, and scabs marked his skin. Len thought he looked like he'd been pecked and nibbled. Then he remembered the gulls and the mice.

"I'll swing at him, "said Len, "and lead him back up front. You get him from behind with this." Len picked up a stick for himself and handed Bennu a part of the shutter that would make a good club.

"I'll be waiting here." Bennu hid behind the door.

Len snuck up on the tremling. His anger, his sense of violation, filled him up. As the tremling reached for a large ceramic canister, Len jabbed him hard with a stick in the back.

Maybe I'll just take him myself, thought Len.

The tremling arched his back and howled in pain. He knocked the canister over, spilling flour over himself. Careening toward Len, the tremling made a fist and swung.

Len miscalculated the tremling's reach. He bobbed away, but not far enough, and the hairy fist caught him on the left shoulder. As flour puffed in the air, Len fell to his right, crashing into the wall.

The tremling shook himself like a dog. In a fog of flour, he swiped at air. He fought through the cloud and ran at Len. Pushing against the wall with his feet, Len thrust his stick straight into the tremling's gut. The monster grunted but knocked the stick away, head-butting Len. Then the tremling raised his head and opened his mouth. The tremling's jagged teeth glistened with saliva. Reeling from the head-knocking, Len felt on the ground for the stick or anything else.

Then Len heard a *clunk*. The tremling's head snapped forward. He groaned and collapsed in a heap on top of Len.

Bennu held the shutter-plank high over his head. "So much for you leading him to the front."

"Uhn. Get him off me. Let's get out of here." The tremling moaned as Bennu tugged at him and Len pushed. "Wait. He's not dead yet."

"That's OK. Let's move on."

Len stood over the tremling on the floor. "No, it's not OK. He could come back after us. He needs to die."

"Leave him."

"He killed good folks from Primus Hook. He should pay."

"He's wounded. He won't hurt anyone now. Let's go. The army is getting farther away."

Len felt sick again. He didn't know if this was continuing queasiness or something new, a reaction to his own bloodlust, his body informing him about the morality of revenge. "I really want to finish him off. I can't believe how strongly I feel it."

Bennu dropped the plank. "I feel it too, Len. I think it's the animal in us—the lion and the falcon." He walked to the door. "Predators don't think much about what's right and wrong. So we have to work to keep that part of us alive. It's not easy."

Len followed Bennu into the street. "If that's the case, it'd be nice to become a whole lion. I mean, we have the disadvantages of instinct without the advantages of the bodies. I don't get it."

Bennu pointed down the road to the end of the thoroughfare, to Fatagar and Gareth on the steps leading to Long House.

Angie leaned against a tree. "My mom and Odin's dad are siblings. It's sick."

"I feel terrible." Lizbeth walked past the tree into the open.

"I guess it's all part of The Acceptance."

"What are you talking about?"

"We have this idea of how things are. Then things happen. If the things are true, we have to decide what to do. Will we put them in The Acceptance or not?"

"Angie, why can't you just say, 'I'm struggling to believe whether this thing about my mom is true'?"

"I guess I could. And I am struggling."

"At the same time, here we are in Welken and we have to deal with MaryMary and the Cutters, not Odin and his dad."

"It's all part of The Acceptance, Lizbeth."

"Now that you say it again, I kind of like that way of putting it. Most of my life is spent in The Resistance. Where are we?"

"I'm not sure. I wasn't awake much before you. Over there, just beyond those trees, I saw a bridge over a river, the Nez River, I guess."

Lizbeth pushed off the tree. "I think you're right. That makes me think of Mook. We haven't seen him in so long, I feel like we deserted him."

"And Vida. And Jacob. What's been going on in Deedy Swamp? Have the Cutters reached Primus Hook? Did they get to Piers and Bors?"

Lizbeth strained her eyes toward the village of the Nezzer Clan. Every once in a while, she thought she saw some movement, but she knew it might be nothing, just branches swaying in the breeze. She looked back at Angie but could only see part of her. Her lower body invisible, Angie swirled her hands in the dark soil. If Lizbeth hadn't known better, she would have been horrified, this half-body sitting on a foot of air, like a poor beggar in India dragging herself through the streets on her hands. Lizbeth tested her own Welken body. The best she could do was to make her head oxen, but nothing else. She changed back. "See anything?"

"Dirt."

"Angie?"

"Yeah?"

"You're not so weird."

"I do feel something, though."

"Do you mean you feel something in the ground, like an earthquake?"

"I don't know. Maybe the ground is shaking a little." When Angie closed her eyes, her mouth and nose twitched. "I feel something in my fingertips. I feel . . . fear."

"Whose? Where?"

"It's getting closer."

"I don't see anything."

Angie's fingers dug into the ground. She created lines and pulled them toward herself. Over and over, she deepened the rows. "It's Mook." She scooped up dirt with each hand and clenched it. "They're gaining on him."

"Where?"

"Vida too. She can't keep up."

"I don't see them."

Angie's eyes flew open. Her body still invisible from the waist down, she stood up and pointed to the left, downriver. "There."

Lizbeth squinted but saw nothing. "Maybe they're coming. Let's get down to the bridge. And make your bottom visible. You're spookin' me out."

"You're gettin' ghostified."

"Yes, 'Vida.' C'mon."

Lizbeth and Angie sprinted down to the bridge. Along the way Lizbeth realized that if they'd waited to spot Mook and Vida, she and Angie would have been seen running into the open. They hid underneath their side of the bridge and looked south down the path on the other side of the river.

Lizbeth heard something before she saw it. And it came from the other direction, from the village of the Nezzer Clan. At first she thought it might be crows, but then she heard for certain. "Angie, it's dogs, *our* dogs I'm guessing, the ones from the huts. The barking gives me chills."

Angie took several steps up the river but stayed underneath the bridge. "I see some dust. You're right, the dogs are charging!"

"Angie, look down here. There's Mook and Vida running. And Cutters, I think, farther back. They're out in the open. Oh, Vida's so slow! She'll never make it. What can we do?"

"The huts," Angie said, "remember the huts, how nothing was as it seemed."

"So?"

"The dogs are coming. It made me think of the huts."

"So?"

"I don't know. I was hoping you'd be inspired."

"You're the inspirational type, not me."

Angie ran back to the south part of the underside. "Mook's pulling on Vida. He's swinging her up every couple steps."

"There must be no archers or they'd have been hit by now."

"The dogs are coming on." Angie ran to the north side.

Lizbeth joined her. "I think Mook and Vida will get here first. Then the Cutters, maybe half a dozen of them, then the dogs." An arrow zipped into the ground just behind Vida. "OK, there's an archer. Terrific."

"Dry water, cold fire."

"How is that supposed to help?"

"Solid air."

"I have an idea. Angie, I can make my head an ox head, and you can make your bottom half invisible. So let's do that—and you sit on my shoulders." Lizbeth knelt, and Angie slipped her leg up and around. "Good. Now grab my horns and lean forward."

"OK. But what's the point?"

"To scare them. The key is for you to lean as far forward as you can. It will look like I have two heads."

Mook and Vida reached the bridge. As Lizbeth peeked at them from her crouched position on the other side, Vida threw a dagger high into the air at the Cutters. Mook yanked on Vida, Lizbeth heard a squeal, and the two Welkeners climbed over the planks of the bridge.

"Keep going!" said Lizbeth as they reached her.

Vida moved toward Lizbeth's voice. "Mook! We've been cavalried!"

Mook turned back, Vida bumped into him, and they both crashed on the ground.

Holding Angie's invisible legs, Lizbeth marched onto the bridge and toward the Cutters who had just reached the other side. She bellowed hard. She snorted.

The Cutters stopped. They stared at Lizbeth and Angie. Backing up, a few of them shielded their faces with their arms.

"Let's go forward," said Angie.

Reluctantly, Lizbeth obeyed. She felt Angie slide her legs up, put one knee on her shoulder, and then step onto her shoulders with both feet. Then Angie yelled. Lizbeth had never heard her make such a sound, like a trumpet blast, like an angel with a bowl of wrath.

Lizbeth joined Angie's sounds of Judgment Day. She strained her oxen throat and let loose with all she had.

The Cutters looked horrified. Some bowed. Some tripped and fell. Then all the Cutters turned and ran. Lizbeth tried to imagine what they saw—just the top half of Angie suspended between the horns of an ox head that grew out of her own sturdy frame.

She didn't have to imagine what happened next. The Cutters ran right into the dogs. Teeth bared, snapping and snarling, the pack of dogs met the Cutters head-on, encircling them, then herding them north along the river, back toward town.

"Yay!" Angie swung around on one of Lizbeth's horns and landed solidly on her two visible feet.

Lizbeth's head returned to normal. "It worked! I'm glad that's over."

"Me too." Mook came up from behind and hugged Lizbeth, his gray foxtails of hair bouncing on his shoulders.

Vida tottered toward them. "I've been marathoned! I'm exhaustionated! You lostlings are a sight for my bo-peepers."

For just a minute Lizbeth felt resolved and at peace.

Then she remembered the Cutters. That Mook and Vida were on the run. And that MaryMary would not stop.

"To Long House," said Mook. "Let's move."

CHAPTER THIRTY-FOUR

THE CONFESSION

It is not the criminal things which are hardest
to confess, but the ridiculous and shameful.

— JEAN-JACQUES ROUSSEAU, *CONFESSIONS*

"What do you think is going on?" Len hopped onto a railing on the Primus Hook boardwalk to get a better view.

Bennu joined him. "Fatagar's excited about something. He's gesturing like crazy—and I can see his knobby head's all red."

Len jumped off. "Let's get closer. I don't think anyone will notice us coming up from the back."

"Let's go around to the right. We'll meet fewer tremlings."

"True."

"I wonder where Sutton is. I hope he's OK."

"Yeah."

"Man, it's getting cold. It's weird, 'cause the sun's still out."

"I thought it was just me because my clothes are still wet."

Bennu took off between two thatched buildings, Len following as best he could. He did not want to say "wait up" or draw attention to his injuries. Even so, they hurt. He wondered if this was what a prizefighter felt like after ten rounds, or maybe a dishrag after being wrung out. Bennu's natural speed gave Len an excuse for being behind, and the cold gave him another. Yeah, that was why he couldn't keep up.

324

The two Misfits ran behind the buildings and into a cobblestone alley, which was by no means straight. Sometimes Len lost Bennu around a corner, and then he would reappear.

Darting around a hedge that bordered a vegetable garden, Len almost ran right into a tremling sniffing garbage. Up ahead, Bennu peered around a house. He must have run by the tremling without being seen. Bennu waved for Len to come.

I'd like to, thought Len, *really I would.*

Bennu turned around. He looked right at Len, over to the tremling, and glanced up and side to side. A line of laundry hung across the alley. Bennu motioned for Len to go around.

Len started to go. Then he saw the tremling lean over into a wooden bin. The tremling got on tiptoe. He tried to pull one leg up over the side. With a swing of his leg, the tremling threw himself up till his left foot caught on the edge. As he bounced on his right foot, straining to get up, Len rushed the tremling. He ran at him like a linebacker and bumped the tremling below the waist in a knock-over tackle. The tremling rolled over the top and into the bin.

Len wiped his hands as if this level of football skill were commonplace for him. He trotted up to Bennu's side.

Bennu pointed at the hill of steps coming down from the veranda below Long House. "Good work, Stud. There's Fatagar. He's been patting Gareth on the back." Bennu rubbed his hands together, then blew into them. "I wish I could see Sutton somewhere."

The scene did not inspire hope in Len. From what he could tell, Fatagar's soldiers of the Wasan Sagad made a ring around the tremlings, threatening them and keeping them hemmed in. A handful of guards stood near Fatagar. Most everyone bore some evidence of the gull and mouse attack, even Fatagar. A tear in his sleeve flapped in the breeze and his flabby neck oozed out gunk that dripped onto his collar. Gareth's open embroidered vest revealed his white shirt.

The cold seemed to be getting to everyone. Tremlings stomped to warm their feet. Soldiers pulled coats out of their knapsacks. And still the sun shone. To Len, the sunlight seemed colder than the shadows. From the north, clouds moved closer, but no wind could be felt.

Just off the steps, at the beginning of the street, soldiers brought out chairs and shelving, then some good-sized logs. Soon, a fire crackled.

Fatagar gestured for someone to come to him. Two soldiers helped the toady general up several more steps so he could be seen above the fire. In the yellow glow and smoke, Fatagar sat down on his blubber. "Primus H-H-Hook has fallen. *Tck-Tck.*" Soldiers and tremlings cheered. "The town f-f-feared us and left!" More cheering. "They should have f-f-feared us. We are a m-m-mighty army!"

The soldiers held their spears in the air and shouted. The tremlings imitated them and slapped each other as they raised their clubs.

Fatagar stood up and picked at the scab above his eye. "Before we t-t-take Long House and declare ourselves r-r-rulers of Welken, I must honor G-G-Gareth."

Len had hoped the warmth from the fire would reach him. He felt nothing. "Gareth. No wonder he sided with Fatagar. He's the greasiest of them all."

Fatagar's head-spikes looked brighter in the fire's light. "*Tck-tck.* Gareth, tell everyone why you j-j-joined us."

Gareth stepped up. His stern chin inched forward. As smoke rose into his face, he rubbed his eyes. In that moment, Gareth's steely features softened. For one second, his eyes registered doubt. Then he hardened again. He drew his sword. "Gladly I will say why I joined Fatagar. He is the strong leader of this army. He made a good plan and carried it out. He stands now at the steps of Long House, ready to assume command."

The crowd yelled and applauded.

"And I'll tell you why I joined him. I'll tell you why!" Gareth continued. "He put a knife to my throat!"

The army began to cheer but stopped.

"He said he would butcher my family if I did not join him."

Fatagar broke a stick in his teeth and stepped toward Gareth.

"He said he would torture Sutton Hoo and my friends from Skinner. So I did the unforgivable. I deserted Welken!"

Fatagar ordered his guards up the steps.

"I was called the Keeper of the Balance. But I left my calling." Gareth raised his sword by the hilt, pointing the blade downward. "And so, I have decided!" he shouted nervously. Sweat uncharacteristically shone on his brow. "I shall never be balanced again!" Just before the guards nabbed him, Gareth forced his sword violently through his own boot. He screamed.

Gareth collapsed into the arms of the guards. They turned him so he faced the ground and yanked him by his shoulders down the steps.

Fatagar's spikes seemed to grow white-hot. "Throw him on the fire!"

The guards dragged Gareth. As his feet banged each step, blood came out from one boot and bathed the stone.

Fatagar raised both hands, thrusting his pointed fingernails into the cold, sunny sky. Flames flickered in his eyes, then a dullness came over his face. A cloud had covered the sun. "To Long House!" Fatagar cried as he turned to mount the steps. More guards ran to him to help him up. Soldiers yelled and followed. Tremlings growled and pushed at whatever marched in front of them.

In the chaos, Len grabbed Bennu's sleeve and moved in closer. The fire burned just fifty feet away. As tremlings rushed by, Len tried to get a good view. He couldn't see Gareth. Looking to his left, Len saw the last of the soldiers coming. He waited. He turned back to Bennu, whispered, "Now," and moved toward the flames. They kept low.

Near the fire, Len saw some slatted wooden chairs that hadn't yet been tossed onto the blaze. He and Bennu ducked behind them. From between the slats, Len saw the guards holding Gareth. They stepped toward the fire, got pushed back by the mob, then stepped forward again. When the last tremling passed them, their sweaty faces shone in the fire's light. Each guard grabbed one of Gareth's arms and legs. They swung him back, then toward the fire. Gareth's head hung down, his eyes closed. The guards moved him back once more, then brought him forward with all their strength. They let go. Gareth landed on top of the burning wood. His weight snapped sticks and slats, lowering the height of the fire, the fire that now became a pyre. Gareth did not cry out.

As Mook reached the protection of the woods, he pointed to a trail. "It's almost straight. To get to Long House, we walk for a short time through the forest, through some farmland, the cemetery, and then we'll see it."

Lizbeth moved quickly to keep up with Mook and Vida. "What's there? I mean, why the rush?"

"MaryMary Hardin Fast." Vida worked harder than the others to maintain the pace. "She wants to mussolini all of Welken. She's got dictatoratin' on her brain, what with all the flotsam-and-foam runnin' around in there."

Mook leaped behind a fir tree, slunk low, and popped back up onto the edge of the trail. "MaryMary does not care about Deedy or any living thing. She does not want reform or a civilization of good Cutters. She wants to be a queen. She wants to rule."

"And that's when I einsteined it," said Vida. "I was researchifyin' the Cutters one day, visual-like. I saw a raft of skeletons all hypnotized and blind-faithed."

Mook held up a hand to stop, then walked on. "MaryMary's got them under a spell. It's not a regular incantation. They've been seduced."

Vida stabbed the air with a dagger. "They're jim-jonesed and gurued, brain-blocked and mobbified. Without MaryMary, they wouldn't be so contrary."

"I see," said Angie. "I see their hearts under a deep shadow, under a veil. Maybe we can lift it."

Angie's words awakened Lizbeth's shard. She pushed on it, like she had a side-ache. The shard reminded her of the veil between dreaming and waking. Lizbeth had thought a lot about veils, between Skinner and Welken, health and sickness, natural and supernatural. She'd mainly thought about how close danger always was, that we can so easily slip toward disease or despair or evil.

But Angie had reminded her that if we could travel more quickly down than we realized, we could also travel more quickly up. That if the veil between right and wrong was thin, the shadows that kept us in the wrong could also be lifted. That if sanity felt frail at times, maybe insanity too was frail. Maybe some veils we ought to make stronger—and others are thin for good purpose.

Mook pulled an arrow from his quiver. He crouched behind a large boulder and waved his arm to get everyone down. Lizbeth obeyed, froze, but heard nothing. She saw that they'd come through the woods. Farmland spread out before them.

"All we have to do," said Angie, scooting next to Lizbeth, "is find a way in and tell our story. That's what Bebba said in the last hut."

"Angie, I'm not sure that's relevant right now."

Vida came between them. "I've been shakespeared many a time in my day. It keeps the thoughts-and-flashin'-lights comin' down in chunks and epiphanies."

"Vida," said Lizbeth. "I'm not sure that's relevant either. Wait. I hear something now, a kind of buzzing."

"Out there." Mook pointed to the crops. "Speckers. A swarm of them. They're tiny creatures, cousins to glimpses. Smaller, but not so shy. Too friendly you might say. Let's keep walking between the crops and the hills. Maybe they won't see us. We have to push to Long House."

"More trekkification." Vida grabbed a stick off the ground and used it as a staff. "Oh, for kelp tea and a watercressin' sandwich."

In a single-file line, the four walked swiftly toward Long House, just above the furrows. Stalks of corn stood tall in the distance.

Lizbeth felt a chill. "Angie?"

"Yeah?"

"I'm cold. Are you?"

Before Angie could answer, a swarm of gnatty bugs enveloped them. Lizbeth felt instantly claustrophobic.

"zippingandsipping."

"safetyfirstsafetyandsweets?"

Lizbeth wanted to swat her way out of the swarm, but she couldn't bear the thought of knocking even one of these little buggy beings onto the ground. "Ugh. These gnats, these speckers, they're everywhere."

"sassysoundsandsassafrass."

"somehelptoyousomehelp?"

The speckers buzzed so close to Lizbeth's eyes that she couldn't see them. She didn't know if the ones she heard were the ones who seemed to be addressing her or the ones by her ears. The buzzing grew so loud that Lizbeth gently flapped her hands by her ears.

"zoundsandzoons."

"swattingatspeckers."

Lizbeth noticed that Mook, Vida, and Angie were all looking overwhelmed. Then a specker flew up Lizbeth's nose. "Hey, get out of there!"

"zoominginzoomingout."

"softandlovelynasalpassage."

Lizbeth shook her head. "Wait up, little speckers. I have a question."

"sayaquestionsayananswer."

"shetalkssoslow."

Lizbeth moved her hand in front of her eyes. "Do you know anything about the Cutters? Or about MaryMary?"

Most of the swarm pulled back like it was getting ready to sneeze.

"What happened?" asked Mook.

Lizbeth itched her ears. "I asked them about Cutters."

For a second, the swarm assembled itself into a horrified face, then it made a ring around the four travelers.

"sickandsullenstaleandstupid."

"spearsandknivesandgreen."

Buzzing loudly, the speckers made themselves into a giant arrow that flew in an arc and exploded in the air. They collected once again, this time into a dense cloud, and they flew away over the corn.

Vida put a finger in each ear. "A bee's bonnet of buzzification!"

Angie got on tiptoe and looked toward the field, as if she missed them. "They might have told us so much more."

"Green," said Mook. "What do the speckers mean by spears and green? Why 'green'?"

Glad to be rid of the irritating speckers, Lizbeth hiked in silence till she saw the cemetery grove off to her left. She wondered where Bors and Piers had gone and what made one Welken plot grow into a crab apple and another a mulberry. As she walked, Lizbeth's eye kept returning to a cedar. It looked familiar, though she doubted she could tell one cedar from another, and it also seemed pale. Was there such a thing as a white cedar?

Lizbeth stopped. She stared at the branches. The tree appeared to be an exact duplicate of the cedar in the Bartholomews' backyard. Even more strange, the tree seemed happy. Lizbeth saw a smile in the branches, then a nose, then soft eyes full of promise. It was Alabaster . . . Alabaster Singing. She grinned widely at Lizbeth and winked. Lizbeth swore she saw it, and once she did, hope rushed through her.

The four walked to the end of the crops. Up a gentle hill, Long House looked like a combination of a temple on Mount Olympus and a cathedral in a sleepy European town. Its magnificence shone in the cold sun.

"It's just as beautiful on the inside," said Angie. "I was there, before, when Vida and Jacob and I were looking for the tile a month ago. The carving in each chair tells a different story, and when I looked at the stained glass, a deep presence bathed me in yellow and blue."

"It looks cold to me," said Lizbeth, "but then, everything does. Could we keep moving?"

Mook nodded. "The sooner the better. We'll be exposed once we get past this hedge. I want to get up the hill as soon as possible."

Lizbeth glanced over to the corn, about an acre away on her right. The tall stalks and golden tassels made her think of bright green husks hiding delicious ears, ears of corn that, roasted, sounded wonderful to Lizbeth right now. Hot roasted corn! Then she saw a tassel move. Then another. The cornstalks were walking, shuffling along. At first, Lizbeth thought it was another wonderful Welkenism—crops that harvested themselves or something. Then she saw feet and hands . . . and the field for what it was. It was an army of corn. "Quick, get behind the hedge. Cutters!"

Vida ran back and squatted low. "Jestered again! And we'd even been schoolified by the speckers. Green, green, greenification!"

The cornstalks marched out of the furrow. A dozen or more Cutters tossed the corn plants on the ground and thrust spear poles under their arms, the tips pointing toward Long House. They charged.

Mook gestured to a path that curled along the edge of the cemetery. "That will take us to the back side of Long House, but we have to get past this open area. They will see us."

"Mook," said Angie. "The Cutters have stopped. They're looking in our direction."

"No," said Lizbeth, "I think they're looking back at the farmland." As the Cutters bowed, a tall, elegant woman emerged from the cornfield. "See, there! It's MaryMary. She's pointing her staff. She looks mad."

MaryMary raised her staff high and brought it down on a Cutter's head. He crumbled onto the ground. Even from this distance, even when being heartless, MaryMary looked beautiful. Once again Lizbeth felt overwhelmed, struck by it as by a weapon. And it was.

Cutters, about thirty of them, stormed up toward Long House. More came out of the corn. But they ran only a few yards before they stopped. Then they waved their spears in the air. They covered their ears.

"Speckers," said Vida, "the whole buzzin' brood! That will molassify their marchification."

Mook crept out into the open. "It's our chance. Run!"

Lizbeth took up the rear, feeling as inconspicuous as a moving bull's-eye. The cold made her run faster. Just as the foursome slipped around to the north side, out of sight of the Cutters, Lizbeth saw a black tendril wisping into the sky from below Long House to the south. It was smoke.

"A fire sounds so good," she told Angie. Then the clouds covered the sun.

CHAPTER THIRTY-FIVE

THE LONG AND THE COLD OF IT

"The trick is not minding."

—GORDON LIDDY,
WHEN ASKED HOW HE COULD TOLERATE
HIS FINGER IN A LIGHTER'S FLAME

 Every second they waited drove Len crazy. Gareth lay facedown on the fire, burning—and all Len could do was wait with Bennu for the last soldier and tremling to mount the steps to Long House. Yet how could he wait? Shouldn't he take the risk and drag Gareth from the flames? But what difference would it make? Surely Gareth had already burned beyond hope. They should be searching for Piers and Bors, doing what they could to sabotage Fatagar's assault. Still, Len had to know. He had to see for himself.

Len and Bennu scooted the chairs to get farther forward. From behind this screen, they saw the last few tremlings march up and felt the heat of the blaze so much that Len shielded his face. He peered beneath his arm at the fire, at the leaping flames, at the impossibility of running into it and pulling a body from it.

Then he bolted toward it. He covered his face with both arms, lowered his head, and made the bounding hop one does before jumping. The heat pressed down on him. It was like wind, a solid force pushing him back. He leaned into it.

The next thing Len knew he swirled backward, lost his footing, and fell on his side six feet farther away from the fire. Bennu stood over him, Len's stretched T-shirt still gripped in his hands.

At last Bennu let go of Len. "We've lost Gareth. It's over. We don't need to lose you too."

Len sat up with his hands around his knees. The heat dried his tears almost as fast as they flowed out. "I judged him, Bennu. I never seriously thought he had been forced into his decision. I thought he should have stayed true no matter what. But what would I have done?"

Bennu said nothing. He picked up a chair and held it over his head, as if he were going to slam it down. But he let it go with little force. It bounced over and landed on its side before it reached the flames. "It's all so pointless!"

Len said "amen" to himself. He also feared Bennu would be heard, that soldiers and tremlings would turn from the steps and throw them on the fire.

No one from the Long House steps looked back.

But something did come. From the smoke and shadows behind the fire a large presence emerged. As tall as a tremling or taller, the being came into the light, first its feet and then its legs. Len saw that it was Sutton. And he carried Gareth in his arms.

Sutton's boots smelled of burned leather. Gareth smelled of burned flesh. The gentle herdsman from Kells Village dropped to one knee and then the other. He placed Gareth on the ground. To Len's surprise, the Keeper of the Balance breathed weakly. His eyes were open in the charred remains of his face.

Len wanted to sob uncontrollably and vomit at the same time. He could not bring himself to look at Gareth's horrific skin—yet to look away would be disrespectful. Gareth deserved this small sacrifice in his last moments.

Gareth said something softly. Len and Bennu and Sutton leaned in closer, their heads almost touching. Though Len breathed through his mouth, the smell crept in and sank to his stomach. It stirred a cauldron there. His ear to Gareth's mouth, Len closed his eyes. At least he didn't have to look. His tears dripped onto Gareth's neck.

"In Welken." Gareth's voice sounded otherworldly, two places below a whisper, yet clear.

"Of Welken," the three whispered back, swallowing almost in unison.

"It's OK," said Bennu. "You don't need to say anything."

Gareth's breathiness continued. "Fatagar is afraid." Len opened his eyes at this surprise. "Fatagar said, 'The four in one is all in all.'"

Len could tell Sutton had lifted his head. Sutton said, "What does it mean, lad?"

Gareth said nothing.

Bennu lifted his head. "Gareth, you're going to make it. Tell us what it means."

Len touched Gareth's shoulder gently. He burned his finger on a metal clip, and something stuck to him. Lifting his head so he could rub his burning finger with his other hand, Len heard a breathy something from Gareth.

"Will you—," said Gareth.

Len waited. Gareth said nothing. Len put his ear one inch from Gareth's mouth.

Gareth exhaled. "—forgive me?"

Len dropped his chin to his chest. He fought back tears. He knew he needed to speak while Gareth could still hear. "Of course I forgive you," Len whispered back. "I already have. You didn't need to ask—but I did think badly of you. I'm ashamed to admit it. I am not a generous person. I didn't think about what you were going through. I don't know what it would be like to have my own family threatened. I would have done the same thing you did. I—"

"Len." Sutton's hand came under Len's neck and pulled him up. "You can stop. Gareth can't hear you. He isn't breathing."

Len wanted to throw himself on Gareth's chest. He wanted to wail over the tragedy. But he couldn't. Gareth's charred body prevented him. He just sat there rubbing his own forehead.

Then he heard footsteps. He looked up to see locals from Primus Hook. They had come out of hiding to carry Gareth away. No soldiers or tremlings could be seen.

" 'Tis a part of the sadness, lads, that we can't stay and do our duty to mourn Gareth's passin'." Sutton helped Len and Bennu up as he himself rose. "There's a battle ragin', doon't ya know. Times a'comin' for mournin', but Fatagar's got to be stopped first. Long House is the center of things. We can't let him have it."

Sutton looked transformed, as if his modesty and kindness had been overwhelmed by his sense of justice. He nodded in gratitude to those who bore Gareth away, then strode to the right, to the east.

As Len and Bennu filed in behind him, Sutton told his tale. "The gulls swooped in on the whole crew just as you departed. They came a-peckin' and a-buzzin'. The deck filled with madness. Then the mice and rats ran and nipped at all those tremlings and soldiers. The army fought back, but they hit each other as much as they did the scurryin' varmints. It was a right glorious scene in its own way. Gareth and Fatagar turned from me—and I thought Gareth sighed for relief at not havin' to cut me. I jumped overboard and swam to Mercy Bay, survivin' I doon't know how. I came out of the water and thanked the namer of that place, and Soliton too."

Len heard noises in the dark and worried that a flank of tremling troops waited in ambush for them. He elbowed Sutton.

"I hear 'em, lad," Sutton said. "It's the villagers of Primus Hook. When I came ashore, I told 'em what was in those ships. They gathered pitchforks and spears and left their homes, awaitin' my call. I passed the word as I came out to get Gareth from the fire."

Len smiled at the mass of villagers assembling. "The odds are getting better, that's for sure." He sighed after he said this, as if he'd transgressed Gareth's passing by sounding hopeful or happy. "Bennu, what about Gareth's words? He said, 'The four in one is all in all.' He said Fatagar was afraid because of it."

"Hmm."

"Yeah, hmm." As Len turned the phrase over in his mind, he studied the sky. Clouds had moved swiftly from the north and gathered in shades of greater darkness. Len felt cold, then colder, and colder still.

Lizbeth wondered if Vida would make it up the hill. Though the Cutters hadn't seen them, Vida's exhaustion threatened the success of their ascent.

Vida sat down about halfway up. "I'm bedrazzled and blood-pumped to my last swath of ugliness."

"You can do it, Vida." Angie held out some water. "You'll be 'Bering Well' in no time."

"Don't go bringin' my namification into the turnstile. If I can't mount-everest it, I'll roll down into the Cutters and strikify them."

Lizbeth pulled on one of Vida's arms while Angie pulled on the other. As Mook pushed from the back, Vida flopped onto her stomach and two daggers fell out.

She rolled over on her back, her belt buckle sticking out as the highest point on her belly. "No need to tugboat my bargification."

"Well," said Mook, "we need to go."

"Yeah," said Lizbeth, "pick up your daggers and walk."

This time, holding out her hand for help, Vida made it to her feet and trudged up the hill with the others.

Long House was indeed just that—a long, rectangular, two-story structure. At the same time, the name's modest description bore little resemblance to the grandeur of the building. A testimony to Welkenian craftsmanship, its architecture reminded Lizbeth of one style and then another. It was like an Olympian-Gothic cathedral, then a magnificent English country manor. But not quite. As with so many things in Welken, earthly forms blended in unique ways. Chinese curved rooflines met Colonial white walls and Roman columns. Arabesque geometrical patterns bordered French doors. A gold onion-dome stood boldly in the center between two round castle turrets. A giant stone chimney broke the symmetry. Lizbeth thought it looked as if it were designed by the architect of the Smithsonian castle who had been commissioned by the United Nations. Yet it worked. Gothic archways and flying buttresses inspired. The marble and gold left Lizbeth breathless.

As Lizbeth stared at the white exterior, the white seemed to grow whiter. It became so bright that she had to look away to the side entrance patio. Then it grew darker. The flagstone on the ground blurred at the edges and connected as it mysteriously turned from tan to gray to black. Lizbeth realized that the patio had become asphalt.

Then a siren wailed, startling her. She glanced back and saw an ambulance coming. She couldn't understand this. The driver honked at her to move. Stepping back, Lizbeth scanned the scene for Angie. She saw no one familiar. And the building wasn't Long House. Its white walls belonged to Sacred Heart Hospital, the place where she'd been born in Skinner.

When Lizbeth walked toward the ambulance that had pulled up to the door, another horn honked her back to the curb. It was the McKenzie Boys' LTD. The car's brakes screeched as the LTD stopped. Tommy and Josh jumped out, then their mom and dad. The family rushed to the gurney being unfolded and rolled through the doors of the Emergency Room. It was Odin. He looked terrible.

A paramedic held an IV up in the air and barked orders. "Get back. Get back!"

Someone grabbed Lizbeth's elbow. "Get back, Lizbeth!" Mook sounded firm and a bit disappointed. "Cutters are coming. You are standing here like a target."

Angie pulled Lizbeth behind a planter. "You OK? What did you see?"

Lizbeth wondered how Angie knew. "I saw Sacred Heart Hospital and the Minks. I saw Odin on a stretcher, and his wretched father. I can't believe he's your uncle."

"Me neither. But we're here now and you need to refocus as fast as you can. It's part of the work of good dreaming. I should know."

Lizbeth nodded. "OK, we got up here first. So now what do we do? Are we supposed to fight off an army?"

"I don't have any great plan, I'll tell you that." Angie got up and joined Mook and Vida behind some tall junipers. When Lizbeth caught up, Angie added, "You have visions of the hospital, but I keep coming back to what Bebba said, 'Find a way in and tell your story.' For the first time, that line makes a little sense." Angie paused. "Maybe we need to 'find a way in' to Long House."

Vida motioned for Lizbeth and Angie to come closer.

As Mook drew an arrow, Lizbeth said to Angie, "You may be right. But what's so hard about getting in? Why don't we go open a door?"

"Keep your eyes visualated, young misfitters." Vida pulled Angie and Lizbeth down. "We might be gettysburged at any moment."

Lizbeth peered around the juniper. It did look like Gettysburg down there, like Pickett's charge, lines of the enemy marching out in the open. Lizbeth looked back at her three comrades, a union of misfits and Welkeners that was not prepared to mow down the rebels. "Mook, what can we hope to do?"

Mook's sternness etched deeper into his face. "The roof. We'll have good cover."

Lizbeth looked out once more at the soldiers. She heard a *thwift* and saw Mook's arrow enter a Cutter in the first line. The soldier toppled back and slowed the charge. Above the rest, toward the rear, MaryMary sat on a carrier. She snapped a whip.

"Quick!" said Vida. "Let's get sniperfied! We don't want to be remembered in some alamoification!"

Lizbeth took the hint. The sight of Mook's arrow made her rub the spot on her hand where she'd been hit underneath. Mook ran to the western wall of Long House and clamored up a trellis. He reached down to pull Vida up while Angie pushed her from below. Lizbeth pitched in.

Arrows, blindly fired from below, landed in flowerpots and bounced off the stone patio. Lizbeth gave Vida a solid shove up, then ran to pick up the arrows, gazing skyward all the while. She hurried back to the wall and passed them up to Angie, who passed them along to Mook. "More ammo," Lizbeth said.

Angie leaned down, extending a hand to Lizbeth. "The first step's the hardest. Come on."

Just as Lizbeth reached up, an arrow skidded along the patio to her left. It slid swiftly on the stone until it stopped abruptly under the toe of someone's boot. It was Piers!

"Angie," Lizbeth called, "come down."

"Mook and Vida are waiting, Lizbeth. C'mon."

"But Ang, look. Piers and Bors are here. They can let us in so we can follow Bebba's command. After that, maybe we'll 'tell our story'—whatever that means."

Angie yelled up to Vida and Mook about Piers and Bors. Then she scooted partway down and jumped.

Lizbeth turned toward Piers and Bors. She couldn't get over how much healthier Piers looked. Even his shoulders looked broader. And Bors seemed the image of an Arthurian knight. His chain mail bulged from his huge arms, and over the silver he wore a kind of purple smock that looked like part of his coat. One hand rested on a broadsword attached to his waist. Piers and Bors stood before an open, solid-wood door.

From Lizbeth's left, several more arrows flew in an arc from below. She cupped her hands over her mouth and cried, "Piers!" Running forward, she felt jerked from behind. An arrow zipped in front of her. Lizbeth stumbled as she fell back and landed on her bottom. "Thanks, Ang." Then she leaped up. "Bors!"

Not seeming to notice Lizbeth or Angie, neither Piers nor Bors looked over. Bors pointed to the west, then stepped through the opening. Piers put his hand on the door.

Feeling betrayed, Lizbeth ran faster toward them. "Wait!"

Piers vanished behind the door and pulled the wooden slab till it shut.

"Stop!" Angie raced past Lizbeth. "Piers!" She got to the door and tugged on the handle. It remained closed.

"What's the deal?" Lizbeth caught up. "Were they an illusion?" Then she heard a solid thud on the other side of the locked door, like a bolt. "You heard that?"

"Yeah."

Lizbeth gestured back to the trellis. "Let's go for it, Ang!"

More arrows came, too many to keep dodging, then the heads of Cutters . . . their shoulders . . . legs . . . and feet. Now they stopped and took aim.

In two steps, Lizbeth and Angie gave up on the trellis and ran to the back side of Long House. The screams of Cutters told them Mook and Vida had sent their missiles flying.

Panting, frightened, and nearly panicked, Lizbeth pressed her back against the Long House wall. "They're going to round the corner, Angie. We've got to hide."

Without answer, Angie led the way, running along the long side of Long House. Occasionally, Lizbeth glanced back. At about a quarter of the way toward the other end, she spotted a Cutter turning the corner. Then another. They carried spears and swords, not arrows, and they pointed them at the Misfits.

Lizbeth and Angie sprinted hard. After twenty more yards, Lizbeth glanced back and saw more Cutters—five, maybe ten. And archers.

A gazebo stood midway down the building. Angie pointed to it. Lizbeth's thighs burned. Her lungs ached. She didn't know what good it would do to get to the gazebo anyway. They were dead, dead.

The cold air hurt. She wanted water. But there was the gazebo, just ahead. Angie ran in and dove onto the floor. Right behind, Lizbeth grabbed a column and pulled herself in. An arrow hit a gazebo wall. She ducked down and threw herself on her side, skidding on the floor till she hit the interior brick wall with her back. Her shoulder hurt. Her legs hurt. Her lungs felt sucked dry.

Angie pulled her up and pointed across the gazebo to the opposite wall. There, slouching low, sat Len and Bennu.

Then Lizbeth noticed it started to snow.

CHAPTER THIRTY- SIX

My Anchor Holds Within the Veil

Our state cannot be sever'd; we are one,
One flesh; to lose thee were to lose myself.

—JOHN MILTON, *PARADISE LOST*

 Although Len tried not to act surprised, his shaking head betrayed his wonderment. "No time to explain. Tremlings are after us. They're about to round the corner." Len pointed to the side he and Bennu had come from. "There, there they are!"

"Ahhhh!" yelled Lizbeth. "They're coming at us from both sides!"

A Cutter arrow clunked against the brick of the gazebo.

"They'll be on us any minute!" Bennu rubbed his hands together. "It's so cold! What's the plan?"

"The plan," said Len, "is to survive. C'mon, we need an idea."

Angie got on her knees. "All I see is snow."

"Yeah," said Len, "but they're in there, coming at us. Trust me, you don't want to fight a tremling."

Lizbeth sat up next to Angie. "Trust me, I don't want to. But how could I fight what I can't see? The snow is really coming down all of a sudden. In buckets. Or blizzards. Or whatever."

Bennu poked his head above the wall. "You're right. I can hear tremlings and Cutters, but I can't see them. Is this what they call a whiteout?"

Len put his hand into the snow. "If we can't see them, they can't see us. This is our chance to get out of here."

Lizbeth stood. "Hey, Bebba said we had to get in. Maybe we should run for the door."

"What door?" Angie grabbed Bennu's hand. "I can't see Long House."

"That's OK," said Len, "we know the basic direction."

Len looked down at Angie and Bennu's clasped hands. It didn't seem right. It wasn't the time to do something romantic. Len did a double take on their joined hands. The hands were merging, flowing into one another. He grabbed them by their "free" arms and stopped them. "Look! Look at your hands. They're blending together. It's like you're vanishing into each other."

The snow floated down in thick white flakes, covering everything.

Lizbeth pulled Len back by the shoulder. "And Len, look at you! Your hand is entering Bennu's arm, and Angie's arm. Wait, mine is too. It's sinking into you."

Len tried to yank one hand out. It snapped back. "What's happening?"

"I don't know." Lizbeth pulled her hand out of Len's shoulder. "I don't like it. And why is it snowing? And why are we stuck here in this tiny building? I can't even see Long House anymore, the snow is so thick. And I'm so thirsty. And—"

"Stop!" Bennu's eyes brightened. "I get it! The lines we've been hearing. Listen to them all together: 'A story's told by day and night / The sun is cold, the wind is white. / When water's dry and land be small, / The four in one is all in all.' It's now, don't you see? The wind is white with dry water, snow. And we're trapped here. And, look, we're becoming one."

"One?" asked Len. "One what?"

"I don't know."

"I do." Angie's whole arm blended into Bennu's. "We're becoming a griffin. We kept hearing about it over and over."

"And maybe," said Lizbeth, "maybe this is why we've only had a fourth of our animal powers each time we've been in Welken."

That led Len to think about just yesterday, when they'd made it to Welken from his backyard. They'd walked into each other as they'd passed through the veil. "OK, I have an idea." A tremling roared from out of the blizzard. "We have to act quickly. Get in a circle. I'm in the north, Angie's in the south. Hurry. Bennu east, Lizbeth, west. Now hold hands and push as you walk into the center."

They did. With frightened eyes, Len watched his hands disappear into Bennu's and Lizbeth's hands. Then forearms merged and shoulders. He wanted to pull out, to not "lose" himself. It took all his willpower to keep going. Nose to nose with his Misfit friends, Len closed his eyes and pushed.

The next thing he knew, all he could see was snow. It was as if he'd passed through Angie and had ended up on the other side. He looked at his arms but saw nothing. He felt them, and they were there—invisible, but there. Then he saw his lower body. It was all lion, slightly larger than usual, and his tail flipped behind him. "What happened? Can you hear me?"

"You don't have to shout," Lizbeth said. "It's like all of me is here, but all I can see is my upper body, my oxen torso and front legs. And Len, you sound so close, like you're inside my head."

"And you're both inside mine," said Bennu, "literally. That's all I've got of my falcon. But I can see your front feet, Lizbeth, and your tail, Len. You're a part of me. I mean, we're a part of each other, but I have the eyes. Hey, Angie."

"I'm here, at least my wings are. I'll flap them down."

"I see them," said Bennu.

"I can't believe it!" said Lizbeth. "This is the most amazing thing yet. So . . . so . . . we're all merged together and we've become—"

"A griffin," said Bennu. "Just like Angie said, a griffin beyond belief."

A Cutter spear flew by them from the white west. A tremling yelled on the other side of the gazebo. Other tremlings roared back.

"They're getting closer," said Len. "Let's start this beast up."

Awkwardly, the griffin walked on all fours into the snow. Len felt the cold through his padded feet.

"OK," said Bennu. "I'm the head, but in a way we all are. For 'the four in me' to be 'all in all,' we have to act as one. We can all see. Lizbeth, you feel all four oxen legs, don't you?"

"Yes."

"And Len?"

"Yeah, all my paws."

"Together then, walk, then trot, then run."

Like a newborn colt, the griffin stumbled at first, nearly fell over, then caught the rhythm of coordinated feet. In a team effort, the griffin began to run.

As the griffin picked up speed through the snow, a group of tremlings appeared. They stopped slugging each other and turned to the creature racing toward them. The tremlings faced the griffin, raised their clubs, and growled. As the griffin came closer, they cowered.

"A few more steps," said Angie, "and I'll take over. C'mon, faster. Let's go!"

Len pushed off as best he could from the back, and the next thing he knew, his feet left the ground and did not return. He was flying. He was a lion flying—well, a quarter of a lion.

The griffin flapped its wings and fought through the snow into the sky. After circling higher, the griffin saw that the snow was letting up. It stretched out its wings and sailed around all four sides of Long House. Cutters swarmed around from the west. Fatagar's army circled to the north of the building from the veranda on the south. MaryMary and Fatagar were nowhere to be seen. Neither were Piers and Bors.

"We need to get in," said Lizbeth.

"I know," said Bennu. "I'm looking. I don't know what to do. Should we try to fight our way through an open door? Cutters and tremlings are everywhere outside."

"I doubt we'd make it in," said Len. "We're so big."

"I could fold down my wings," said Angie. "We could make it."

"Wait, I know." Len tried to keep his legs from galloping through the air. "Look at the chimney. It's huge."

"Yeah," said Angie. "I was in that fireplace during my quest for the tile a month ago. I came through the back of it with Vida and Jacob. It's the size of a small room."

"Getting in would be easy," said Bennu. "It's making the turn at the bottom I'd be worried about."

The griffin cruised by the south side at window height, knocking a few tremlings off the veranda with Lizbeth's hoofs and Len's claws. From there they could see the Council room and Tholl Table and the giant fireplace that Angie had told them about. They could also see Piers and Bors fighting Fatagar and MaryMary. Bors flashed his sword around him like the steel of ten men.

"We've got to hurry," said Angie.

After flying up, the griffin swooped down on the chimney.

"Let's not dive into it," said Lizbeth. "Let's land on top, then drop down. That way we won't build up too much speed."

"OK," said Bennu. "Here we go."

As the griffin soared above Long House, Bennu screeched a falcon war cry. It chilled Len to the end of his tail.

The chimney stood like a tower between a golden dome and a castle turret. Swiftly, the griffin descended onto it, Angie cupping her wings, Lizbeth extending her hoofs, Len preparing to dig in with his claws. Len could feel all these motions, though he could only see his legs.

The griffin landed cleanly enough, but its hoofs skidded on the wide rows of brick.

Lizbeth yelled, "I can't stop!"

With all the strength of his claws, Len worked at the brick. He felt his front legs sliding and his head dip down. He could tell that with his beak, Bennu had snagged the end of the chimney they slid toward. Desperately, Len gripped on to some loose mortar. He felt Angie's wings flap at his flanks.

The griffin held. It righted itself from the clumsy landing and looked into the flue.

"Everybody ready?" asked Bennu.

Before anyone could answer, the griffin's head leaned into the chimney and the rest of its body followed.

In the back, Len saw nothing. He felt his body hitting the sides.

Then Bennu shouted, "Tuck and roll!"

The griffin hit the embers hard, turned on its left shoulder, held in its wings, and rolled through the blanket of ash into the room.

Len's lion body felt fine, but his shoulder hurt. "Lizbeth, you OK?"

"I think so," she said.

The griffin got up onto its four legs and shook off the ash. Len could see that plenty of soot remained on his lower body.

The now-black griffin screeched its piercing cry again. Its wings spread out, then Len saw what he had been longing to see—a frightened Fatagar.

MaryMary slipped behind two Cutters and pushed them in front of her. One carried a spear, the other, a long knife in each hand. "Kill it!" she screeched. "I came here to be Queen."

Fatagar looked up in surprise. "W-w-we'll see. *Tck-tck.*" He poked a dagger into the side of a tremling to urge it forward. Three of his guards ran through the door behind him. They charged Piers. Then a tremling roared and raised a club over Bors.

When a Cutter launched his spear at the griffin, Len pushed off on his lion's legs, and the spear hit the back of the fire pit. Len got worried because his feet couldn't find the ground. Then he realized that the griffin had opened its wings like a sail. Len was flying. The griffin reared back as if standing in air and dove at the Cutters.

Len saw Fatagar duck behind two tremlings. Bors thrust his sword through one tremling's chest, then pushed him back with the chain mail of his forearm. The griffin dipped at a Cutter and pulled up. Lizbeth hammered him with her hoofs. As the griffin pressed through, Len grabbed at the Cutter with his claws, snagging his coat and lifting him off the ground. The griffin flew up into the many banners that hung from the high ceiling. Len shook the Cutter. Digging his claw into the Cutter's shoulders, he swung the Cutter toward MaryMary and let go. She sidestepped quickly, and the Cutter landed at her feet with a thud. She stepped on him and waved her short sword at the griffin.

Piers was in trouble. Backing up, he fended off the slashing blades of Fatagar's guards with his staff. He swung high to the right, then low to the left, blocking thrusts each time. When one spear caught and tore his vest, Piers flicked his staff quickly, smashing a guard in the head.

But more came, and Fatagar stepped up, stabbing at Piers with his limited reach. The griffin left the Cutters and charged at Fatagar's army. Guards and tremlings backed up into Fatagar, knocking him down at the stairway door. Guards farther in swung wildly at Piers. His back against a stained-glass door, Piers defended deftly with his staff, parrying jabs and clubbing hands and heads. Then Cutters streamed in from the west door.

"We have to stop the flow!" said Bennu.

As Cutters filed in, Fatagar's troops recovered and pushed their way in from the stairs to the south. The griffin flipped around in the large room. It landed on Tholl Table, just missing the open Book of Quadrille in the center. Len crouched and pounced off the oak. Bennu hacked at tremlings with his beak. Lizbeth stomped on shoulders and heads, and Angie flapped her wings hard, holding the griffin aloft just above the encroaching army.

Then Len's left flank got hit squarely with a tremling's club. The griffin rolled over in the air and landed on its back by MaryMary. She snatched a spear out of a Cutter's hand and raised it for the kill. All at once, Bennu screeched, Len roared, Angie screamed, and Lizbeth bellowed. Len's throat felt warm, and he saw a flame in front of his face. A flame!

MaryMary lurched back. She dropped the spear and stumbled into the Cutters coming in the door behind her. The griffin looked over at Piers and Bors. They seemed to be holding their own against Fatagar. So the griffin turned over on all fours and leaped, bowling MaryMary out the door. It shot fire into her unprotected face. She screamed, and Len saw her hair burning. It curled up on her head rapidly. She flailed at it and at her singed eyebrows. Cutters in the line swatted at the flames on her hair and clothes, burning their hands while hitting MaryMary's head.

"Stop it!" she screamed. "You're killing me." As the pungent smoke rose above her, MaryMary touched her head and winced. Her fingers groped for her hair but only found wispy strands here and there. "I have nothing left!"

To Len it seemed a ridiculous thing to say. In the middle of a battle for Welken, MaryMary mourned the loss of her hair—her beauty. And he felt impatient. He wanted to finish off MaryMary so he could get back to help Piers and Bors.

The Cutters froze. With MaryMary's head bowed, they seemed unable to move, to keep fighting. Holding her face in one hand, she wept. As the griffin approached, the Cutters stepped back.

"You've killed me," MaryMary screamed through her tears. "You've robbed me of everything." The griffin glanced quickly to see that tremlings stood on Tholl Table. Piers and Bors weren't there. The griffin turned back to MaryMary's wailing. Just when she seemed overcome with grief, she leaped up, grabbed a knife from a Cutter, and jabbed the griffin in the shoulder, drawing blood from Lizbeth.

The griffin shrieked and jumped back. As the Cutters took one step forward, the griffin charged at MaryMary. Bennu snapped with his beak, piercing her shoulder. Angie swept Cutters back with her wings. Then Len stood on his legs and Lizbeth slammed one hoof firmly down on Mary-Mary's exposed head. She dropped the knife.

Impatiently, Len watched MaryMary. He thought she would flop to the ground from the blow or order the Cutters to attack. She did neither. Wearily, she stood up. She wobbled from her wounds but managed to glare hatefully at the griffin.

Len couldn't bear waiting for her. Piers and Bors were just a step away, needing their help, and here they were, waiting to see what MaryMary would do.

MaryMary scrutinized the griffin up and down. She seemed to be deciding something, or trying to gather the courage to act on a decision. Somehow, in this instant, something drained out of her. She seemed to die in some sense, to lose the will to fight, maybe even to live. Her willfulness floated from her almost tangibly, like vapors off hot pavement. Then she reached down and took her burned and tattered shawl and threw it around her neck. With bruised elegance, MaryMary turned her ravaged head. She held her injured shoulder, pushed Cutters aside, and walked deliberately back to the west. Then, with similar resignation, one Cutter near her adjusted his belt and followed her. Then another, and another. Soon all the Cutters followed her. Len couldn't believe that she—they—simply gave up.

The griffin swiftly turned around toward the center of the room. Tremlings stood on the table like gorillas, clubbing the sides and pushing each other off. One held the Book of Quadrille over his head. Through the stained-glass windows, Len saw Piers and Bors on the veranda, surrounded by Fatagar's army. Back to back, Piers with his staff, Bors with his sword, the two Welkeners fought bravely in the slushy snow.

"Through the window!"

Len spoke first. "Did you all hear that?"

"I did," said Lizbeth. "But which one?"

The griffin flew up above the tremlings.

Angie said, "It's coming."

"What is?" said Bennu.

"The sun."

Piers's voice grabbed them again. "Friends! The window!"

The griffin hovered, waiting. Len saw Fatagar raise a dagger over his head. The circle drew in on Piers and Bors, step by step. Piers and Bors spun around back to back, Piers swinging his staff and Bors his sword. That sword! Bors moved as if he had trained all his life for just this moment.

A shaft of light hit the fourth of the eight windows.

"Now!"

The griffin dove hard toward the glass, knocking tremlings off the table, crashing into and completely through it. The window exploded into a thousand shards, the glass shooting out all over the veranda. Then, like shrapnel, the broken pieces took aim and sliced into the army below. Soldiers and tremlings screamed out and fell to the ground. But the missiles kept coming, a fuselage of pointed judgment, a rain of sharp-edged terror. Then more screaming. Then silence.

The griffin flew above the shattered glass and then around the circumference of the veranda. Len extended his claws for more battle—but only Piers, Bors, and Fatagar remained standing. Glass blades stuck out of Fatagar's knobby head. Blood mixed with grease and slime as it oozed down his body. The griffin landed on the railing of the veranda, Len digging his claws through the snow and into the wood for balance. From the roof, Mook and Vida waved.

Fatagar plopped down on the floor and moved his hand to rub his head. It recoiled as if bitten, and Fatagar screamed. His slaughtered-pig squeal rose in volume before breaking off like a leg caught in a trap, like one of his own sticks snapping. Fatagar dropped his head. Rhythmically it bobbed up and down. "*Tck-tck,*" he said, but nothing else. His slime dripped into the melting snow.

Piers raised his staff. A Moses in the wilderness of fallen soldiers, he brought his staff down. The staff did not become a snake, but it trembled. He let it go and it turned around and around, picking up speed. Faster it spun. And faster. The snow melted away and the wood of the veranda smoked. Then the staff drilled down into it until the top was about two feet off the ground.

Fatagar sat in a stupor. "*Tck-tck. Tck-tck.*"

"I told you," said Piers to the Misfits, "that Bors has a good and true judgment. We need this more than his arms."

Bors walked around bodies back to the broken window. Suddenly Len remembered the tremlings on the table, their clubs raised in triumph. Looking through the opening, he saw the tremlings standing in a line, facing outward, all malice gone from their faces. Then Len noticed that one image in the stained glass remained unscathed in the casing. It was a scale. Bors tugged on the scale, then lifted it up and out. As he carried it back to Piers, the weighing platforms and chains became three-dimensional. Bors nodded to Piers, then jammed the center post of the scale onto the sunken staff. The scale swayed till Bors steadied the platforms.

Then Bors's eyes seemed as strong as his arms. He widened his stance and shouted, "I am the Guardian of the Veil."

Len thought it odd. Bors spoke as if proclaiming his authority before a multitude. Yet there was no audience on the veranda, none that could listen anyway. And the tremlings. How much could they understand?

Bors swept his purple tunic behind him to reveal his chest armor and black belt. He turned toward the griffin. "I guard the dead, but as I do so, also the living. I hold the veil between those who go on and those who do not. It is my charge, my duty. I must show a good and true judgment. It is the office assigned me by Soliton. I hold the veil by his will and generosity."

Then Len realized that this speech was for him, for all of them, the Misfits, joined together in the griffin's body. And, he supposed, for Fatagar. An audience of five was enough.

Bors picked up his sword and held it at his side by the hilt. Seeing him lift it so effortlessly inspired awe and some fear in Len. Then Bors said, "Come, Griffin."

Angie extended her wings, and the griffin bounded to the leaders of Primus Hook in one leap. Piers reached up and scratched the griffin on the back of its neck. Len wanted to purr.

Fatagar growled softly and scooted back on his bottom.

Piers smiled. "So. The Welkening began a reckoning. It set in motion a resolution. The war was over, but one more battle had to be fought."

Bors held one side of the scale to the floor. "Fatagar, the time for your accounting has come."

With no hint of resistance, Fatagar crawled on hands and knees and blubber over to the platform. His knobby spikes glowed weakly. Then he reached out with one hand and grabbed the chain holding the platform. As he yanked with his remaining strength, the scale tilted slightly. Fatagar slimed himself onto the platform, secreting defeat from every roll of fat. He sat awaiting his accounting. He opened his eyes but looked at no one. "*Tck-tck.*"

"Griffin!" Bors's voice blasted through Len, his tail standing stiffly behind him. Bors approached and Len's tail dropped between his legs. "Pluck a falcon feather."

The griffin did not move.

"Len," said Bennu, "*you* have to do it. I can reach back to Angie's wing with my beak but not to my own neck."

Somewhat dazed, not wanting to be responsible, not wanting to get any closer to his or anyone's accounting, Len lifted his right leg forward. He stretched hard and made an awkward stab at Bennu's neck. He plucked out one feather and held it in his claws. After he drew his leg back to regain his balance, he held up the feather to Bors.

The knight stepped up and took the feather. He walked back behind the scale. He bowed his head and looked up. As if he expected an answer, he said, "Whose heart is light as a feather?"

Len gasped. The question came at him like a wire squeezing around his neck. He felt short of breath.

The griffin started to pant.

"Len," said Angie, "are you OK? I don't think Bors is asking us."

But Len knew more than this. He felt a sharp pain in his stomach, a piercing pain—and he realized that in this griffin's body he sensed Lizbeth's shard. "Lizbeth," he said, "it's moving, isn't it?"

"Yes," she answered.

Bors held the feather up to the sky. "One kiss of sunlight." He placed the feather on the scale.

It did not depress the platform. Fatagar did not rise. And Bors did not place his finger on the scale. There was no compensating weight for Fatagar—only himself, his weight, his deeds, his heart.

As if molten lead were being poured on him, Fatagar sank in on himself. He collapsed under the pressure, his body condensing, compressing. His face barely recognizable, Fatagar eked out one last *"Tck"* before the whole platform bored right through the veranda floor, creating a hole into which the platform's chains stretched. The scale did not look strained, but the chains on Fatagar's side rattled as they extended down and down and down, into a pit, into the abyss.

Then they stopped.

Bors held the chains and looked down. Then he let go and the chains retracted. Finally the platform emerged onto the floor of the veranda once again. The metal shone in the sunlight, bereft of Fatagar, clean of his ooze and spiky head. "It is right and just," said Bors. "It is what Fatagar wanted, to go where he could rule, to be away from Welken's ways."

As the platform slowly rose above ground level, the tremlings cheered. They hopped over the sill of the broken window and roared their approval.

Len couldn't take his eyes off the feather. Fatagar's side of the scale came up even with the other side. If the feather side dipped slightly, Len could not tell. Then a gust of wind pushed the feather off the scale and toward Len's direction. It floated up, twisting in the breeze. When it twirled down, Len snatched it with his right paw.

"Going to put it back in?" asked Bennu.

Len said, "Yeah, that's it. I don't want you to lose one feather."

Bennu laughed.

Piers put his arm around Bors and walked up to the griffin. "You four have served us well again. By faith, you have lived out what you know and, by faith, you have acted in trust when you didn't know." Piers placed one hand on Bennu's giant falcon head, as if extending a blessing, then ran his hand slowly down the back of the griffin's head and neck. "So, Bennu, you are a thin-boned flyer—and you soar with grace and purpose. Though you are thick with thinking, you have become as clear as a riddle unriddled."

Len felt struck by the line. He knew it came from Lizbeth and Angie's experience in the huts, but he had never thought of it in relationship to Bennu.

"Lizbeth." Piers put his hand on the griffin's shoulder. "You are the solid earth, sure-footed and strong. When you rumble, you find your way in and you have the courage to tell your story."

Lizbeth sighed. "But I thought we hadn't told our story yet."

"Justice will be yours, Lizbeth."

Wait, thought Len, *"justice" was the word given to me at our commissioning in Ganderst Hall a month ago. Lizbeth's word was "power."*

Piers's hand glided onto the griffin's wings. "Angie, your water flows and flows. You have found the spring and filled your bowl. This power will never run dry."

Len stiffened. He couldn't figure out how Piers could make this mistake. Then Piers's hand slid off Angie's wing and onto Len's lower back. He could feel the pressure more directly, more distinctly. He could distinguish each finger and also Piers's palm. Len thought a hand imprint would remain there forever on his back, as if he had been branded, as if he had been claimed as one of Welken's own.

Piers said, "Len, you are a fire bringing warmth and healing. You have learned how to burn in the cold as well as in the heat, and that the source of your power is not anger but peace."

Len enjoyed these words. They tasted sweet and nourishing. He closed his eyes and tried to savor each syllable, to let them swirl in his mind before swallowing. Now he understood what had happened as Piers had spoken: each quality announced to the Misfits had shifted a quarter turn from the original commissioning. Bennu had gone from peace to grace. Angie had gone from grace to power, Lizbeth from power to justice, and Len from justice to peace. Maybe eventually Piers would say each of them had grown into all four qualities.

When he opened his eyes, he was not part lion anymore—or griffin— but fully his Skinnerian self, and so were his three friends.

Piers addressed them. "You found me and rescued Bors. You fought tremlings and Cutters and warned Welken of trouble to come. And we are grateful."

All Len could think to say was something trite, like *"glad to be of service,"* so he held his tongue. He nodded to acknowledge the praise. "Piers, your words sound so final. But what about the Cutters and MaryMary?"

"When Sutton left you, he took the townspeople of Primus Hook and joined them with others from Kells Village, including Zennor Pict. They are moving now to the west. Prester John and Ellen Basala also march from the north. The Cutters won't resist for long—if at all."

Angie touched the scale. "Are we leaving then? Are we going back to Skinner?"

"Yes, good friends, yes," said Piers. "Your gifts must stay in motion."

Bennu ran a finger across his forehead. "What do you mean by that? Don't you want us to stay and help with the Cutters? And what about the homeless guy we keep seeing in Skinner? We don't know how that's supposed to help Welken, or what we should learn from Mom's drinking that will make a difference here."

Bors stepped forward. "I have seen the veil between health and sickness. The distance is not as great as it might appear. The same with strength and weakness, choosing good and choosing evil. You four have begun to see yourselves as saviors of our world. Be careful. You may undo all that's been done in you. You think that everything in Skinner is shown to you for Welken's sake. And while this might be so, you cross the veil in the other direction as well. This time the questions in Skinner have answers in Welken. Your journey is not over. You must take these answers back to Skinner. There is a Welkening of sorts to be accomplished there."

"So," said Piers. "Now you see why I needed my Bors, my friend."

In that moment, Len felt his wooden perspective change to glass. He had only been seeing doors into Welken and events in Skinner as keys for opening doors. Now he saw a window that could be seen through from both sides, a much thinner veil. He had been searching for locks and knobs and panels when he'd been given sills and frames and transparency. Now he put on a new lens, a new way of seeing. And if true, then how did all of Welken prepare him—them—for events in Skinner?

"I have to ask you," said Lizbeth. "I mean, Piers, I've been thinking." She paused. "You always seem to know, like about Prester John and Sutton stopping MaryMary and the Cutters, and about our coming to get you, and about how we still have things to do in Skinner. If you know these things, why not tell us? Why drop hints when you know the answers? Why should we suffer as we figure out what to do when you could just tell us what to do? What's the point of all your mystery?"

Piers gestured to Bors. "Let us hear from the 'found one.'"

Bors bowed gratefully. "The point, dear Lizbeth, is something you understand better than you think you do. I will tell you this. You reckon that your main work is the finishing of tasks and getting to whatever destination you've been given. But 'what is happening' is less some list of work achieved and more, much more, about who you are becoming. Your transformation is more important than things you need to do and have done. And it's also about love. The story's always about love."

Lizbeth sighed. "So I've got the story all wrong?"

Piers put his arm around her. "Your story is rich and full. You just need to learn to tell it."

"Another way to put it," said Bors, "is that you have come to Welken to help reunite Piers and me, so I could join soul to body, so I could fulfill my role as Guardian of the Veil. But this mission also shows something of equal or greater importance—that you are guardians too. You are protectors of what passes between Welken and Skinner. You are guardians for others and for yourselves—guardians of so many veils, veils between running strong and running scared, between passing gifts along and hoarding them for yourselves. Some veils we shore up and others we break down. And to learn which is which is the work of our lives. In our dreams and in our waking hours, we are all guardians of the veils."

"*We* are guardians of the veil?" asked Bennu. "I don't see myself as someone like you, Bors, so strong and sure. To be a guardian sounds so important, so weighty."

"Hey," said Lizbeth, "I know all about being weighed down."

Len felt something in his shoe. He slipped it off, saw the feather, and put it in his pocket.

Angie opened her arms. "Hugs all around before we go!"

As Len embraced Piers and Bors, he noticed that Bennu and Angie had added a hug of their own.

"Come now." Piers pointed to the scale's platforms. "Have a seat on these—Len and Angie on one side, Lizbeth and Bennu on the other. Squeeze in and hold the chains."

Len did not like the idea of getting lowered into an abyss, especially this one. Would they meet some ghoulish Fatagar at the bottom? Len swallowed hard. He "let" Angie get in first. She smiled and patted the metal next to her. As Len settled in, he hung his feet over the edge until they touched the ground. Looking at his toes, he wondered if the platform would drop down like it had when Fatagar had sat on it.

But it didn't. In fact, the platforms didn't budge.

Now Len knew what would happen. In a flash, he would find himself on the platform at the tree house, the place where their journey to Welken had begun. Then he paused and thought that maybe the journey had begun well before then. Maybe the journey had always been there, that the veil had always been thinner than he'd realized. Had his whole life been a preparation for Welken? Could he look back at his life and see clues when he was six or eleven? And how could he put these thoughts together with what Piers had said about transformation?

Len held the chair on the platform with one hand and the feather with the other. Then Angie pushed off with her feet, jerking Len back. What was the matter with Angie? How could she treat the scales of judgment so frivolously?

The platform rocked back and forth. Len could see that Bennu and Lizbeth's platform did the same.

CHAPTER THIRTY-SEVEN
DRINKS ON THE HOUSE

How many times it thundered before Franklin took the hint!
How many apples fell on Newton's head before he took the hint!
— ROBERT FROST, *COMMENT*

 Lizbeth swung high until she reached the arc's zenith. As the platform came down, her hair flew up into her face on both sides. She felt exhilarated by the height and motion, then pinched by Bennu's presence on the seat with her. On the descent, she dropped her feet into the bark-o-mulch below the swings. Looking out, she saw LaRusso Park. On the swing's forward movement, she lurched off, stumbled, and fell on her side. "Ouch. That's where I got stabbed."

"Sorry," said Bennu, still holding the swing. He skidded his shoes against the ground.

Len and Angie jumped off in unison, Len surfing the bark to a stop, Angie running out and circling back.

Pushing herself up, Lizbeth walked over to the plastic border of the playground equipment and sat down. "It's weird. We're home again. Welken one minute, Skinner the next. So dependable and unpredictable at the same time. And—so far at least—I haven't continued the nightmare. I wonder if that means it's over."

"What did you dream last time?" asked Len, hands on hips. "Bennu and I never heard." He sat on a bench and pulled chips off a larger piece of bark.

Lizbeth sighed. "I've wanted to tell you. There just wasn't time in Welken." She paused. "I dreamed that the son came to the new home to visit the mother and daughter. He was terrible. He wanted money. He came into the house and wrecked things. And on his way out he said something amazing and horrifying. He said his last name was Mink."

"Wow." Bennu's eyes flitted back and forth. "So, if Dear-Abby is the mother in the story, and your mom is the daughter . . ." He drew a breath. "That makes Odin's dad Charlotte's brother. I'm freaking out. This is too bizarre. Then Len and Angie are cousins to the McKenzie Boys." He frowned. "I don't know if I can handle that."

Len threw the bark pieces down as he stood up. "You don't know if *you* can?" Looking no one in the eye, he brushed off his pants. He seemed in shock, angry and afraid, steely-eyed and teary-eyed. Then, without warning, he took off. He jogged a few steps before bursting into a sprint.

Bennu stood up too. "Let him go. He needs to work this one out. We all do, well, providing all this is true."

"Why would you doubt it?" Angie grabbed the side poles of the swing set. "In Welken, everything plays out. I mean, it's hard to swallow, but there's honey to be made."

"What?" said Lizbeth, still on the ground.

"There's a sweetness that comes." Angie swung slightly on one pole. "We have to work at it, but eventually there's honey. We can't taste it yet." She stopped swinging and kicked the ground. "Actually, I'm struggling too. I can't bear the thought that I'm related to him." Angie walked off. She left not so much in a huff or in her typical dreamy state but in a furrowed-brow determination, as if she were reviewing an argument in her mind. She looked so un-Angie.

Before Angie reached the street, Bennu caught up to her. He put his arm around her. When he squeezed, Angie started to rest her head on his arm. Then she pulled back. Lizbeth couldn't tell what was said, but she must not have been pleased with Bennu's comment. She walked away from him.

As Bennu chased after Angie, pleading with his hands, Lizbeth rubbed the wound in her shoulder. Then she picked up a handful of bark dust and let it drift out slowly from the bottom of her fist. When she brushed the remains off her hand, she got a tiny splinter and winced. It lodged in her hand where the Cutter's arrow had tagged her.

Figures.

She pushed herself up and headed for home. Everything seemed so fragile. She half-expected a bike to run her over or a meteor to strike her from the sky.

How can I go from happiness to despair in a heartbeat? Why can't the Welken feeling linger?

Then she thought about how with every step she was getting closer and closer to her mom.

And the shard poked into her gut.

Len sprinted down the street toward his house and trotted onto his front lawn. He wiped sweat from his brow. He tried to catch his breath, but inside he kept racing.

What am I supposed to do with this? I hate Odin and his brothers. I can't remember not hating him. I guess people hate their cousins. And what about Mom? Does she know? Does Grandma know? Have they been keeping this from us? And, I wonder, is the dream even right? It's just a dream, isn't it?

Just then Percy strolled onto the lawn and plopped down next to Len's feet. Stretching his front paws, Percy clearly wanted to be petted. Len bent over and slipped his hand under Percy's midsection. When he did so, the end of the feather in his pocket jammed against his leg. Straightening up, Len pulled out the feather and ran his fingers with and against the grain, causing separations. Then he put it back in his pocket. When he looked at the ground again, Percy was gone.

Len went inside to the kitchen and opened the fridge. He checked out a few containers, found some leftover Chinese food, and put the box in the microwave. Staring at the sweet-and-sour pork to make it heat up faster, Len pulled the door open before it dinged. "Ouch! Too hot." After he poked the meat and licked the sauce off his finger, he put a piece in his mouth anyway, chewing with his mouth open and exhaling over the bite to cool it down.

"You sound like the little train choo-chooing up the hill-hill." Dear-

Abby put some water in the kettle. She placed the kettle on the left front burner, then turned on the right front burner.

Len watched to see if she caught the error.

"I like my tea hot, hot, hot," Dear-Abby held her hands over the flame like it was a campfire. "My friends call me Hot Tea Abby." She walked away from the stove. "But sometimes they just call me Hot Abby. Ha!"

"Grandma?"

"Yes, Lenno."

"Your tea is not going to get hot that way."

Dear-Abby studied the stove. She looked at one burner, then the other. She picked up the teakettle and put it on a back burner. "You're just trying to make me look stupid."

"Grandma, I wouldn't do that." Len put the kettle over the flame.

"OK, dear-heart."

"Grandma?"

"That's my name-o. Don't wear it out-o."

"Do you know a family by the name of Mink?"

Dear-Abby closed her eyes with a pained expression. She rubbed one eyebrow repeatedly. "Mink, mink, like the stole?"

"Yes, Grandma."

"Did they steal anything?"

Len gobbled down several pieces of food. "Actually, they have. But I don't think it has anything to do with their name."

"I can't remember a Mink. I remember a Fox, I think. Lenno, I have a good memory, just short. I tell you, it's not my fault."

So her short-term memory was getting worse. And, now, the stove. He would have to tell his parents that Grandma shouldn't live alone anymore.

"I mean it, Len-o, it's not my fault!"

"I didn't say it was, Grandma. C'mon, don't take it out on me."

Dear-Abby hummed three notes, then sang, "He's got the whole world in his hands."

"That's one of your favorite songs, isn't it, Grandma?"

"He's got the whole wide world in his hands."

"Go, Grandma, go."

"He's got a hole in his heart."

"What?"

"He's got a great big hole in his heart."

"Grandma, what are you saying? Bebba, who are you singing about?"

"Jesus, of course, you ninny."

The teakettle's whistle hit full blast, scaring Len and shooting steam out with billowing force. Len dodged around Dear-Abby to turn it off. He poured the water, dipped the tea bag, and left the cup on the kitchen table. "Grandma, I gotta go."

"Me too, Lenno. I drink, therefore."

Len grabbed the keys from the rack. "Mom?" He opened the door to the garage. "Mom!"

"Yes, dear?" Charlotte's voice came from upstairs.

"I'm taking the Skylark."

"Thanks for asking nicely, Len."

"Grandma just turned on the stove and put the teakettle on the wrong burner."

"Oh?"

"Yeah, you better watch her. She could burn a hole in the house."

"What?"

"Nothing, I'm leaving."

"Bye."

I'm such an idiot, thought Len as he started the car. *Burn a hole in the house? Yeah, but Grandma knows more than she lets on.*

Backing up, Len passed Bennu and Angie talking on the front lawn. Maybe they were arguing. He saw Lizbeth on her front porch. He hit the gas. An awkward delay later, the Skylark picked up speed.

Len drove. He didn't know where he should go. All he could think about was finding the McKenzie Boys, his cousins. But where? He didn't want to drive to McKenzie Butte. So he drove downtown. Maybe he'd get some coffee. He needed to sort things out.

My options right now are pathetic, thought Lizbeth. *I could sit here and mope about being left out. I could go referee Bennu and Angie's argument. Or I could go inside and deal with Mom. I feel like a spy. I'm going inside.*

All was quiet on the parental front. Unless her mom and dad were gone, Lizbeth knew this was a bad sign. She braced herself. Sometimes she imagined armor growing over her, moving up from her toes to her helmeted head.

I wish . . . I wish it were that easy. Mom always has a way of zeroing in on the gap in the metal. What can I do? If I protect myself, I become hard on the inside too. If I don't protect myself, I become a pile of mush. Hey, maybe I should do something more Egyptian. Armor is for Len and Angie.

Lizbeth walked softly past the living room and kitchen, and into the family room. Darlene lay on the couch, her head propped up on a pillow. She had one leg stretched out on the couch, the other bent at the knee and hanging over the edge. Lizbeth did not think it an attractive position. On the wooden coffee table, a glass sat in a pool of water, its ice cubes long since melted.

Lizbeth felt the armor "chink" into place. Her arms stiffened and her hands became fists.

Darlene laughed at the TV. "I like this show. I think it's funny."

It was a documentary about the Civil War.

"Hello, Honeypie." Darlene picked up her glass and showed it to Lizbeth. "Be a sweetie and make me a drink, will you? Sniffles says we want Scotch and water."

Lizbeth looked over at the cockapoo asleep on the bare tile. "Mom."

Lizbeth's voice rose barely above a whisper. It simmered there. "I am not going to make you a drink."

"Sniffty-piffle, Lizzy won't make Mommy a drink."

"OK, fine." Lizbeth snatched the glass out of Darlene's hand. "You want Scotch and water, I'll get you Scotch and water."

"Oh goodie, Sniffles, Mommy gets another drink."

Lizbeth clutched the glass, walked to the kitchen, and slammed the glass hard onto the island. She banged open the pantry doors. Though tears clouded her eyes, she read the labels. Johnny Walker, Jim Beam, vermouth, tonic water, vodka, margarita mix, Jose Cuervo, merlot, chardonnay. Bottles, bottles, more bottles.

Reaching up, Lizbeth grabbed the Scotch whiskey and put it on the island. She took down the bourbon, the tequila, the vodka. She opened the Scotch and poured some into her mother's glass. She held the glass at eye level and swirled the amber fluid. It was beautiful in its own way, but deadly. Like MaryMary. She sniffed the whiskey and wondered what the attraction was. So she took a sip. She swished it around in her mouth, then spit it out in the sink. One drop slipped down her throat, and she felt the burn.

Making a face, Lizbeth put the lid back on. She grabbed the bottle by the neck and turned it upside down. She liked the feel of it.

Her tears flowing now, she stepped back into the family room. "I made you a drink, Mom."

Darlene kept watching the TV. "Why, thank you, sweetie."

"Here it is, Mom." Lizbeth held the bottle over her head. "Here's your drink." Lizbeth flung the bottle onto the tile a few feet from the end of the couch.

With the crash, Darlene screamed and sat up. Sniffles ran out of the room. Glass flew up, some pieces coming down in the puddle of Scotch, some pieces shooting over in Darlene's direction. She pulled both feet up onto the cushion. "Lizbeth, what are you doing?"

Lizbeth said nothing. She stomped back to the kitchen and grabbed a bottle with each hand. She rushed back to the family room. "You want it, Mom? Here it is!" Lizbeth dashed the vodka on the floor, on the other side of the couch. She threw the bourbon down. Then she got three bottles of wine and sent them crashing onto the tile. Shattered glass flew everywhere. Red wine flowed to the area rug and soaked in. The stench of alcohol filled the room.

Darlene screamed. She blocked her face with her hands. After the glass settled down, she dropped her head into her hands and sobbed. Then she lifted her head one time, appeared to size up the mess, and wailed.

"What's happening?" Martin came up behind Lizbeth. "What's going on?"

Lizbeth turned back to her dad. With a bottle of tequila raised over her head, she looked at him, her lips quivering. "I'm . . . I'm showing Mom what I think of her drinking."

Darlene wept with abandon.

Martin swept his hand over the scene. It shook fiercely. "Lizbeth, stop this now!" His voice rose with every syllable, his anger more evident in each added decibel. "Look what you've done!"

"Yes," said Lizbeth, "I see."

"Broken glass is everywhere!"

"Yes!"

"You've ruined the rug!"

"Yes!"

"You've scared your mother half to death!"

"I hope so!"

Martin grabbed the tequila bottle in Lizbeth's hands and wrestled it away from her. As his face clouded with rage, he raised the bottle above his shoulders. Lizbeth thought he would hit her with it. She stood her ground and waited for the blow.

But it didn't come.

Martin extended his arm till it was straight in the air, the bottle nearly touching the ceiling. Then he tossed the bottle hard onto the floor by Darlene. It crashed into dozens of pieces. "And that's what I think," he said. He looked at Lizbeth. Tears flowing down, he dropped to his knees. Lizbeth followed him down and threw her arms around him. They hugged and wept and breathed hard.

Lizbeth pulled back a little. She wiped her father's cheeks.

"I haven't had the courage," he said.

"I haven't either." Lizbeth hugged him again. "I needed help. We all do." She held him tightly and wept till she was tired. "What are we going to do, Dad?"

Martin patted Lizbeth's back. He tapped it rhythmically, like the tapping was more for him than for her. Lizbeth felt both of his hands on her back. Then she felt another hand.

She glanced up and saw Darlene bending over her. Their eyes met. Though Lizbeth had prayed hard for this confrontation, this telling of truth, she couldn't fix her eyes on her mother's. Love and hatred, joy and sorrow swirled in her.

And then Darlene knelt right next to her. Lizbeth noticed that her mother's feet were bleeding from stepping in the glass.

Martin sighed and embraced his wife. Lizbeth held her mom.

After the sobbing slowed to gentle weeping, Lizbeth sat up on her knees and held both of her mom's hands. "You don't have to do this, Mom."

"I know."

"And Mom, I love you."

"You can't," Darlene's voice cracked. "I'm terrible. I don't deserve love."

"Yes, you do. And it doesn't matter because I'm going to love you anyway."

"Really?"

"Yes, Mom."

Martin put his arms around both of them. "I'll be there for you too, honey. I won't hide in my office anymore."

Darlene let go of Lizbeth's hands and kicked her feet out to the side. "I want to stop. I do. I'll need a lot of help, but I'm going to stop."

Lizbeth saw a glass sliver sticking out of her mother's foot. She reached over. "Don't move, Mom. Let me pull this out." As soon as Lizbeth touched the glass, she felt the shard inside of her. Carefully she pinched the sliver. She cut herself and let go. And when she did, she felt her own shard go deeper in. She sucked the blood off her finger, then wrapped it in the bottom of her shirt so she could pull again on the sliver. To reach Darlene's foot, she had to bend way over. Her ear almost touched Darlene's mouth.

Darlene whispered, "I've been waiting for you."

Then Lizbeth gripped the glass sliver. She pulled on it. As the glass in her mother's foot moved, Lizbeth's shard moved. Gingerly, she kept pulling. The shard kept moving. She held the sliver as firmly as she could in her shirt. Then the glass came completely out. Lizbeth dropped it on the floor. When it fell out of her hand, she felt the shard leave her. Cautiously, Lizbeth felt her own ribs and stomach but could not find the shard. She poked hard where it used to hurt, then smiled. "Mom, your foot will feel better soon."

Darlene applied direct pressure to her wound. "I know it will. I want you to keep me company while I get better."

"OK."

"I will be, Bennu, I will be."

Mom, look at your foot. Are you OK?"

into the family room. His eyes widened. "Who went crazy? Are you OK? the kitchen. "What's going on?" He sniffed the air and leaned past them Just then the front door slammed. A minute later, Bennu walked into other up. Darlene winced as she put weight on her foot.

out of her. In the empty space, hope came in. And then they helped each All three let out big sighs. Lizbeth sensed her bitterness and anger rise

"I guess so. Maybe I do have a story or two to tell."

"You can tell me stories."

PART FIVE: AWAKENED, THE FAMILY

CHAPTER THIRTY-EIGHT

THE FOURTH LIE

I will remove from you your heart of stone
and give you a heart of flesh.

—EZEKIEL 36:26b

Len parked the car in a ninety-minute space and car-ried a yellow pad half a block to Java Jive. Although he liked frappuccinos and caramel macchiatos, today he ordered an Americano straight. He felt more manly with this drink—at least until he added cream and sugar.

At his bistro table, he wrote down Loose Ends. Under this heading, he listed what he'd learned lately about the McKenzie Boys, that Odin was sick with tetralogy of Fallot, that the Boys were planning some kind of ac-cident, that the homeless guy had made three out-there statements: "You have more to give than you know," "There is pain beyond yours," and "We are all broken." Len could see how these statements all said something about suffering, but he couldn't figure out how they applied to him. He doodled on the page, hoping to stumble into meaning.

Then he thought about what Piers had said about Welken setting them up for Skinner. He didn't know how becoming a griffin would help out in his hometown. But maybe his experience with Gareth would come in handy. Maybe he should be less trusting.

With intense anticipation, he sipped his Americano. Then he stuck out his tongue and got up to get up more sugar. Since the condiments were by the front door, he looked out onto the corner of University and Eleventh. Even though it was summer, the intersection bustled with students. A guy with dreads and a loopy smile bounced by. Two beauties in short-shorts waited at the light. It turned green, and Len watched them cross the street. As they moved up University, Len moved to the door to get in his last looks. They turned their heads back in his direction. Clearly they were upset. For a second, he thought they'd seen him gawking. They raised their hands in complaint about something or someone.

Then Len saw why. Tommy Mink. He said something back to the women, and they shook their heads with disgust. Tommy turned away. He smiled.

I can't help it, thought Len. *I really hate that guy. He is such a loser. I don't care if he's my cousin. The whole idea makes me want to vomit.*

Tommy drew on his cigarette and hit the Cross button four or five times.

He's such an idiot, thought Len. *One push is all that registers on those things.*

A man in a suit bumped Tommy slightly, and Tommy flipped him off. He flicked his cigarette disdainfully in the direction of the suit. Then he punched the button over and over.

"You're an idiot," Len realized he'd said it aloud, so he smiled sheepishly to the other Java Jive customers. He took a sip of coffee and looked back at the street.

Before the light turned green, Tommy hopped off the curb. A Ford Mustang screeched and stopped just into the crosswalk. Tommy jumped back, then went around to the driver and yelled. The driver rolled his window up. Pointing to the now red light, Tommy hit the hood with his fist. He stopped in the middle of the crosswalk, pulled out another cigarette, and lit it. Then he tossed the match at the Mustang and slowly finished crossing the street.

Maybe I'll throw this coffee on him, thought Len. *Maybe I'll have a little "accident,"* and this Americano will end up on his face.

Len took another sip. He pushed open the Java Jive door and watched Tommy from under the awning.

Where's Josh? Len thought. *Those two are inseparable. Together they add up to half a brain.*

About a dozen people stood on the corner. Others filed by. A young couple pushed their baby in a stroller. An old man shuffled along with a cane. He wore a broad-brimmed straw hat and dirty brown pants wet at the crotch.

Len shook his head at the old man. Then he studied Tommy. The McKenzie Boy just stood there on the corner, like he was going to go back to the side he'd come from. Len couldn't figure out what he was up to. Tommy didn't act as if he'd forgotten something and had to go back. But he did look nervous.

Maybe this is his way of being worried about Odin, thought Len. *Maybe he's scared, so he's punishing everyone who gets in his way.* Len shook this excuse out of his head. *On the other hand, maybe he's just being his jerky self.*

Len walked onto the sidewalk. He didn't know what possessed him to go out there. He didn't know why he couldn't leave well enough alone. People streamed by. A girl with earphones. A guy holding a skateboard. A middle-aged couple in matching shirts.

Len walked into the flow and tried to think of something to say. Nothing came. Tommy stood in profile, cigarette ash floating down onto his jeans. Len studied him. The light turned green, but Tommy did not budge. Then the light changed and the cross-street traffic moved. Tommy didn't. No question, he was waiting.

To Len's left, someone cleared his throat loudly, so Len looked in that direction.

With hands in pockets, two men in suits shook their heads in irritation. "Make everyone walk around you!" said one. "Some people!" said the other.

Len sneered at the back of their heads, then he realized he *was* in the way. As he scanned the pedestrians between him and Tommy, Len saw a familiar face, one that startled him deeply. It was the intensely pale, homeless guy. He sat on a bench with a sign that read, Anything Helps. God Bless.

I don't have time for you, Len thought. *I've got business to attend to.* But he really didn't know what business he had confronting Tommy. How stupid was that? Had he forgotten the size of Tommy's fists?

Len swirled his paper coffee cup. He took the lid off. When he threw it in a trash can by the bench, Len saw the homeless guy lift his chin in his direction. Len turned away and walked toward Tommy. He wanted to stay focused.

Three more steps and he would be there.

Two.

Len put on his toughest tough-guy expression.

Taking a long drag on his cigarette, Tommy peered over Len's head, down the street to the left.

Len stepped toward his enemy. Standing on the curb, he blocked Tommy's view. Tommy appeared not to see him. The McKenzie Boy hooked his arm around a streetlight and scanned the oncoming cars. He looked expectant.

Nothing brilliant came to Len's mind. He glanced down at his coffee and raised the cup for another sip. Just then, someone bumped his elbow hard. Coffee splashed into his face. In one motion, Len hopped back and thrust the cup forward. More coffee flew out, landing on Tommy's wife-beater undershirt.

"Yeow! Whatter ya doin'?" Tommy brushed at the coffee with his hand. His angry eyes met Len's. "You! I'm so sick of you showin' up and wreckin' things."

Tommy pushed Len with both hands, knocking him into the trash can and spilling coffee on Len's pants. Gathering his balance, Len saw a good inch of coffee left in the cup. A loud engine roared in the distance. When Len saw that Tommy was intent on the approaching car, he threw the coffee in Tommy's face. The McKenzie Boy grabbed Len's hair. He pulled it back and slugged Len square on his right cheekbone. The car came on, revving its engine. Tommy slammed his fist in Len's stomach. Facing the street, Len fell to his knees, holding his gut.

As the Chevy Monte Carlo rushed toward him. Len saw Josh at the wheel. The car hit a pothole too fast, bottoming out with a clunk. Sparks flew.

Len got up on one knee. He heard comments from the crowd.

"What's he doin'?"

"That junker's goin' way too fast."

"He's going to kill someone."

Of course, thought Len. *This is it. This is "the accident."*

Then Len felt one hand grip his pants and another grab his T-shirt at the back of his neck. In a second, he was off the ground.

"You'll do," Tommy said, then threw Len toward the street.

Instinctively, Len stretched out his hands. He hit the asphalt hard and rolled onto his right side. He saw the oncoming car, the underside and the rusty bumper. He heard the brakes screech. At the same time, he tried to push himself up. He knew he wouldn't make it. The car closed in. The brakes locked. The tires smoked.

Fear was all he felt. Was this how he would die, crushed under tires? Knees bent, his left hand in the air, his right hand pushing off, he stiffened for the hit.

To his surprise, Len felt a sharp tug on his arm. He flew off the ground, then hit the sidewalk, crashing into the trash can. As he collapsed onto his side, pain came, intensely. He saw blood on his palms and knees . . . and the Monte Carlo taking off.

A woman screamed.

Another woman said anxiously, "I'll call 9-1-1." Then, "C'mon, c'mon. Go through!"

Len lifted his head. "I'm OK. I don't need an ambulance." Shielding his eyes from the sun, he saw someone crouch down beside him.

A man in a gray suit bowed his head. "The ambulance isn't for you. It's for the guy who pulled you up. I don't think he's going to make it."

Len grabbed the man's hand and struggled to get off the ground, his knees nearly buckling from the pain. Len limped through onlookers till he got to the curb. On the pavement, flat on his back, lay the homeless man. He moaned with every breath.

Swallowing hard, Len felt tears coming. He sat down and leaned in. The homeless man's shirt was open, his white chest beaming in the sun- light, a red welt showing where he'd been hit. Heart racing, Len slugged his own thigh. *"What a waste. Please don't die, don't die. No! No! What a complete waste!"*

The homeless man coughed. "This," he said in a rattling whisper, "this is your fourth lie."

Len couldn't believe what he was hearing. He saw the man's closed eyes pinch in at the pain. Len shook his head. "You don't need to talk. It's OK."

"This is your fourth lie." When the homeless man repeated these words, a small stream of blood dripped out of his mouth, the red line contrasting sharply with his pale cheeks. "You think you don't need to be died for." He tilted his head back, as if trying to swallow. "Listen."

Len bent farther over. He heard nothing, so he put his ear close to the homeless man's lips, just as he'd done with Gareth. Strained breaths puffed out. One gasp. Then another. In the hush, the ambulance's siren screamed closer and closer. Len plugged his right ear and lowered his left closer to the face growing paler below him. He heard another faint grunt of breath. Len leaned over so far his ear touched the man's lips. The lips moved. To Len, it almost seemed like a kiss. Then one more puff. Then nothing.

Gently Len shook the homeless man's shoulders. Len sat up straight for a second, then put his head on the man's chest. Quietly weeping, Len whispered, "Your heart, old man, your heart is light as a feather."

Without resistance, Len let himself be pulled away. Two paramedics attended to the homeless man, lifting him onto a stretcher. Another turned to Len. "Do you want to hop in? We'll get you checked out too."

Len nodded.

The paramedic helped him up and put his shoulder under Len's arm. He half-carried Len to the open doors of the ambulance. "Can you strap yourself in? We need to get going."

While Benu held the dustpan, Lizbeth swept in the last of the glass. "I don't feel the shard in my side anymore, Benu."

Benu dumped the glass into the trash can. "What do you make of that?"

"I thought all along that its purpose was to help me remember the boy and the mother—and everything they went through." She opened the door and grabbed one end of the area rug. "But now I'm not so sure." She and Benu dragged the rug to the backyard. "Now I'm thinking that, well, of course it was about Dear-Abby and the Minks but also about Mom and my bitterness."

Bennu turned on the hose. "I've been watching you shut down, Lizbeth. Angie has too. It's not just about Mom. You've been building walls. We've felt it."

"In a way, it's kind of cool. What if we all had something poking us whenever we started to do something stupid?"

"I think we'd get poked a lot."

"I suppose." Lizbeth kept the spray on the red wine spot till the water bled it out. "On the other hand, I feel incredibly blessed. I mean, Soliton or Piers or Somebody made this happen so I'd stop turning myself into a kind of prison."

The click of the latch on the side gate drew Lizbeth's attention.

Angie ran in. "Len just called. He's in the hospital."

With ice packs on his knees, Len watched a nurse clean his palms and pick out tiny rocks. He said, "I feel so bad for the other guy."

The nurse did not look up. "Were you in a fight?"

"No." Len paused. "Well, yes. I mean, it started with a fight, but then it led to an accident." The word rang with irony. On the sidewalk, Len had realized this was what the McKenzie Boys had been planning. In his mind, he reviewed the scenes in the pharmacy and the Minks' backyard. Then Len heard doors slam and many voices. Orders were shouted out. Methodically Len's nurse opened the drape. "I'll be right back."

Len picked up the nurses' tool and picked at his knees. The voices got closer. As a gurney rolled past him, Len saw the patient's face. It was Odin.

Len thought about how stupid the whole plan was—to run over someone in the hopes that his heart would be a match for Odin's. Such idiots! A doctor stopped right in front of Len's open drape. He said, "Keep checking the monitor. I have to examine the other one that came in, that homeless man."

After a brief flurry of activity, Len stepped off the table. His knees hurt with every step. He wanted to go see how the pale, old man was doing, but he also felt sure the guy was not going to make it . . . that he had already not made it. And he just *had* to pull back the drape of the next room. So he did.

A nurse sat in a chair. "You can't come in here."

"It's OK," Len took two steps in. "I'm . . . I'm family."

"How so?"

"First cousins. I've known Odin all my life."

"That's not his name."

"I know. It's Oliver. But he goes by Odin."

"OK, but only for a few minutes. He has a high fever."

Len approached the gurney. He'd always dreamed of finding Odin helpless before him, and now his dream had come true. Here was the cruelest person Len knew, breathing weakly, his arms at his sides under a blanket.

Len looked at the McKenzie Boy's bluish face. "Odin. It's me, Len."

Odin tightened his eyelids. "Yeah."

Len wanted to tell him about how his brothers had almost killed him, how angry he was, how stupid Odin's brothers were, and what the Misfits were going to do about what Tommy tried to do. But the sight of Odin's face staring at him like a death mask unnerved Len. He wanted to hang onto his malice—but compassion rose in him. Biting his lip, he fought it off. He thrust his hands angrily into his pockets.

"Len."

The Misfit felt the feather in his pocket.

"Len, I have a hole in my heart."

"Yeah, I know."

"No, just listen." Odin worked hard at breathing.

The nurse sat up. "Maybe you should go."

Odin lifted a hand from under the thin blanket. "It's OK." Each breath sounded like a deep sigh. "I've always had a hole in my heart. I need a new one. I need—" Odin stopped. He pulled out his hand and ran it over his chest. "I need to start over."

The nurse walked toward Len. "That's it."

Len held up a finger. "One more thing."

"Hurry."

Len reached forward. His hand landed on Odin's hand. He saw Odin's tiger-snake tattoo on his arm. Still growling on his skin, it looked limp and less fierce. Len tried to think of what to say, some rebuke or empty threat, but what came out was, "I forgive you."

Len couldn't believe he'd said it. But when he did, his hands felt like paws. He felt every inch of his mane and his long canines resting in his mouth. But his body had not changed.

Odin said nothing. He closed his eyes.

Len took the feather from his pocket and put it in Odin's hand.

Waving to the nurse, he walked out of the room. At the drape, Len turned back for one last look. The nurse angled a fan so the air hit Odin more directly. The air caught the feather. In Odin's hand, it twisted back and forth. Then it flew out and drifted up and up.

The doctor rushed back and asked Len to move. To the nurse, he said, "The homeless guy, he died. Intestinal injuries and heart failure. Too bad. We were hoping he'd be a good donor candidate for this one here."

CHAPTER THIRTY-NINE

Mr B

Some things wilt thou not one day turn to dreams?
Some dreams wilt thou not one day turn to fact?

—GEORGE MACDONALD, *DIARY OF AN OLD SOUL*

A week later, the world seemed a different place to Lizbeth. So many circumstances had changed, but then so had she. How much of the difference could be accounted for by what had happened to her and how much by what had happened inside her? She didn't know. After The Wakening, Lizbeth had thought that nothing could be improved upon, that she was living in a kind of perfect space, an idyllic moment. Now she knew better. She had not "arrived" then, and she was not now in a state of perpetual fulfillment. She was on a long journey, a steady hike of many steps.

On this Saturday afternoon, at the kitchen table, she read a newspaper article that announced, "Oliver Mink Still in Intensive Care." The paper had decided to feature a story every day on "Oliver's Quest for a Heart," the need for it, how "Oliver" was such an unusual case, such an old person to have survived tetralogy of Fallot, and the failure to find a match.

From Lizbeth's perspective, the most amazing thing was that Len kept visiting Odin. She could barely process this turn of events. Len came back excited when Odin was lucid, and depressed when Odin looked more ill. At times, Len seemed to have forgotten what the McKenzie Boys had done to him.

He said that the homeless man's death had changed him forever. Len vowed he would never stop being grateful, that gratitude would mark his life, that someday he hoped his heart would be good enough to be given away. But Len also talked about how he couldn't manufacture this transformation as quickly as he felt it. Some days he came home upset about arguing with Tommy and Josh at Odin's bedside. Sometimes he felt furious that Odin's dad had suffered so much from his father, from Len's own grandfather. Len told Lizbeth that he worried that the cycle might never be entirely broken, that violence would mark the Minks for generations. And he said that, whenever he thought himself superior, he saw himself in a cycle too, and he knew how hard it was to change. They needed help, and so did he. We were all like the homeless, pointing each other toward the next generous hand.

Darlene walked in. "I'm getting some iced tea, honey. Would you like some?"

Lizbeth said yes. She couldn't imagine saying no to any offer of a non-alcoholic beverage for the rest of her life. From her mom anyway.

Darlene filled the glasses. "That Mink boy. What a story. It renews one's faith in human nature."

"So do you, Mom."

"Oh shush." Darlene sipped her iced tea, then cut a lemon wedge and dropped it in. "Look, my hand is shaking."

"It's OK. You've had a great week." Lizbeth hugged Darlene.

"I signed up for that recovery group. Sometimes I just want a drink so bad. . . . I don't know how I'd survive without you."

Martin cleared his throat as he entered the kitchen. "I've been thinking. A motto might keep your motivation up, dear. How about 'One little drink and I will sink' or 'My oh my, it's good to be dry.'"

Lizbeth rolled her eyes.

Darlene gave him *that look*. Then she said, "Those slogans alone might drive me to drink!" She laughed.

"OK, OK, back to the drawing board." Martin left, humming to himself.

Lizbeth made lines in the condensation on her glass. "Mom, I feel awkward asking this. I mean, if you don't want to answer my question, that's OK, but I just keep going over things in my head." She waited until Darlene's eyes met hers. "Why did you do it? Why did you start drinking so much?"

Darlene poked the lemon down, let it rise, then poked it down again. "If I say I'm not exactly sure myself, you won't be satisfied, will you?"

"Not really."

"It's partly true, though. Somehow the whole business begins to take on a life of its own—and you just feel trapped. But before that, well, I think I was afraid."

"Afraid of what, Mom?"

"Of so many things . . . that you and Bennu were growing up and you'd leave me behind, but also that you already thought I was pathetic." Darlene touched Lizbeth's hand. "No, don't say anything. Let me finish. I was afraid your father and I were drifting apart, into our own worlds. I was afraid of getting old, of getting wrinkles and varicose veins and a sagging stomach, of needing surgery to keep my figure." She laughed. "I was afraid Martin would not make enough money for us to go on a cruise someday. Oh, it all sounds so silly saying it out loud."

"No, it doesn't. I have so many fears, it's crazy."

"You're such a sweetie." Darlene pulled her iced tea in closer. "And I worried that you would discover my secret."

"What secret, Mom?"

"That I've been struggling off and on with drinking since college. I've been hiding it pretty well, until recently. It's funny, isn't it? I drank more and more to cover up my drinking problem. Smart girl, eh?"

"Oh, Mom." Lizbeth took a sip and gathered her thoughts. "What matters is that you're starting over. That's one of the happiest phrases, isn't it? 'Starting over.' Sometimes I think we're meant to say it every day."

A "hello" came in through the screen door. The voice was Angie's.

"In the kitchen," said Lizbeth.

Darlene poured another glass. "Angie, if you get any more beautiful, you are going to sprout wings and float up to heaven."

Lizbeth and Angie exchanged smiles.

"Honestly," continued Darlene. "The men must weep and faint when you walk by."

"Oh, Darlene, stop it. I'm just Angie."

Lizbeth sighed. "Yeah. And how do you think that makes me feel? You're going to drive me to drink." As soon as Lizbeth said it, she wanted to take it back. "Stupid me. I'm sorry, Mom."

"Don't be sorry. If I couldn't take some ribbing, why would I keep acting like a dingbat cheerleader from Mars?"

Everyone laughed, then Darlene picked up Sniffles and left the room. Angie reached out across the table and took Lizbeth's hands. "Lizbeth, I have two things to tell you."

"OK."

"First, Mom and Dad have decided to move Grandma into an assisted living place. They think she can't live by herself anymore."

"I'm sorry."

"I know. It's just so sad to see her keep going downhill. We're going to move her into Autumn Years. You gotta love that name."

"It's so weird, 'cause Dear-Abby is Bebba."

"I know. I used to think that the fabric of the world was tearing. But now it seems that things are getting mended, like everything's getting pulled closer together."

"And I used to think of Welken as this far-off place, this amazing world that I couldn't get to. Now, well, we can't get away from it. We can't go back to it because, in a way, we've never left it. Piers would say, 'Soliton's joys extend beyond the map of this world.' I love that idea."

"That whole way of thinking changes everything." Angie gazed out the kitchen window. "We're not going to sit around and wait for someone from Welken to come to us. We have to get eyes to see, glasses to see what's been here all along."

"Huh."

"What?"

Lizbeth tinked her iced tea glass with a fingernail. "Glasses, glass, chips of glass."

"Yeah."

"So what's the second thing?"

Angie sat back in her chair. "Bennu and I are taking a break."

"Really? Are you OK?"

PART FIVE. AWAKENED, THE FAMILY

"Yeah. We both think it's a good idea for now. Things were happening too quickly. I mean, we'll still be friends. You can do that, right? You can stop dating and still be friends?"

"Why not? Makes perfect sense to me—but what do I know about boyfriends?"

Someone banged on the screen door. "You guys in there?" It was Len. "You gotta come out and see this."

Lizbeth raised her eyebrows at Angie. She raised them back and stood up.

Len held the door open. "C'mon. You won't believe this."

Lizbeth and Angie followed Len out to the sidewalk. There, kneeling down, Benau petted a basset hound puppy. He looked up at the other Misfits. "He's just ridiculously cute, isn't he?"

Leash in hand, the owner smiled.

Lizbeth sat on the sidewalk and lifted the basset's loose skin as far as it would go. She laughed. "This is so hilarious. He's adorable."

Angie held his ears up. "What's his name?"

The owner, a young man in his early twenties, dropped the end of the leash. "We call him Mr. B."

"That's so precious," said Lizbeth, exchanging glances with the Misfits.

"What's the B stand for?" asked Len.

"Oh, whatever we feel like calling him that day. Bosco, Butterhead, Braveheart, even Boogers. For some strange reason, when we run out of Bs, we call him Rose. Not a very masculine name, but he has such a sweet disposition, it fits."

Lizbeth leaned toward Mr. B's head. "We know it's you, Bones. We know you're in there."

The owner picked up the leash. "What did you call him?"

"Bones. Bones Malone. He's a character in a story. He's a basset hound."

"I like that. Well, Mr. Bones Malone, we need to be going. Thank your friends here for all that attention. OK, come along now, Mr. Bonesy Maloney. Oh dear, Oh dear, I love that name. Good-bye."

The four Misfits turned toward the Bartholomews' house. They walked into the living room and out into the backyard. Lizbeth saw Percy stretching in the sun on the back porch. When she picked him up and petted him, Percy meowed softly and pushed his nose up to Lizbeth's chin. They nuzzled each other so hard that Lizbeth felt Percy's teeth. Then she put him down. She looked at Angie, Len, and Benn sprawled out on the grass, soaking in the summer sun.

Lizbeth noticed the cedar standing majestically beyond the grass, its branches full. The tree swayed slightly in the breeze—and when Lizbeth squinted in just the right way, she felt quite sure she could see the smile of Alabaster Singing.

About the Author

Gregory Spencer has loved fantasy for as long as he can remember. In the fourth grade, he wrote a thirty-page short story about a collie and a magic eight ball. Much to his dismay, the story was thrown out when someone in his family "helpfully cleaned out" his desk one day.

After college, to his delight, he married Janet (his First Editor par excellence), and they were later graced with three daughters—Emily, Hannah, and Laura. When the girls grew old enough for bedtime stories, Greg often recited the adventures of Percival P. Perkins III, Detective Cat, inspired, in part, by the antics of their own ginger cat, Percy, who has since gone on to the Great Sandbox in the Sky. Years afterward, he decided to write down these tales. Inexplicably, the orange cat and his sidekick basset hound receded into a backstory as Len, Angie, Lizbeth, and Bennu emerged. Set in the semifictional town of Skinner, Oregon (Eugene, Oregon, was founded by Eugene Skinner), the "three-dimensional tales" took shape. *The Welkening* was the result, and *Guardian of the Veil* soon followed. For the most part, he wrote the first draft while sitting on his front porch, recording the stories in longhand on lined yellow pads. He says he "needs a view" when he writes.

Greg is Professor of Communication Studies at Westmont College in Santa Barbara. He has written another book, *A Heart for Truth: Taking Your Faith to College*, dozens of articles and poems, and was interviewed in the Disney film *C.S. Lewis: Dreamer of Narnia*. He loves to garden, hike, play tennis, and mentor students. For more information, visit www.threedimensionaltales.com.